Skin
Room

Skin Room

Sara Tilley

PEDLAR PRESS | TORONTO

ACKNOWLEDGEMENTS
The publisher wishes to thank the Canada Council
for the Arts and the Ontario Arts Council for their
generous support of our publishing program.

LIBRARY AND ARCHIVES CANADA
CATALOGUING IN PUBLICATION

Tilley, Sara, 1978-
    Skin room / Sara Tilley.

ISBN 978-1-897141-20-5

    I. Title.

PS8639.I554S54 2008   C813'.6   C2007-907115-5

EDITED for the press by Stan Dragland

COVER ART from the 2002 collection
entitled *Blue Bird and Sedna* by Sarni Pootoogook
(deceased). Etching & Aquatint, Edition 50;
77.1 x 88.3 cm

DESIGN Zab Design & Typography, Toronto

TYPEFACE Galliard, Carter & Cone Typefoundry

Printed in Canada

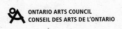

This book is dedicated

to all my living ghosts, wherever you may be
I dream about you

and to Craig

Here's much to do with hate, but more with love:
Why, then, O brawling love! O loving hate!
O anything, of nothing first create!
O heavy lightness! O serious vanity!
Mis-shapen chaos of well-seeming forms!
Feather of lead, bright smoke, cold fire, sick health!
Still-waking sleep, that is not what it is!

William Shakespeare, *Romeo and Juliet*

I

It's been eleven years. I haven't written a single letter to you. I haven't spoken at all about that place. I never mention it, but it's with me every day; it's the place of my dreams. If I dream that I'm chopping tomatoes, I am chopping them there, where tomatoes are fictional. In dreams, you're with me, and I don't know why. I don't remember why. You're usually chopping cucumbers.

That's a joke. You've probably never tasted cucumbers. They're delicious. They taste like stained glass. And fresh tomatoes. They're firm, like meat, with these juicy shocking pockets of ooze and seeds in amongst the flesh. If I thought it wouldn't rot by the time it reached you, I could send you a tomato. But after the trip to Sanikiluaq the juice would be gone, the fruit shrivelled or frozen or split open and ravaged by the elements. Sa-ni-ki-lu-aq: a word that means nothing in my language. Syllables with no sense, strung together aimlessly. Impenetrable.

I have two dreams every night. In the first I'm an old-timey martyr, complete with Jesus' crown and His nails through my hands. My parents both had a classic Catholic upbringing, nuns and the works. For Mom this meant ecstasy and obsession, salvation, fallback plans. The lilt and race of the rosary. Someone to whisper sweet nothings to, at night. Dad always associated religion with the strap, so my brother and I weren't allowed to have any. God, that is. Dad says he has too much guilt, didn't want to pass it on to his offspring. He calls it 'Catholic hangover.' He's a real card.

In the second dream you come to marry me. I want to but I'm scared, I'm not ready. I say: soon, soon. This isn't what you want me to say. You're big and strong and you take me anyway. You turn into a tulugaq and carry me off to your lair and I'm your slave princess, your chained-up bride. You force me to eat the dirt off the floor in order to keep the house clean. While I do this I'm allowed to wear a beautiful embroidered gown made of caribou hide and coloured beads with soft white fox fur in the sleeves. But after I'm done cleaning I must take it off and sleep outside the door in the snow, naked and huddled, tied to the house like a dog or a small child you're afraid of losing. I manage to escape, and start swimming towards a boat out in the harbour. There's a man fishing in his open boat and I can't see his face. He's blocking the sun. I'm sure he will see how desperate I am. He'll save me.

I reach the boat and start hauling myself over the side, but the man spears me in the eye with his harpoon and rips it from the socket. I hear the plop when it lands in the water. I keep hanging on to the boat. He cuts off my fingers as they grip the side. They drop one by one into the ocean like Vienna sausages. I fall back into the water, deep, deeper. I'm looking up and the man with the harpoon is falling away from me. When I reach bottom my hair is turned to seaweed and I have a tail like a narwhal. My sausage fingers have turned into seals and walruses and char, all the creatures of the ocean. They procreate around me into a beautiful bounty. They love me, and will do anything I ask them to.

I like to have this dream last. The first dream makes me feel small, a sweat stain on the world. In the second dream I've got a purpose. I'm the mother of the ocean, a goddess for all the animals and the Inuit. The People. I am the hard heart of Hudson Bay. I live for the letting of my own blood and the pleasure this sacrifice gives me. I am your water goddess, your Sedna. I know this dream is at the centre of things. Through me the world will heal itself.

Atausiq. Makkuq. Pingasut. Quyanaq. Ii. Appak. Qimmiq. Takatak. Tulugaq. These are all the words I remember of your language. One. Two. Three. Thank you. Yes. Father. Dog. Caribou. Raven.

I remember how everyone was baptized with Christian names. John. Jim. Sarah. And how some took back those names and made them Inuit: Johnassie. Jimassie. Sarassie.

And you.

Your name.

Willassie.

2

I've made a fascinating scientific discovery. If I look at something red and let my eyes go all funny and relaxed, I can see the inside of my eyeball reflected in my glasses, complete with all the fluids moving around and the criss-crossed muscle of the socket. Like an overhead projection in the clear surface of my glasses, lash-length from my eyes. Dad took me to the optometrist, who said it was impossible to see the inside of my eye and told me to stop lying, at which point I bit him. I know I'm too old for that kind of behaviour and it's a disgrace and all that, but I can't stand it when someone says I'm lying and I'm not. Plus, his hand was on my jaw, pushing my head back so he could shine his light into my cornea, and it was too tempting. I couldn't help myself.

The fold-up trays on the back of the plane seats are bright red. As I stare straight forward at my tray and let my eyes unfocus, I can see their insides squirming around, just like in a science book. This makes me feel sick, like I fell and hit my elbow really hard, but it's better than looking out the window and seeing nothing but ice.

We're leaving civilization behind. Dad says we're on a Great Adventure, which I'm sure is code for Buck Up and Take It Like a Man, even though I'm a twelve-year-old girl. The adventure tales worked on Evan, though. He can't wait to get out there and wrestle some polar bears. At least he couldn't before we got on the plane. He's been puking nearly the whole way, and this is a teeny little twelve-seater, so it's gross and sour in here. And the engine is so loud I think I might get an aneurysm. And if I look out the window and see nothing but snow I'm sure I'm going to cry, and once I get started I might never be able to stop. So staring at the nerves in my eyeball seems pretty damn good, at this point.

The other people on the plane are used to this type of travel. They're the nurses for Sanikiluaq, all flying back from some conference. Also the dentist, who comes up three times a year to look at everyone's teeth. Even though it's freezing, they've taken off their coats and are playing cards in the back. Dad was talking to them earlier and tried to introduce me, but I really wasn't in the mood. I've been sneaking peeks at them, though. There are three nurses, all wearing pink. Lame. Maybe it's a uniform or something, but I don't think so, because one of their shirts says My Other Body Is In The Shop, and I don't think that's the sort of thing that goes on nurses' uniforms. The Other Body woman is fat. She's got brown hair in a stumpy ponytail. She's winning whatever game they're playing. She's kind of pretty. At least I think she'd be pretty if she weren't fat. Maybe that's why she's waiting for the Other Body.

The other two nurses are blonde. One has braces. I wonder if the dentist put them on for her. Her pink shirt is a button-up one and she's got the top two buttons undone. She's got these little sharp collarbones sticking out of the neck of her shirt. The other one is wearing a plain pink cotton t-shirt. She's got a birthmark on her cheek, the shape and colour of a pine cone. From my seat, I can see the dentist rubbing her leg under the tray, but he thinks he's being really top secret about it. I'd pick Other Body, myself, but Dentist is rubbing away and Birthmark is blushing slightly to match her shirt, perhaps emitting a faint piney-fresh scent from the brown splotch, who knows. No one says anything. They must notice. The tray is too small to hide it. So everyone's pretending that no one else knows about the love affair, but everyone does. Royal Flush. Four of a Kind. Grown-ups are so transparent.

The pilot has a handlebar moustache. His name is Dale. This plane doesn't have a separation to the cockpit. Dale just spilled coffee on the switches, but he doesn't seem to be concerned. Earlier, he asked if I wanted to go up and sit on his knee, like I'm still five. No way would I sit on his lap. I'd rather puke my guts out with Evan, thank you.

To think that yesterday I was still in a civilized part of the world, where you can see trees and buildings and people who don't wear pink. Where there are grocery stores and libraries. Swimming pools. Restaurants. Theatres and parks. And the planes don't rip your head open with the noise of the engines. Instead, they show movies. They have cramped little washrooms with vacuum toilets and runny pink soap which I never fully appreciated. This plane has no washroom at all. There is no carefully made-up stewardess, no tiny pillows, no newspapers or thin blankets. Nothing to put on the fold-out tray: no apple juice, no peanuts.

3

I am changing everything lately. It used to be mostly landscapes, mostly cliffs and trees, sky and sea. Small outport communities. The fast-shrinking remains of our natural environment. I used to be passionate about presenting Newfoundland with a dedicated heart, an open eye, and not leaving out the ugly stuff—the garbage off the wharves, the graffiti on cliffs, superstores, the drunkard's Disneyland that is George Street, kids fighting. Once, a pair of women fighting too, right out in the road in Bonavista, the man's suit coat they were scrapping over getting ripped to shreds rather comically in my series of stills. I wanted to document the dying rural life of the province, magnify it, show it off with all its scruffiness, all the makeshift solutions, the cracks and chips. Lately, however, I'm finding myself obsessed with blurring—deliberate lack of focus, just soft blendings of shadow and light that could be anything.

I've been taking this photographic journal, kind of, each night when I wake up shaking, still half in the nightmare lands. I grope around on the bedside table for the remote cord. With my other hand I find the light switch. I flick the switch and click, suddenly exposed in the overwhelmingness of light. My camera looking down at me from where I tied it onto the ceiling lamp.

This is the closest I can come to articulating what is obsessing me. I leave the camera in a soft focus that blurs my figure. You can't see much of anything, just a white-skinned girl, naked, with near-white hair, in a white-sheeted bed. In the photograph all these whites blend together. There is only the topography of my body—faint suggestions of hips, breasts, nose, feet. A different-textured blur where the hair grows. The dark striation of wrinkles in the bedclothes, the black of my pupils. White is the absence of colour. The void. The figure in each shot is white as the bedclothes, white as the tundra, and just as vaguely sexual. Nothing is hidden. All is seemingly laid bare in the blurred stare, the naked torso, the bleached flatness of the landscape/bedscape. The possibility of reversal between land/sky, flipped on the horizon's axis. An image so vague you can see anything you want to. The figure is floating over snow, or lying in it, or standing on it, or drowning in a sea of liquid clouds. She is asleep, her body twisted with nightmare, desire, or a fucked-up hybrid of the two.

The prints are never satisfying. I can never really take a picture of myself that properly expresses what happened on that day of total pivot, the swing-around—the day I got my first camera, first put my eye up to a lens and slowly turned the barrel, bringing everything into focus and back out again. First felt the slight resistance of the shutter, the satisfying, heavy click. My camera is really the only thing I managed to bring out of Sanikiluaq and hold on to all these years. The only thing I could make use of, back in the city. Maybe because it was so new.

It's impossible to take a picture of something that happened a decade ago, but I have to keep trying, because the thirteen-year-old girl that used to be me is more and more in my head these days, and I don't want to give in to all the crying she wants me to do. She's demanding buckets, bathtubs full of tears. She wants whole reservoirs.

She should be dead, and isn't. She should be afraid. She should have given up by now. Instead, her stare goes on forever. She looks up at me from each cool, blank print, immersed in her little ocean of chemicals. Pleading? That's what it seems like, but she's so blurry I really can't be sure. I stand hunched over the stop bath with my glasses slipping down my nose, afraid she'll never change. I'm still trapped in the tundra, naked and pale, thirteen years old. Even after all the shit and all the crying, I refuse to leave. My body wants to freeze and ache. No matter what I do, I can't lug it into a more temperate climate. A night of sweet dreams. A warmer place.

4

We're landing. It's real. The sick crunch of gravel under the airplane wheels proves it. I stare at my red lunch tray one more time. Take comfort in my eye-guts squirming. Look out of the window.

It's beautiful. It's white and flat and goes on forever. The white has blue inside of it. The sky is blue, and the blue has bits of white floating in it. There's nothing else. The two colours meet each other in a perfectly straight line. This is not a place where people belong.

Dad's hustling me out of the plane. He needs to get out into the fresh air, away from the closed-in smell of engines and barf. He's got a hand on the concave part of my back, he's pushing me forward. With his other hand he's dragging Evan behind him. I'm like Neil Armstrong, but a girl, the first of our family to land on what might as well be the surface of the moon. The wind whips past my face when I step through the airplane door and onto the metal stairs. The wind is so strong and cold and steady that it takes my breath away. I can't move, can't inhale or exhale. The wind sucks the air out of my mouth. It forces itself against all the bones in my face, marking me as an obstacle. Dad pushes me forward on the slippery stairs. I catch hold of the rail. It burns my hand, it's so cold. I get my feet down the stairs. I breathe through my nose and hurry into the dirty metal building next to the greyed-up snow of the airstrip.

Our bags are thrown off the plane into a pile. So are the three wooden crates that hold our food supply—the cans of corn and beans and mushy peas that Evan won't even eat, cans of fruit cocktail and boxes of spaghetti and oatmeal. Powdered milk. Prunes. Corned beef and tuna. Welfare food we wouldn't eat at home.

There's a truck coming now. We're getting our stuff put into it. A big white man in an army-coloured parka with a furry hood comes over to Dad.

"Nice to meet you! Welcome to the Great White North. I'm Maurice Levy, and you're James Norman, and these are…?"

"Maurice, this is Evan and this is Teresa."

He shakes our hands. He's got mittens made of some kind of animal.

"Evan. Teresa. Yes, of course. It takes me a few days to get the hang of new names, but I'll remember your faces for sure." He laughs. "No worries about that."

The men have put all our stuff in the truck. It's the only truck or car on the island, Mr. Levy says, and belongs to the town council. The people all drive skidoos in the winter, he says, and three-wheelers in the summer months. I don't know what a three-wheeler is. Mr. Levy says it's an ATV, which hardly makes things any clearer. I get in the truck and am relieved to find that it has a red vinyl dashboard. I stare at it and will this whole cold place to disappear.

21

5

The Metrobus sucks. Truly. They keeping winning this Canadian Public Transportation Award, but I think the person who makes the decisions on that must be comatose or something. Or the rest of the mid-sized cities in Canada must have the shittiest public transportation of all time. Buses that come bi-weekly. Rickshaws.

The bus is frequently late, or broken down, or, worse, so early that the schedule ceases to mean anything. It helps to bring something to do. I make lists. Things I have to do, have to get at the supermarket, people I should really write letters to, grant deadlines, what room in my cramped apartment to clean up first. Various options to somehow rustle up enough money for another car, any car, to replace my poor dead Pontiac 6000. The lists don't make the bus come faster, but they serve several purposes: #1, getting my head in order, and #2, making me look serious and busy so as to deflect attempted conversations by various bus-waiters, usually punk kids, senile old women or the lower echelons of middle-aged masculinity. There are those bored old people who sit up front and criticize the young ones for their ripped-up clothing and their gangsta-talk, so out of place on Harvey Road with the smell of fish and chips wafting past and all the Irish-blooded, pasty-faced kids giving each other complicated handshakes, their rings and chains and assorted bling clinking together when they punch fists like true brothas. The old people wear pleated pink jogging pants. Rain bonnets if it's either bit damp out. They pick their noses openly, and have no right to judge.

Freddy has Down's Syndrome and will try to put his hand up your shirt. If you make eye contact he will glom onto you, sit near you, whisper dirty stuff in your ear: tight twat on you, my lover, I'd like to put my fingers in your bush and squeeze. New girls on the Metrobus don't know what to do with him. They can't tell him to fuck off as they would a normal sicko, because he's got Down's. They look forcefully at the filthy floor, fiddling with the clasps on their thrift-store handbags. He occasionally manages to cop a feel, the girl in question sitting still and terrified, wishing to God she could afford a car and never had to take the wretched bus again. Freddy rides the bus all day. I'd say he squeezes more titty in a month than most men will in a year. When I see him coming, I look the other way. As long as you never meet his gaze he'll pass you by. I know every detail of the stitching in my shoes. They're the safest thing to focus on in such situations.

I ride the bus once a week, on Sundays, when I tell everyone I go to tai chi. I have purchased a tai chi video and learnt the movements in my living room. I use this skill as my ongoing alibi. I carry a bag with leotard and sweats and bottle of water and I get on the bus and go, not to tai chi, but to the Waterford, telling myself that this elaborate cover-up has nothing to do with shame. I walk down those familiar hallways to the small white room with the single bed where my mother now has to stay, whenever she quits with the meds and lets the darkness catch up with her, pocket knives flashing in its hands.

No personal touches here. No photos, paintings, no flowers, stuffed bears, heirlooms, bags of chips. An oasis after the constant threat of suffocation in her cluttered house by Bannerman Park, full of trash masquerading as souvenirs. Broken things. Stuff you couldn't fob off on someone at a yard sale.

The only bits of colour in her hospital room are the light blue stripes on the fresh-pressed pillowcases and the flowers on her nightdress and slippers. I can't remember a time when my mother didn't wear something flowered. She was always a garden, lush and fragrant. Generous. But too much has been pulled up and rooted around. I can see that today. Too many weeds pulled out, too much topsoil washed away, my mother so spare in her blooming now, even in her good times.

Mom was always extreme, all one way or the other. Either talking your ear off or shut up in her room and sobbing audibly. Little cuts on her thighs from the hidden sharp things. I grew up in a fucking Movie of the Week. Neat rows of little cuts I was never meant to see.

That one night. Evan racing dinkies down the hallway. Vroom, schreooom. The door ajar. My eye to the crack. Mom's in there. She has razors and she's cutting herself, rocking back and forth a little in the sag of the mattress. I don't know that that's what she's doing. Hair over her face. She has no face.

Evan crashes the jeep into the door and it blows up, ka-boom! He jumps on me, protecting me from the imaginary explosion. We hear things drop inside the room. Mom pulls the door open and we fall in on her feet. I can see up my mother's skirt for a moment, and she's bleeding. There are three parallel lines on the inside of each of her thighs, way up. Horizontal. They are as long as a thumb and not very thick. I wouldn't even know that they're lines of blood except they're dripping. It's not even a very serious drip. I mean there isn't blood running into her socks or onto our faces. It's not a horror-movie gush or anything, just a little dribble, a little drip, just enough so I can't ignore the fact that my mother is bleeding. She's hastily pulling her skirt down, daisy-print fabric sticking in the blood, or so I imagine. Everything I imagine for weeks after that has to do with blood. Every time my mother goes into her room and shuts the door, my first thought is: razors. Blood. She's rushing in to fix our dinner, shaking enough to spill the vinegar, putting the bottle down with a rattled hand, too quickly, and more slops out the top. She's swearing softly under her breath and we never heard her swear before.

"Fuck. Sugar sugar sugar."

Balsamic vinegar in a brown splotch on her shirt. Yellow, I think. Daffodils.

"Fuck fuck sweet Jesus fuck. Judas Christ."

Rubbing with those shaking hands, making it worse, still swearing, now in a single stream of air. All the words start running together and she's got tears running down her face.

"Fuck fuck sugar fucking Goddamnfuck shittyshit GoddamnitallforJesussake."

Evan making car sounds in the hallway. Vreeoom, screeachhh. I take the bottle of vinegar and measure out the teaspoons, get the oil, the salt, basil, oregano. I make the dressing for her, put it on the spinach, put in the sunflower seeds and dried apricots and bean sprouts. I've seen her make salad so many times that it isn't hard, and she just sits there pawing absently at the stain on her shirt, swearing a little, but starting to calm down. By the time I'm done making the salad she's just breathing kind of heavily, that's all. We eat and read *Charlotte's Web* out loud to Evan—I read Wilbur and Mom reads Charlotte—and we go to bed and it's fine, nothing's wrong, and Mom is Mom is Mom, same same as always. Easy to forget about the cuts and things, because I want to forget.

When I think about The Vinegar Day I wonder where Dad was. I think there were exams or he was coaching his teams at school. Basketboring or Volleyboring. Dad coming home sweaty and exhausted and going straight to bed. He was overworked and tired and she was lonely and sad and I could do nothing but help make supper, try to keep Evan occupied, and pretend that nothing was wrong. The last days of the Norman Nuclear Family.

Just because a person cuts themselves up doesn't mean they're bipolar, a.k.a. crazy, schizo, psycho, PMS-ing big time, manic, fucked. Self-mutilation is, however, a warning sign, as are: significant changes in weight, insomnia or hypersomnia, fatigue, feelings of worthlessness or inappropriate guilt. Recurrent thoughts of death/dying/killing oneself.

Did he not care that she was doing this? Cutting herself? Had he not seen her thighs in months, did she keep them hidden, was it easy to do this, did they never touch each other anymore, was it over, were they just beating a dead horse, going through the motions, was it all a terrible routine? How relieved he must have been to get out of there just in time, the children unharmed, untouched, no cuts on our little bodies. Soon after we left, she tried cutting lines down her arms, through the wrists. More dangerous than her usual thigh places. She tried all those clichéd ways of ending things while sobbing so loud, luckily, that the neighbours called the cops. The thin walls of downtown housing allow no rocks, no islands.

We didn't rush to her rescue. In fact I didn't really know, not then, how badly off she was. Or I did know, and did my best to deny it.

I knew she didn't talk like other mothers, when she was having an episode. She talked in parable then. Her particular parable was that of her namesake, St. Elizabeth of Hungary. She could go on for hours in precise detail about the life of St. Elizabeth. I heard the story with increasing frequency and it became like code to me. It was when she started in about the bread becoming roses that I'd really start to worry. Sometimes she'd think she was Elizabeth herself. Sometimes she'd call out 'Ludwig' in a voice like a cartoon floozy, pacing around, crossing herself, whispering shit about the joys of the world, the shaking limbs of lepers, and the penitence of man.

Once she cut off all her hair in the kitchen, sitting in an old Captain Beefheart t-shirt of my father's. Me and Evan standing just outside the doorway, my hands on his shoulders. Mom said she had to make a hair shirt. St. Elizabeth used to wear a hair shirt under her brocaded, princessy gowns so she could do penance constantly, without her husband finding out. Mom said if she made a hair shirt then God might accept her into His gracious bosom, despite her flaws. Her hands were trembling so much I went in to help her with the cutting, afraid she'd lop an ear off by mistake. She didn't have enough hair to make a shirt. A bra perhaps. A necktie or thong. Her hair had fallen just past her shoulders and made a pitifully small pile on the blue and white tile of the kitchen floor. She scooped up some of it and spread it across her chest where it hung limply off Beefheart's dementoid grin, strands of it falling to the floor with every laboured exhalation, her face worn and wet, tears flowing copiously onto her lips as she said again and again: "I have failed him." I didn't know who she was referring to: God, Dad, Ludwig, or some other, nameless man.

This is what it means to be raised by an artist, I told myself. They're supposed to be emotional and strange. I told myself that this was just my mother, just her creative temperament.

But: crazy. It was hard to think of my own mother that way. Even when I used the word myself, I never really meant it, not in the dark way in which it was true. And by the time I came home from the Northwest Territories and saw the red, slug-trail scars up the soft parts of her arms, that sort of thing no longer disturbed me. I was used to it.

They pump her full of various drugs—fluoxetine hydrochloride, sertraline, bupropion, chemicals with commercial names like Prozac that are just syllables with no etymological meaning. Side effects include: anxiety, drowsiness, sweating, nausea, lack of sexual appetite, tremor, dry mouth, insomnia, irregular heartbeat. All better than the fist in her throat. The drugs keep her from wanting to hurt herself—when she takes them—but they also deaden her emotionally. That's what really bites about all this medication, because she used to be so vigorously alive when she was happy that it almost hurt to look at her. She would take a moment by the balls. No half measures.

We'd drop everything to go to the beach if the mood hit her, shrieking and shuddering in the frigid water but getting in anyway: "It would be a sin to pass this up, Teresa, to pass up this visceral experience." One afternoon we played tag on the lawn in our good summer dresses, after church, on one of those special treat days when I was allowed to go with her. I was maybe eight, and it was in the middle of a rainshower so warm it steamed back up at us from the grass. Earthworms crawling under our bare toes, my bow dripping purple dye into the white of my skirt, Mom saying, "What odds, don't worry about it, honey, come on and dance with me, we'll never have a rainshower this gorgeous again." We danced with our arms up to channel the rain in towards our chests and down our fronts and legs and bare feet onto the earthworms around us, catching water in our mouths and gulping it down. Dad in the window with Evan in his arms, calling out occasionally that we'd both die of pneumonia, Mom yelling back for him to stop acting like an old woman, for God's sake, me just spinning in that bright warm rain, feeling out my contours in the glove of water coming down my arms, down my forehead, coating me.

And in her third floor studio, sitting on the hardwood in my underwear, watching her paint. My own scrap of canvas on the floor. Her hair and clothing streaked with paint, distracted, so immersed in her work that she'd forget I was there and I could see what she looked like totally unguarded, with no mother-mask. Her face a clean, smooth slate.

Now she does nothing. Not in the Waterford. While she's in here she sleeps between bouts of electroconvulsive therapy and the nurses come and smile because she's finally resting, poor trout, and her so exhausted and sad. She's subdued, thanks to the ECT. So calm after the anaesthesia, the pulses through her head. Asking only to have the bed moved so she can see the trees in Bowring Park, their green tops shimmering in the wind. Very *One Flew Over The Cuckoo's Nest*. They probably shove a piece of wood between your teeth. Best not to think about it. It's the only option left when she flushes the pills and takes the razor blades to her skin.

Today, she's still under. I can see how she's getting thinner, her eyes sinking a little into her face. She looks old. Her skin has that shiny red look to it, like a burn with butter rubbed in. New bandages on her arms, taped down firmly. I hope she doesn't wake up. It's better when she's sleeping. I will still have done my duty and made my visit, but I don't have to hear about St. Elizabeth of Hungary, with her retarded useless miracles and itchy secret undergarments, her self-flagellation and adopted orphans, how she gave a leper her bed and was generally some serious fanatic hell-bent on discomfort and abasement in order to get to sit next to God at His dinner table, or whatever, once she kicked it. I swear I know so much about St. Liz, I could teach a course at the university. Thanks Mom, I love you, but please don't wake up. Please don't start talking at me.

I sit for twenty minutes listening to the uneven, damp pattern of her breathing. Two days more and she's home again, with Aunt Cack sitting in my old bedroom and listening with a baby monitor for sounds of suicide, forcing the sertraline down Mom's throat at mealtimes, running her bath and sitting with her while she scrubs herself to make sure she doesn't slip under the water and try to stay there. There are cycles to these things. Aunt Cack and I know this and we wait and wait for the upswing.

I look out over the park at the tiny families walking dogs there, bright spots. I leave my mother an apple and a Dairy Milk, and tiptoe out, slinging my tai chi bag over my shoulder, back out to the bus stop where the day patients wait, more insane and less invasive than normal bus-waiters. One guy with a pink windbreaker is always here on Sundays too. He paces in a line behind the bus shelter, patting his right thigh with one hand, over and over quite softly and syncopated, like the heartbeat of a dove. He's a big guy and sometimes he drinks a can of pineapple Crush, in little messy sips as he's walking. I don't faze him, I'm part of his landscape. He never talks to me, preferring to mumble his catechisms and mission statements to himself.

"He said to take it and I took it. He said to take it and I took it. He said to take it so I did."

6

The house is small, but not as small as I thought it would be. Corrugated metal on the outside. There's no carpet except in the living room, the rest is just that smooth white specked floor like they have in hospitals in St. John's, so cold it burns the bottoms of your feet if you don't have three pairs of socks on. I have a bunk bed to myself. I don't think they're used to such small families. I stack my books like a moat all around my bed. They're arranged by colour, and I have enough to make a nice wall about a foot high the entire way around. Although I've read most of these books already, I wanted to bring them all. Dad hoped I wouldn't, because we had to pay to fly everything up here, and books are really heavy, once they're in piles.

He was the one who taught me to read when I was four. First word: Sears. He taught me to write too. Sentence #1: I am good. He's the one who got me so addicted to words I could be happy doing nothing but reading, all day, all week. But as soon as money is involved, Dad turns into the biggest hypocrite that ever lived and the reading thing makes him grumble and growl and rub his eyes with the heels of his hands. Proof of idiocy? He asked me why I couldn't like Barbies more and books less.

I am who I am, Dad. Evan plays with my Barbies more than I do. He makes them go on dates with Ken and clean their houses and talk about their vacations to Honolulu. When he begs me to play, and I do something halfway interesting, like make Barbie a serial killer or a photojournalist lost in the Himalayas with frostbite, forced to amputate her own leg, he gets sooky and starts crying and then neither of us has any fun. So I much prefer reading, in my secret fortress on the bottom bunk.

I have tucked Mom's quilt with the hearts on it around the bunk, so I have a little cave on the inside. The hearts face outwards and the soft white underside of the quilt surrounds me and glows when I turn on the night light.

I'm starting in the yellow section. *A Wrinkle in Time, Wuthering Heights, The Adventures of Huckleberry Finn,* two Roald Dahl books and my thesaurus are in the first pile. I pick Huck Finn, always good company in lonely places.

I can hear Dad out in the living room, grunting as he shifts the couch around. He could ask me for help, but he doesn't. I'm never going to come out of my fortress into the frozen nothingness he's dragged me to.

Not only is it freezing and bleak and treeless here, but we don't have proper plumbing. We don't even have a toilet. True, we don't have to go outside and pee in a snowbank, but nearly as bad. The Honey Bucket, a pretty sick joke. A garbage can with a toilet seat on top of it. You pee or crap into the bucket, which is lined with a garbage bag. When the bag is full, you carry it outside where it freezes by your house until the Honey Truck comes by and takes it away to be thrown in the ocean or whatever it is they do with garbage around here. Not only is this so-called Honey Bucket really smelly, but you have the pleasure of seeing everyone's feces each time you have to go. I don't want to know what my dad's shit looks like. Or Evan's. And I sure don't want them to see the clots of blood that have started coming out of me. The smears of red on the toilet tissue. Civilization is not having to look at everyone else's excrement on a daily basis.

Dad had an accident with the Honey Bucket today. He was carrying a full Bag O'Honey through the house and snagged a corner of it on the coffee table. Which is why he's moving the couch, to hide the stain on our one good piece of carpet. It still smells like diarrhea. Another reason why I'm never leaving my fort, not even the next time the Honey Bag is full and Dad wants me to hand it out to him through the bathroom window, to save the perilous journey past our little mounds of familiar things from home.

We couldn't bring much. Besides my books and my quilt I brought lots of paper and markers and board games that Evan likes to play with me. Pictures of my mother and Nanny Norman. Seashells and rocks from Middle Cove beach. My microscope. That's about it.

Evan brought dinkies and some of my Barbies and lots and lots of action figure toys, Lego and building blocks. He likes to build forts too. But usually he wants someone on the inside with him, and that's usually me. Not that I won't let Evan in my fortress. He's the only one I ever let into my special places. I just won't let him bring any crayons or else he'll mark up the walls, and I like them white.

White and cool with tiny paint bumps, like a snowstorm.

7

Mark called at midnight and said: let's go out walking. I knew something was fucking him up, but I wasn't sure what. There's a long list of possibilities. My bet would be either his looming exhibition next month that he still hasn't started working on yet, the shitty production job on his band's new EP and how it just doesn't sound like them, his closet manuscript of prose poetry never seeing the light of day, or, worse, people actually reading it. Or angst over being pulled in too many creative directions at once. Or of a financial nature, all aforementioned initiatives still leaving him living below the poverty line and considering going back to school to become an electrician. Or it could be a girl problem. Maybe a 'she wants commitment and I'm allergic' situation, though I doubt it, as I haven't heard of any recent flings, and I'm the first to hear, normally.

In Bowring Park they've been doing major landscaping. We both prefer the old dirt paths to these pressure-treated board-walks. For the longest while Mark doesn't say much. It's mild out and Orion is showing off his fancy three-star belt. He and I walk over the tunnel the train used to run through when we were kids, in the seventies and eighties, respectively. Mark's breath, heavy, like a happy dog. Slither of wind in the long grasses.

"Did you ever lean out over the bridge and watch the train go by underneath it?"

"What," I say, "upside down?"

"Yeah. Me and my buddies would hang off and you could feel the vibrations. I was always half afraid of getting my head knocked off, to tell you the truth."

He's trying to scooch under the railing but he doesn't fit. The back of his shirt gets hitched up. Patch of exposed flesh at the base of his spine, little dark hairs on skin pale as soap.

"I wasn't a tough-ass like you," I say.

"You probably didn't even come down here at night."

"Not allowed. We shouldn't be here as it is."

"Hiding from the patrol cars is half the fun."

"Seriously."

"I had to jump in the pool once."

"Mark."

"June. Had my wool sweater on. Hid ten minutes in the water and it was so cold I thought my balls had retracted for good. I walked home soaking wet, 2 AM, but they didn't catch me."

"I've never been in the park at night before."

"I was sick for a week."

"I was a very good little girl."

"There was a wheeze when I breathed and everything."

"If we have to jump in the fucking pool I'm going to fucking kill you."

I help him up and we cross the bridge. We climb down onto the rocks by the river. Skitter of animals. Wind in the trees. I've brought shortbread cookies and lemonade in a thermos. Mark feeds a piece of cookie to a duck.

"This one duck is over here while everyone else is down by the Peter Pan statue having themselves a nice time."

"He's the lone wild duck," I say.

"Yeah." He's sounding weird. I push his shoulder. He's got that dark look I hate. Like he's going into a funk that could take days to clear. A black mood, is what Nan would call it.

"What's going on?"

He laughs. A cold, sharp little bark. "Well. My sister's getting married."

I shove him. "Fuck off."

"I've never been more serious." And I know it's for real, because his Cape Broyle accent has begun to creep back into his voice, and that only happens when he's really upset about something.

"She met the guy a month ago and they're madly fucking in love and now she announces at Easter dinner with my cousins and aunts and the works that her boyfriend she'd introduced them to not an hour before was actually her fiancé. Mom dropped the rum sauce all over herself and had to get treated for burns."

"Jesus."

"I know."

"I hope she's going to invite me."

"It's in two fucking weeks. Yeah, you're the fucking brides-maid. She's calling you about it tomorrow." Mark chucks the rest of his cookie in the river and the duck disappears after it. "Perfect or what?"

"I didn't even know she was dating anyone serious. She said there was a guy she met at a benefit…"

"His name is Curtis. He's from the Mainland."

"Wow."

"You know Vanessa. We don't know who this person is, or what he's like, or if he's going to fuck her over, or what. If we only have her word about this guy—she's hardly the most reliable."

"Her opinion counts a little more than yours, I'd say."

"I mean, meet the guy, fine. Fall in love, okay. Two weeks, whatever. Maybe it could happen. Who am I to judge. But don't fucking marry him. Get engaged, if you must. If you really have to make a lifelong commitment, just get engaged. Set yourselves a year or two to give things a try. Why insist on suicide?"

"I don't know. I don't want to say anything till I've talked to her about it."

"Like that'll do any good. She's over the fucking moon. He's The One, for sure this time. The rest of them were apparently target practice."

"Could be true."

"Hand me a cookie. It's not true. You can't love someone you've just met. You don't know anything about them yet."

"Maybe it's there right away and it just takes most people a really long time to admit."

He snorts.

"Maybe not everyone works the same way you do. You and Vanessa are miles apart."

"About to get more distant."

"Mark."

"I felt like hitting her. And poor old Mother there with the rum sauce in her lap. What a scene. Jesus."

I pass him the cookies. I cut them out in stars, like Mom used to.

"You'd better eat it this time," I say. "That duck doesn't need my shortbread stogging him up, as my Dad would say. He can't digest it."

He throws half the cookie in.

"Really Mark, we shouldn't feed that to him. If I totalled up the number of times me and Mom came down with a bag full of bread heels, we probably killed two dozen ducks between us, when I was little."

He takes a bite and throws the rest. I whack him one.

"Are you listening to me?"

"I'm sick of seeing her fuck things up."

"It is her life."

"Over and over again."

"Did you actually talk to the guy?"

"You think it could be real."

I don't say anything.

"Well, sure, she might think so, but come on. Remember what happened with that last guy? The welder? She could have died for him. When he broke up with her, she got his blowtorch out of the shed and burnt through his mountain bike till it was in pieces no bigger than my fist. I mean, I know she's my sister, but this is a serious nutbar we're talking about. I said, what about that welder you were so in love with you wood-chipped his bike and she said, he was nothing. She's learned a lot since then. "

"If we keep expecting her to be miserable, it's inevitable."

"It's inevitable anyway. Christ, it's like believing in frigging fairy tales."

I take a swig out of the thermos. "So, love's impossible. Awesome."

"No, just non-existent. This thing that Vanessa thinks is

happening to her just doesn't exist. You know? I mean, she's always chasing this idea of Love, and she doesn't even realize it's just an idea. It's like watching a lemming running at a cliff. Throwing herself headfirst like that."

"Ever try it?"

"No thank you."

"Feels nice to fall in love, that's what I hear, anyway."

"Feels like being drawn and quartered is more like it."

"Well, you don't need to worry. You never let them stick around long enough to mean anything, but no girl would, anyway, when all you'd do is tell them they're hallucinating when they say they love you."

"Oh, fuck off." Mark says.

"Fuck you. You don't know everything, you know, especially about this shit. You don't know anything. And besides which, she's an adult too, even though she's your sister. And Vanessa should be allowed to make her own decisions, even if they're shitty ones, which they may not be, you know. Maybe she's doing exactly what she should and you should stay out of it."

Mark's looking at the cracks in the leather of his shoes.

I can see you in my mind, Willassie, parts of you.

Mark's clenching everything. Breathing hard through his nose, and I hate causing that sound to come out of him.

Your eyes. Those depthless mushrooms. Your skin a different mushroom brown.

"Sorry," I say.

"Whatever."

"I shouldn't have said that, that way."

"Don't worry about it," he says, and I know I've hurt his feelings. "You win, okay."

"Okay, dicksmack," I say. "Race you to the parking lot."

I take off down the trail. Dark of the night, slap of my boots on the boardwalk. I figure Mark should pace around by himself and smoke a bit. That's what he usually has to do when he's coming to terms with things. I lean on the Art-Van and wait. I write my name in the dirt on the windshield. I nearly forget what you look like again. The patrol car comes by and swoops its beams on me, but I'm outside the park limits now. Olly olly oxen free. Mark finally emerges from the shadow of the dogberry trees, walking grimly, his hands shoved way down into his pockets, his eyes on the ground. I hate arguing with him, but he just shouldn't challenge me on love. Love, loneliness and guilt, these three things are familiar to me, inside out.

I could write books on the subject. I could head committees.

8

It's all very well here for Evan. He's five. When you're five you can get along with anybody. And he has brown hair. And he tans to a peanut butter colour in the sun. Even his eyes are brown. He's like a little nut all over. Brown is a good colour to be if you want to blend in here. The Inuit are all various shades of brown. My eyes are so light they're almost clear, rabbit eyes. My hair is whitish-yellowish-see-through coloured. I'm the colour, all over, of a cut-out paper snowflake, not even a freckle to call my own.

Mom says I'm really one of the fair people, the Fairies. She says that I'm her changeling child, switched in the womb with her actual dark-haired baby, who was brown and tan like the rest of the family. She says she's honoured to be raising a genuine Good Person. The switch must have happened when she was about six months pregnant and she went berrypicking with Aunt Cack on Bell Island, which is known to be maggoty with Fairies. Aunt Cack told her to turn her socks inside out to ward them off. Mom didn't touch her socks, and wouldn't put bread in her pockets either. She wasn't scared, even though she'd heard the stories of grown men touched in the head, unable to say anything before they died except *the Fairies got me*. Sores that eventually broke open to reveal small mounds of river grasses, fur, human teeth. The boy led astray for seven days in winter. He began to starve and ate his own sweater. All of his fingers and toes were lost to frostbite. He lived to be eighty-seven and never said another word besides the name of the marsh he'd been found in at age nine. He never focused his eyes and was continually running his fingerless palms over his forehead. The Bell Islanders called him The Lump. He sat outside the convenience store and muttered the name of the marsh, over and over, pawing at his scalp with his finger-stumps. Proof enough to keep clear of it, the locals said.

It wasn't that Mom didn't believe. She actually wanted to meet those Fairies. She wanted to get as close as she could to all the mysterious things, even the scary ones. That's why, she said, when she was led astray by beautiful singing that time on Bell Island and woke up a few hours later at the side of a riverbed, all alone, she didn't panic. She knew the fairies had come to christen me, in utero. To bless me with their powerful magic.

Mom tells me not to listen to the kids who poke fun, pull hair. Don't listen when they talk about my thin white skin with the veins showing through, my see-through eyelashes and eyebrows, my quick pinkness in the sun, the paleness of even the blue of my eyes. She says of course I'm not an Albino or some other kind of freak, don't listen when they say that, if I was an Albino I'd be disabled, wouldn't I, unable to see properly and with many other disadvantages. My eyes would be blood red. Instead, she says my Fairy blood will protect me if I'm ever in danger. But even I can see that she's just trying to make me feel better about being such a freak. I am total circus material, creepy as a bearded woman or a chicken-chomping geek.

So, I have no chance of hiding in the corner of the classroom and hoping no one will notice me, but I sit in the back anyway, because, as Mom also says, you never know when God might decide to grant you a miracle. Each classroom has two grades combined. I'm in 5 and 6, in the 6 part. But I'm learning out of a different book from everyone else. Math and science from the grade eight books, English from grade ten. The grades are set up differently here and I'm way ahead of everyone else my age, which I guess is helped by English being my first language and not my second one. So I suppose I'm in the 5 and 6 classroom for the social aspect, even though I'm ignoring the teacher and doing my own thing. Hilarious.

There's nineteen kids in my class. Most are girls. The girls wear headbands, the plastic kind in pretty pastel colours, the ones I can never wear because it hurts behind the ears where my glasses are. They all have long, beautiful, shiny black hair, like heavy sweet drippings from the spout of a molasses container. These girls smile a lot, and laugh a lot too. They have round faces and hidden eyelids unless they're blinking. They're curious about me, and keep staring at me, I guess trying to figure out how I got to look the way I do. I'm trying my best to stare right back, but really I'm blushing and feel like I've got no skin at all, and they can see right through me, into my guts.

The boys are at the back, where I've foolishly chosen to sit. I think I may actually be taking someone's seat, and if I wasn't sure that everyone would laugh at me, I'd get up and move to the front right now. I don't want to make enemies on the first day. Some of these boys look older than me, some look really old, maybe sixteen or seventeen. The desks are too small for them. The boy next to me is dirty, he smells of dirt. He's got a stain going down his shirt. He's really brown and really big—tall-big, not fat-big—with shiny white teeth. Some of them have missing teeth but his are all there and they're really shiny. He's caught me looking at him. He's smiling.

I say hello. I say my name is Teresa and I am very pleased to meet him. His face loses all expression. Everyone's laughing. Two boys in the corner start chanting something, and then all of them say it. They knock their palms on the desktops. I can't make out what they're saying: Margaret? Marguerite. Some girl's name. The big boy looks around him. He's laughing too. His buddies are kicking the sides of his desk. All of a sudden he picks up his pencil and breaks it in two and throws the sharpened end right at me, hard. Smiling, like he's handing me a chocolate bar.

The boys have this look of admiration and disbelief on their faces. They're yelling, and the girls have turned around in their desks. My cheek is stinging and hot. I put my hand up to my face and feel the pencil sticking out. Bull's eye. When I touch it, most of it falls out, but there's a big broken piece still inside my face, rubbing up against my cheekbone.

The room is getting smaller, all the laughing and the yelling is sounding farther and farther away. I'm getting that stomach-sick, tunnel feeling, and I think I'm either going to faint or throw up, so I put my head on my desk, pencil side up. I think there's blood running into my eye, but I can't be sure, because now I'm crying. I can't help it.

I think they're still yelling but I can't hear them anymore. It doesn't matter. I'm going to go to sleep now and wake up in Camelot or Narnia or someplace else, someplace nice with hot apple cider and pale people in ermine capes riding horses. I call on my Fairy Cousins, or Parents, or whoever, to transport me now to their Fairy Land. I will eat of their food, renounce my human upbringing and join their tribe if only they will rescue me. I don't care what kind of twigs and bones they have to stick inside me. I'm closing my eyes, and when I open them I shall see trees, miles and miles of them, and strange, half-human figures, pale like me, dancing in circles all around. I scrunch my eyes shut, hold my breath and hope the strength of my need will somehow make the wish come true.

But I know it won't work. I open my eyes and the boy is still looking at me. His face is taking up the whole room. He's got pretty eyes so white and brown next to his brown skin. Pupils like mine shafts. Black as the pitch. I can't stand seeing him look at me.

Someone takes me to the Nursing Station when I pass out again. When I come to, Other Body is leaning over my head. She smells like hand cream. She has a new t-shirt on, one that says Bingo Hoedown and there's a cowboy hat and a pot full of cash on the back. It's white, not pink. There goes the uniform theory.

She smiles and tells me that after they get the fragment of graphite out of my face it'll only take three stitches. She's getting these tweezer things, a needle and thread and some scissors. Other Body is quicker than she looks. She had a feeling I might bolt. She pins me to the bed and calls for help. I'm choking under her. She's got Braces to hold me and they're heading straight for my face. Other Body clamps her hand down on my forehead. Braces takes my glasses off. The blur of a silver needle comes right for my eye. I vomit and then blissfully pass out.

9

Do you remember the little bird you carved for me, an apology for the scar on my cheek? It was small enough to fit into my pocket and I carried it around all year, rubbing and rubbing the soapstone with my fingertips until finally the feathered etching wore off. In the end it came in pretty handy. I didn't think I still had it. I didn't think I had anything left of you. We tried to throw it all out. But there it was, in the bag of rags Mom gave me for making quilts. For his birthday I'm making Mark the Ultimate Macho Quilt out of leather and denim with cowboys and motorcycles and a toreador on it, these t-shirts I found at the Sally Ann. I guess Mom had all my old shit. That bird. It was in the pocket of a lavender shirt with frilly cuffs and a Peter Pan collar, my favourite shirt for years. I felt pretty in it, like the icing on a birthday cake. It was crumpled, having been in that bag for ages, with plastic buttons, cheap-looking and not mother-of-pearl as I thought when I was twelve. It's a child's shirt, soaked in the scentless sweat of a body not yet fingered and groped by puberty. The elbows are threadbare, one cuff is stained a little with something brown. It seems improbable that I could ever have worn it. How could my wrists ever have been small enough for those tiny cuffs?

Did you think I looked like a birthday cake when I wore it? Did it bring out the blue in my complexion? I hold it up to my face in the mirror. Next to the lavender cotton the veins pop closer to the surface, the ones in my temples, my chin and neck—all those places where the skin is thin. In the harsh combination of daylight and 100-watt glare I can even see the veins leading toward my mouth, snaking along under the pellucid blanket of skin as I go eye to eye with myself in the mirror. It's pretty freaky, but kind of beautiful too. My blood runs so close to the surface.

I drop the shirt and back away slowly from the mirror-girl, drawing my sharpshooters and firing double-barrelled: doosh-doosh, doosh-doosh! I twirl my imaginary guns, blow on the barrels like you're supposed to. Sling them back into their holsters. You can be as weird as you want to when you live alone. I pick up the shirt, fold it along its decade-old creases and put it back in the bag. It seems impossible that anyone small enough to wear this shirt could do something terrible. Also that a body so small could be capable of that hot, itchy feeling that arises from the proximity of another person's body, their arm so close to yours that you can feel the heat through the thin purple cotton, the knock-off mother-of-pearl.

I pick up your little stone bird and put it to my cheek, which remembers the feel of it. The bird is surprisingly heavy. Its eyes have long since been rubbed away, but the edges of the wings are still sharp. I'd like to try soapstone carving again sometime. I tried that year, but the file was too heavy for me, my arm unused to working powder off of stone. I used to watch you carving rock into animal, first from the hole in your shed wall, later from the tire in the corner with the canvas piled on top of it, my special Willassie-watching spot. You never spoke while you worked, you were all shoulder and hacksaw in your green t-shirt, your breath blossoming into clouds, the light falling blue on your hair. At least that's how I imagine it. I can't resurrect you and can only picture you in fragments, broken. Tiny fragments no larger than an ear, an eye, whorls of skin on a fingertip. The soft cleft above your lip. Not enough to cry about, even.

I'm tempted, though. I'm seriously contemplating water-works of Las Vegas scale, when fortunately Gay Stevie comes in without knocking, like all my friends do. Gay Stevie is sporting a mohawk today. Well, a hybrid thing, mohawk in the front and mullet in back. Or what a mullet becomes once it's in pigtails. He has a safety pin through the middle of his septum. He's wearing false eyelashes made of tinsel and a navy business suit. On the tie are many tiny pairs of bright red lungs, smoke-free, full and healthy, like cherries on stems.

"What's the occasion, Fancy Pants?" I say.

He coyly bats those sparkly lashes. "Oh, nothing."

"Nothing?"

"Well, maybe."

"Let me guess. You got voted onto the *Newfoundland Herald's* "Fifty Most Beautiful People At Home and Abroad" list and next week's issue will feature your glamorous Teresa Norman Original Headshot next to photos of Brad Pitt, Britney Spears, all the members of Great Big Sea and that guy who hosts Open Mic Night at Madgie's."

"No, but that would be hilarious."

"Yeah."

"Like all my aunts and uncles would think I finally Made It."

"No. First you have to get on the CBC."

"Sad but true. But if I really want to impress them, it's the soaps for me." His eyes get wide, reflections of iris breaking into millions of tiny bits all over the tinsel lashes. "I confess that it's a sick wish of mine to be on the soaps. Like a guest doctor on General Hospital who secretly switches all the main character's brains."

"With hilarious results."

"Naturally."

Gay Stevie pirouettes and smacks his head on the lamp. He spins around with his hand over his head, clutching at things. "I'm dying!" He collapses on my couch and expires over the course of several minutes, uttering Shakespearean parting lines: thus with a kiss I die, et tu Brute, etc. He even manages a death rattle. I rush to him and listen for breathing. I swear profusely for good measure. Finally I ponder aloud the right way to go about mouth-to-mouth resuscitation. This has the desired effect. His eyes pop wide open.

"Okay, my lover, no need to take it too far, now."

He pokes my belly where I hate to be poked. I blow on his eyes. Don't ask me why. I just have this urge to blow on his sparkly tinsel eyes. He's outraged. We wrestle a bit. It's good to be able to wrestle with someone as an adult. Simplifying. I flip him onto his back and lie on top, wriggling furiously with the full force of my weight. This is the funniest thing you can possibly do to someone, if their ribs can take it. Gay Stevie's can. He's got ribs by Brinks, for fuck. We lie back, exhausted, our hands to our foreheads. He wriggles around on the floor like a carpenter bug. I grab his tie and tuck it into his pocket before he chokes himself. He licks the inside of my ear and I squeal like a kid on a SlipN'Slide. He tells me his news: he's been hired on for the summer out in Trinity.

It's acting, which is good, and it's a beautiful town. The sweep of the harbour, the beaches, the old church with the red-rimmed, stained glass windows and the gravestones from the eighteenth century. Like living in a dream. But we also know the truth of it: rubber bootery in the extreme, silly wigs and salt-and-pepper hats, mummering in June. Forcing out all those poorly written, sentimental lines: the smell of a salt cod dryin', b'y, dere's nothin' sweeter. Unless it's the whiff off Nan's pork buns. The aim seems to be to make the tourists jealous at how worked up we locals get over our fatback and molasses, our dead Beothuks and our rum. Shows go up with two days of rehearsal, it's perfectly acceptable to write your lines on your props. The actors are all depressed. They congregate at night to smoke copious amounts of drugs. They drink a hell of a lot. Still, it's steady work, and for most actors, that's enough.

Gay Stevie grabs my boob. "Lattes on me, baby. All the nutmeg you want."

He waits for me to get my hat and mittens. It's way too warm out for anyone but pussies and hand models to be wearing mittens, but I put mine on anyway. These are my Mittens of Invincibility that this kid Laurel made me. Her mom's on the board at the gallery and Laurel worships me for some reason. She said the mittens would protect me from anything bad. We walk down Duckworth, looking into all the windows on the way. I love the barbershop window. The guy in there always waves, and I wave back. There's a kid getting a trim with electric clippers, sucking on a Popeye cigarette.

We stop for a moment of silence next to the parking lot with the big concrete wall graffiti'd over with terrible bright cartoons of American celebrities, but we haven't stopped because of that. We've stopped because underneath that, under the shit that's there now, was the most profound and brilliant graffiti of all time:

MY HEART BEATS
KELLY WITH BLOOD AS
RED AS THE ENVY
OF EVERY OTHER
MAN

Neat letters, green housepaint, thick brush. No adornment. Just the words. It was there for years. I used to stop and look at it every time I walked by. I had to, because here was proof that the true romantic poet was still alive, still kicking. The Romantic Soul: Not Dead. Grand Gesture: Still Allowed. This was real graffiti to me, it was public expression born out of true need, need to tell not just Kelly, but the entire world about the redness of your blood as it pumps through your heart every second of every day. The redness of envy in green housepaint. There was something so beautiful about that. And totally strange. Was this an expression of triumph? Did he paint it the night after he and Kelly first had sex, was it written in that brief euphoria? I would try to imagine him, this anonymous poet, his heart feeling like it might burst right out of his mouth if he says anything, so he paints it on the retaining wall instead.

Everyone I knew was outraged the day they painted it over. We grabbed each other's sleeves in the street: did you see what they did to MY HEART BEATS KELLY? I thought it'd be there forever. I took it for granted and didn't take a picture of it, not once. I bet the kid who painted those fucking movie stars on top got the serious beats, or maybe he's on the run. Probably hiding out in the Southside Hills in an abandoned tree fort, snivelling into his second-hand sleeping bag, abducting puppies for food.

Gay Stevie genuflects and solemnly crosses himself. We continue on down the courthouse steps and past the Superman phone booth to Hava Java. We always go there; it's the best place to go. The people who work there are all body piercings and asymmetrical hair, and are nice, and calm too, but Delith is the best. We like Delith. Gay Stevie flirts and she flirts back. She's cool.

We sit in the window and watch people walking by. We make up stories about them. That kid there with the skateboard and the purple hair, tripping over his own pant legs, that kid just had his first French kiss. It was on the War Memorial, of course, the girl was a straightedge, totally hot. Her tongue all the way in like a scalding snake's head burying itself in his mouth. He panicked, couldn't help it, took off in the opposite direction, didn't know anything could possibly feel like that.

We stare out the window. "He's gay," we say, at the same time. Everyone is a potential gaylord to us.

I dig out my camera and focus on Gay Stevie's profile. He's the only one of my friends who lets me do this. I'm going to make some kind of exhibit out of him. He adores this idea. I say, tell me about all those other people, and I focus and wind and shoot and focus again, capturing the elegant series of exaggerated hand gestures Gay Stevie makes while talking, and also his mouth, moving delicately, forward and out. The light picks up the shine of his eyelashes and the safety pin in his nose. In black and white they will glow like sacred objects. Gay Stevie turns and I get a good shot of the bizarre pigtailed mullet/mohawk from behind. He turns back towards the window, and in the frame of his body I get this gorgeous shot of Delith with the cups. She's looking right at me, her hair slipping out of its ponytail and into her mouth, just one strand. These crazy-huge eyes. She puts down our coffees. "Hey, you. I'm shy."

"Sorry," I say. "I couldn't help myself. I'll give you a copy."

"I'd rather have one of him." She puts her hands in Gay Stevie's hawk and you know he really likes her because he lets her do it. "I'm not hot on pictures of myself."

"Okay. It's a deal then. I'll bring you a print when I get them done."

We shake on it. After Delith leaves, we look out the window again. It's started to rain. The skateboard kid runs by again, the opposite direction, his hair running purple dye into the collar of his shirt. He's got a balloon. Red, plain. Just a balloon. There are an infinite number of possible reasons why.

10

There's thick black thread coming out of my face, like I'm Frankenstein's Daughter. I feel so ugly I just want to pour boiling oil all over myself and make it official: I am not fit to be looked at. I might as well have a lazy eye, or pus-ridden, oozing sores all over me. My skin is even whiter than usual, which gives a nice contrast to the black twine stitches, like a witchy grin of something evil about to pop right out of my face.

I read once about this guy who went to the hospital in the States somewhere to get a cut stitched up and the doctor didn't sterilize everything properly. Somehow or other this larva thing got in his cut and got sewed up, and the swelling was supposed to go down after a week, but it didn't. His face kept puffing up like a blowfish. Finally, when the doctor went to remove the stitches, out came a caterpillar thing, with millions of legs, crawling down the man's face and over his mouth. This was in a hospital in the United States where the doctors are so good you have to pay lots of money to go see them. I'm in the middle of nowhere in Northern Canada, and there better not be any bugs oozing out of my face in a week or I will have to just give up, lay down and die.

Not a bad idea anyway. Everyone here hates me for no reason at all. I barely said two sentences in school before I was scarred forever. And all I did was say hello. I mean, I've never exactly been the most popular girl in school (read geek, freak, weirdo, lame-o, loser, major ug-fest, total dog), but at least kids used to have a conversation with me before deciding I was worth picking on. That boy can go stick his head in the harbour and die of frostbite on the brain, it'd serve him right.

Dad has set me up a bed on the couch. I told him I'd rather just stay in my room and never come out again, but he wants to be able to see me and talk to me while he's making supper and helping Evan with his spelling. Even though the couch literally smells like shit and I'd really rather be alone, I let him do it anyway, because I can tell he feels bad.

I don't really need to be taken care of, though. I mean, I'm not sick, just scarred for life and mortally depressed. Still it's nice to have someone make you tomato soup and Jell-o and ask if you need your blankets tucked any tighter. Dad even let me choose the music, but I picked the Beatles because I know that's what he wants to hear, and Evan knows all the words. I love hearing Evan sing. I do backup vocals, when I feel like it, and he dances around the room, singing into a paper towel roll like it's a microphone. Dad is trying to get him to learn to write his name, but he's laughing too and enjoying the sight of my stupid brother being hilarious.

"Love, love me do! You know I love you! I'll always be true! So pleee-eee-eee-eeese, love me dooo!" Even though he's about fourteen octaves above the Beatles, he's in tune with them, waving the microphone in the air and twirling around on one foot. I'm pretty sure Evan is going to be an international singing sensation when he's older. I'll go on tour with his band, which will be called Evan and the Double Dares. I'll write their biographies. We'll travel all over the world except the Northwest Territories. *National Geographic* will read my book and ask me to be a journalist for them, and what with my great writing style and keen cultural eye and three degrees in archaeology, I will soon be the Head Journalist In The World and get to do stories on whatever I want. I will also discover the ruins of a Beothuk camp and it'll be the most complete Beothuk site ever found. I'll have contributed immeasurably to Newfoundland history. There'll be a female skeleton discovered and they'll name it Teresa, after me.

Mom and Dad will be back together. Mom will be really happy and working on her paintings again and will win the Governor General's Award for Visual Art and maybe the Order of Canada. Dad will be principal of a school in St. John's, but a cool principal who high-fives the kids in the hallways. Evan and I will come back, every Christmas and for everyone's birthdays, but other than that we two will travel the world. I just need to make it through the couple of years Dad said we'd stay here and everything will turn out wonderfully.

Someone's knocking. Dad splatters himself with soup as he goes to get the door, cartoon blood on his yellow sweatshirt.

It's Ms Ikusik. She teaches girl stuff to the older girls. Sewing and cooking, which they call Nutrition. Ms Ikusik introduced herself to me early on the first day of school. She said that her name, Ikusik, meant 'elbow' in Inuktitut. If I couldn't remember the Inuktitut word, I could call her Ms Elbow. That would be fine. She had smiled and gone down the corridor toward the staff room, her bracelets jingling softly and her teacher shoes making heavy clicking noises on the floor.

Dad is smearing the soup stains into his shirt and letting Ms Elbow into the house. She has a plate covered in tinfoil.

"Nancy, how are you?"

"I'm good, James. Is Teresa hurting?"

"Come in and see for yourself, Nancy. Please."

Why is Dad letting the sewing teacher into our house? I don't want anyone to see me. The ooze. I hide under a pillow, but Dad yanks it off me with a big grin, the kind with gritted teeth that means I'm being counted on not to disappoint him.

"She's just a bit shy, don't mind that." And, to me, "Behave yourself and say hello, Teresa."

"Hello, Ms Ikusik." Of course I remember how to say her name.

"Hello, Teresa. I made you some brownies."

"Do they have nuts?"

Dad smiles again. "Teresa. Don't be rude."

"What? I just asked if there were nuts."

"Walnuts." Ms Ikusik says.

I smile. "Well, thanks but no thanks, I don't eat chocolate and nuts together. I can't stand the combination of flavours."

"Oh."

Dad is turning red. "Nancy, please forgive her. She's injured. She's tired. Evan and I love nuts and chocolate together, don't we, Evan?"

"Yes, we sure do!"

Stupid Evan always sides with Dad, and he doesn't even like

walnuts all that much. Just because Ms Ikusik is pretty and curls her bangs and wears dresses even though it's freezing. Evan has always been a sucker for glamorous stuff like scarves and perfume.

"Apologize to Ms Ikusik, Teresa."

"Sorry," I say, and put the pillow over my face.

Dad's sighing. "Nancy, I apologize. I'll see you tomorrow, all right?"

"Sure. No problem. Feel better, Teresa, and see you in the school, Evan."

She's wearing bracelets. Evan is a huge fan of jewellery. He thinks any woman wearing jewellery is as cool as Mom.

I don't say goodbye and hold my breath until I hear the door shut.

"Teresa, how dare you be so rude?"

"Well, I don't like nuts and chocolate together! You know that! What am I supposed to do, lie?"

"Grow up!"

"Dad, do you even know what Ikusik means? It means elbow. How can I possibly be expected to like anyone whose last name is Elbow?"

Dad is angry now. "Sometimes I can't believe we're related."

"Well, me either! Why don't you just marry Ms Elbow and kick me out and then you and Evan can eat brownies all day long and roll around on the floor because you're so fat!"

Evan is starting to cry. He hates it when we fight. So do I, but sometimes Dad is just so dumb I can't help myself. There's a knock on the door.

"That's probably your bride-to-be. I'm going to my room."

"No you're not, Teresa, you're going to stay here and be

59

civilized to someone who only wants to do something nice for you, for God's sake! I mean it." He says this in his most serious voice. No sense arguing any more. I could tell I'd only end up with no supper at all. Grounded for a week. So I heave out a big sigh, flop back down on the couch like a dying flounder, and wait.

"If she's got more brownies, I don't want any," I say.

The door opens.

"Oh. Hello." Dad sounds surprised.

"Is Teresa there, sir?" It's a girl.

"Yes. Hello. What's your name?"

"Mina Ippaq. From Teresa's class."

"Nice to meet you, Mina. I didn't know Teresa already had friends."

Evan's joining in. I can hear everything, even the squelch of her boots on the linoleum.

Evan is saying that he's pleased to meet her too. Little traitor. He brings the Mina girl over to the couch. She was sitting in front of me today. She's very small and has pierced ears with tiny pink earrings shaped like wristwatches. Skin that crinkles up around her eyes when she smiles. She's smiling at me.

"Sorry you got hurt. We's sorry about it, the class. I bring you something from Willassie, because he's sorry too."

"Who?"

"He's my brother. He throw the pencil. He's seventeen and not so good in the schoolwork and don't want you to think he's stupid so he mean to scare you, like a joke. When he really hurt you, he get mad at hisself and leave the school."

"I thought you all hated me."

"No, but my mom say not to play with you because you's

60

white so I don't say nothing to you."

"Oh." I don't know what to say. Mina doesn't either. She's looking around our house like it's the Taj Mahal or Nefertiti's tomb or something. She puts her hand in her pocket and brings something out into the shine of the lamplight. A stone bird, tiny, complete with etched feathers and eyes. She puts it in my lap.

"Willassie make that for you. I give it to you because he's too embarrass. I's embarrass too but I would do it anyway."

The bird is heavy and also soft, smooth. It fits right into my closed fist.

"Thank you."

Dad interrupts. "Mina, do you want to stay for supper? We're having spaghetti."

She shakes her head at him. "Mr. Norman, I gotta go home to my mother now. She don't know I come here."

"Well, take these." Dad hands her a couple of brownies. She stuffs one in her mouth.

"Bye, Mina," I say.

"I gonna come see you tomorrow Teresa, if you want."

"I want. Sure."

"You got any Barbies?"

"I got lots of Barbies."

"You look like a movie monster with the string in your face." She goes out into the wind.

Dad closes the door behind her. "Well. You've made a friend."

"We'll see," I say.

I hope to God he's right, for once.

II

I get to Dad's house. He's got raisin buns in the oven.

"Hello, Teresa. Bun?"

"No thanks. I'll have tea, though. You want any?"

"Not for me."

He turns away. Starts wiping down the counter in long, even strokes. Sink's filling up with water. Dad does his dishes the minute that he's finished with them.

I reach for a mug in the cupboard above the stove. It's the flowered mug I gave him as a kid, after going to a flea market out in Port Union or somewhere with Nan. I've never seen him use it. He doesn't use any mug except the same plain white one, over and over, rinsing it out as soon as it's empty and thus avoiding ever having to wash it with soap, which would ruin the taste of his tea forever.

I do the crossword while he finishes his dishes. We talk about recipes. I try not to notice the stoop in his back. Moving slower. I try to keep Dad in soft focus and just concentrate on something else. The newspaper, the crude, stamped design of my teacup.

Peonies bright as meat, crowding in on one another. The murky brown liquid sloshing around inside.

We watch old movies, twice a month. If we had more of a sense of humour we might call it a club or something. It was Mom who made me promise. "You're the only one left. He needs somebody." Engrossed in the black and white jitter, hands in popcorn. Separate bowls. Then the ghosts show up. They're not dead people, not exactly. The ghost of my mother sits among the ghosts of Sanikiluaq people she's never met, all of them still living beyond our reach in their own worlds, which no longer have much to do with us. Evan's there too, slouched on the floor in the corner, his ghosty thumbs nimbly flicking over the surface of his video game thingamajig, even though the real him is still in Port Rexton, in Nan's living room.

Damn, I think of her and she shows up. Dear Nan. Her ghost there, leaning over Evan's shoulder with a grilled cheese sandwich and a glass of Tang. Him reaching up. The room is full. They choke us completely, the air filled with forbidden words they long for us to speak. They hunger for us to speak their names. We never do. We sit, with one couch cushion apiece, and one between us for the comfort in it. I try not to look at Dad in my periphery. I concentrate on Clark Gable. Dad snorting a bit when it gets too romantic. If I look sideways at him a ghost might decide to take the opportunity to squeeze between us, hold our hands, stretch their feet out on my lap.

I am clenching my jaw so tight it hurts. The movie going on in front of me has turned to blurs from all the misty shapes between me and the screen. I picture smashing the teacup to the floor, spreading hard, cutting shards of lurid pink peony all over the room. Something to do. To clear the air. Something that would maybe change things.

We sit through the whole movie, silent, however many million hours long it is. When I get up to make more popcorn, he sits with it on pause, not doing anything. Looking out the window at the neighbour's identical trim and siding. I put his bowl near his elbow and press play again. He smiles in my direction with half of his face. My own face tightens. We don't cry when Scarlett gets left alone. We know she'll carry on. She'll make it.

12

We're in the skin room.

I know I'm in a different world from my regular one because this school has a skin room, and we're in it. The whole school is here, all one hundred and twenty of us. We're lined up on the tiled and sloping floor, around all four sides of the room. The little kids are in the front. Evan is getting excited and karate-chopping his friend Tom-Tomas in the bum. They're both wearing jogging pants and t-shirts, but with belts tied around their shirts.

Evan refuses to wear anything but jogging pants, because other pants restrict his ninja moves. He wears the belt around his shirt like with a martial arts uniform, except instead of being a black belt, it's a blue belt with red boats. You only get the Red Boat Belt when you're really lethal. The sight of it causes women and children to hide in the corners of kitchens. It makes men go running for their shotguns. Tom-Tomas's belt is a tan one, the same colour as his skin. He's obviously the Red Boat Menace's trusty and dependable sidekick.

Today was hunting class day. Every two weeks, on Fridays, the older boys and men teachers go hunting. If they catch anything, we all shove ourselves in here and look excited. There's a drain in the middle of the floor, for the blood. If you get too near the drain, your socks get sticky with it. The bottoms dry out and harden onto your feet and you have to soak them off in the tub, later. I know better now, so I'm standing in the corner.

There are two seals today. Someone brought out a big salad bowl, for the guts. The bowl is shiny silver with roses etched into it. It was probably a wedding present for one of the teachers from their relatives in Calgary or Kelowna. Now it's being used to throw intestines into. They look nothing like they do in science books. Neither do lungs, or hearts, or kidneys. The books leave out the sliminess of everything, the wetness, how it's all mushed together like Jiggs' Dinner boiling on the stove. They leave out how hot everything is, how when you slice open a seal's middle and pull the guts out, steam rises as well. And the smell. There is nothing else that smells like the steam off a freshly skinned seal. It sticks in the back of your throat for hours afterwards, so if you eat a cookie or some bannock it tastes like blubber, like rawness, and hot, thick blood.

Lucassie and Larry from Grade Ten are skinning the first seal. The skinning is important. It must be done in a very specific way, or else the pelt gets ruined. First the skin around the neck is cut, like you're giving the seal a necklace. Then a cut is made right down the belly, from necklace to flippers. Another little cut goes around the flippers, and the upper ones too, and then you pull hard and the whole thing comes off like a winter jacket. The seal's eyes are open while this happens, staring around the room. It's got all its skin gone and is a depressing-looking thing, all pink and chunky but puny too.

One of the Grade Ten girls is scraping the blubber off the inside of the skin with an ulu, her shirt sleeves rolled up and knuckles greasy. Larry is hauling the insides out of the carcass, the stomach yellow and heavy in his hands. He's tossing the hot insides into the beautiful bowl. I want that bowl. I want to float flowers in it, or put chocolates in it, anything but the slimy gut-slop that's in it now.

He's got the heart. The little kids are crowding in on top of him, so I can only see his right arm and knee, both smeared black with blood. He's cutting the heart up quickly, like one of those TV chefs, and passing the pieces out to the little kids, who take them eagerly into their mouths and suck the blood out. Evan is stuffing his piece into his cheeks, chewing greedily. Lucassie is slicing off pieces of the seal's flank and handing them around to the rest of us. Benny and Willassie from my class are lying on the greasy floor, having an arm wrestling contest to see who gets the left eyeball. Benny should know better. Willassie has arms like the Incredible Hulk and is the toughest boy in school, even if he's only in grade six. He smashes Benny's knuckles into the tiles. Larry throws him the eye which he pops into his mouth like a Gobstopper. Larry's eating the other eye, and grinning.

I am passed a small piece from the seal's left flank, above where its lung used to be. Mina is looking back to see if I will dare to put the meat in my mouth. Every second Friday I vow to try it, but I haven't done so yet. I tell her to mind her own business, then look at my brother, who's crowding in for seconds. The blood is running into the cuff of my good lavender shirt. I put the meat into my mouth before I can think about it too much. It's warm and fills up my whole mouth so I feel like I'm suffocating. There's thick blood going down my throat and it tastes like pennies. I start to gag but I chew instead and the meat is so dense it's making my jaw hurt.

I swallow the whole lump, and it's hot going down my throat. I'm giddy from all the blood. I'm laughing and they've never heard me laugh before. Mina and Lucy turn around and stare at me. Everyone's staring now, and I'm still laughing and everything is hilarious, including the taste of raw seal and the blood on my face and how I'm the black sheep in this room but I'm actually really really white. And I don't care that everyone is staring at me because now I'm staring back. Oh, isn't everything funny.

Benny starts laughing too. Everyone does. Benny says I'm the polar bear who is so white and likes meat so much she must laugh. And then everyone calls me Polar Bear. Polar Bear Girl. I'm not like everyone else in this room, but I belong too. The second seal is brought out. It's a big one. Instead of Johnny or Leo or Paulassie skinning it, it's Dad. This also causes everyone to laugh. It's like Christmas in the skin room, everyone's so happy.

Dad looks a little nervous. It's the first time he's killed. Larry hands him the knife. He hesitates and his cheeks are flushed. We wait for him to make the necklace cut. He puts the tip of the knife to the seal's throat like he's wiping a dribble off its chin. He thrusts the blade in and makes the first cut. They take the carcass from him and tell him to take off his shirt. He's trying to get out of the room. Mr. Takatak and Mr. Levy are grabbing him, they're pulling his shirt off. They toss it and it lands in the gorgeous guts bowl. They're making him lie down where the drain is and he looks really small and pale. The hairs on his chest look like scars, from where I'm standing, lots of little black scars from a billion razor blades. He's turning red from his face downwards. I can practically hear him panicking. All the little kids are giggling in the front.

Leo and Johnny have the carcass. They drag it over Dad's chest, up over his body like tucking him into bed. They drag it over his head and onto the floor. There is silence in the room. He's covered in the blackness of the seal's blood. I have an urge to go and draw in it with my finger. He lies there for a moment, and I think maybe he's going to cry from the suddenness of it all. Then Benny calls him Big Hunter and Father of the Polar Bear, and everyone laughs. Dad stands up, and when he smiles his teeth are huge and white in the dark red muck of his face. He gives Evan a hug and gets guts on his shirt. They stick together at the middle like an Oreo. I stand in the corner and watch it all. My belly is warm and I'm smiling.

13

Vanessa's wedding. I'm wearing a hideous orange bridesmaid dress with a two-tiered skirt, left over from the eighties. And shit, I'm high. Everyone looks like a cake decoration. Vanilla icing bride, licorice icing groom. Motley fruit flavours for the rest of us. Vanessa says she hopes I'll catch the bouquet. I hope I don't. She's two years younger than me. Married at twenty-one. Mark is still up in arms about it, but he promised he'd refrain from making any fuss.

When we all met I'd just finished high school. Vanessa and I both worked at Coles. I'd start getting twitchy about five hours into my shift. My 'Can I Help You' smile would start to shift into a sneer and Vanessa was all that was stopping me from losing control and going on a berserker rampage, whipping hardcover editions of Anne Rice and Danielle Steele at gawking passersby. We became friends. She introduced me to her older brother, who'd come in to buy a copy of *Alice in Wonderland* with gilt edges and full-colour plates of the original illustrations, leather-bound. For their niece, Vanessa informed me.

He also bought a bodybuilding magazine.

"To impress you," Vanessa said.

"Actually, it's to use for collages," Mark said. "I'm making a series of collages based on masculinity and food."

I said nothing, but my ears got hot. I rang the sale through and handed him the bag. I had grown up in galleries. Mom and I had gone to his first solo show when I was fifteen. Hundreds of china teacups full of urine left out to grow skins of whitish mould, laid in parallel lines on the gallery floor. An aisle down the middle. A microscope on a plinth at the end with a slide of one of Mark's pubic hairs.

Mom said, "I don't have much hope for this new generation." At this point she still made oil paintings of angels in gardens with glowing hearts.

Later that night, Mark came back to the store.

"Vanessa left two hours ago," I said.

"I know," he said.

"Can I help you with something? We're almost closed."

He smiled. His hair was messy. He was twenty-six and had dark circles under his eyes, which made them very brown.

"Actually, I'd like to give you this." He handed me the Coles bag with the *Alice in Wonderland* book inside. "Because you're the White Rabbit."

I didn't say anything. The book was heavy, straining my forearm.

"Don't get mad. I just mean, you know, you're cute like a rabbit."

"Cute like a rabbit?"

"And I bet you're always losing your gloves, too, aren't you?"

"I'm a mitten girl."

I put down the bag on the counter. I pulled out the sliding wall, running it along the track and closing us in. Mark flipped through *Chicken Soup for the Christian Soul*, swearing softly to himself, and I went back to counting the cash.

"Well, it's a great book, a classic, if you're any kind of reader you should own a copy."

"*Chicken Soup?*"

"*Alice*. And you're not really the White Rabbit. I mean you don't have his neurotic personality. Not that I know what kind of personality you have. And I don't believe you can categorize people with astrological signs or numerology or any of that shit. No offence if you believe in that stuff, but I think it's just a pile of, well, shit. Shit, I should really stop saying shit. I'm not usually cursing every third word. Sorry for startling you. You don't have to keep it, but you can. I wrote my phone number in it. So I guess it can't be returned. So keep it. But you don't have to call me. If I were you, I wouldn't. I mean, I approached you out of nowhere and compared you to a rabbit and that's probably not the kind of person you're interested in telephoning."

His mouth was beautiful, once he stopped talking. The moment seemed to have its own smell: glue off the bookbindings, and deodorant, his (sporty) and mine (organic peach). And the metal of the cash register, that smell that's almost more of a taste under the root of your tongue. He turned to go. I cleared my throat.

"So, is this like a Happy Un-Birthday present or something? How'd you know?"

He waited while I closed up. I got my coat and we walked out into the night, which was foggy and warm and starless, the kind of night which makes me want to go wandering.

And now we're at Vanessa's shotgun wedding to Her One True Love, For Real This Time. Curtis looks nice in a tuxedo. He has a firm handshake. Drinks bourbon. During the ceremony, their kiss was warm and shy. Finally he put her bouquet in front of their faces. I thought, this may really be the one time Vanessa is right.

I'm her bridesmaid and life is fucked. I don't know how I ended up here. How did I end up in the Masonic Temple dance hall with a cake stain on my stupid orange dress and too much wine and pot in my system, Mark watching me from every conversation with those cartoon stars in his eyes? Which is funny. Which is hilarious, because we started out so well, so patently romantic, and I thought I knew what was going on. I mean, I thought for sure that if a guy you don't know gives you an expensive copy of *Alice in Wonderland*, complete with ridiculous explanation for doing so, well, I thought for sure that meant the beginning of something serious.

But not with Mark. Master of the Mixed Signal. Man Who Knows Not What He Wants. Who never once tried to kiss me, hold my hand, grab my ass, nothing. He didn't make a single overt move in those first few months when I expected it and wanted it, or even later, through all the years we've been friends. The kind who lend each other money, who hold each other's hair back over toilet bowls. The kind who argue like family. Bosom buddies, minus stray thoughts of stroking aforementioned bosom. This is good, fine, and for the best. I'm glad we didn't have a silly, brief affair. Mark is, after all, hugely immature and emotionally stunted, even if he's nine years older than me. He's more trouble than he's worth. Still, sometimes I see him seeing me and I'm afraid of those stupid stars he's got in his eyes. They change everything.

I look at the reflection of myself in the window. I'm only here as a double exposure, Willassie, superimposed on this happy scene as someone's idea of a joke. If I took my picture in a mirror tonight—a focused, sharp-lined picture—I wouldn't recognize myself. This pale girl in the Tangerine Travesty and Matching Sateen Pumps with her head thrown back over the top of her neck is not the same girl you knew. She could never have survived the temperature, the isolation. This frivolous girl only knows the word 'blood' as an abstract concept. Those diagrams with the platelets, the white cells, the red.

If you were here tonight, you wouldn't recognize me. You'd say I smelled too much like city things. Makeup and soap. But really I'm a different person in every new location. I couldn't be the same me here as there. If you came here, you'd change too. You'd have to. There'd be traffic and alcohol and purchasing of produce. You wouldn't know the language. You'd change too. Alice has to do all sorts of strange things in order to make it through Wonderland. She eats that growy stuff and drinks the shrinky stuff too.

Shit. I need a quiet place. I wander upstairs where the Masonic meeting room is. Women aren't supposed to come in here—there's a sign. Fuck you, Masons, and fuck your patriarchal rules. I tromp inside. A big gilded eye protrudes from the ceiling. The walls are covered in life-sized oil paintings of elderly white men. There are red light bulbs on tall wooden stands placed strategically around the room. Red plush chairs that fold down, like the ones in rundown movie theatres. Two pipe organs and thick, abstractly blood-coloured carpet. I take my shoes off and feel it beneath my feet like the moss of the tundra. I lie down under the eye. I watch it watching me and feel my heart thudding out into the silence of the forbidden room.

Mark's downstairs wondering where I am. Happy party noises are coming softly up the staircase and mixed in is the chorus of White Wedding. I raise my hand and salute Billy Idol, blocking out the pupil of the golden eye with my fist.

You're very young, Teresa, you used to say. You are small and pretty and young like a snowflake. I am still very young. I will always be snowflake-young, even when I'm eighty. And you'll always be young for me, curled up in my fist and thrust into the eye of the sky. It's a weird night. I'm feeling lonely. There's too much fluid in my body. I've got to puke or piss or cry. That old carpet smell. I want to sink down to where you are dormant in my mind, Willassie, I want to sink all the way down to where I'm thirteen, sleep a bit on this carpet that feels like moss. The eye continues to stare at me. I can hear pretty well up here. The song is turned off. The acoustics of this building are really something.

"Get off of him!" I hear. "Get out of here! Get out! Get out! Get going!"

It's Vanessa. I get my shoes on with difficulty and hurry down the staircase. A rushing sound that is a lot of people inhaling at once. The front door slamming. Curtis is standing in the front hall, his corsage scattered in pieces around him. White petals like exploded doves. He has a cut on the bridge of his nose. Vanessa with her hand on her heart. She shoos the onlookers back into the party.

"What's the matter? Never seen a dust-up at a wedding before?"

"It's tradition, sure," someone calls out, and then there's laughter.

Everyone goes back inside. Elvis puts on his blue suede shoes. I go to the washroom and dampen a few pieces of paper towel, but when I get back Curtis has gone out for a smoke. Vanessa is standing in the hallway by herself, in her borrowed white dress, safety-pinned under the arms.

"What happened?" I say.

"Mark jumped my husband. You know how he gets."

"He didn't."

"He ripped the corsage into pieces. I think some of it he did with his teeth."

"Jesus."

"It was like a wild animal."

"He must have been loaded."

She sighs. "He has to let me change. It's stifling everything. I shrink when he's around."

"He's an asshole."

"I don't want to see him again. It's unhealthy. This time I'm serious."

I tuck a piece of Vanessa's hair back into her veil. "I don't know how your mother ever survived raising the two of you."

"I'm sure she'll be sainted after she passes on."

Vanessa goes to find her blessed mother. I go out after Curtis. His wedding is full of strangers with mixed wishes. His family is in Alberta and the States. He hadn't thought being in love would be this lonely. Not two hours in and the brother-in-law is swinging punches at his face.

"Smoke?" He holds his pack out.

"No thanks. This is for you."

I give him the paper towels and tell him where to wipe. He didn't even know he was bleeding before that. I put out my hand.

"So, Curtis." I say. "Nice to meet you. How's it going. You having the night of a lifetime yet?"

14

Me and Evan and Mina and Lucy are using the food crates as a playhouse, outside. We've got them stood on their ends and propped up against the side of the house. You have to crawl in, but it's big enough for a few people to sit. It smells like wood. The wind whistles through the knotholes and makes your face really cold when you press it up into the gaps between the crates to spy on the outside world.

We were forced to bring Evan along, but I don't mind so much. We're making him dress up like a girl, for badness. We don't have much to play with. If I brought Barbies out here, the plastic would get so cold it'd snap. That's what happened to Evan's GI Joes. So we have bits of soapstone and a big rusty file that I'm trying to carve with, and a pencil, and a box that someone can sit on, like a throne.

We're writing all over the walls of the playhouse. First, our names. English letters and syllabics too. I write mine and Evan's. Teresa Norman and Evan Norman. Mina writes Mina Ippaq and Lucy writes Lucy Arnataq. Mina and Lucy write boys' names with hearts around them. They tell me to do it too. I say I don't like any boys here, so they tell me to write the name of my boyfriend from home.

Teresa Norman + Romeo Montague, True Love Forever.

They ask me if we've gone all the way. I say sure. Evan starts writing numbers on the wall and I help him make the fives go the right way around, with their fat bellies sticking out to the right. Mina won't stop talking about my boyfriend and if he's a good kisser. I say he's the best kisser ever and even had a kissing booth on Valentine's Day. Last year, he made enough money from it to buy a red dirt bike, so it was totally worth the whole week of chapped lips. He kissed every girl in school and all the lady teachers too. I lent him my Cherry Chapstick. He had a giant shiny mouth twice the size of his normal mouth, because the zillions of kissing booth kisses had in reality chapped his entire lower face. It hurt him to smile, but he still smiled at me. His lips bled when he talked, but he still talked to me. He'd walk me home and at my door would plant a shiny kiss on my forehead, leaving an imprint greasy as a fried egg. I wouldn't wash it off. Dear sweet Romeo Montague. What an amazing boyfriend he was.

Mina likes this story as much as I do. Lucy asks if he gives good hickeys. I ask her what a hickey is. She takes the pencil, licks the eraser, and jams it into the side of my neck. She twists it in, deeply. I try not to cry.

"This is a hickey?"

"It's what boyfriends do to their girlfriends to show them that they love them." The eraser pushes harder into my throat. I can feel my pulse throbbing against it.

When she stops there's a hot place that hurts to touch.

She says, admiringly, "'Cause you're so white it gonna get nice and purple. Mine just are brown."

She and Mina give each other whole necklaces of hickeys. Strands of hot brown pearls that Lady Diana might wear. They've started in on Evan. They're putting one on his forehead.

In class the next day Lucy and Mina wear turtlenecks. Lucy's is aqua and Mina's is lime. They're not looking at me but everyone else is. My hickey is bright blue. I'm wearing my Peter Pan-collared shirt. Willassie keeps dropping his pencil on the floor so he can lean over and get a better view. His ears are red. He's just jealous. They're all jealous of my one true love. I think tonight Romeo might give me hickeys on my legs and arms as well.

After school I'm walking home, going around the edge of the town, past the church and the police station. I'm crunching my boots down in the snow, stepping on the slippery river stones and singing.

I'se the b'y that builds the boat
I'se the b'y that sails her
I'se the b'y that catches the fish
and takes 'em home to Lizer

Lizer is a horrible name. I wonder if she was pretty. She probably had ten kids and watched *The Young and the Restless* and was wicked at crib. Made bread a lot. I bet she wore a flowered apron. The bread they make here isn't real bread at all. It's fried in long coils, deep-fried so it looks like a crispy golden worm. The best bits are the ends because they have more crunch. But it's not real bread, it's bannock. You can't put peanut butter and jam on it and call it a sandwich.

I stop suddenly, on a rock in the middle of the river. I can hear someone behind me. Breathing. The rock knocks against the riverbed. A crack outwards in the skin of ice. I don't know if I should look back. Dad says to ignore troublemakers and they'll leave you alone. But maybe it's Evan. Maybe he'll fall into the river and drown if I don't turn around. I start to slip. My leg is going to go through the thin ice around the rock. Someone grabs my arm and pulls me back. Big feet in dirty, scuzzed-up sneakers with the laces gone. A hand on my arm. Breathing into my scalp.

"Who give you the hickey?"

It's Willassie. Jesus. I start to slip again. He keeps his grip. I lose my balance and now I'm leaning back against him. He's not falling.

"Can you talk?" he says.

I can't breathe, let alone speak.

"Tell me who give you the hickey or I puts you in the river."

"Lucy," I say.

"No shit."

"Lucy did it. She's got a bunch. So does Mina. So does my little brother. I only have one. Don't put me in the river, Willassie."

"I give you a hickey."

"No. It hurts."

"I give you a hickey, Teresa."

"But I don't have a pencil!"

Then: this hot, wet touch on my neck. I think it's his mouth. His nose is cold above his hot mouth. He's pressing his face into my neck, sucking my pulse out. I'm sure he's got my pulse in his mouth. I can't stand up. My back is against his chest. I'm looking up into the sky at the turrs that are circling each other, making a racket in the quiet afternoon. My eyes are closing by themselves. There's a roaring feeling inside my ears, and I think this might be the noise that lunatics hear. Willassie stops sucking and licking me. His breath is wet in my ear. He lets go of my arm, and I teeter a little on the rock.

"That's going get real purple 'cause you's so white," he says.

Then he's running fast back the way he came, jumping from rock to rock like Superman. As he gets farther away, he doesn't get smaller. He's a giant in my line of vision. His spit dries cold on me below the dent his nose made in my neck.

Dad is furious about Evan's hickeys. I change into a turtleneck before he yells at me. It doesn't matter that Mina and Lucy did it. Dad says that because I was there I should have stopped them. I say Evan liked it.

"I don't care if he liked it, he's five."

"But…"

"No buts."

"But you're the one who made us play with him!"

Dad's getting red. "So it's my fault, is it? It's funny how everything's my fault. Your poor brother has bruises all over his face and arms, for God's sake, and it's my fault!"

"They're hickeys."

"Excuse me?"

"They're not bruises, Dad, they're hickeys."

"Hickeys?"

"Yeah, Dad. Hickeys. You know, for decoration. Everyone has them."

Dad rubs his face. "Teresa. I don't know what you and your friends are doing, and I don't want to know. I don't know where you got that word. That word doesn't mean what you think it does, you got me?"

"What does it mean, then?"

"You're pushing it."

"What does it mean? How can I ever learn anything if you keep it all from me? Mom would tell me what it means."

"I refuse to have this conversation. You're acting like a child, so you'll be treated like one. Do not dare start to cry, or so help me."

But the tears are lined up and ready to fall, and I can't stop them.

Dad rubs his neck. "You're grounded for a week. Go to your room. No arguing."

Dad's left me a secret weapon. My dictionary. If he thinks I'm stupid and won't find out what a hickey really is, then he's dead wrong. I'm sly. I'm wily.

Hickey/hiki/n & adj. (pl—**eys**) N. *Amer informal derogatory* **1** a red mark on the skin, caused by biting or sucking during sexual play. **2** a gadget (DOOHICKEY)

He's right. I had no idea. Now I know why Dad was so mad about Evan. I should tell him we did it all with a pencil. Are hickeys really not the same as bruises? Are they little hurts that people in love give each other? Does Willassie love me?

I touch the sides of my neck, each with their own sore spots. I get in bed and pull the covers up around my face. I won't cry. I like being grounded. I grit my teeth and start reading *Anne of Green Gables* for the hundred zillionth time, the words 'sexual play,' 'sucking' and 'biting' dancing like sugarplums in my head, till I can't even see what I'm reading.

15

I wish I could document you somehow. I wish I could summon you for a day, position you in an indirect afternoon light, and shoot my way through a few rolls. Enough photographs to last me. But you've slipped too far into the past, and I don't have the skill to bring you back. I'd need to hack you out of stone to really do you justice, although I catch myself focusing sometimes on a man's back, his tanned neck, the curl of his earlobe. If I take pictures of strangers, at oblique angles, sometimes I can almost convince myself that they're pictures of you. The men don't need to be Inuit. I can't really remember what you look like, so nearly any substitute will do. I ripped up all my pictures, when we got back. Or Dad did. We both thought we'd never want to remember Sanikiluaq. We decided to start again, to pretend that year was some sort of mistake in time, easily whited out, erased by blizzard. Bleached through to bone. Scoured of identity from the inside out. Is this what we did to you, Willassie? Is this what My People did to Your People?

I'm changing into my red terry cloth dress. It's Mark's opening.

Even though he knows I have to be at the damn gallery anyway, he made me promise to be his date, with a hand on my heart and everything. Since he and Vanessa are on the outs I'm his only backup in case things get ugly. At his last opening, one of the Old Guard threw a wine glass at his feet. "This isn't Art." Mark rolled up his shirt sleeves, eager to scrap with the guy. "What, not enough puffins for you? Have I offended your provincial sensibilities?" It'd been a bad idea to start the bar service before his talk began. I was chastised at the next board meeting: "You know our crowd. They're a bunch of rowdies. Always start with the talk before proceeding to the drinking." This will be the first time Vanessa isn't here with him. I put on mascara and striped tights and mess around with my hair for a bit, working it into knots, threading bits of wool into it.

Mark's show is called *Tanked*. He's constructed a large glass tank inside the gallery with just enough room for people to walk around it. I've polished it, publicized it, sent out the invites, put the title on the wall. The tank is filled with water. Immersed inside is a replica of everything normally found in the gallery, floating or anchored to the sides with bits of rope. You're encouraged to punch the sides of the tank to make ripples. You can climb a stepladder and stir the water with a paddle, making hundreds of slides float by in schools like fishes, or surface as flotsam on the top. The diligent may cause enough movement to stir the gallery desk into wobbling on the bottom. A duplicate of my pink cardigan is sometimes sucked up off the plexiglass floor. Its sleeves swell into arm-shapes as the water goes through. The comment book has already started to disintegrate.

This is Mark's most ambitious work yet. He had to employ an engineer to make sure that the tank was structurally sound.

He didn't want a lawsuit if it burst in the gallery and a shard of glass the size and shape of a badminton racket stabbed into the arm of some poor, wine-grubbing Exhibit Opening Attendee (EOA), pinning him/her to the wall as the mighty wave of water sloshed past. The poor EOA pinned through the wrist of his/her writing hand, and he/she was working on A Novel, imagine. He/she is the only one of the crowd not swept up in the escapee wave as it bursts through the doors, tearing them from their hinges, swelling forward with an intimate, yet horrifically loud liquidy noise, an amplified version of the phlegmy sigh that Dad, undoing the top button of his pants, likes to let out after dinner. The wave then rushing madly across the traffic on Harbour Drive and leaping into the welcoming, stinky arms of Great Aunt Atlantic. Reunited at last! cue violins! Leaving the sodden Artists and Artists' Mothers in a lurid, bruised pile in the parking lot, like a bowl of last week's fruit, sucking their thumbs and feebly calling out the names of loved ones in their Post-Wave, Pre-Stiff-Drink Shock.

Not that any of that will happen. Mark has hired the engineer and the tank won't break. It's perfect.

When we came last night to clean, I walked slowly around it, admiring the size. The welding on the frame smooth and shiny, slightly blue at the seams. The refractions through the water making Mark on the other side look like he was shooting light from his torso, shooting it out in these delicate waves. He was like a merman or something, wavering there under water, his limbs melting into loopy shapes, his head swelling and curving in impossible, freak show ways, with giant forehead and giant eyes. It was quite beautiful. I didn't say that. I said, "Mark, your piece is lacking something." I told him he should have a few gulls, for

God's sake, maybe a harbour seal. Or synchronized swimmers in smoke-damaged costumes and not quite in sync. They could be attempting to keep a cake aloft and lit in the air. Also they could be juggling.

He said that I don't take installation work as seriously as I should, and that photography was a perfect medium for those not daring enough to make actual Art, with a capital A. Who choose to hide behind their telephoto. That my work is a weak and unnecessary attempt to resuscitate a dying practice that should just be left to waste away. Evaporate. Let's euthanize the sucker and get it over with. No one wants fucking black and white landscapes, or pictures of out-of-work fishermen. I should get myself a digital camera, at the very least, and join the ranks of the living. Stop being so prehistoric. The disadvantages of the darkroom. Haven't I heard that 35mm film isn't even going to be available within the next ten years? Gone the way of betamax, the laser disc, floppy disks, the ditto machine. Dot matrix. Cassette tapes. If I'm going to refuse to move forward, then I should just stick to my day job, stencilling other people's exhibit titles onto the gallery wall.

I said, "Holy defensive, Batman," and left it at that. No way am I going to fight Art-Man on a subject he knows nothing about, the sort he fights over most passionately. I don't want to fuck up our friendship because stupid Mark can't understand that the archaic quality is part of what I love. I love the darkroom. I love the science involved, the slowness of it. I love seeing my images developing in the tray, submerged. I love the chemical slop, the headachy smell. I like how easy it is to ruin negatives. All it takes is one finger of light through the crack of the door. The fact that it's dark. That there's ritual and mystery. That it's expensive and bad for my skin and probably cancerous in the long run. Wouldn't surprise me. This digital shit, this click and you're done, time to download, time to alter in Photoshop, so the art is not in the photography but in the manipulation—all fine for someone else. I prefer to be medieval. Mark said I'm going to have to start hoarding film. I could bury it and draw maps, that would be just like me.

I didn't say, hey Mark, you jerk, why don't you have a little respect for my medium. I didn't say, just because I don't fight with you doesn't mean I don't have my own opinions. It doesn't make my work devoid of meaning. I'm not less of an artist than you because my work is sellable. Or that I don't shock people, usually. I'm developing a metaphor—it's a metaphor in metamorphosis—that all art is like a mirror, but a selective and warped one, a scientifically sound and specifically designed one, that picks out various elements of life, perhaps magnifies or distorts them, perhaps arranges them in patterns or abstracts them into unrecognizable forms, perhaps transfigures them entirely, but ultimately throws a fragment of life back at us to examine. Artists make these mottled, wonky mirrors to show us what it is to be a human, now, in this world. A photograph is physically incapable of summing up everything the photographer is seeing or experiencing. The interest is in what she chooses to focus on and keep. How much more you can see when the familiar is shown back to you through some static patterns on a piece of glossy paper too delicate to touch with your fingertips.

I told Mark none of this. I just smiled and changed the subject. He'd love for me to say something like this, he really wants to argue theory with me. I won't. I don't want to hear whatever cruel things he's waiting to throw my way. But I'm wearing the dress he likes and making a bird's nest of my hair for him. I'm bringing white chocolate 'brownies' to the opening because they're the only kind of brownies he'll eat. He's freakish like that.

Maybe I'll make an installation piece called *Missing Person*. It'll consist of all the things about you that I can still remember. There'll be a bag of dirt for smelling. An arm cast in bronze. A piece of sandpaper stapled to the wall, nearly worn through to nothing. A thin green t-shirt, soaked in apple juice for a year. A husky dog allowed to roam the room. And everywhere, the sound of breathing. People can reconstruct you in their minds as I've had to do. They'll hail me as an artistic force on the cusp of genius. They'll say, finally, she quit hiding behind that silly camera. Finally, something with Meaning. Taking up the mantle of the Norman Tradition. Finally, thanks be to God. Some motherfucking Art. I'll have testimonials from various Legitimate Artists congratulating me on my leaps forward. I'll get someone else to put them on the wall. I know it won't fix anything. What's done is done. But maybe I'll make this installation anyway, just for fun. Just to make Mark mad. I can think of worse motives for doing something.

16

Me and Evan are going to build an igloo today. We've taken the biggest knives out of the kitchen to cut the blocks with. Dad'll never notice. The snow next to the house is too soft, so we are walking away from the community, out toward the open tundra. We stop when all the buildings are as big as our fists. I have to wipe Evan's nose for him. He's become a real little Inuit kid, snot in two thick streams down into his lip. I do like the mothers do and squeeze his nostrils out into my hand with two fingers, then wipe them in the snow.

I tell Evan to stomp out a circle that we'll use as a guide for where to put the blocks. He makes it too big, so we move again, another twenty feet, and this time I mark out the path to put the blocks on, my skidoo boots crunching into the crust of snow like teeth into toast. This only needs to be a little igloo, for just the two of us.

I tell Evan to cut some rectangles, big ones, in the snow. It's like cutting up Rice Krispie squares. The hard part is getting the blocks up whole, without crumbling the edges. I make a shallow trench around my first block to pry it up better. The crisp white hunk of snow comes up in my hands and I place it carefully on the circle of footprints. Evan is singing and hacking at the snowdrifts. I can tell he's not going to be much help, but that's okay. It's the company I want.

Evan stops me from thinking about confusing things too much. Alone in my room, with my books spread uselessly on my knees, all I can think about is hickeys. Licking. What Willassie might look like underneath his jeans and Boston Bruins sweatshirt. It's better to be out here with my brother, making igloos. It requires concentration. I must focus to put the blocks together snugly, to cut their sides on the proper angle so they lean slightly inwards and eventually slope into a dome, the whole thing supporting itself with gravity.

The church in Sanikiluaq looks like a big, permanent igloo with a little cross on top. I wonder if this is on purpose, to make the Inuit feel like this white God is theirs too. As though He's more accessible inside a familiar shape. I haven't been there. It's Anglican, not Catholic. I'm not really sure what the difference is, except for the lack of incense. When I was little, I used to go to mass sometimes with Mom and Aunt Cack. I thought the incense smell was coming from the big statue of Christ on the cross. I thought that old, flowery, secret smell was His breath coming down around our heads, protecting us. I used to breathe it in so deep I'd get dizzy, waiting in the pew for Mom to get back from taking communion, too little to understand why I couldn't go too. I wanted to know what His body tasted like, and His blood. I wasn't baptized. I couldn't eat of Jesus. I knelt on the worn red velvet of the fold-down bench, elbows on the pew in front with my hands folded, chin on top, looking up at all the beautiful windows with their saints and sad people, the lambs and lions, the doves and angels and snakes. All those violent stories. John the Baptist's head coming clean off. People turning to pillars of salt. Parents sacrificing their children, agreeing to cut them down the middle in order to share them around. Those who loved Jesus sending Him to His death in the end. The Romans forcing the vinegar down His throat. And all those saints, centuries full of them, getting killed because of their convictions, dying gratefully. Girls burning up in public fires, men stoned to death, getting pierced through the heart with arrows, in loincloths, tied to trees. It was like watching a scary movie, peeking through my fingers, despite myself, at the strange things going on. Horrified, but hooked. Later on, dreaming.

I wonder if the kids in my class feel the same way when they go to church. Do they sit there in awe, jaws dropped into laps, when the minister talks about Judas and the hanging tree? Maybe Anglicans leave all the gore out. Maybe they only tell the happy parts of all those stories.

I cut into the snow, leaning down onto my arm to get some force behind it. I look up and see that Evan has wandered a little way off. He's eating a fistful of snow, the knife sticking out of the ground beside his knee.

"Come back and help me, Evan."

He bounds back and jumps on me, cracking the block I've just cut and nearly falling onto my knife, stuck in the snow.

"Be careful, little monkey. That's sharp."

"I'm a Ninja. Nothing can hurt me."

He kisses me. His face is wet and cold. We drag over enough blocks to make the bottom layer of the igloo. I thought it would be quicker than this. I get Evan to come inside the circle with me.

We lie on our backs, looking up at the clouds. The row of snow blocks keeps the wind out.

"What's that one look like? A dragon?"

"It's He-Man and his tiger. See, there's his head and there's the tiger head. They're talking. He-Man is telling jokes to the tiger."

Once he points it out I can see it too. We lie and make pictures in the air for a while. Evan falls asleep, his cheeks rosy in the cold, all snuggled up to my side in his snowpants and big blue coat. I keep staring up, making cloud pictures of lips and eyes. Necks, bums. Willassie pictures. The sound of Evan's quiet breathing beside me.

And then there's more breathing. Louder, faster. It isn't human. I lie still, my heart pounding so loud now that the breathing sound is covered over, and maybe I imagined it.

I wait for my heart to calm down a bit, until I'm sure this isn't a case of Teresa's Wild Imagination Running Away With Her Again. Then I hear a crunch in the snow of something shifting weight, close by. The seconds are long and strained and Evan's soft baby snores seem as loud as thunder, or ice cracking. I want to put my mitten over his mouth. Finally I decide to peek. I slide my feet up a little to give myself leverage, hoping to sit up very quietly.

The polar bear looms above us. We are caught in its shadow and my brother doesn't wake. The bear blocks the sun. At first I see only its outline. I shut my eyes. I pray to God that it will pass us by, think us dead or too strange to prod at. It smells sharp and sour and not like anything else. Many seconds go by, and the bear and Evan breathe. I open one eye a sliver, a crack. It's so big. It takes up all the sky.

It has Evan's knife in its mouth, like a bear in a dream. I don't know why it would want the knife, except that it's shiny. Dad's old kitchen knife, with the splintering wooden handle and the three golden rivets. Each of the bear's paws is as big as my head, the claws long and sharp. Fur the colour of my hair, clumped and matted with snow, blood on its front from something newly killed. It looks at me. I whimper. I try not to, but it happens anyway. The bear just looks at me. Its eyes are not like people-eyes, and not like cartoon-bear-eyes, but wild, wet, dark. They investigate me. It sniffs, shifts weight, pitches forward, lumbers over us. The bear's walking right over us and Evan's still sleeping. Its legs are huge. They're telephone poles. It moves lightly, the snow squeaking and crunching under it.

I wait, shuddering, tears silently running into my ears. I lie as still as possible in the snow, praying the bear won't turn around and come back for us. One touch of that paw and we'd be finished. I sit up slowly. The bear is gone. There's nowhere for it to hide so I know it isn't hiding. I shake Evan. I make him get up and head for home. He's grumpy and disoriented. He asks why I'm crying.

"Just thinking about home. Nothing."

"I miss Mom, Teresa."

"Me too, baby. Let's go and eat something."

He doesn't think to ask about the missing knife, which is lucky. If Dad ever notices, I'll tell him I did something stupid with it. Dropped it in the river, broke it while carving. I'll take all blame. If Dad knew about the bear, we'd be locked in the house till the end of our time here. Better that he doesn't have a heart attack.

I think about the skin room, the day they called me the Polar Bear Girl. It no longer seems very funny. I think about those cutesy animal posters some of the girls at home used to put in their lockers. The ones with captions under the animals: Bad Hair Day, Just Hangin' Around. Stupid jokey phrases under pictures of tigers and orangutans and polar bears, framed in pink or with borders of cartoon clouds.

Tomorrow, at school, they'll talk about the bear that came into town, how it ate a husky dog. How it got up on the front step of Larry's house and tried to open the door, snapping off the doorknob in the cold. Larry's brother had to climb through the window to let them all out in the morning. They'll talk about the tracks it left. Easy work for hunters. This bear means meat, fur, money.

I will thank my lucky stars it found the dog before us, that it wasn't hungry. This place so near to wild that anything can happen. Death as close to us as anything else, as sunlight, wind, breathing. So close, it makes no sense to waste any time. I will follow all my impulses to their endings. Tomorrow I'll sit in school with the bear-talk around me. I'll figure out how to talk to Willassie again. I'll sit quietly in the classroom and plan how to get him to touch me. I must find a way to talk to him, to ask about the pencil in my cheek and the hickey on my neck. Which one was something real and which was meant to trick me.

I can't wait for things to happen. Those claws could've come across our faces. One lazy swipe and Evan and I would've been suddenly dead, our faces split and red at the claw-seams. Our chests opened up and innards gone. Steam coming off us like a pair of seals, helpless on the ice.

17

My mother has told me the story of how she met my father, over and over, with little change, for as long as I can remember. If our family had an oral tradition of any kind, this would be its pièce de résistance, no question.

She was eighteen and in Bowring Park. She was wearing a green cotton dress with tiny yellow flowers, and a cardigan with pink buttons, and had gone to the park to sketch. It was July. She climbed the willow tree and was busily drawing the pairs of mothers out strolling with kids in tow, enjoying the roundness of the women's heads as seen from above. She was swinging her legs, totally absorbed in her sketch pad, swinging and swinging her legs, one and then the other. Her left shoe fell off onto the head of a man who was passing by. He stopped and picked up the shoe and then looked up into the tree, his hand to his head, just like Chicken Little: the sky is falling! Mom grabbed her own head in shock and cried out, "Dear Lord, I am sorry! Sorry!"

He squinted up and she called down, "Without my shoe you're going to have to help me." And then, "Watch out." She dropped her book and pencil and proceeded to lower herself with one foot and both hands, the useless, shoeless foot just dangling. I can picture this so well. My mother's little bobby-socked foot floating in front of Dad's face, like a carrot. He has no choice at all. He's suckered in by it.

He caught her waist and held her as she lowered herself toward the ground. He stooped again for the shoe. Found her foot in front of him. From his crouch on the grass, he seized it firmly. Put the shoe on, tied the laces. He looked up as she looked down. They caught each other looking.

He had little metal-framed glasses and a tweedy cap like down at Wm L. Chafe and Son. Eyes that looked like they saw everything. Fresh into the city from Port Rexton. Mom said that with the dappled green light coming through the new leaves of the tree they were both transformed. They seemed to each other like figures from a dream, or a past life, or déja vu. Perfect and surreal, with changing faces.

They sat in the park and talked for hours, till the sun went down and Mom had to get home, where Boiled Dinner awaited. When I was small I always made gagging noises at the Boiled Dinner part—totally sickitating—all that waterlogged, mushy cabbage and turnip with flecks of salt beef in every crevice. The mustard pickle, the pickled onion, the beet. I'd rather have gone without dinner than eaten any of it.

That first afternoon my parents talked with voraciousness, with the kind of immediate hunger that Mom says has been lost to every generation since hers, the last to truly believe in The Power of Love. Nowadays, she says, it isn't acceptable for a person to say they love someone until they've dated for at least three months, for God's sake. She says you know right away if you love someone, and all this waiting is nothing but fear. And fuck fear, Mom says, if it's getting in your way.

According to legend, Dad and Mom said they loved each other that very first day. By the time the sun set, they'd said they loved each other, and had made plans, too. He would pick her up the next day in his truck and take her to the secret swimming hole out by Petty Harbour. You had to pull over off the highway, and walk fifteen minutes through the woods while blowing the blackflies out of your eyes, but it was worth it to get to this still little place with smooth rock sloping down into the water, and no sign at all of any other member of the human race. Mom knew she'd marry James Norman within half an hour of meeting him, she said. Which I guess could be why I didn't freak out as much as Mark did when he heard Vanessa's *Shotgun Wedding to a Mainlander* plan. I'm preconditioned to believe that love at first sight can lead to happy marriage, at least for a while, for a decade or so.

At sundown they kissed each other briefly, but with such intensity that her lips were bruised the next morning, purple and huge, "throbbing exquisitely." My mother said she loved my father so much that she would have thrown herself into the dirty mess of the harbour if anything were to happen to him. She said she loved him so much that life before him seemed to be nothing but a rehearsal. My mother said that my father was the magic that kept the insides in and the outsides out. In later years, the insides and outsides got mixed together. Sometimes she couldn't distinguish between what was real and what she was making up. Sometimes every thought came out of her mouth raw, in strings of syllables, often without sense. Or in whole memorized pages from some Catholic encyclopaedia, fermented in her chemically imbalanced brain, spewing forth, a geyser.

"Ludwig and Elizabeth of Hungary married when he was twenty-one and she was fourteen. They were raised up together from childhood, and it wasn't mad love. No bodices were ripped during hurried horseback fornication after having accidentally lost sight of the rest of the hunting party. They loved each other devotedly and warmly, not hotly. But Ludwig never understood Elizabeth's need to mortify herself. He was not a spiritually astute man. He couldn't understand why she put those sharp little rocks in the soles of her expensive slippers. Beware those heathen men, Teresa. They'll drag you into compromising situations, and not all of us have the moral fortitude of blessed St. Elizabeth."

I don't know my father's side of the story.

Mom has finally given in and let Aunt Cack put her in a home. Though only fifty-eight, she hasn't aged well and looks much older. She hates taking her meds because they swell her up — it's called edema, a build-up of fluid under the skin. She's edematous just about everywhere, even on her tongue. Swelled up and emaciated all at once, a pretty sick joke. Her hands are so bloated that it hurts to hold her brushes, her skin all raised and reddened, a permanent itch. Feeling things as though through a blanket, muffled, unclear. It's hard to see her like that, hard not to agree: go on, stop taking that shit. It's killing you. Then again, so are the recent suicide attempts. There's no way to win when you're crazy.

The home is the closest we can come to being fair. Aunt Cack has her own family, she has her own children's monitors to listen to. Mom will have nurses on call in quiet rubber shoes. There'll be flowers, I'll make sure of that. She'll rest, and be safe, and maybe happy. I'll switch my Sunday bus route and continue the tai chi charade and nothing much will change, for her at least. I myself will have some adjusting to do.

Mom's left me her house and all its contents. This is supposed to happen when a person dies, but this morning she took hold of me by the ears. "I'm halfway there already," she said. "So you might as well take it now. Stop wasting money on rent. Lord knows it's hard enough to scrape along. Quit the gallery if you want. Rest for a while. Fool around with your camera. Get a car. Have to get back out to the country, don't you, and make some work." She said things which made me think that maybe she was sane again. She had her thumbs on my earlobes, squeezing them, appealing to my ears to listen carefully. She told me to call Evan. "He might think he doesn't have parents anymore, but he'll always be tied to you, Teresa. Whether he likes it or not." She said it's my responsibility to call him, to keep on calling him, whether he actually talks to me or not. Sitting with the phone near his ear, breathing sullenly into the receiver. She said, "Teresa, it's up to you to wear him out. He needs you to be there, even if right now he'd rather someone gutted him."

Aunt Cack tapped her on the shoulder and jangled the car keys. Mom kissed me on the forehead like I was a little kid still, or sick, and climbed into the passenger seat. She looked relieved to be leaving.

I'm twenty-three and the owner of a house full of things no one needs. Useless objects that mean nothing. I wade through stacks of old magazines, Mom's bedsheets strewn across the floor. Stems of old flowers arranged in dusty vases with the powder of fallen petals in circles on the tablecloth. A half-finished painting on her easel upstairs, the brush uncleaned, its bristles clogged with paint and covered in a furry layer of dust. The predictable detritus. Other aspects of the house are less expected, at least to an impartial observer. The murals, vibrant and throbbing with colour, and by now taking over most available surfaces: walls, ceilings, bookshelves, doors. The collection of dressmaker's dummies heaved in on one another in my old room with the rainbow wallpaper, the height of cool when I was nine. The neat stacks of rusted car parts, salvaged from the roadside for their beautiful feathered edges. No doubt meant to become a sculpture someday, they fill an entire broom closet.

And the door to the master bedroom that she plastered over, trying to bury the room inside the wall. The plaster job ragged as a wound. She painted angels over it, pale green ones and scarlet ones slumped as though they've been deboned. Sad angels lying down, maybe to die. Eyeless angels weeping from their empty sockets. Soon I'll go one better than Mom and shove a dresser in front of it, sagging angels and all. I'm going to have to. Otherwise waves of sad/madness will crack that plaster, burst right out of there and drown me. I should crawl in through the window and throw out all the crap I bet is piled inside: paperback romance novels (Mom's guilty pleasure), her rose-pink negligee (permanently retired), a whole laundry hamper full of used Kleenex (saved from the 2, 312, 489, 721 times she blew her nose after Dad left her), that pair of briefs he left here by accident (bronzed), and the painting she did of him lying in bed in that golden Sunday Morning light (with his mouth hanging open so realistically you could almost hear the lawn mower rumble of his snore). There could be anything in that room. Things could be rotting and polluting the air. I really should just grit my teeth and hack through the plaster. Get it over with.

But I want to document everything first. To remember her. To pore over later, trying to discern meaning from the objects my mother lived amongst. Those murals like prehistoric cave paintings. The garden. The box of razors and other precious heirlooms that I'm sure are waiting for me underneath the bed somewhere, in Evan's old room, where Mom has slept since we left her here.

To Dad, Mom died over a decade ago. For years he's thought of her as a ghost. Attending her funeral, when the time comes, will be unnecessary. He long ago completed his period of mourning, after the person he married ceased to resemble the girl whose foot swam through the air with more grace than any other foot in the history of bipedal lovers. I'm unsure whether Dad left Mom because she was losing herself, or if she lost herself because he was leaving. I guess it doesn't really matter, in the end. We do what we do, and that's the way of it.

Today I spent too much money on flowers, but it was all I could think of. To send my mother away with flowers, with the soft translucent petals she likes to touch to her cheeks as you'd feel a baby's fingers. I got every kind of flower except the common carnation, which she could never stand. Roses, dahlias, begonias, violets, pansies, tulips, anemones. A sunflower and baby's breath and forget-me-nots. Even orchids, lilies, bleeding hearts. The colours colliding with each other, fireworks. She grasped my ears. I said "I love you" and "Goodbye," the only two phrases I could get out because she was talking my ear off. With her it's either silence or avalanche, on or off.

I sit on the edge of Evan's bed. I can't go back to the rainbow bedroom that was my haven as a child. That would be harder than sleeping here, where my baby brother used to sleep before our family spontaneously combusted. Where my mother slept, post-explosion. I'll need a new box spring and mattress. All that dead skin. And the Sacred Heart on the ceiling is going to have to go, as soon as possible.

I trail through the rooms, touching things, listening to the shower through the left-hand neighbour's wall. Someone calls out, "Bring in the mail, Rodney, would ya?" I hear feet pounding down the stairs in a familiar rhythm as Rodney leaps the last three steps. His bedroom was the one next to mine. He liked GnR and Poison. I peek out the sheers in the living room and catch him on his front step, all grown up, but still the same old gawky Rodney with the bad haircut. That's comforting.

I go out into the garden, through the back porch stacked haphazardly with boxes of sewing materials and old shoes. The descendants of the poppies I planted before Evan was born are taking over the back fence, bursting forth in ridiculously vibrant orange glory, with no one to admire them for it. It's pretty late for poppies, but they're still going. Global warming is really kicking in. Soon there'll be no winter at all, and we'll have to walk around in special sun-shielding suits whenever we step outdoors. I read in the paper that in something like thirty years the permafrost of the tundra will be defrosted, permanently. There'll be radical changes in temperature. The treeline will move northward. Birnam Wood! I don't want to think about what that'll do to the delicate balance of things. Buildings meant to stand up in frozen ground will buckle at the knees, begging for clemency from their new environment. All those polar bears lost in the new forests, panting in their thick fur, waiting to die out. The narwhals slowly cooked alive in the simmering sea water, the walruses, the seals. They're talking about flooding. Will you sink into the ocean? Even if you don't, you'll be lost. There'll be no reason for the white people to keep out of the North, once it's not freezing cold. You poor fuckers: doomed to inundation, no matter how the coin is tossed. It's all because of pollution and land overuse, that's what the paper said. In Sanikiluaq, there is no pollution, beyond cigarette butts ground into the gravel, garbage kicking around. The tiny island is hardly overused. Even if the population has swelled to seven hundred by this point, there's still lots of land to go around. You can safely say, this change in climate is not our fault. But here's the rub: you're still the ones who'll sink in the mud, you're the ones who'll have to claw your way back out. When your world transforms, how will you be forced to change? Before the transformation starts, it's impossible to tell.

I kick my shoes and socks off and swish my feet through the long, coarse grass of my mother's backyard. I need a scythe. I picture a lawn of tangled grass growing up the map of Canada like a thermometer, the mercury rising, green and soft. It laps at your feet where you stand, some way below the Arctic Circle, on an island so small you appear to be floating on the ocean itself. You've never seen grass like this before. There's flowers from southern climates taking over the tundra, covering it in glossy spots of colour that get denser and denser till there's nothing else left. You're afraid to move, stuck in the middle of the map on your little sinking dot of land.

I walk around in my bare feet for a while. The squish of things dying every time I take a step. I must resign myself to being a murderer if I'm ever going to move. Impossible to pick up every blade of grass and rescue every insect. I walk quickly to the back fence, holding my breath. I sit in front of my mother's flower bed, take a poppy petal and rub it on my lips like I used to as a child, pretending to make myself up. My old sad game. Playing at being a grown-up.

18

School is stupid. I hate it.

All right, I don't hate it. I like learning stuff. In fact, I think I love it. But I really, insanely, hate being in school, with everyone staring at me, the pink and white pencil scar on my cheek getting redder and tighter the more everyone looks my way. Mina and Lucy and the other girls don't exactly exclude me, but they don't include me either. When the school day is done and they want to play Dress-up or Barbies, they love to be around me. I'm everyone's bosom companion. And I don't really mind if they want to come over to play with my stuff and not me at all, because they don't own anything. I know they like me, mostly. But they don't show it in school, because everyone else would make fun of them. I don't really blame them for that, either. I would avoid that kind of attention too, if I could. If I was an Inuit girl with glossy black hair and smooth brown skin and no reason to be a loser, then I wouldn't exactly throw myself in the path of ridicule, especially for a stupid whitey-white girl with cowlicks and glasses and absolutely no social skills. I guess why I'm hating school has got nothing to do with this, either. I wish Willassie had never shown me what a real hickey was. I wish he'd never put his cold nose on my neck, underneath my jacket.

I can deal with being excluded by the girls. But, after what happened in the river, every time he jeers at me with the other boys it feels like a rope burn going all the way down the inside of my throat. Stinging. I finger the stone bird in my pocket, its beak, its clawed feet. I know Willassie doesn't want to make fun of me. All the time he's calling me names in his own language, I can see in his eyes that he's sorry for what he's saying. I have stopped looking at him because I can't bear to see the pitying look in his eyes while the mean words come out of his mouth.

He won't talk to me by myself. He won't say anything that isn't rude or mean. Who gives a care. I could care less about stupid Willassie who is still in grade six even though he's seventeen. I could care less what he thinks about me. I hate him more than Dad and more than Hitler. I hate Willassie so hard I might throw up from the bad feelings it's giving me. But I still have to sit next to him. I can still smell him, I can smell the outdoors on him. I can still see his feet stretched out in the space between our desks, can hear him scratching words into the veneer of his desk when the teacher isn't looking. Probably more crap about wishing I was dead. Eternal Rest for Teresa, Die in Hell Bitch, that kind of thing. He's got several nice inscriptions done already, the letters neat and scratched really deep, for posterity. I'd rather join a convent or dig trenches in Ethiopia for twelve hours a day than sit next to him for the entire year. It's unbearable to contemplate.

It's science class. We're learning about centrifugal force, which makes things go outwards from a centre of rotation. Like a rock on a string, when you swing it around. The rock is experiencing centrifugal force. This is what Mr. Levy is saying. Even though he's the principal, he's also our science teacher, because Ms Jenkins went bonkers and had to go home to Lethbridge. She couldn't take the kids always making fun of her in Inuktitut and not paying any attention. One day she kicked a hole through the wall. She broke her toe and told us we were little shits. The next day she disappeared and Mr. Ilsat gutted her desk. Since then, all the teachers have been covering our classes. Dad now teaches us Health and Reading, to perfect my happiness. He read out that Judy Blume book *Just As Long As We're Together*, including the part where the girl first gets her period. He didn't notice that all the kids turned around and stared at me, and that it was the most embarrassing thing a father could possibly do to his daughter. He's totally without a clue. Science class with Mr. Levy is what I look forward to, while I stare at my desk during Health and try not to hear whatever mortifying shit about pubic hair or mammary glands my dumb-ass Dad is saying, out loud, to everyone.

I like Mr. Levy. He's really tall. He has red hair and a red face to boot. He usually wears a purple sweater with a polar bear on it. Mina said his daughter made it for him. Marguerite. They chanted her name that day that Willassie threw the pencil. Don't ask me why. She's like a superhero. Mina won't tell me much about her, and I'm curious, I've got to admit. All I know is she's in university in Toronto but grew up here. I've seen her picture and she looks really normal. She has red hair, and is almost as pale as me. Everyone in school talks about how great Marguerite was and how pretty she was and how she was friends with everybody. So it can't just be that I'm white.

Mr. Levy likes to demonstrate. He likes active lessons. He

understands that everyone will pay more attention if they're not just reading from a textbook. So he does stuff like make doorbells to learn about electrical circuits, even though no one in this town actually has a doorbell on their house. He showed us how to capture snowflakes on plate-glass slides in this special solution that keeps them frozen. We looked at them under the microscope. These teeny little specks of white turned into gorgeous lacy designs too complicated to simply fall from the sky. I showed Mr. Levy my little microscope after school and he helped me slice up and dye part of a fruit fly so it was easier to see. It wasn't as beautiful as the snowflakes, but it was really cool. All dyed red, the parts of the fly became distinct. All these hairs and joints on something so small it can fit on top of one of Evan's freckles. And its strange, bejewelled eyes. I started thinking about how complex something that small is, and how, to something much bigger than us, like God, it must be amazing that something so small as a human can be made up of so many parts. To something way bigger than a human, the many parts of a fruit fly must be mind-blowing.

Mr. Levy likes me. He doesn't want me to be excluded from the class, even though I'm not even learning the same things. But I can't make him understand that singling me out doesn't help my situation.

"Teresa, could you come up to the front please?"

"But?" I gesture towards my Grade Ten science book. While everyone else is studying laws of motion, I'm learning about the periodic table. What all the code names mean. Mr. Levy doesn't care. "Up to the front, Teresa, if you please."

I shut my textbook and walk down the aisle towards the front of the class, my eyes on everyone's sneakers.

"Lie on the floor, please," Mr. Levy says.

There are hoots of laughter.

"Teresa, I'm serious. Lie face down."

I get down on the carpet. It feels like old man stubble grazing my face. A thunderbolt striking me dead would come in handy. I'm lying on the fucking carpet while Mr. Levy talks to the class about how an object experiencing centrifugal force is temporarily freed from the laws of gravity. This magic force lets the object go through the air horizontally, without being drawn downwards towards the earth. He's gotten the boys to move all the desks back and now he's picking up my ankles. Everyone laughs when they see my bunny-print socks. He's swinging me through the air in a big circle, by my ankles, yelling the whole time about centrifugal force. I'm not listening. My entire body is taken up with the effort to keep from sobbing hysterically. I can't see anything but a coloured blur. I close my eyes because the blur makes me want to throw up. Closed eyes are better. Suddenly I feel like centrifugal force is the answer to everything. I can't see the smirks on anyone's faces, can't really hear anything except my own pulse. I am flying free of my body, free of this classroom and this frozen place. I start grinning and the movement through the air chills my teeth. I vow to become a physicist.

Then the calm stops. Mr. Levy's hands lose their grip on my ankles. This happens in stop-motion, like a claymation on television, jerking to life. First his fingers loosen slightly and slide further down my ankles, then loosen and slide again. This is accompanied by equally jerky noises, both from him and myself. And then, I'm really flying, free of centrifugal force and gravity both. Free of his hands. For one entire second I'm in the air, alone.

I land face down on the carpet, skidding across the room, skinning my nose and forehead and chin so bad they start to bleed. My glasses are broken, the bridge cracked in two. This is the worst tragedy. I run out of the room, hanging onto the bits of my glasses, banging my knee on the door frame because I can't see properly, letting out a howl of pain so loud that Ms Elbow in the room next door comes out to see what's going on as I pelt down the hallway, bleeding and burned. I feel like asking someone to shoot me and get it over with. This can't be my life. I'll be scarred from this, too. I should just declare leprosy and go live in a cave right now. Get it over with. I'll be the world's youngest hermit. I put my sleeve up to my face and it comes away wet with blood and whatever else is inside, under my skin. The smell of carpet burn on my face. I feel like blowing chunks and wonder if I will.

I can hear Mr. Levy calling out to me, exasperated, as though it's my fault that he dropped me. Nancy's coming down the hallway, I can hear her teacher shoes. I crouch down near the staff room. Maybe Dad's in there. I call out for him and lie down before I pass out, going down the dark tunnel, where I'm flying again, without my body, leaving it behind.

Down in the dark cave, cheating time.

19

I know I haven't written to you, but that doesn't mean that I don't wonder about you or hope you're okay in all the ways a person can be. Given the circumstances, I mean. I think about you a hell of a lot, some might say obsessively. Certainly you've infested my dreams and fucked me over in the relationship department. My dead heart full of sand, the numbed-up sex organs. I can't help it, I have a hereditary tendency towards martyrdom, and these were the only things I owned and could therefore sacrifice. I pay the price. No lovesickness, no orgasm. Cross my heart. Not one. Isn't that a modern fucking tragedy if you ever heard one? If I were a country singer, my most heartbreaking songs would all be about you, although I'd have to change your name to fit the lyrics. I hope you understand. As it is, I'm more of a St. Elizabeth of Hungary type, which means doing without pleasure. Do you have the Internet now? I suggest you look her up. She's fascinating.

I had too many India beers tonight and not enough to eat, and I did a lot of crazy dancing at CBTG's, and now I'm so loose on the outside that the insides are spilling out. You know. Well, maybe you don't, since alcohol is banned in Sanikiluaq. Unless you've moved, or you make your own. Or maybe you smuggle, or buy from a smuggler. I don't know. That's not the point. I'm like a dog chasing its tail. All right. The reason I am mooning over you more than usual, tonight: I was walking home from downtown, in the falling snow. It was extremely quiet. All I could hear was my own breathing and my feet crunching into the street. That never happened in Sanikiluaq. It was never that still. There was always the wind. It made a roaring in your ears and forced itself against your mouth, sick and hard, like a tired mother smothering her crying child. I hated the snow because it never fell down. It flew straight at your face and made stinging marks, and when it landed it formed itself into huge crusty drifts, too hard to swish through and too soft to stand on. I hated the snow and the fucking wind. It was a struggle to go against this strength that it had. You had to harden yourself and shrink yourself up into a little creature with a shell made of your own compressed muscles. A limpet. And you couldn't breathe all the time you were outside. At least that's how I felt about it.

So, walking home, I was amazed to discover that, although white stuff was appearing out of the sky, I wasn't panicking, and I didn't hate it. In fact it was as beautiful as anything I've ever seen: the fjords in Gros Morne, orchids, or your naked body.

I felt like I'd shaken my molecules into new formations, what with the vigorous dancing and all. Like I'd danced myself hard enough that I was a new person. It was an exfoliation, a sloughing of unnecessary layers. I thought about all the different words there are for snow in your language. How, if you came to visit me, and you were walking in this quietude beside me, past the darkened windows of the souvenir shops, past the barbershop with the red neon sign illuminating the inside like a Tom Waits album cover, seedy and gorgeous, past the orange and pink row houses and the statue of the child playing hide and seek with no one—well, I thought that if you were here with me you'd need to invent another word for this experience, and it'd be a word of mostly vowel sounds, with no Ts or Ds or Ps in it. My word for this snowfall is *calm*. Or, *alone*. A combination of the two: *Calone. Alalm*. That's pretty.

Willassie. I want to see you in the lines of snow falling through the pools of lamplight. I need to see your skin against that night-brightness. You, grown older. Intact. You wouldn't have to say anything. Just stand and be seen. I'd take a picture, and that picture would last me till I quit this earth and shuffle off into the atmosphere.

Are you married now? Are you dead? Do you have children? How was that time at the group home? Did it eat at your pride? Do you forgive me? Are things any different, now that you live in Nunavut and not the Northwest Territories? Does the rose by another name smell as sweet? If I went back up there, would you agree to see me? Could we touch? Did I die back then? Is this a dream?

I'm sorry. I'm drunk and maudlin tonight. Snow-dazzled. I've been half of myself since I left you, I grew up that way. Half a girl maturing into half a woman, the outside completed but the inside still raw, unfinished. A cavernous, lonely hole, my cockpit from which I gaze out at the world I'm in, that you've never visited, which doesn't belong to me.

Or I don't belong to it. I have no sense of belonging.

I think of you. I think of you daily. Do you feel it?
Can you feel me?

20

Dad powwowed with Mr. Levy and Mr. Levy was a snitch. I listened through the door to the staff room after school today, with a glass pressed to my ear. I know all the best tricks for uncovering top secret information. Mr. Levy told Dad that I was getting 'a little too much attention' from the boys in my class. As though I were some kind of irresistible beauty, and not scrawny and awkward, with no boobs at all, and a *Night of the Living Dead* complexion. Not to mention the dental tool with a mirror on the end tied to the top of my glasses frame with fishing line, a glamorous souvenir from my lesson in centrifugal misery. It was the best way Dad could think of to fix my glasses until we get back to St. John's in June and I can get a new pair. I look like a character in a bad science fiction movie. When I turn my head I send shiny reflections off to the side. I'm probably signalling Morse code without knowing it: I AM A PINT SIZED FREAK STOP DESPERATELY NEED MAKEOVER STOP SEND HELP STOP IT WILL SOON BE TOO LATE STOP SAVE ME AND I WILL GIVE YOU ANYTHING

Of course these retards don't see things properly. They think I'm somehow in danger of being seduced, 'taken advantage of,' whatever that means. Dad has formally declared that I'm not allowed to play with any boys in the town without asking him first. By this he means Willassie. Mr. Levy told him he's caught Willassie carving my name into his desk. Mr. Levy apparently didn't notice that my name was below a skull and crossbones and above the words Rest in Peace. He thinks Willassie is becoming infatuated with me and that the situation should be watched. He's seen this before, it's not an easy matter. What with the cultural chasm. Not to mention Willassie's Burgeoning Adulthood.

What a stupid-ass. Willassie's not even talking to me. Playing Medical Examination is not exactly a danger that Dad should be concerned with. We'll probably never even talk again, the way things are going now. The way he's acting.

And as far as I'm concerned, there are no other boys in Sanikiluaq, except Evan. The other boys are like the crowds in old movies, there to make noise but you don't care enough about them to ever want to see their faces in close-up. They exist simply to incite riot, to egg the main characters on. They exist to keep Willassie from speaking to me. In close-up, Willassie looks sorry for hating me. Mixed in with the background crowd, he looks like he's having the time of his life.

My face has healed, after a week and a half. I don't have any scars where my skin hit the carpet. If anything, it's smoother than before. Maybe carpet burn should be adopted as a form of beauty treatment. Movie stars could pay millions to be thrown across the room so they land on their faces. After I forgive him for the tattling and the glasses-breaking and the face-skinning and whatnot, Mr. Levy and I could go into business. In Hollywood.

Where it's warm and there's fresh fruit all the time. I'll wear big sunglasses and no one will even notice where the pencil entered my cheek.

Not only do I not want to play with the boys, I don't want to see the girls either. I'm sick of being so sad about myself because no one likes me. I will spend this time reading and drawing and exploring my surroundings so that when I'm a famous beautician, begged to write my memoirs by a detail-hungry public, I'll be able to recall everything perfectly. I'll be the world's first beautician to win the Pulitzer Prize.

There's a lot of fun to be had by yourself. I've always known this. In St. John's I wasn't exactly the most popular girl in school. I had a few friends, but mostly my life was like it is now, mainly solitary except for the time in school and the time I spend with Evan. But it was different, too, because there was lots more to do, and Mom would take me out to the country. There were beautiful tall trees and the ocean. Beaches, fields and woods. Those spots with the orange toadstools, the moss and the tree trunks covered in old man's beard, and everything sappy and golden. Places that lend themselves to the imagination. When I go out onto the tundra and attempt to play make-believe, my mind gets as blank as the prairie of white rolling out in front of me. Sometimes I can't breathe because the wind's so strong, and even turned backwards it smacks into my hood so hard it takes my breath away. I don't know how to relate to the tundra; so empty, yet full of danger. Full of bears. We're having a translation problem. We don't have each other figured out yet.

So, I'm sticking to activities inside town for now. I've decided to take up spying, like Harriet from *Harriet the Spy*, which I didn't take up here with me, but should have. I have a notebook with a pencil attached to it with string, and I'm going to spy into people's houses, into their porches and sheds. I'm going to sketch floor plans of where each object is located, and make detailed lists of personal effects. This is a dangerous pastime. I'm pretty sure I'll get tarred and feathered if I'm caught, or whatever the Inuit equivalent is.

First, Mr. Levy's living room. This isn't so exciting, because I've been there before, but it'll give me practice. Besides which, I know he's at school in the darkroom.

He has a brown couch and a matching chair, facing one another. The walls are light green, like toothpaste. There's a bookcase next to the chair, with mostly large books about science and medicine. Dictionaries. Books of maps and books about different places around the world. Mr. Levy reads to know stuff, not to fall into a story. He has only one picture on the wall. It's of the Queen. On his bookshelves he has smaller photographs, mostly of Marguerite and her dog, Spiffy. Marguerite's really pretty. That long red hair. There's one picture I can't see from outside the window, but I remember it from when we went to dinner on our first night here. It's of Mr. Levy holding Marguerite when she was a little girl. She's wearing a pink dress with little puffed sleeves. His face is the same colour. She's looking solemnly into the camera and he's helping her to wave. It's my favourite thing in his living room. I write about it in the spy notebook even though I can't see it from here.

Now that I've warmed up a little, I decide to move on to the next house in the teacher's area of town. It belongs to Ms Ikusik, the Elbow Lady herself, a.k.a. Nancy of the Disgusting Walnut Brownies. Before I look in the window, I try and guess what it's going to look like. Pink and lilac. No books at all. A calendar with puppies on the wall and embroidered things she made herself. Lots of flowered material.

I'm surprised at how sparse the room is. There are two carvings on the plain veneer coffee table. One is a walrus, and one looks kind of like a mermaid. Definitely a half-woman, half-animal, but from here I can't tell what animal, exactly. Her kamiks hang by the door. There's a braided rug covering the cold vinyl floor. It's green and blue, with little stripes of black, and coiled like an enormous sleeping snake. I got one thing right. There is a puppy calendar. She probably lives alone. The single pair of kamiks, on a single hook. I'm sketching the floor plan. Where the rug is in relation to the rocking chair, covered over with a plain green cushion. I look up to get the proportions, and she's in the room. Shit. Do I leave now, or do I peek? Harriet would peek. I hold my breath. It's not like she's going to hear me below the windowsill, but. Slowly, I raise my eyes above the ledge. Dad is in the living room with Ms Ikusik, and they're kissing.

Dad is kissing the Nutrition teacher. He has his hand on her waist and his other hand in her hair. He has his hand in her glossy black hair, where it curls around her ears. She must get up extra early to curl her hair every morning. Does she do it just for him? If Mom had been spying instead of me, she would've keeled over into the snowbank and died by now. She'd slice herself into ribbons and let her blood pool out and freeze. He probably wouldn't care. He said he was going to develop pictures with Mr. Levy in the darkroom. The latest hunting class trip. I know he doesn't love my mother anymore, but I never guessed he had no manners. That he'd actually lie to me.

I head towards the other side of town. I'm going spying somewhere else. I need to sketch some objects, no people.

Certainly no fucking grown-ups doing things you don't ever want to see them doing, with women who don't know anything. Adults are horrible. They have no morals. I don't want to grow up. I don't ever want that to be me. I pick a shed. It's my first time stopping in this part of town. I don't know whose shed it is. No windows. There are cracks and knotholes in the wood. I pick one and squish my eye up to it, cold against my glasses. Any distraction will do.

A tire in the corner, bits of machine scattered in a pile, probably skidoo parts. A pile of stone. Saws and chisels. A mug of tea on the floor and the bones from a meal of something. A man with his back to me, working with a file on a piece of stone.

I watch the movement of muscle beneath his shirt. It's nice. The shirt is thin and maybe a little damp. Green. It clings to the man's back like green skin. It's nice to see how muscles work. To watch them when they're working. He stops for a break, puts down the stone, looks around for his tea. I catch sight of his face and run.

It's Willassie.

21

Last night I dreamt the same two dreams as always. St. Liz was first. Then you came, in the form of an arctic wolf, with white fur soft and dull as Sundays. You dragged me to your island, your teeth in my arm. They left bright little cuts, two moon-shaped constellations, pretty beads of blood on my snow-white skin. I didn't have to do the housework but you let me wear the beautiful dress, with the fur-lined sleeves. Tiny mirrors stitched into the bodice, reflecting your yellow wolf eyes all over my breasts. I was breathtaking, more like Cate Blanchett than myself. You asked me to sing. I sang the old throat-singing songs for you, the goose calling songs the way your mother and sister sang them. A flock of giant geese landed all around the sod house, huge ones, big as me, with intricate patterns on their feathered throats. Evan was on the back of one. He was dressed up in his Hallowe'en costume, the white bunny one that fit on over his snowsuit. He held out a can of peaches in his fist. You pierced his body with your claws. You sliced him into a million ribbons, bottom to top. You hung him by the rabbit ears on a flagpole.

His shredded body waved in the wind. When I ran away and caught onto the side of the boat, the man turned away from me. His back looked familiar. I could've seen who he was if he hadn't been in the sun. When he held the axe above my fingers, preparing to strike, when the terrible chop went through the bones of my hand and into wood, he said, quite clearly, "Why don't you ever make me proud?"

He sounded familiar. I remember thinking Pierce Brosnan. I tried to speak and he ripped my tongue out. I could see that he was sorry for what he'd done, but he couldn't help himself. There was a microchip implanted in his forehead, which I could see quite clearly now that I was drowning. Mr. Levy and Willem Dafoe, hunched over a control panel in some Batman-esque location, piping their instructions into poor Pierce's head.

Mr. Levy:
Good work, Mr. Brosnan. Now for the easy part. You will bring the harvest to us.

Willem:
(*grabbing the microphone device and scat-singing into it, with great enthusiasm but very little skill.*) Yessirreeeeeee Bob, ya slob-di-dob-she-wob! Hot diddly squat-di-dot-she-wot!

Mr. Levy:
That's right, Brosnan, pick them all up.

Willem:
(*continuing to scat*) Zeedobbity boo bop, she-wop a-clock-stop!

Mr. Levy:

All ten digits, man. Make sure none of them fall in the water or you'll become useless to us. And that would be very dangerous for you, my friend.

Willem:

Zrriiing, beding-beding-dong!

Mr. Levy:

(twisting Willem's nose off and stuffing it inside an arctic hare.)
Hurry up! We fancy a snack of...finger sandwiches! *(he laughs maniacally)*

Willem:

(noseless and jovial) Now *that's* comedy!

Willem Dafoe did a little tap-dancing number. He clapped his hands and his nose grew back. He high-fived Mr. Levy who mutated into a mailman the instant their palms slapped. They lifted their shirts and banged bellies. The letters in Mr. Levy's bag came tumbling out and floated around them and into the sea. Pierce started fishing around for my fingers in the bottom of the boat, his ass sticking up in the air with a target tragically painted onto the shiny seat of his cords.

I am left alone, without allies, half-dead and forgotten. Evan is shredded into ribbons and hung by his bunny ears to rot in the sun. Pierce Brosnan is broken. It is my fault these things have happened. Like Helena in *All's Well*, I am the cause. Sedna after the animals have gone: fingerless, depressed, unable to help myself, to cook, to clean. Unable to comb my hair. The filth of the world trickles down and catches in the tangles. My head hangs heavy with the weight of it. I sit helpless on the ocean floor, waiting for the tiny people up above to remember that I'm here. I grow greasy from their waste. I cry from my single eye and bang my stumps together. A forgotten goddess is a singularly forlorn creature. I'm inconsolable, even after I wake up.

This is the reason I've got to go back. I'll have this evil dream every night, in endless, fucked-up variations, until I do.

I don't think I can survive it for many more months. When I wake up and take my nightly photograph, I feel like I've been scoured with acid on the inside, unable even to cry. My admission of guilt does nothing to relieve it. The ridiculous subplots should make the dream easier to take, but they don't. The more ludicrous the guest stars get, the more I shake. I yank fast on the light cord with the camera at the ready, exposing myself in a short bright oasis within the awful catacombs of night. I try to capture myself filled with vaporous dream-likenesses of you, as close as I can come to once more filling myself with touch, your touch, on all those deadened places.

Do you dream about me, Willassie? Do I figure in your nightmares? Or have you somehow managed to forget? I hope you have. I wish you peace of mind. I hope you're happier than I am. I can't sleep. I don't know what I'm doing in this city with this huge pile of stones on my chest that is invisible to everyone else and never mentioned. The burial mound that should have been mine, heaped onto my unresisting body, sinking me into sleeplessness, into isolation.

God. Pierce was right. When will I ever make him proud?

22

I'm outside Willassie's shed, trying to squish my glasses as hard against my secret knothole as they can go without breaking the delicate dental-tool contraption, as though my sight is better with my iris pressed right up against the lens. But no matter how hard I squish, I still can't see any better. It's dim in there. It's only from memory that I know for a fact that the t-shirt he's wearing is the exact colour of the door to the Emerald Palace in *The Wizard of Oz*, that it's been worn so often it's transparent, and that underneath it you're able to see his skin, even the faintest trace of dark nipple. It's only from memory that I know this t-shirt like a lizard's eyelid pulled down over his body, slightly damp.

And I know the face he'd be making if he turned around, if he weren't facing away from me with his breath going up around his bent head. It would be that stone face, that sleeping face. Mom gets it too, sometimes. It's an artist's face, the kind they get when they're so deep inside what they're doing that the whole world around them ceases to exist. When the thing they're making becomes everything.

I want to see that look on Willasie's face. That's why I'm standing on an oil can behind his shed for the third day in a row, my heart pounding in case I get caught, like spying on him is the same as stealing, or sniffing, or drinking, or any of those other things I'm not supposed to do.

I'm not spying, now, I'm just looking. I'm observing. Admiring. Appreciating. I am appreciating the artist at work in his studio, the same as if he was Chagall or Bosch or any of those other famous guys that Mom likes. Maybe someday Willassie'll be a famous artist with glossy picture books made out of photographs of his carvings and they'll ask me to write the foreword, because I was the first to appreciate him. I still don't like him. I'll never forgive him. But I can appreciate everything about him when he's carving. I appreciate the way his shoulder works so hard to make the grooves in the stone. I appreciate the way he doesn't have to look to find the hacksaw on the floor, how he just picks it up with one hand as the other holds the stone up to his face to blow the dust off. There's no sensible shape to it yet, he's just feeling his way in. It's amazing to me how he can look at a rock and tell what animal is living inside it. Every rock I look at, I see a bird.

I fumble for the stone bird in my pocket. I take it everywhere with me. It's small enough that no one knows I've got it. I can just slip my hand in at any old time of crisis and feel the smooth stone with the delicate lines of etched feather, the sharp edges of the wings, all warm from pressing up against my thigh. But now I've shifted my balance, trying to get at the bird, and banged my knee against the shed, and toppled over the stack of cans beside me. My cover's blown. Willassie turns to see what's going on, like maybe there's an animal inside with him. All I see is the not-peaceful, not-sleeping look on his face. His eyes huge and white, the red of the hacksaw above his head as he heaves it too high in his surprise. He lifts it too high. The red and the hardness of the metal make a beautiful contrast so close to his face. And I know right away that something bad is going to happen and I'm going to have to watch it, because it's my fault.

The hacksaw, falling. Funny what a few extra inches in the air can do to a tool in a hand. The saw is falling, it's falling onto the stone Willassie was working on and onto the hand that is holding it tight in front of him. There is no more red added to this picture. The blood that comes out of him is dark. It looks almost black against the blade and the skin and the stone, and especially the green of his shirt.

I watch without breathing. I stumble around the corner and go inside. I say, "Willassie." He doesn't look surprised to see me. He looks at me with hope. The bone is visible. His thumb is at an awkward angle. There's a lot of blood. I don't know what to do about it.

"Willassie, I'm going to be sick."

"Teresa."

"I'm going to pass out, I think."

"Teresa."

"I think I might pass out. So first I'm going to wrap my mitten all the way around your thumb. I'll squeeze to stop the blood. And if I faint, then you hold onto my hand, hard. Okay?"

"It hurts."

"I know."

"I don't feel so good."

"I know, Willassie."

Then I'm in the dark place where everything is floating, the place you have to earn by going through the sick feeling, the nauseousness of the faint. It is open and bare and smells of nothing. I'm sure if I float long enough, I'll forget my own name. There's singing but it's not in words. Or it's a hum. And then there's a catching, a holding-on that I don't want to be there, and it's pulling me back up the disgusting, stomach-sick tunnel. There's too much light beyond my eyelids, and that horrible crackle sound like bugs frying on a light bulb. I have only one second to choose between the darkness and this otherness, and I choose the otherness because of this pressure on my hand, this thing that won't let go.

I open my eyes. Willassie is there. Somehow we're sitting into each other, shivering. His hand is around mine, knuckles white. We must have been in the shed for a while. The blood on his shirt is dry.

"Teresa."

"Hello."

"We stick together."

The stripy yellow bits of my mitten have turned black with his blood. When I try to move my fingers, he draws his breath. The blood has dried or frozen us together. We get up slowly. I try to wipe a spot of blood from the corner of his right eye, by the soft, slight pit of his temple with my unstuck hand. He attempts to smile, and this attempt is so weak that I put my hand up to wipe it away. I'm touching his mouth. It's heavy underneath my mitten. I remember the day Willassie showed me what a hickey was. How soft and hot a mouth can be.

"Teresa. We have to go."

"Okay," I say.

"Okay?"

"Where are we going?"

"You got a first aid?"

"Okay?"

We are going to my house, for band-aids and my father. Who can either fix this or take us to the nursing station.

"We're sticking together, Willassie, okay?"

"Yes. Let's go."

His mouth is moving bits of warm air through the cold air towards my face. His breath is like that hot air around a campfire that makes everything look all wavering. I half expect to see sparks floating up around us. As we stand up, his cheek brushes mine. We walk quickly down the road to my house, all the while stuck together like I was dumb enough to try and arm-wrestle the greatest arm-wrestler in all of Sanikiluaq.

Dad's face is so white that it's green. He doesn't like blood much, especially when it's covering his daughter. He doesn't like the stuck-together look of me and Willassie, exactly who I'm not supposed to touch, to look at, to let look at me. Dad looks sick. Even though it was his idea to come to this island in the first place, I can tell that it scares him to see me touching one of the locals. Which I'd laugh about if there wasn't still blood coming out through my mitten.

We're running our hands under cold water. This hurts to the core. My mitten is getting so heavy and wet that our hands drag a little into the pink cocktail of water and blood that is swallowing itself down the drain. For once Dad isn't asking questions. He's satisfied with "the hacksaw fell." He doesn't want to know anything else. But when you don't want to know the truth, your imagination creates scenes much more horrible than what actually happened. You can't stop replaying your own made-up versions of the facts, and eventually your mind gets infected, like a worm eating out a peach from one small bruise, and you completely lose your marbles, and your eyes roll back into your head, and you become a raving lunatic, filled with jealousy and looking for revenge, sweet revenge. In the movies anyway. Or *Wuthering Heights*. Which is my favourite book right now. I've read it twelve times. That doesn't mean I want Dad to turn all Heathcliff on me, roaming the tundra, gnashing his teeth and soliloquizing about how I've ruined him.

He's gone to phone the nursing station. I can hear him in the living room, beyond the sound of the tap and Willassie's breathing. The pain of the water on my frozen hand, like the sympathy pains that men get when staring at their screaming, bursting wives in the delivery room. I'm feeling dizzy. I don't know if it's from the water or how close we are, how every time he breathes I feel the outline of his bicep and forearm pressing deeper into mine. I don't know if it's because he's in my bathroom, and can see the box of maxi pads glowing pink like a beacon of embarrassment by the Honey Bucket, but in any case I'm getting dizzy again.

"Willassie."

"Yes."

"I don't feel so good."

"I know."

"I don't want your thumb to come off."

"It won't."

"I'm sorry I made you cut your thumb off."

"Teresa."

"I'm sorry, Willassie."

He's touching my face with his free hand. It's wet, like a dog's nose on my cheek. He's making me look at him. I don't want to. I want to crawl inside a book and tear my hair out for the loss of Catherine. I want to weep at her grave and have her haunt me in the night. That'd be easy. I don't want this stomach-sick, hideous feeling, this demand that I look him in the eyes. Because I get this feeling when we really look at each other, like all my insides are falling away into a bottomless pit I didn't know was there till it ate me up. Now I've got nothing. I'm no one.

"Teresa. It's going to be okay."

There are jagged things in my chest and they're all rigged up to his breathing.

"What if you lose your thumb and you're a War Amp and you can't ever carve again? It's my fault. I ruined your life."

"Teresa. Quanniq. I forgive you."

"No."

"You gotta stand up some more. Quanniq, come on, stand up."

"I can't."

"You gotta stand up or we gonna fall over."

I can't keep on struggling, I can't put in the effort. I'm falling into the black pits of his eyes. I can see two reflections of a small pale girl, a white girl, a kid. She can't control the movements of her trembling limbs and torso. She's holding onto a hand and that hand is attached to a strong, nut-brown arm under a thin green t-shirt and the rest is hidden from sight.

I've fallen onto the floor. I think Willassie's fallen too. Maybe I dragged him down there. My face is pressed against the cool linoleum. Willassie's body covers mine like a fierce blanket. I am somewhere between him and the lino, lukewarm. Somewhere in the centre of my ear I can hear him, trying to call me back with the low, throat-scraping sound of my new nickname. My little Inuit name. "Quanniq. Quanniq. I'm here still."

23

It's Valentine's Day. Or, as Mark puts it, Black Thursday. He hates Valentine's Day. So do I. I hate it because I think that people in love shouldn't need a special day of commercialism to honour it. The real thing is so rare that, when found, it should be worshipped, constantly. Mark, on the other hand, hates Valentine's Day because he doesn't believe that love exists. Or even if it does, it only complicates things. He thinks it's better left undiscovered, a lost and mythical continent, Atlantis of the heart. Mark likes flings, casual little things with a short shelf life. In all the time I've known him, he's never had a girlfriend who lasted more than five or six weeks. He insists this is the ideal way to conduct one's life. He's even named the principle. His infamous Two Month Rule.

I guess I'm his opposite in this respect, having clung to your memory like a nun clings to Christ throughout years of solitude, penance and devotion. Flagellation and the works. I'm like Mom in a lot of ways. We've both spent the past decade in thankless loyalty to a memory that's been aggrandized into myth. However,

Mom's fervour has shifted from her pagan love of the golden idol, my father, back to a righteous marriage with God. Her heart beats just for Jesus, like it did when she was small. I don't have the luxury of a sanction for my obsession. Like Mom, I know my little heart is full to bursting, numb as it is. But I don't worship God. There isn't room for Him or anyone else. I've made your shrine from the whole of my heart, and that's a lonely fucking feeling, let me tell you.

Today there are couples everywhere. The shop windows are done up in pink with fat-bottomed Cupids in shiny red vinyl. There's two-for-one everything, desserts piled on top of each other in a sugared orgy: tiramisu and tunnel o' fudge cheesecake, strawberries dipped in chocolate, then dipped in whipped cream. I'm getting a toothache just thinking about love, and a stomach ache from the thought that no one loves me. From how small this city is. Every man I've gone on a date with in the past three years is bound to be at the Bung reunion show #33 tonight, all within ten feet of one another, surrounded by legions of loaded ex-girlfriends in the sticky, tangled web that somehow connects us all. There's no one in this city for me to love. If there were, he'd be a Curtis, an idealist, fresh from the prairies. Former cattle rancher, future mussel farmer. Building himself a solar-powered cabin in Spaniard's Bay. Everyone here already thinks they know so much about me, there's nothing left to allure them with. I'm as ordinary, as inoffensive and plain as Ivory soap, nothing to rub lavishly on your naked body. My secrets are not the delicious kind you can dab on your wrists like expensive perfume, with beaver semen or beluga pancreas or deer spit or whatever, added for the hormonal pull. You can now buy human pheromones to cut your perfume with, extracted from live specimens and guaranteed to incite mania in the opposite sex. Maybe I should give it a try. No sexy wild-animal sweat has been coming off of me, lately.

I'm in a period of nothingness. A void. I don't want to work. I think maybe smashing up my camera would be a satisfying way to spend an afternoon. The noise of it. I want to wreck anything in reach. I want to carve your name into my arm then peel the scabs off and mail them to you as a symbol of my affection, of the lengths I'll go to.

To what? What do I want? Why am I still thinking about you? Even if I were Nancy Drew, I wouldn't be able to sort through all the contradictory evidence. I know, logically, that you and I don't fit together in this world. We didn't. Our worlds themselves didn't even really fit. I tried to live in yours, and failed. Jumped ship. Maybe we could blame that on the fact that I was twelve, going on thirteen. Or say it was because my father didn't understand, no one did, or—yes—that I betrayed you. I've been telling myself versions of that story for a decade, but it's not satisfying. No matter how I look at it, we never really fit.

We fit the way that Heathcliff and Cathy fit, or Romeo and Juliet: so fierce that life in the face of this love must extinguish itself, or the lovers must be separated. I'm glad you're not dead. Not that I know if you're dead or not. Maybe you are. But I prefer to think, like Heathcliff, that I'd know if your life were coming to an end. I'd get that eerie wash of sixth sense. I'd feel it on a cellular level.

You'd laugh at all these outdated, impossible notions: True Love, Consuming Passion. They're fictions. They are too clean. I wipe my nose on my shirt front and let the snot just sit there. It's gotten to that point again.

I hate Valentine's Day because it makes me feel sorry for myself. I'm sitting on my living room floor thinking about going to bed out of it when Mark comes in. He's wearing a tweed coat and a fedora with a yellow feather on the side, the spit of his father as a young man, though he'd hate my saying so. I wipe my snot on my knees. He sits on the coffee table and hands me something wrapped in a paper napkin. One heart-shaped sugar cookie, broken down the middle in a perfectly straight line. He probably used a ruler and cut it with an X-acto knife.

"Have half my heart," he says.

"Awww."

"I don't need the whole thing. Eat it. Put some meat on your bones."

"Nice to see you've pulled out your most romantic material for the occasion."

"What? It's Black Thursday. Anything could happen."

I give him back half the cookie and go to make tea. Mark takes off his jacket and follows me. We Hansel and Gretel our way into the bright kitchen, a trail of crumbs behind us on the dirty hardwood. I blink in the glare, like a star-nosed mole. There's one down at the museum, nearsighted and tiny. Its nose a star of flesh like a miniscule pink sea anemone. Creepy, like all taxidermy.

"I'm fucking hungry," Mark says. I get out the mortar and pestle. No food processors came with my new digs. Mom and I both like to do things the hard way. Mark rolls a joint on the kitchen table while I make pesto. We listen to sad country music. Mom's murals loom over us. On the ceiling above the stove, the Last Supper is getting dished up. Mark loves it, but he doesn't live here. He doesn't have John the Baptist's severed head on the toilet seat leering up at him every time he has to go.

The meditative act of cooking helps me block out all the paintings, the mobiles and collections, souvenirs of my mother's madness. I need the quiet I find inside the rhythm of cooking, inside the repetitive, purposeful gestures my body has to make: the smash, the chop, the stirring and sifting. Kneading, grating, layering phyllo with a brush of oil in between. The rich smells: fresh basil and garlic, cilantro, toasting pine nuts, roasting vegetables. Damson jam from Nanny Norman's plum trees, brought over from England as seedlings by her great-great-grandfamily. A smell to die with. And the sounds: the clean pop when you pry out the mushroom stems, polenta farting away gently on the back of the stove. The only piss-off is the dishes. I achieve my most zen-like frame of mind doing two things: cooking and developing photographs. And since I don't have my darkroom set up yet, cooking has lately been all that helps me maintain my grasp on sanity while living among all this evidence of how easy it is to crack up.

"Isn't it amazing!" I can't help exclaiming. "Newfoundland in February and fresh basil to be had. There's something to be said for superstores after all."

Mark pokes around in my cupboards for something to drink. He pours scotch into juice glasses and passes one to me. My fingers leave smears of garlic on the glass, the smell cuts like acid. Stop bath.

"Here's to all happy couples," Mark says. "May they die together, in bed."

"Is that a curse or a toast? I can't tell."

"Don't put too much parmesan in."

I point my knife at him. If there's one thing I can't stand, it's a backseat chef. I tell him about the sparrow that's dead in the studio. The window was open when I moved in, the little bird stiff on the damp hardwood. I knew it had died of natural causes, but still. It'd be just like my mother to leave God a little something on her way out. I ask Mark to remove it. He likes to take care of these things for me, it makes him feel mature and manly, as opposed to the sissy he normally is. I can't stand little dead things, especially birds. The open beaks, the dulled eyes. The smallest ones are the worst. Since I've moved in, I've kept the studio door shut and haven't gone back up the stairs. But sooner or later I'm going to need somewhere to develop my prints, and Mom's already had the proper plumbing put in. It's ideal. Mark gets a baggie from the drawer and heads upstairs. I take the opportunity to remove the Valentine's Day card from the counter. It's the only one I received, and it's from Vanessa. He'll be fit to be tied if he sees it. An astronaut with hearts for eyes: *To T love V. You Send Me Over the Moon, Baby.*

Mark comes back downstairs holding the bird out in its baggie like a prize.

"Put that somewhere, quick," I say.

"I think I might use it in something."

"Oh no." I avert my eyes. The pesto needs pounding. I won't get sick.

"If only I'd kept that mouse we found in the basement."

"If only."

"*Corpses Collected at Teresa Norman's House.* It'd be so beautiful. Don't throw out any of the other ones."

"You are sick. You're sick."

Mark humbly bows his head. "Thank you."

"I hope there aren't any other ones."

The water starts boiling. I tend to the pot. I threaten Mark with no supper if he won't get rid of the bird. He puts the clear bag in a paper one and lays it carefully on top of the coat rack so he won't forget it when he goes. He washes his hands and finds his scotch. When we sit at the table he raises his glass again.

"This time it's my official toast. Here's to beauty. Feathers, pesto. Your eyes, dear Teresa, your eyes. This scotch. You never do skimp on your liquor, I admire that in a woman. Here's to all the good shit that's got nothing to do with love. Happy Black Thursday."

"Word, brother. Word."

We clink glasses, sip our drinks and pick up our forks. Mark winks at me across the table. We decide to get drunk and play Scrabble. Five buck wager. It'll be a tight match. He's good at strategy but I make better words. Mark gets up for seconds. His wake in the air is enough to knock the paper bag off the coat rack. It floats towards the tiles. At the last second, the baggie slips out, a magician's trick. The little thing is on its back, cocooned inside the baggie. Minute talons prick the plastic. If Mark weren't here, I'd have picked it up in the dustpan, stuffed it in the fireplace and set it on fire. That's what I feel like doing. Don't ask me why.

24

I'm in Willassie's shed, on the tire. He has ten stitches in his thumb. The stain of his blood is gone from my hand, but I remember where it was. He's wearing his green carving shirt, the bloodstains long gone, and making something so small I can't see what it is. It's not stone, though. It's ivory, from a walrus tusk. He doesn't say anything while he works. Neither do I. It's not polite. I have a book, *Gulliver's Travels,* that I sort of pretend to be reading, only I keep thinking of Gulliver's Taxi back home, and imagining the Gulliver in the book driving down Hill O' Chips and talking about his missus and her Bingo winnings, like the guy did that time me and Mom broke down at the supermarket and had to take a taxi. The driver wore strong perfume that I think was meant for ladies. He had a homemade skull tattoo beside his thumb. He asked Mom if she ever played Bingo, saying that his missus treated Bingo just like church. He can't say nothing bad about it or else she smacks him up the side of the head for being lippy. Although Mr. Swift's Gulliver was never a taxi driver, the whole time I'm reading I can't help picturing him like that Gulliver taxi man. That's what's known as Word Association.

But I'm not really reading. I'm watching Willassie in my periphery. Even though I can't see what he's making, I can see him making it. He uses every visible muscle. Some to actually carve the bone, the others as backup, a cheering section. His face is the only relaxed part of his body. His breath comes out in one long stream, like he learned the trick of breathing in and out at the same time, like the aborigines in Australia. The didgeridoo players. I focus on the rhythm of his muscles and try to breathe the same way. My breath still comes out with gaps in the steam. I wonder if this is maybe a racial thing, a genetic difference between us. I wish I had black hair like Willassie, and brown skin like Willassie, and brown eyes like Willassie, and breath like Willassie that can go in and out at once. I wish I had a name like Willassie. I wish I could speak Willassie's language. I wish I could do something, anything, as beautiful as his arm moving downwards with the file, making snowflakes out of walrus tusk. Light as air.

That's what he's making: a snowflake. It's small, maybe as big as a quarter. He's blowing the dust off with his magic in/out breath. He catches me watching him. Although I'm sure he knows that's why I'm here. This tire isn't exactly the ideal reading chair. We haven't really talked about it, but ever since I made him cut his thumb we've been keeping each other company. Doing our own things in the same space, close enough to hear the other person's breathing, not saying much. I think we're both afraid that any talking we do might mess with this thing that is happening. I don't know what comes next and I don't care. Even if we got stuck in this moment forever, if Jabba the Hut came here and dipped us in carbonite and we were frozen forever in these exact positions, I would feel I had accomplished something. A comfortable, shared silence is pretty rare.

I can't concentrate on the book. My eyes are skimming the same paragraph over and over, catching on the pattern of capital letters. "The Artist himself was at that time busy upon two great Designs; the first, to sow Land with Chaff, wherein he affirmed the true seminal Virtue to be contained, as he Demonstrated by several Experiments which I was not skilful enough to comprehend. The other was, by a certain Composition of Gums, Minerals, and Vegetables outwardly applied, to prevent the Growth of Wool upon two young Lambs; and he hoped in a reasonable Time to propagate the Breed of naked Sheep all over the Kingdom." I have no idea why anyone would want naked Sheep, except maybe as some ugly, skinny sort of Dog Substitute for people with Dog Allergies. Half my brain is thinking this, and the other half is listening to the sound of the file. In my periphery I can see Willassie's foot in his shoe. Even his toes are scrunching and tensing with the effort. All of his energy is going into a little piece of ivory no bigger than a gumball. I'm amazed. It's amazing.

"Quanniq."

"Willassie."

"I'm done."

I look up. I let my eyes trail lazily from his shoe to his knee and waist and chest. His neck and his face. I have a visual pig-out, looking up at Willassie. He's holding up the snowflake. The light from the open door shines through the ivory.

"What do you think, Quanniq?"

"What does that mean? You keep calling me that."

"I wondered when you'll ask."

"Well?"

"Guess."

"Is it a trick? Is it bad?"

"No."

"Are you making fun of me?"

"I won't do that."

"Yes you would. You make fun of me all the time: *Teresa Rest In Peace, Go Home Ghosty...*"

"I write those to write your name."

"Well, it's not very nice."

"Sorry."

He's got melty eyes and I relent. "You're not making fun of me now," I say.

"No."

"Do you promise?"

"Yes."

"Cross your heart and hope to die, stick ten thousand needles in your eye?"

He's grinning now. "Yes, yes, yes. Guess!"

"Okay. Does it mean...little?"

"Not really."

"Not really? What do you mean?"

"It means little and also other things."

"What other things? You're not being fair!"

"Falling down."

"I give up."

"White."

"I give up, Willassie."

"Pretty...do you give up yet?"

He thinks he's so funny.

"Yes, yes, I give up, Willassie, just tell me what it is!"

He's so pleased with himself. "It is in front of your nose. It is snowflake, Teresa. Snowflake: Quanniq."

He pulls a piece of yellow yarn out of his pocket, and threads it through.

"I saved this from your mitten. I washed most of the blood out. The Inuit are not going to throw out anything we can use again. Like seals, you know that, we use everything after we kill them. The guts and everything."

He's walking to the back of me. I feel the itch of the yarn around my neck. "That is your special thing, Quanniq. So you don't forget your name."

His fingers are touching the back of my neck. The clouds of breath have stopped coming out of me. I can feel each goose-bump individually, all over my scalp.

"You already gave me a present, Willassie. The little bird."

He puts one hand on the back of my neck, then takes it away again.

"That is not a present. He tells you that I'm sorry. This time I don't do anything to get sorry about."

He reaches around from behind to touch the scar on my cheek where his pencil went in. He gets a finger in my ear, then leaves it there. I feel for the bird in my pocket, where I always keep it. It's warm from my leg.

"Thank you for the snowflake," I say.

"Quyanaq means thank you."

I try and make that q sound I'm no good at, so far back in my throat I feel like I'm about to hawk a loogie. "Qqqu-ya-na-qqq." It makes me cough.

"You're funny," he says.

He puts his nose on the dent where my soft spot used to be.

"You gotta go now, Teresa. If you don't go now you gonna forget."

"So?"

"Your dad will fail me, or kill me. You gotta go."

"Okay. I'm going."

"Okay," he says.

"See you tomorrow morning."

"Okay then."

I leave. I forget my book. There is nothing in the world. There is me and my necklace. The yarn is stained on one end with Willassie's blood. I put this part in my mouth. The faint taste of pennies.

25

Somehow I've crashed a cast party that Gay Stevie was throwing and have recently discovered that I'm missing a sock. I don't know how or when this tragedy occurred; it's been that kind of a party. People are trashed and passed out in the porch on piles of shoes. I go to sit cross-legged in the corner and hide my naked foot up my other pant leg. The play was *The King and I*. The party has an "oriental" theme, with egg rolls, geisha, paper lanterns and garish, gelatinous sweet and sour sauce. There's a portrait of Buddha done on butcher paper, his face cut out for you to pose behind. Gay Stevie is wearing a kimono with a hoop skirt on top and can barely get through the doorway to the kitchen. He knocks the spider plant onto the floor and dances in the dirt.

Stevie's house in the Battery is excessive, layered in sheer fabric and doilies and mirrored objects from exotic locales. When I think about your house—so spare, the gyproc walls, that seal oil lamp on the floor—Gay Stevie's excess of ambiance makes me feel slightly ill. But only slightly. He's putting on the dish gloves.

The yellow really compliments his highlights. He's gripping Janice's cheek with the dripping glove, whispering "So glovely to see you…you're looking simply glovely tonight, darling" and then toasting his own brilliance. Janice looks like she might be reconsidering A Life in the Theatre: all night the insidious smell of damp latex will refuse to leave her personage.

I have no one to engage me in scintillating repartee. In the hallway there are too many Theatre People, and, worse, Progressively Multidisciplinary Artists. It takes so much effort to be witty and interesting. I don't have the right clothes on. I cut my own hair and I'm pretty sure it's uneven at the back. I can't compete with those put-together, martini-drinking, asymmetrical-shirt-wearing, multimedia artist women who stand at strategic points in the hallway and allow the legions of admirers to circulate wide-eyed around them, bouncing from one to the next, fetching new drinks, asking questions about their slick new projects, hoping to casually brush up against bare, elastic, freakishly unblemished skin. I've stencilled all of their names on the gallery wall, at one time or another. When I walk by, I actually lower my eyes and look interestedly at the floorboards. I'm the chick who prints the press releases and finds the money. Isn't it cute that I showed up. Alone. Again. That's me, cute as a fucking button.

Mark refused to come. He doesn't like how Gay Stevie's always touching people when he talks to them, how he insists on looking in your eyes. He doesn't like the characteristic exuberance and chummy qualities of Theatre People. He likes to say that he's allergic. And Vanessa and Curtis aren't answering the phone. Undoubtedly holed up in bed, talking in baby voices. Sucking each other's faces off.

I end up in the living room. The Theatre People have gathered in a circle to trade horror stories. Theatre is always on the verge of total collapse. There's always a high-alert situation going on: never enough money, or time, or press. Burning off your bangs in the curling iron two minutes before curtain. Getting rigged out in safety pins because your pants had to be let out and the overworked costume ladies didn't have time to sew them back up before opening night. "It's only for one show, my love." They're not the ones out singing "The Darby Ram" when the sudden stab of an opened safety pin in the scrotum makes its unwelcome appearance.

There is a game of Musical Chairs happening, with Boney M on the record player. People viciously bump each other out of place with their asses. The neighbours come by with a pot of fresh meat soup and a bottle of beer in every pocket. They've lived in the Battery for four generations and can get a good price on weed. Salt of the earth. They pose for pictures as Buddha while the art-kids scream.

I'm writing on a napkin. A list of anagrams for my name: an Easter morn/a matron sneer/a ranter's omen/a near monster/a sore remnant. I rub my numb foot. Getting nearer and nearer to the truth of things.

Someone hands me a glass of Sangria. I'll drink anything that's put in front of me. I try to think of anagrams for your name. I write it on the napkin twice, but it doesn't help. Willassie Ippaq. Willassie Ippaq. I know I've been at it for a while, because Gay Stevie has changed into his paisley cords and a casual blonde wig, and all the young chorus girls have gone home to their single beds in their parents' houses in Airport Heights and Paradise. I think about the anagrams for a long time. The q in your last name, minus partnering u, is getting in my way. Anagrams work best with Anglo-Saxon names. The familiar, stodgy letters are easier to push around. I must be drunker than I thought, because I fall asleep holding the pen, sitting on the floor of Stevie's party with my bare foot tucked up into the leg of my pants, the ankle stretched and cramped so badly that when I wake up in the morning I have trouble getting around.

On Stevie's floor I dream I'm St. Elizabeth, come straight from Japan. I sit in the lotus of meditation. I have long black hair wound into buns with chopsticks. A sheer orange kimono coyly reveals the strap of my hair camisole, which is very chic, with lace made of pubes at the neck. I'm at the hilltop where Jesus has been left. I climb the ladder. Bits of kimono tatter away to nothing in the wind. I'm all rags and threads, the hair slip. My skin gone scabby with the rub of it. I lift the crown of thorns from off of Jesus' head. Come on, buddy, let me take over for a bit. By a miracle of God, we switch. The orange rags wind round the nails. The blood soaks in and turns them red. They flap out like wings in the wind, and I turn into a butterfly, pinned onto a piece of index card inside a glass case, with other insects. Red and orange and white and black, big as a man's hand, but still with my human genitals and face. The label is in a language foreign to me, maybe Arabic. Jesus is the lepidopterist. He sticks the pins in with a solemn face.

In the morning, I'm the only one left, besides the boy Gay Stevie lured into his canopied bed. The poor thing has to call his mother for a ride home. His voice still hasn't finished cracking. Gay Stevie sees him off at the door with a chaste peck on each cheek, and one on the nose. The boy has a beautiful nose, and it's important not to neglect it. I help Stevie clean up, even though my ankle kills. Shaking my head, trying to clear it of the image of myself inside that glass case, those wings. I limp around, wiping up all the sticky patches in the hallway where the put-together, statuesque artist women slopped their martinis. This is a calming action. Humbling and hopeful at the same time. I may have been trashed, depressed and missing a sock, but at least I didn't spill anything.

26

My father has become a real Inuit Art Expert, or so he likes to think.

He has a small collection started: two black soapstone geese with elegant necks nestled over green stone eggs on a bed of real eiderdown. He also has a carving of a man in a kayak about to throw a wooden harpoon with a tiny, lethal point made of ivory. "Look at the detail," he says. There's sinews threaded through where the ropes would be, and miniature buoys made of sealskin.

Most of the men and some of the women here make money by carving soapstone. They also make some money selling things like furs, seal pelts and woven baskets. The girls in my class knit hats and mitts to sell to the Hudson's Bay and the Co-op. Families get by on this, they make enough to buy their smokes and teabags, their tinned milk, sugar and flour, blue jeans, bullets and gasoline. All bought from the same two stores; there's nowhere else to buy anything. Survival is possible because the government gives everyone money to build their houses, which are small and plain and can't cost too much anyway. They get along all right because they spend a lot of time hunting and fishing, which doesn't cost anything either. Most of the things that the Inuit eat are taken from the land. They gather berries in the summer and ice-fish in winter. In spring they gather eggs and build traps to catch foxes and rabbits. The men hunt for seals, walrus, narwhals, for polar bears, geese, ducks and caribou, wolves, foxes, anything that's alive out there. They live at the mercy of migratory masses of animals. There are quotas to make sure that the animals keep surviving. The quota for polar bears is about twenty-five a year. The number changes according to the size of the population. After twenty bears or so are killed, all the hunters put their name in a lottery. Every day, two names are drawn and those two men go out on their skidoos and try their luck. Every night they draw two more names, until the rest of the bears are killed, and then the killing is illegal, unless for self-defence. Willassie has had two days, but hasn't shot a bear on either of them. He had to skip school to go out hunting, but Mr. Levy doesn't mind. He believes in the attempt to integrate Inuit and white ways of life. The quota days are just as important as math class. Maybe more important, considering where we are and how we have to live to survive here. Willassie still gets all the homework, though. I ask him, "What happens when the bears decide to turn around and go to Greenland one year? If the animals don't show up, what happens then?" "Those are the years," he says, "when little babies die because we don't have nothing. The mothers are starving. Some men go off to hunt. We make a lot of carvings. But most years it isn't like that. The animals go the way they like and we know about the path of it. We have to wait, but they always come to us."

They call themselves carvers here, not artists. There is no word for art in Inuktitut. Mom used to say the first step to being an artist is admitting it. She likens it to mental illness. According to her, there's no artists at all in Sanikiluaq, since they won't confess. These sculptures on our coffee table, therefore, don't exist. They look real enough to me, though.

The stone has been polished and heated with wax in the oven, then buffed with a soft old rag to bring the shine out. Some of the soapstone is a deep black-blue with rare, thin veins of white. Some is a light green colour, mottled with dark flecks and small clear specks that reflect pink and white depending how you turn it. There's a greyish stone that warms up fast when you touch it. My little bird is made of this. It has one undulating stripe of lighter grey bisecting its soft stone neck. I asked Willassie to tell me the names of the different kinds, but he didn't know them. He said "This is the green rock and this one is the black." He has a few chunks of raw stone in the corner of the shed, under an old piece of tarp, jagged and rough, their colours greyed with dust, and unremarkable. This is because they aren't waxed and polished yet. Waxing makes the stone look like it's underwater. It brings out the depth.

The carvers sit in unheated sheds wearing thin t-shirts, oblivious to cold. They carve their rocks and take them to the Co-op. Some of the carvers have specialties. A lot of women carve birds or family scenes. There's a man named Samuel who makes everything with two heads, as a kind of a joke. Sometimes one of the heads is eating the other, or one head is where the animal's bum should be. "Qallunaat think I some kind of magic," he says, and laughs with the other men outside the store, drinking Pepsi. The Co-op sends the carvings down south to galleries where white people pay lots of money for them. But, if you're like Dad, and you happen to be able to buy directly from the source, so to speak, you can get about ten carvings for what one would cost you in an Indigenous Art Gallery in downtown Toronto or Winnipeg. He's tickled pink.

His new favourite carving is a large rectangular woman with mismatched breasts and the face of an ugly old man, with stubble and everything. She is dressed in an old-style amautiq, which is the traditional thing that a woman wears, a big long coat made of white canvas or skin, with two solid bands of colour going around the rim. It hangs down low in back and front, but is cut up to the hip on the sides to make it easy to sit down in. In the carving, the coloured bands are etched in with skill, and show up white on the black stone, like in a negative from a photograph. There's a big hood on the amautiq. It's how the woman carries her baby around. This stone woman and her baby look angry. They both have the same face, and it's the face of a scruffy, grumpy old man. Their eyes follow you no matter where you go. From the corner of each of their mouths dangles a tiny ivory cigarette, and they stare at me with their ugly eyes, mother and child, both smoking. Dad says, "This is real folk art." He says, "It's indicative of the subconscious state of the Inuit at this current point in history, when their identity is changing to cope with factors forced upon them by the outside world." He thinks it's profound, as well as clever and whimsical, but I think creepy is really a better adjective. The amautiq woman was made by Willassie and Mina's mother, who is one of the most respected carvers around. I've never met her. Mrs. Ippaq is an infamous recluse and never leaves her house. Lucy told me that she makes her kids get her anything she needs, and that even after all these years of being Mina's friend, she's never seen Mina's mother once. Looking at that ugly carving I think maybe Mrs. Ippaq should meet Mom, they could hang out and gossip.

Dad has even bought one of Willassie's carvings, although I don't think he knows who made it. He can't read syllabics yet, and that's how the carvers sign their names, etched into the bottom of the stone. Willassie's carving is a bear with a man's face, looking upwards. If you turn it upside down you can see his signature, scratched in the triangular and snaky shapes I'm learning to read. Since Dad doesn't have a clue, syllabics have become a secret language. Mina can write me notes in my exercise books that my father will probably never be able to decipher. So far, I only know the basics, numbers and the names of animals and simple stuff like mother, father, boat, sky, tent. Every night I touch the bear's back. I imagine Willassie is in the living room, looking upwards, watching me climb the stairs in my flannel nightie with the pink lace at the neck. I wish I could think of his bear as a dream guardian, protecting me, but I'm no longer that naive. I know that no one's watching over me while I sleep.

Every night for the past two months, I've dreamt of myself as St. Elizabeth, saving the Saviour. I know this was Elizabeth's greatest wish. It's what she was constantly punishing herself in preparation for, like training for the Martyr Olympics. I've tried every thing I can think of to make myself happy before I sleep, so I won't dream about it, but nothing works. I've tried reading Roald Dahl, counting sheep, even picturing the sheep all naked and Gulliver-style and then counting them. I once tried staying awake as long as possible, but finally, at five AM, I fell asleep anyway and dreamt that I'd become her again. There were the nails, the weight of my body on the cross. The heat of the sun on my snow-white skin. Everyone I knew came to see me be crucified. They stood in a blur before me, filling up the tundra with human-coloured spots, breaking the monotony. They were relieved that it was only me who was going to die, not someone important. I saved nobody. It was meaningless. My body was eaten by ravens. The tulugaq. And the ravens were tame, they were pets.

Last week I asked Dad if I could get baptized. He said, "You have no idea how lucky you are not to have the church influencing the development of your mind." That's a laugh; Jesus switches places with me in my sleep. Maybe if I was baptized this would stop happening. Besides, I used to go to church with Mom when I was little, and she lectured me incessantly about it all. I still have all those Catholic martyr stories walled up in my head, as well-known as fairy tales, and just as big an influence on the development of my imagination. Though without the benefits of being a bona fide Christian.

It's five minutes to the end of school. Willassie is sitting in the next row, pretending I don't exist. I know I'm not exaggerating, because this morning when I said hello to him he looked at me, then pretended he hadn't seen me, that he was talking to Carla instead. He hasn't looked my way since. Who gives a care. I hate everyone on this island, except Evan, who's just annoying. I hate being the freak that no one talks to when other people are around. I wish I looked like everyone else. I wish I spoke better Inuktitut. I wish I was better at making friends.

School's finally over. No one says goodbye to me as we're leaving, except for Benny, and he says it to make fun of me, pretending to cry.

"I gonna miss you, little bear. I gonna miss you tonight!" he sobs at me, clutching at the door frame to remain upright. Some little kids laugh and I kick gravel at them.

"Go home, white girl!" this kid Randy screams at the top of his lungs. He's in Grade One and is the kind of kid who's always making a fuss about something. His older sister Annie is really tough. She's having a smoke on the step in view of the staff room window. She and her cool friends spit at me.

"Go home!" Randy shouts again.

"I'd love to! I'd love to!" I shout back at Randy, startling him. "Who needs this shithole place?"

We're all surprised by my outburst, and it leaves things at a standstill. Okay by me. The sleep deprivation must really be getting to me. I've never yelled at anyone like that before. And what a stupid thing to yell at somebody, anyway. I walk into the wind, past the playground, and out across the frozen river. I feel like I'm suffocating. I'd love to go home, Randy, you snot-nosed frig-ass dick. Under the ice, the water's still moving, blood under skin. I pause in the middle of the river and turn around so I can breathe in the lee of my hood. I have to lean back on my heels into the wind in order to keep from falling.

I half hoped to see Willassie coming up behind me when I turned around. I was hoping he'd heard what had just happened and wanted to say he wasn't like that. "This is old hate that is taught to the children. There is a fear of what the whites can do and you are the whitest of anybody. They don't know what to make about you." And then he'd kiss my forehead.

But of course he's not following me. He's probably making out with Carla in the gym or something. Mina said that Carla's already done it with lots of guys. They're probably doing it now. Girls mature a lot faster here, they do that stuff before they're teenagers. I know nothing besides what I've read. I haven't really done any field research, to date, except for the hickey Willassie gave me. And that time he touched the scar on my cheek, tying on the necklace. The kiss on my head.

I turn back into the wind. I lean forward and walk like I really want to get to where I'm going. Determination is the only way that I can make it. I pretend that I'm not walking to the other end of Sanikiluaq. I'm walking home, Randy, home to St. John's, to the house with the yellow clapboard and the clean blue trim. The trees across the street in Bannerman Park. The big wooden playground and the crowded swimming pool with the green water marks. Mom's cooking, Linzertorte and curry and her homemade yogurt, and even those paté sandwiches that used to embarrass me at school. She used to take us to Mary Jane's for groceries, for saffron threads and green tea and that peanut butter they crushed out of peanuts in front of you and spooned into plastic tubs. When other kids were bringing tuna on Wonderbread, I was carting around quiche, crepes, hummus and kiwis. Not that Randy would know what a kiwi is.

I pretend I'm walking home to a world that isn't frozen, to a home that no longer exists. I didn't think it was all that great when it did exist, but, now that it's gone, I miss it. I miss how happy my mother was, now that she's sad. It's more complicated than the words happy and sad. The thing that's wrong with her goes beyond the meaning of those words, but that's as close as I can come. I can't even draw it. If I was a real artist I'd paint my mother with a thunderstorm inside her, the opening to her throat sewn shut. I'd paint the knife she's contemplating holding to her own throat, because she's so sick of having thunder and lightning trapped inside her. This is what I think about in order to fight the wind and make it "home" to where my father and Evan are, at the edge of Sanikiluaq, in the middle of nowhere. There's only room on our skidoo for two, so I get stuck trudging in the cold. Having kids spit at me. Having them scream in my face.

I get into my pyjamas as soon as I'm in the door. I say I'm sick, and crawl into my fortress. I take out my sketch pad and draw a close-up of a hand with a nail through it. I use my own hand as a model, but improvise the nail. I've been teaching myself to draw from a book, *Drawing on the Right Side of the Brain*. It helps that I'm left handed, as left-handers are automatically more in tune with the right, creative side of their brains, but the pictures I do without looking are still no better than the drawings that Evan makes. In fact, his are better, because he uses lots of different coloured crayons, and mine are just grey pencil lines on white paper. Nothing special. I write the words to "Jesus Loves Me" on top of the drawing in blue ballpoint pen. Then I scratch out the word "me" and replace it with "you." Jesus doesn't give a shit about me. I wasn't allowed to eat His body or drink His blood when I used to go to Mass. Which means I'm going to have to deliver myself, I guess.

I start drawing angels. I draw them with nanny wings, the lovely cool drapings of flesh that hang from the undersides of old women's arms. They wobble if you poke them. These are the wings that old women get to Heaven on. That's what I told my Nan once. She looks just like Dad, except with more wrinkles, and plucked eyebrows drawn on again with an orange pencil. She got mad, because she thought I was making fun, but I wasn't. Nanny wings are beautiful. They show how much work a woman's done. My Nan worked hard. She had six kids, a few head of cattle and a sizeable vegetable garden. She used to go out and fish with my dead Pop, when it was needed. Thus, her nanny wings are very large. I wish she were here to wrap her soft, whispery wings around my head. Maybe if I had her arms around my head I wouldn't dream that when I die no one will save my body from the scavengers.

There's a medicine ball where my brain once was. It feels like Evan is pulling on both my hands, my shoulders are so heavy. I wonder if complicated emotional problems are hereditary. God, grant me a night of peaceful sleep. One night is all I need. If tonight I can sleep and have pleasant dreams, I'll dump all this excess shit and surface free. Weightless. So relieved that I'll be laughing, permanently.

27

Sometimes I feel like I really only lived during that one year. Everything else seems like it was just a shadow of that one time I lived totally within my body and used myself to full capacity, loving, hating, being violently jealous. For a decade, all the emotional extremes have passed me by. I dated for the sake of it, the casual fling, just to have an arm around my neck for a while. Hoping stupidly that love might jump out and surprise me if I waited with someone's arm around my neck like that. I have a box of careless snapshots of me with various ex-boyfriends, all with their arms slung over my shoulder in the same old way. Casually possessive.

There's the ones from high school, when I dyed my hair green and wore magenta eyeliner in a thick, solid band that extended into my hairline. I had blood-red high-tops with satanic stars drawn on the toes and long black laces which I wound up around my fishnet calves and tied in bows, like ballerina ribbons. Dog tags. Safety pins in the arms of my sweaters. Boyfriends at the time tended to be fans of Nine Inch Nails. Melvin played racquetball.

He had a smell I couldn't wash off, no matter how hard I tried, like a locker room and mentholyptus. I never liked to kiss him. JJ was the school drug dealer/public speaking champion. The nerd front kept him from getting busted. I'd peddle to the punks for him at recess, dealing ready-made joints as well as regular smokes out of my Mary Poppins lunchbox, though I myself partook of neither.

Veej was East Indian. There were only two or three Indian kids in school, one black girl, a dozen Asians. Veej glowed like a hot toddy next to all the pale things he waded through in the hallways. What's more, he used to read real books during lunch. *The Catcher in the Rye* and all my other favourites. In my pictures with Veej, I look vaguely towards the camera with a scowl, having compulsively removed my glasses. I was convinced of my own hideousness with glasses on. That is to say, how I normally was. I'm slouching forward, like the weight of his skinny arm is somehow going to break my neck.

Later on, there's the snaps with Lyle, who had moved up from Vancouver; Grant, the bartending sociopath; Rick and Mike, who were brothers, neither of whom lasted more than a month with me; and Marty, my photography professor, who propositioned me while forcing open the door to the school darkroom, holding out a bottle of warm vermouth. "Miss Norman, have a drink, have pity on me." "Marty, you old lech, come in, and for shit's sake close the door." He put his hand on my breast right away. I let him do it but continued with my work. He'd fucked up my best exposure, and I was pissy. Marty was friends with Mom. He'd taken shots of me as a kid. He had a wonderful sensitivity for light and shadow. He was one of the few who didn't abandon my mother when she started to lose her shit. He put his hand inside my shirt as I stood swishing the paper in the developer. With his other hand he touched himself, looking over my shoulder at the shapes that were distinguishing themselves gradually, like magic, a flower blooming. "Ahhh," he said, "it's done," and then he came. He had a powerful erotic connection to the physical process of developing. I admired it. The pictures taken with Marty's arm around me are more artistic than the others. They are in black and white, and we are wearing a variety of ridiculous ensembles. He insisted on switching clothes at portrait time. Every time we fucked, we had to photograph ourselves afterwards, dressed in drag, sitting like that, chastely, his arm around me. His bullish neck straining in the tight collars of my vintage dresses as I swam around in his sweater with the moose stitched onto the front. He rarely wore anything different. I think he passed away last year or the year before. Mom told me it was testicular cancer, poor old fuck. I prefer these photographs to the others, but, even so, there's always this look of endurance on my wan little face, because it wasn't ever you, it wasn't your arm. No one had the magic touch, not even horny Marty, for whom I did have an honest affection. My breasts and vagina were still carved from soapstone. I'd eventually float out from under the weight of all those arms, alone again, adrift, my camera the only thing keeping me in the world at all. It was very easy.

All that remains of reality in its sturdy massiveness is the year I was twelve, going on thirteen. When the world was a snow-storm, a hurricane, and you were the eye. Open eye, watching out for me. The light so bright I barely dare to look, then so hooked I can't look away. Closed eye and I'm off the hook. The wink in between. You're taking yourself too seriously. Yeah, I know. It's my tragic flaw, but my life has been hard. And before you start going on about that, Mr. Closed Eye, I know what you're going to say. Lots of people have hard lives. They learn to move on, and I should do the same. I'm trying, Mr. Shut-Eye. Really I am. Wink. Blink. Flutter. Settle. What are you doing in there? Why won't you let me in?

Outside of my daydreams and sad old boyfriend reminiscences, in the half-reality, the almost-reality, in which I spend my waking life, I am sitting with a latte waiting for Vanessa to get back from the can. We've just had our first real talk since the wedding and Mark's berserker attack on the groom. I guess the newlyweds have been face and eyes into each other. I was worried that if much more time passed without our seeing one another, she'd think I was choosing sides, picking Mark. Which I wouldn't, and I'm not.

Vanessa asked if I thought she was crazy for making such a quick decision. I said I wasn't sure I could argue with her gut. "All the family is still really awkward," she said. They haven't taken the time to get to know Curtis, to see how it is. They just mistrust him and that's it. Mark hasn't said a word. She said, "I suppose I'm dead to him now."

I said, "He's massively depressed, Vanessa. The fact that you're happily married disproves all of Art-Man's theories about love as modern myth. If you're happy, he no longer has impossibility to console himself with. He's finally forced to admit that it's himself at the root of his own shit."

"When I told him I was engaged, the first word he said was alimony. It's like we're talking two different languages. He can continue to avert his disapproving gaze. You can tell him he's broken my heart. I've gotta piss, excuse me." She walked upstairs, winding her scarf around her hands, which were purple with cold, and shaky. Vanessa has always had terrible circulation.

There are four or five Theatre People coming into the coffee shop. One was dressed as Elvis at the *King and I* party. Actors are so fucking funny. I avert my eyes lest they should see me and decide to get kissy. With my spoon, I draw stick people in the spilled sugar. It gets too complicated and then turns into nothing. I dread these unforeseen moments of silence in the day. It's only when I'm idle that I start to think about you. If I could arrange the present, I would eradicate these little slips in activity and continually stimulate myself with tasks and conversation, thereby decreasing my tendency to dwell. What good does it do?

Delith is clearing tables. I watch her through the mirror: the stoop, the bend, legs and arms moving in counterpoint. An interior pas-de-deux. The stretched blue fabric of her shirt accentuating her spinal column like a garden hose. God, she's thin. Her scapula. I want to order her a sandwich. She's clearing thirty crumb-encrusted plates at once, in a precarious, tottering pile. She can balance anything. She's a magician, superhuman, made of finer stuff than me. There's something remarkable there, it shows up in that shot I took. She's got these eyes, big with experience. She's fragile-looking but you know she's tough. Like a monument. There's not many people who could live up to a name like Delith, but Delith can. She turns towards me, and smiles when I catch her eye. "Refill?" I shake my head and cover my cup with my hand, struck dumb. Her left canine is chipped a little. Brown eyes. Maple syrup. The blue shirt is buttoned up the front. She bends again, and through the folds I catch a glimpse of something pink. Her nipple. Is it? She bends again. This time I'm sure. Taut with the cotton brushing into her skin. The weight of her breast pushing out against the fabric. I'm biting my tongue without realizing it. I start to blush and look away, wipe the sugar off the table. Is this a crush? Am I lesbo? Is there anything I actually know about myself?

Vanessa comes back, wiping her hands in the hem of her skirt. "They're out of paper towels." She sits quickly, like she's embarrassed for anyone to see her moving from one place to another. My head is full of exclamation points.

"Look. Do you think it's possible for me to be bisexual? Now, I mean?"

She is scraping her chair in, and says nothing.

"I mean, aren't you supposed to figure out your sexuality early on? Like, in high school?"

"I guess," she says.

"I don't know. While you were peeing I came to the conclusion that I think I could fall in love with anyone, whether they're a dude or a…dudette. Excuse the language."

"I see."

I grab her hand. "Really, though. Couldn't love happen with a woman just as easily?"

"I don't know. I'm married."

"I know. I was there. And good for you. But maybe I've been going the wrong way here. Maybe the reason that I'm still single and loveless at the incredibly old age of twenty-four is that I haven't…broadened my horizons."

"Are you serious?"

"I think I'd have to kiss a girl to know for sure. But my guess is that, yes, I am a fisher of all seas, and I've only just discovered it. Now. Today. Isn't that fantastic?"

"Shh."

I have little sense of appropriate public volume.

"It's a bit odd," she says. "This just occurs to you, this minute. I mean, lots of people go through the whole lesbian phase. Maybe you just need to try it out to see that it isn't your thing. If you really were gay, or bi, or whatever, don't you think you'd have known when you were small?"

"Being gay is one thing. You're still strongly oriented to one sex. That's easier to identify than feelings towards both. And you never heard of bisexuals when we were growing up. I think any feelings I'd have had toward girls would've been subverted and turned into something else."

"I guess it's possible."

"I had these really intense friendships. We'd bite and hit each other a lot. Pull on hair, snap each other's training bras."

"That's not really a sign. We all did that stuff."

"Maybe everyone's a pervert."

"Ha ha." She's not amused.

"I've been hanging out with Gay Stevie too much, I think."

"What, he's turning you? Besides, I thought there was no such thing as too much Stevie."

"There isn't. It's statistically impossible."

Vanessa has that constipated look that means she wants to say something but she's trying to hold back, for my sake.

"What?"

"Nothing. Just, I was wondering what Mark is going to think."

"I probably won't tell him. I mean, not unless I'm going steady with a hot chick and having her babies. He has his head up his ass half the time anyway. Won't notice."

"Yes he will."

"He didn't when I cut all my hair off."

"He noticed, Teresa. He just didn't say anything."

"If you'll excuse me, I have to tip the waitress."

I can tell by the mothering look Vanessa's giving me that I'm acting like a ninny. I don't care. My feet, stupid slugs, carry my body to the cash. It takes about a year. Delith looks up. Her hair and eyes are both the colour of molasses. For some reason I picture her wearing a yellow plastic headband, it digging into the backs of her ears. She smiles. It's like watching a print in the developer. That slow.

"Can I get you anything else?" she asks.

"I'm okay at the moment."

"Good to hear."

My stupid feet don't want to move. They're made of concrete. I'll never escape. I stand there. Clear my throat.

"What's the soup of the day?"

"Mediterranean vegetable garnished with feta and kalamata olives."

"Nice." My heart is pounding at the back of my throat.

"Cup or a bowl?"

"Look, I don't give a fuck about the soup."

"What?"

"Sorry. Look, don't get freaked out by this, or anything, but I was just wondering, would you like to go someplace with me? Like, for a coffee?"

She's wide-eyed.

"I'd be honoured to escort you to a Fine Dining Establishment other than your place of work."

"Well…"

"Really. Your grace stuns me."

"Uh huh." She's looking at the man standing in line behind

me. I'm a boob.

"Okay, I've said too much. I'll just la-la-latte myself away and let you get back to your job. Sorry. Bye."

Vanessa has my coat and has already left the building. She's looking back through the plate glass with a pained expression, embarrassed for me while I, inexplicably, can do nothing but laugh. I keep laughing loudly. I look back once, to see Delith going for the broom, sweeping up shards of china from the cup she just dropped. Coffee running over the side of the countertop. The man who was in the line behind me cursing and wiping his expensive pants.

"Well, Nessie, that was a disaster," I say.

"Then why are you practically skipping down Water Street?"

"I don't know. I just feel better. Than I did before. Cheesy as it is, I feel way more alive than I have in ages. Years."

"You're going to have to work on your pickup lines, T. Even Mark is better than that."

"Yeah, but he's had years of practice with the ladies. Maybe he'd coach me."

"Maybe, but I think he'd rather you punched him in the kidneys."

"Both can easily be arranged." I crack my knuckles.

Vanessa smiles. "Well, give him one from me while you're at it. And a matching one from Curtis on the other side."

I skip a little down the sidewalk. I can't get into more talk of the feud right now, it's too depressing. The eye is opening. I'm giddy with the thought. Anything can happen, can't it?

At this point it doesn't matter whether it's your eye or not.

28

It's Evan's birthday. He's turning six. I remember six: popping sap bubbles with a stick, knowing right from left, tying my shoes. Reading books by myself. Finding pebbles that looked like animals. Six is about possibilities beyond the familiarity of the front porch, beyond the small circle of adults who previously made up the world. No more baby stuff. Six is limitless.

I'm making Evan a picture book for his birthday, about a little boy who finds out he is actually a pirate prince and heir to pirate gold. He becomes the captain of a pirate ship and goes on all sorts of adventures far and wide with his trusty crew of humorously diverse misfits, like Stumps, the first mate, who has two peg legs, and the cook, Quiet Sam, who is covered in tattoos of random words. He is a mute and points to his tattoos to tell the others what he means. Instead of a parrot, the boy captain has a talking hamster named Gregory. I think Evan will find this hysterical. In fact, I'm pretty sure that when he reads about Devon, the Boy Pirate King and his talking sidekick, Gregory, he'll laugh so hard his apple juice will come out of his nose. I'm looking forward to it.

I used every single colour of my pencil crayons to make the cover. There's a ship with complicated sets of masts and a pirate flag. It's sailing around Signal Hill, drawn by memory. At the bottom, on shore, are all the people Devon is leaving behind. I put Dad in there, and Tom-Tomas, but not me, because I'm on the ship as a stowaway who emerges to save King Devon by fighting a giant sea monster made of clear mucousy stuff. I do this by using magic to turn a regular Kleenex into one seven hundred times the size. We throw this on the slimy thing and vanquish it. I become one of the crew and get to sit in the crow's nest with a telescope, while antics ensue down on deck. It turns out that the monster was actually made of boogers and, although gross, is good-natured and kindly. His name is Gloopulus. He keeps the sharks away.

Evan loves pirates. In fact, this is a pirate party. Dad made a cake and everything. It's pretty good, covered in white icing with a chocolate chip drawing of a skull and crossbones in the middle. Everyone coming has to dress up like a pirate, and we're going to play games like Pass the Pirate Booty and Pin the Peg Leg On the Parrot. I made a piñata with newspapers dipped in flour and water and wrapped around a balloon. You pop the balloon when the paper is dry and paint the outside. Then you fill it up with pirate loot, which is actually candy, although some of it looks like gold coins. Doubloons. Dad had them sent up here especially.

All the little kids from Evan's class are coming. Most of them don't have proper costumes, so I've made a bunch of eye patches and construction-paper pirate hats. Dad said I could invite some people too, but I didn't want to, so I'm the Door-Answering Pirate, in charge of giving a hearty "Arrr, Matey!" when each kid comes up and knocks, and then making sure they get a hat or an eye patch. It's more fun than I've had in a while. Little kids don't care how dorky you are. In fact, the dorkier the better. It just makes them laugh. Lucky thing my best friend in the whole world is turning six today.

There's a knock.

"Arrr, Matey!" I yell, and fling the door open.

Ms Nancy Ikusik is standing on the step, dressed as some sort of glamorous girl pirate, carrying a cake like a treasure map, X-marks-the-spot done out in licorice.

"Hello, Teresa."

"This is a kid's party, Nance."

She doesn't flinch. "Your dad asked me to come."

I smirk. "Did he come over to your house and ask you in person or did he send you an invitation soaked in cologne?"

"He came over." Nance seems to be an expert at playing dumb.

"Well, in that case, come on in. You're the guest of honour. Should we all bow down and salute you?"

"No thanks."

Dad is in the bathroom putting coffee grounds for stubble on his dirty pirate face.

"We already made a cake, Ms Ikusik," I say. "What flavour is yours?"

"Mine is chocolate."

"Oh. Evan always has strawberry for his birthday. I'll put this in the fridge. Maybe they'll want to take some home."

She's taking off her stupid kamiks, with the beading around the tops. More like a gypsy than a pirate. When I tell her this, she says she never liked pirates much.

I snort. "Evan likes pirates more than anything."

Right on cue, Evan comes tearing out of his bedroom, chasing Tom-Tomas with a cardboard cutlass. He sees Ms Ikusik and runs up to her, jumping for a hug like he does with me. He loses his paper hat.

"Ms Elbow is here!" Evan yells. "You're the prettiest pirate ever!"

Nancy's face is glowing like the teddy bear night light in the hallway with the chipped-away eyes. I hate that stupid night light. Evan sinks his face into Nancy's hair, under her scarf with the bits of tinsel threaded into it.

"Ms Elbow, you smell better than anybody!"

Gag me with a spoon, for God's sake. Puke-tastic to the max. Everybody knows that my mother smells the best in the world, and she never had to put any kind of perfume on to get that way. She was born like it.

I carry Nancy's cake towards the kitchen. Dad is coming out of the bathroom, his coffee-ground stubble looking silly underneath his real moustache. He growls fiercely and all the little kids around him scatter, screaming. Tom-Tomas runs in my direction and smacks me into the wall. The treasure map cake slides off the tray, hits the wall and then splatters all over the floor. I don't say anything, at first. Tom-Tomas is laughing and scooping cake straight off the wall and into his mouth. He's licking the door frame. Dad's getting red under his moustache and smelly fake stubble.

"Teresa, what have you done?"

Evan is crying. "My cake! My cake! You hate me!"

"It was an accident!" I say. "You've got another cake, Evan, one that Dad made."

"I want Ms Elbow's cake!" Evan cries.

"Tom-Tomas banged into me. I'm sorry," I say.

Dad is getting a cloth to wipe the mess up. "He barely touched you, Teresa."

"I barely touched you, Teresa," Tom-Tomas mimics. The stupid little kids all start to laugh.

Dad makes me go to my room. He thinks I did it on purpose. Just because I don't like Nance and don't want her to suck face with my stupid father who's still married to Mom doesn't mean I'd stoop to sabotage. I wouldn't have to anyway. Our cake was better, hands down.

I throw my eye patch across the room. Who wants to be a pirate other than total dorks and babies. From my room, I can hear the screech of little kids high on sugar. They're having hot dogs and French fries, glasses of ginger ale. Strawberry cake with three birthday candles lighting up each eye socket of the skull and crossbones. I get in my secret cave on the lower bunk, and take off my clothes underneath the covers, shivering from the cold touch of the sheets. I can hear Dad out in the living room. He's reading my storybook out loud to everyone. Suddenly I'm crying. He's getting all the voices wrong. Letting fucking Nancy read my character. I bite into the soft side of my wrist. If I don't, I'll cry so hard the sonic waves will knock the house down.

I turn over and sink my face into the mass of pillows, gasping for air, biting in. I'm praying, even though I don't know a single real prayer. Dear God, let me escape this place. Send me a friend or let my mother come here or let me go home to her. I don't care if I have to give up everything else in my life that's happy and good, just let me get out of here. God, I didn't do anything. I don't know why everyone hates me. Don't let them hate me anymore. I'm sorry about being rude to Nancy and everything else mean that I've done in my life. If you fix this I promise I'll never be mean again. If I can go home, I promise I'll never forget you. I'll get Mom to teach me the rosary and I'll say it every night, cross my heart. Thanks God, amen.

I lie and let the snot in my face drain out into the pillow, later to dry into faint brown markings, blending into the topographical map of the world I have already painted on this pillowcase from nights of bawling. The door to my room opens. I pretend I'm asleep in my fort.

"Teresa. I am sorry." It's Nancy. "I want to tell you that I love your family and I want to spend time with you but I am afraid of being in the way. So I don't try very hard to make friends with you. Do you want to be my friend?"

I can see Dad's hand in her hair, in her Inuit living room. I refuse to say anything. I just lie there and wait. After a short silence, she starts in again. "I know it is hard to be the outside one. Maybe you are not going to believe me, but I too am outside of many things, because of my personality and what I am doing in my life. Lots of Inuit think that the school is a waste of time. They want the kids to learn to hunt and fish and make their clothes and have kids. They want the old way of life to keep going and don't see why learning English is important. The older people think I am a fool to spend my life teaching someone else's language and rules. But this is what I want to do, so I do it, even though I know I will be alone. It is too important for me. We have to keep up with everyone else, we have to be ready for the changes. Even though this is a little island, it is still inside the bigger world. We are still connected. And I will tell you a secret, Teresa. It is okay to be alone. Sometimes there are friends. I could be a friend to you, if it's okay. You know Sedna, the story?"

She tells me about this girl, Sedna, who gets married to a half-god/half-guy who can turn into animals and who treats her badly. When she runs away and tries to climb into her father's boat, he stabs her eye out and cuts her fingers off, even though she's his daughter, because he's afraid of what her husband will do if he knows that he helped her. And although she sinks to the bottom of the ocean, Sedna doesn't die. She grows a tail and her severed fingers become all sorts of animals that the Inuit can hunt. She saves her people from starvation. Her fingers become all the animals in the Arctic. Nancy tells the whole story. It takes so long that I can hear the piñata getting smashed, the squeals as everyone dives among the furniture for the spray of treasure. Dad calling out, "No fighting."

"See how Sedna was so lonely, but in the end everyone loved her. She was important. But it is hard in the middle, when you feel no one is on your side." Nancy sucks some breath in. I can hear her shifting weight. "You want to come to my house some day, I'll show you a carving of her."

I've seen it. On her coffee table. I decide to say something, at last. "You sure talk a lot, Nancy."

"Yes. I am Little Miss Chatterbox." I think I can hear her smiling.

She leaves the room. I'm alone again, naked under my quilts, my face damp from snot and tears in the lumpy mass of my pillow. Sedna. I like this story. I like that Nancy didn't spare me any of the gory details, just because I'm a kid.

I hope I won't have to cut any fingers off in order to be needed, though. That's a little too extreme, even for yours truly.

29

Out in Ferryland with Mark and Vanessa and all of their relatives. Talk about an awkward situation. It's their Poppy's ninetieth birthday, and we've come to pay a visit with the rest of the well-wishers. They both begged me to come, saying the same thing. "I won't make it through without you." Mark got down on one knee, Vanessa pressed my hand to her sweet, flushed cheek. A flair for melodramatic gesture runs in the family.

They have to keep up appearances of civility for the sake of their mother while they'd like to get at each other's throats like savages. Nearly a year since Mark went berserk at the wedding. "What about Curtis?" I asked Vanessa. "He'll have the flu," she said. The three of us got in the back of their mom's minivan, looking breezily out the windows. Their mom seemed oblivious. Mark kept his headphones on.

I've only met Pop once before, at the wedding, when he insisted we shuffle together to *The Tennessee Waltz*. He held my waist so tight he left a bruise. Today, when we come through the door into his kitchen, he looks at me like I'm a Christmas ham on display at Halliday's. "Come here," he says. The room is stifling with heat from the woodstove, yet the aunts all have their sweaters on. The outport constitution is more accustomed to temperature extremes than that of us Townies. I cross the floor slowly to Pop's chair by the window, with the rolling papers and tobacco on their own special stand, an objet d'art. He takes my hand and turns me around. I make suicide faces at Vanessa. Pop smacks my thigh.

"Are you after putting on weight, or is you pregnant?"

I get very red in the face. I can feel it happening. It starts at the sternum and shoots straight up to my soft spot, which gets hottest of all, till I imagine it as a scarlet target that God is using for pissing practice. I sit down quick on the daybed and put a pillow in my lap. Some of the uncles are laughing, and Mark's mother turns to her sister Vi.

"That's shocking," she says.

"Actually, Pop," Mark says, sombrely, "the baby's mine. Aren't you going to congratulate us?"

Pop stops rolling cigarettes. There is a general round of gasps. Vanessa comes in from the doorway and shoots Mark a death-ray look. He glares back. I'm ready to pass out with embarrassment. Vanessa takes Pop's arm.

"No one's pregnant. Teresa hasn't even put any weight on. Sure she's thin as a stick."

They all want me to twirl around on the slanting linoleum so they can judge my weight for themselves. Even Vanessa. It's diverting the attention away from her, for once, from her rash life decisions. But I can't be her martyr, not today. I rush back out the front door, which swings open behind me. I can hear them halfway down the road.

Vanessa:

Now look what you've done. Always have to stir it up.

Mark:

She's just too sensitive. It was a goddamn joke, for Jesus' sake!

Another chorus of gasps from the relations as he takes the Lord's name in vain, on top of everything.

Well. At least they're talking. I'm walking fast, scuffling gravel in a trail away from my shitty friends and their shitty grandfather. At the shore I pick up a handful of beach rocks and throw them as far as I can. They land with a distant plop.

Why do I overreact to every little thing? Why is my first impulse to sob or run out of the house, rather than laugh or poke fun back like a normal human? It was a joke, for fuck's sake. Now that I've bolted, it's not a joke anymore. It's an issue. Sometimes I really hate Mark.

The wind is whipping off the water. I turn so that it slaps the back of my neck. It's a wind full of salt, a cold, sad wind, like the breath of a new-made widow. The beach is empty, except for me and some pieces of broken glass, and a line of dried kelp the tide has left. Three sandpipers flirt with the waves, their thin legs implausibly carrying them out of danger. They always manage not to drown.

I sit on the rocks. They're cold. I'll probably get frostbite on my ass. My hands are chapping from the wind. I don't care. I can't go back into the smallness, the hotness of the room, I can't face the smug-ugly wallpaper and the smell of salt beef and tobacco, and the innocent criticism of my elders, and Mark's assumption that my skin is three inches thick. Even Vanessa just wants to hide behind me. My comedy act.

They must be laughing to kill themselves right now, all of them, doubled over, smacking each other's knees, their lips glistening with the sheen of a good joke.

My pale, moon-shaped abdomen shows itself over the top of every pair of skimpy underwear I try on. So what, so what. I'm not one of the masses. I do not believe the shampoo commercials. I don't have subscriptions to women's magazines. The women in all those ads look the same after a while: wrists like spun glass, neck the trembling stalk of a lily. Bathed in a sheen of expensive studio lighting that illuminates her perfect contours. From beneath her pert, taut breast, the message: if this isn't you, it should be. Buy this two thousand dollar necklace. Buy this lipstick, it's the best.

I hate myself for hating myself, am ashamed of my shame. I know it shouldn't matter. I never watch those sicko programs. I have read *The Beauty Myth*. Still, every time I get dressed, it takes four or five changes of clothing, with critical analysis in the mirror—back, front and side—before I can get out the door. Everybody knows that the only thing less attractive than a pseudo-albino is a fat pseudo-albino. I'm the last of the White Rhinoceros. Goodbye, logic! Hello, self-loathing, my old friend! Let's peer into the warped mirror once again. I should advertise. Some cosmetic surgeon might take me on as a charity case. Tint my skin the nice, healthy beige of a normal girl, dye my hair to match. I'll choose a dark brown that's almost black. Extensions please. Let the brown hair fall in a torrent down my back. My surgeon will produce the Sharpie and proceed to draw me up: nose, cheekbones, breasts, thighs, ass. My ears have always been a little weird. My fishbelly irises, colourless. Not to mention the sad old flabs. A lesser surgeon might balk at the task ahead: "This is a tough one, all right. There's not always a Beauty in every Beast. But, what can I say, I'm tender-hearted. Pass the scalpel, Doris, and get me a coffee, double double. Looks like we've got an all-nighter here." The cool ink drying on my skin, a promise of where the knives will cut in. I'll be unconscious while he or she does the actual carving and will awake as someone unrecognizable. I'll offer myself to the surgeon who has transformed me. I'll fall in love with him/her and have his/her babies.

A stone skips out into the water, five skips. It's Mark. He's wearing an expression I've never seen before, something between determination and shame. Chagrin. I turn back towards the water.

"What?" I say.

Seven skips.

"Are you okay?" he asks.

"Yeah."

Four skips.

"Are you sure?"

"Yeah."

Six skips.

"I'm sorry, Teresa. We were just fooling around. Pop's a funny one."

"Runs in the family," I say.

"I guess."

Ten skips.

"That was a good one," I say. He grunts.

Mark sits down next to me on the rocks. He has a mussel shell in his hand which he passes to me, iridescent inside facing up. I shove him once, hard. He topples to the side, then sits back up. Where our shoulders and knees are touching there are two imperfect circles of heat on the cold beach. We sit like that for a while, watching the water make its way closer and closer until we can feel the salt from the spray in little stings on our skin.

"I forgive you," I say.

"I like you even though you're enormous." Mark says. "Even though you're the size of an entire KFC outlet, I'll still be your friend."

He pinches my forearm, through to the bone. "I was going to tell you that dinner's ready, but maybe you'd better skip it."

"You're funny."

"Fatty."

"Jerkface." I push him over again and take his hat. I throw it and it lands in the ocean. Mark makes a mad dash for it, going in past the ankles, soaking his shoes. He runs back and wrings the water out over my head. I scream at the coldness of it, hopping around on the rocks. We're both laughing to kill ourselves, screaming like kids. Clutching our guts.

"Seriously, though, T. If I catch you on some kind of stupid-ass diet, I'm going to kill you. 'Cause that's just Pop. Last time we came here, he asked if I was 'one of them homosexuals,' if you can believe it."

The word doesn't seem like it could ever apply to me. Not even the sexual part, minus the homo. I think I'm maybe asexual. Except for maybe twice in my life, I can't remember ever experiencing a feeling of arousal. I can't remember feeling sexy, wanting sex. Isn't that a sign of being dead already? Why don't I just jump in a lake or, hell, the ocean's right here. Why don't I just drown. I'm sure Delith thinks I'm perverted. I probably make her sick.

"Well, what did you tell him?" I say.

"I said I was keeping my options open and put my hand on Wilf Chafe's knee."

"Who's Wilf Chafe?"

"Pop's neighbour. Last of the salt-stained fishermen. Does three weeks of crab a year and wins money off Pop playing crib the rest of it. You should have seen it. Fit to be tied, the both of them. They couldn't do anything but wheeze for about ten minutes. That's what you've got to do with these old people, you know. Turn them on their heads for a while. Shake them up. Shake n' Bake them and chew them up for dinner. Speaking of which, pea soup, moose stew and fresh bread await."

"We're vegetarian, " I say.

"Like I said—there's bread. And bakeapple jam. Pop made it himself. If you don't have some he'll never get over it."

He takes my hand and leads me towards the house, letting go as soon as he sees that I'm coming. I follow half a step behind, studying the pattern his hat left on his hair. I want to say, thank you, Mark, now forgive your sister for being happy. Let's make a day of it. I want to touch his head, smooth out the ridges of hair at the nape of his neck. I nearly do it. I only just catch myself in time. He notices nothing.

30

This is the most exciting day of my life so far. Today I am On Assignment for the *Northwest News*, which is the brand new school newspaper that Mr. Levy and Dad have started printing out on the ditto machine. Dad lets me turn the dittos around. I like the chemical smell. I like the rhythm and the pages that go in wrinkled and get their words messed up, stretched and tragically separated. I like how it makes you tired to turn it, how you really have to work pretty hard. And the leftover inky pages that me and Evan hoard, pressing each fingertip into the blue and then onto the back of an old math test, lining up the swirly little ovals in neat rows, pretending to be cops, arresting each other.

Some of us students get to be reporters and write about things that are happening. Dad and Mr. Levy make enough copies for everyone in school to read. In the first issue I wrote about the bake sale the Grade Nine girls were having, and Mr. Levy wrote an article asking for evidence of who busted out the windows to the library with a slingshot. There was one thousand dollars' damage, and now there are pieces of wood nailed up in the windows. He also wrote about a break-in at someone's shed this weekend. Two cans of gas were missing. "Your brain and body are important," he wrote. "Don't let anyone drag you down."

Now there's real news to report, and I get to report it. There is a team of archaeologists here. They are digging up the Tuuniq houses on the other end of the island, looking for clues about the ancestors of the Inuit. I don't get to do any interviews, but it's even better than that. For the whole day I will be an apprentice archaeologist, digging in the ground and looking for artifacts. Dad arranged this, Dad the Loser, with Occasional Streaks of Alrightness. He remembered how much I've wanted to be an archaeologist since forever, and he arranged this one beautiful day. I used to have all these books about uncovering the tombs of the Egyptians. Probably Dad just wants me far away so he can do it with Nancy, but still. It's pretty great.

This is a day just for me. We're leaving Evan behind. We tied him onto the outside of the house like a crackie dog, a little midget madman screaming in his baby harness. He's so mad his face looks like a broiled tomato. I don't know why he's so upset. It's beautiful out and he's got enough rope to move around. I even left him a bag of raisins.

We're going by skidoo, and the wind is turning my ponytail into a pot handle off the back of my head. I've brought my notebook and pencil. I'm holding onto Dad's waist, where the spare tire is. It jiggles a little when we go over rough spots. The buzzing feeling of the treads on the snow jarring up into my teeth is making me stomach-sick, but the air is refrigerator temperature and it wakes me up as it whips around my head, past the pot-handle ponytail. This is the most beautiful day since

I arrived in the Northwest Territories.

We go for a long time until, finally, colours pop out at us. There are white people on the flatness. Strangers. They wear bright coats, new and clean, which give away the fact that they are white and they are strangers, way before we get close enough to pick their faces out. Dad introduces me to the team, a husband and wife, Chuck and Marla, three others, and two Inuit assistants, Gary Inuktaluk and Elijassie Mannuk. Dad's leaving me here.

"See you, T-bird. Get the full scoop. I have to go home and let your brother off his leash before he bites someone." He puts a baggie full of dried apricots and chocolate chips and peanuts into my hand. A frozen granola bar, the biggest of treats. He raps his knuckles on my forehead like I'm a coconut—"Still not ripe!"—because he knows I hate it when he does that. He gets back on the skidoo and drives back to Sanikiluaq. It takes him half an hour to disappear completely.

The archaeologists remind me of aliens landed on a strange planet, delicately prodding the landscape as if they might discover that it is really the skin of a sleeping Colossus, ready to gobble them up. Like in the *Star Wars* movies, when they fall down that tunnel that is really the inside of a gigantic worm with millions of razor-sharp teeth. The team has dug down to the earth, and put the snow in a big pile on the side. Probably they got Gary and Elijassie to do this for them. The pile is huge, and the snow is hard and packed heavily. I'd think it would be easier to excavate stuff in the summer, when the snow has melted, but who am I to decide. The archaeologists have roped off pieces of earth underneath. I ask how they know where to dig. Marla, the one in charge, says that they know because of the faint circular indentations in the ground. She shows me one that hasn't been excavated yet. It looks flat to me. I guess I'm going to have to improve my eyesight considerably to become a bona fide archaeologist in my grown-up years.

Marla is explaining how the digging process works, how you start from the perimeter of the indentation and only move inwards after thorough excavation. Her voice is strange. The vowels sound flat. I guess that's what makes her an American.

Chuck gives me a trowel, and some rough brown gloves that are too scratchy, so I put them in my pocket. I'm more used to living here now, so my hands aren't really even cold. I'll do without.

We dig for hours through the hard, grey dirt and then we eat our pocket treats and drink some tea out of a thermos and dig again. There are actually two thermoses, one for the archaeologists and one for the local guides. The archaeologists would probably puke because of the huge amounts of sugar in the other thermos of tea. I take American tea when Marla offers it to me.

I find three flint arrowheads. The archaeologists don't seem too excited. They've already found lots of arrowheads. They no longer appreciate the look of them, so hard and sharp and small, like badger teeth, but since these are my first arrowheads on my very first dig, I'm thrilled with the idea of them. It's amazing to think that someone made these, centuries ago, that they chipped them out of stone with another stone. Someone figured out how to do that, the right angle to strike, the right amount of force, the exact type of stone needed. Flintknapping. I bet Willassie can flintknap perfect arrowheads, without looking, in his sleep. I draw what they look like in my notebook and make a note to write about flintknapping in my article.

Even though the archaeologists aren't excited about the three arrowheads, they take them anyway, and catalogue them, each one in its own separate baggie, with a number corresponding to a diagram of the Tuuniq house we're excavating. They're Artifacts. Marla draws the diagram on a pad of yellow paper with green grid lines. She uses a ruler and a measuring tape and a very sharp pencil to mark her coordinates.

I'm digging with my trowel. I used to help Mom in the garden, when I was Evan's age. I had gardening gloves with pink flowers on them and every year I got to pick out some seeds and bulbs to plant. I had a special patch of the garden just for my flowers, out by the back fence. Tiger lilies, pansies, poppies, scarlet tulips. Bright-coloured flowers that Mom would help me put in the ground. And everywhere the smell of dirt and my mother's smell: Ivory soap, lemons and anise, clean cotton, and the metallic smell grown-up women sometimes have. This digging with the archaeologists is good, but it's sad too, because it reminds me of my mother, who isn't here, and it reminds me of home. And this place isn't my home. I might as well put on a mountain-climbing jacket with armpit zippers in seafoam green and tell it like it is: I belong here as much as these Americans do. I am as out of place as they are, poking at the earth as though picking its scabs. Nosy Parkers.

My trowel hits something. I put my hands into the soil and feel around. Black pieces of something light. I call out to Marla. There is Christmas eagerness in her face. Then she sees what I've got. Her eyebrows huddle together and she smacks my hands.

"Chuck! Fucking kids. Fucking stupid kids! She's ruined the whole thing! You don't touch charcoal, ever. If you touch it we can't date the find. It won't be half as accurate. Do you understand? This is the fireplace. This is the charcoal in the fireplace.

This is what we've been looking for all day. This is why you're supposed to wear gloves when you're digging. You've ruined the whole thing. Do you understand that?"

"Honey…" Chuck's trying to interject.

"We might as well go home." She's talking to herself now. "What's the point of anything."

I'm trying not to cry, and so is Marla, but in different kinds of ways. Chuck takes her by the shoulders and leads her to a camp stool. He gets her a cup of tea and pats her on the head with his mitt. She didn't tell me about the carbon, before. I guess she thought I wouldn't find anything. I get up and walk. It doesn't matter how far I go, I can still see them. No one's coming after me. They're all huddled around the hole, trying to salvage my mistake, except for Marla, who's sitting on the camp stool looking blankly off into the blank landscape.

I slump down on my knees. Even though it's wet, I lie down on the snow, facing away from everything. Underneath me there are probably more Tuuniq houses, spreading themselves like pancake batter in an iron pan, underneath the snow and mint-green lichen and the thin layer of dirt. Who cares how old they are? They're old, period. They're markers that people were here and that they saw the same sky I'm seeing now, that they chipped weapons out of stone and caught their food, and maybe dug in the ground looking for clues about the past. But I doubt it. I'm sure they had more important things to do. Who cares about the year, and the exact circumference of each dwelling, and its relationship in inches to the other dwellings? These stupid scientists are dredging up the magic of this place and ruining it. They're leaving nothing to the imagination and they're putting holes in the tundra where there shouldn't be any. Fuck the archaeologists.

They'll never know how beautiful the line between the ground and the sky is when you're lying on your side, because they'll never lie down and find out. They look at the Inuit and they don't see people, they see specimens. Interesting cultural phenomena. They'd take a measurement of Willassie's head, they'd count his teeth, but they wouldn't ask him what he dreams about, and they wouldn't want to see his art. Not like I would.

I compose the headline of my article: Archaeologists Should Get Out and Stay Out. Rude-mannered Americans Berate Child Reporter. I'm going to stay here until Dad comes back. I don't care if I'm making a scene. I'm just going to lie here and ignore the world till he drives up on the skidoo and carries me home to some oatmeal and *Charlotte's Web*, and plans to become something other than a retarded soulless scab-picker archaeologist when I turn into an adult, at some point in the distant future.

God forbid.

31

St. John's is a strange place. Correction, St. John's has some strange people in it. I am surrounded by them in the tiny upstairs area of the bar in a humid, tight-knit, interwoven cloud, as textured and intricate as the hooked mats made with grasses and human hair which have replaced Mark's big glass tank at the gallery. In front of me are half-dressed women with drastically applied makeup and plastic fruit in their hair. A boy in a Zorro mask. A drag queen is singing "Lean On Me" and accompanying herself on the hand-drums. Someone's hauling out a Twister mat and calling it performance art. This is a Night On The Town, Gay Stevie Style, and I have to get really tanked to deal. I'm on my third Ass-Kicker, extremely strong but tasting of Freshie and bright blue as 2000 Flushes. I'm hitting my comfortable, warm, lushed-out zone, like looking through a layer of finger-smeared plastic.

Gay Stevie is leaning on a table, having naturally sought out and obtained the most well-lit spot in the room. Directors love this. They never have to tell him to find his light. He was born with a natural sense of how best to expose himself. There are little clusters of people chatting around him, each group waiting for his present conversation to end so they can hug enthusiastically and squeal each other's names, or pat forearms with firm palms and ask about upcoming projects like the Theatre People they are. So sincere. And Gay Stevie is the king. He is pretty and charming and overwhelmingly nice, and eccentrically dressed and outrageous. He gives the best parties and the most bone-crushing hugs. He is the kind of person who has to stop thirty times on a walk down Water Street, in order to talk to everyone he knows, to invite them to yet another elaborate shindig, to ask about their haircuts or their solo shows or that gorgeous black guy everyone's seen but can't figure out where he came from, we thought we knew all the black people. His overwhelming range of acquaintances makes him either the best or the worst person to go out on the town with, depending on your mood.

Right now, I am not enjoying being Gay Stevie's date for the evening. He's taking off for his second summer in Trinity on Monday so everyone in the world wants to give him their phone number, first. He is withheld from me by a fence of bodies in various synthetic outfits that resemble figure skating costumes. Indecently short, or tight, or both. I feel like my Nan, in comparison. I am being sucked into various Pre-Stevie Conversations (PSCs) with clumps of Theatre People I barely know. I recognize them all, of course, having either seen them in shows or taken their headshots. An easy way to make a buck, if you ask me. They come over all done up and sit in a nice light, making sexy faces into my lens for half an hour, and then fork over quite a decent chunk of change. I print them up some eight by tens. They gush over how professional it all looks, and I agree.

I am nothing if not professional, even if I'm gritting my teeth and mentally flagellating myself.

There are about five Theatre People looking to have a PSC with me, and every one of them is under the impression that taking their particular headshot was the high point of my photographic career, a memory I hold so dear to my heart I'm in danger of smothering it. They don't understand that I whore myself, just like they do. When Mr. Actor in the yellow shirt there did that Cohen's Furniture commercial, I'm sure it wasn't for the artistic fulfillment. It was for cash. Cold and hard, plain and simple. Dude also played Hamlet, for fuck's sake. Still, they think these hired gigs I do are what I do, that I live to take headshots. Soon that little bit of easy money will be gone too. Everyone's going digital, you can get rid of blemishes so easily. In every PSC I start off asking about upcoming shows. This keeps us all occupied nicely.

All conversation stops when this chick comes out as a clown wearing a lot of ponchos and a bright blue bathing cap. It has to, as she is viciously heckling anyone still daring to make a peep. "I'm sorry," she corners some sad schmuck drinking a White Russian, "would you like to come up here and do this instead? Sir? Yes, you sir, yeah you, the one with the visible ass crack. Put that thing away, honey. No one needs to see that shit tonight." She sings "Let Me Fish Off Cape St. Mary's" in a strange, androgynous falsetto, and takes her clothes off, layer after hideous layer, staring us down, till all she's got on is several pairs of grandma-style underwear, on top of each other, and what look like clown noses on her nipples, and cowboy boots. The panties bulge grotesquely into a weird, jagged paunch or a swollen penis shape, because of something she has stuffed in there. She hauls it out, yelling "Who

193

wants to see my enormous package?" The room erupts in cheers. She waves around a slightly soggy parcel wrapped in newspaper. She makes us play Hot Potato and sings "Eternal Flame" into the microphone. The heat of multiple poncho layering has made her sweat, and the black of the newsprint has come off on her slick white belly, which is wobbling slightly, soft and rounded, and almost obscenely feminine. A moon. This chick with the sad clown face is standing there in her underwear, clown noses on her nipples, yelling at the crowd to toss the hot potato faster; with her smooth, round belly and her slightly mismatched breasts and her slumpy shoulders, all imperfect and brave, brave and scary and sad and potentially insane and lovely and great. The Ass-Kickers are kicking my ass, all right, because, suddenly, even though I find this all so stagy and uncomfortably sincere, and even political, in an abstract, feminist kind of way, I'm also loving it. I wish I were more like this girl. She appears not to give a shit what people think about her. I wish I'd brought my camera, after all. The hot potato slips out of my hands into the dude's next to me and we're both laughing. St. John's is so weird.

She's done. She's picking up her clothes and stuffing them into a suitcase. Before she leaves the stage area, she grabs the microphone again and whispers into it "Take off your clothes. I love you all. Try hugs not drugs. One life to live. Freedom, freedom, my sisters and my brothers."

The guy who won the Hot Potato game is sucking on his new candy necklace and matching strawberry-flavoured ring. I decide to go downstairs and get another fancy drink. It's that kind of night. I leave the PSCs and walk slowly toward the stairs with what I hope will be interpreted by all as a look of Dignified, Alluring Unattachment. Not Snobbery or Boredom or Plain

Old-Fashioned Drunkenness. Come Hither tempered with layers of Reserve. I walk slowly and keep my hand on the wall. I'm starting to get spinny with the ass-kicking. Chicks whipping out their enormous packages and passing them around. It's crowded tonight. People are backed into awkward configurations against empty shelves, sitting on each other on tables in the back. I recognize nearly everyone, but only as vague acquaintances I've met at some other Gay Stevie Occasion (GSO), or in black and white, drying in the darkroom, in either case sporting the serious, calculated smile meant to suggest a balance between intellect and sexual possibility. That cocktease look. I actually *know* no one. Except, as I scan the room again, I see one familiar face, way off in the corner. I blink to be sure, and I'm sure. There he is, Prince Asshole. King of Cats. Dear Mark, hiding in the corner of a performance art cabaret. The world's biggest hypocrite.

He hates this kind of thing. He rants about these kinds of Events. But now he's sitting under some girl with a peasant blouse and chunky highlights who's talking to some other girl.

The other girl is Delith. In any other place this would have to be made up. But this is St. John's, and this is the youngish arts community of St. John's, that sticky, inbred, amorphous pool where everyone gets around to everyone else, eventually. I hope they haven't been talking about me.

What to do. I put my body on autopilot and send it down the stairs. It leans up against the bar and asks the bartender (cum fashion designer, stage manager, line cook, bass player, and even mascot Buddy the Puffin for the defunct St. John's Maple Leafs) for the opposite of an Ass-Kicker. I say, "I don't care what it is, as long as it's not a shooter. I'm morally opposed. Food and drink should be ingested slowly. We have been blessed with the gift of taste and should luxuriate. I'm a sensualist. My mother trained me." He nods. My arms prop themselves on someone's velour scarf. If I were more of a badass, I'd take this scarf, because it feels so nice, so soft. But I'm no badass. My ass is dead from too much kicking. The bartender hands my right arm something like a milkshake, all coconut, mocha and cream. I propose marriage and hand him my money. He declines. I leave the change on the counter and go back up the stairs, my fairy-tale milkshake slopping a little over the side of my glass and onto my arm, which I must stop and lick, of course, like anyone would if they had an alcoholic dream parfait dripping down their arm. It's with my tongue out, sopping up the creamy stuff like a piece of bread in spilled tea, that Mark sees me. Correction, this is when Mark and Delith and even Girl With Massive Highlights see me. A skinny white boy with a lopsided Afro is now singing songs in German while playing a cheap synthesizer. A guy coming up the stairs with his ladyfriend says, "See, I told you synth wasn't dead." She rolls her eyes and they stop and proceed to fondle one another's necks on the landing. "You have my heart," she says. He backs me into the corner of the stairwell with his frisky, amorous ass. This is embarrassing. I edge past the couple, now really going at it. Mark and Delith are talking with that girl in the corner. I can't hear their conversation but I can see them seeing me, and their faces are all so wide open that I can read them like the most rudimentary of books. Dick and Jane and little dog Spot. And of course I've got to go over. It's required. Mark stands, shunting Girl of No Known Name or Origin off his thighs and into the corner, where I suppose she's protected if I go bananas and try to peck out her eyes. Like I'd ever. Delith there too, mysteriously knowing Mark somehow, like Mark actually knows people.

"Mark. You poser. Thought you hated the Theatre Scene in this, North America's oldest colony."

"Funny."

We punch each other. Upper arm region, but I miss slightly, and punch his chest instead. Girly-Girl's hand shoots out, like an ambush wire snapping into place, latching onto his abdominal area with strictly territorial ferocity. I know the stupid game we're going to have to play now, and it exhausts me, the predictability of the whole thing. (1) she's wildly jealous of our friendship, (2) forbids him to talk to me under any circumstances, (3) he then has to choose, (4) ignores me for a while, (5) realizes that's Crazy Talk, we're best friends, ain't no Flavour of the Month gonna get between us. He then (6) issues an ultimatum to her, she's gotta (7) put up with me or Get the Hell Outta Dodge, she (8) packs up her bags and leaves. And that'll be the end of it. I don't even know her name, and already I can tell this is how it's going to go. He grips her wrist and removes it from his rib cage. He's grinning in that sheepish way men grin when they know they're going to get in trouble and want somehow to diffuse it with charm.

"Who is this, Mark?" asks Girl Staking Claim.

"That's Teresa. Norman. She's a friend of mine."

"Work acquaintance," I say.

"Fuck off, T."

Delith is to the right of me and I'll be okay as long as I don't look that way. She's wearing something short and black and there's the white skin of her arms and her throat in my periphery. Chickie extends her hand to me—so formal!—and her palm is soft and cold.

"I'm Mark's girlfriend, Solange. I recently moved from

Vancouver. Coast to coast. I'm an actor. I don't believe we've met."

"Nice to meet you," I say. "He's told me all about you."

She's getting more jealous by the minute. Poor Mark. I forgive him for keeping this one a secret. He has foolishly forgotten his own cardinal rule. I paraphrase: Never Get Involved with a Mainlander, Especially on Your Home Turf. They're too fucking serious.

I decide to act like I didn't ask Delith out, and that this didn't make her break things. Like I went back in time and lost my nerve before I reached the cash that day. I decide to ignore the grating, tooth-grinding, napkin-shredding presence of Mark's latest find. Her name is Solange, and she's an actor. For fuck's sake. I force my head to turn in Delith's direction and will the muscles in my face to stop jumping around.

"Well," she says, as Mark turns to whisper with Solange about why I'm absolutely no threat to their budding romance, all that "hey baby, it's okay baby, I only have eyes for you baby" shit that's probably true, but never sounds like it.

"Well," I say.

"This is awkward," she says.

"Insert nervous laughter here."

We laugh, nervously, which makes us really laugh a little.

"Look, Teresa…"

"Yeah?"

"I'm not…of the lesbian persuasion, okay." She's not quite looking at me, speaking to the inflatable guitar decoratively duct-taped to the wall behind my head.

"I figured. Me either, really."

"You're not?"

"No. Want to go for lunch sometime?"

"Inserting nervous laughter again," she says. "No. Sorry. I can't."

"Don't worry," I say. "I couldn't either. I've officially gotten the hint."

She puts her hand on my arm and applies slight acupressure to places I didn't know were hurting, before. That is to say, she digs her fingers in. "I've got to go. I'm next."

"Wait. You're a Theatre Person?"

She takes off her dress, unzippering quickly. I dare to watch. Well, my neck won't turn and she's there in front of me. It's a forties cocktail dress, black with a satiny bow. Underneath, she is wearing some kind of costume made entirely of sequins and fringe. Red and gold and silver.

"Hold onto this for me?" Delith hands me her dress, which is still warm, and which I hold lightly so as not to wrinkle it. She disappears in the thicket of bodies and resurfaces in the light.

32

When I get to the playground, Mina's waiting with the other girls from my class. They say they're going to show me something. I say okay. Mina pulls out a tube from her pocket and hands it to Carla. It's a Vicks Inhaler, one of those things you stick up your nose when you have a cold and it makes the snot go away. I've used one before, and am not particularly impressed with its worth as a treasure, but I smile anyway, to remain on everyone's good side.

"You know what you do with this?" asks Lucy.

"Put it up your nose, for colds."

Carla tells me to take off my glasses. She says they put it in their eyes, for fun. That it's fun to rub Inhaler in your eyes, and, what's more, it's how you get into the club. She's coming near me with the stick. I don't want Inhaler in my eyes, but Mary is saying that all the girls do it, and if I want to play with them then I should too. I can't see anyone without my glasses. The whole group of girls has blurred into one big shape. I can't tell whose arms are holding down my shoulders and who is bringing the Inhaler up to my face. The minty, chemical smell is making my nose run. Someone's fingers are spreading and holding my eyelids open. They smell like they've recently petted a dog. I try to remain calm, but as the Inhaler touches my eyeball and goes right through to my brain, I can't breathe and I can't do anything but start to cry—of course, little baby—as they burn my other eye too. I grope to put my glasses on my face. It doesn't help. All is red and the world is burning.

"You okay, Teresa?" I hear Mina's voice, and I can't tell if she thinks it's funny or sad that I'm crying. Everyone with mock concern in their voices, pushing me. They have to take a trophy from me, then I'll be part of their group. I'll be part of their circle if they take something special away. I'm blind and oozing tears, scorched. I have nothing special to give and tell them so.

"Take her glasses." It's Sarassie.

"Please don't take my glasses. Take anything else. Take my boots, anything. You don't want them anyway, they're cracked." I clutch them by the dental tool bridge, holding them to my face. I'd barely make it home from here if they took my glasses.

There are hands feeling my body, searching for treasure. Some are not so gentle. They jab their fingers into my rib cage. They pinch me. They get my nipple and twist it around. I start biting at them, at any hands I can reach. I start kicking. They find my snowflake. They pull it out through the neckhole, and they've got it, my special thing. They have me by the shoulders and rip the yarn from my neck. Carla pushes me back.

"Willassie make you things?" Her voice is as angry as the Vicks shit in my eyes.

"I stole it. I stole it from him. He didn't give it to me, I swear." For some reason I'm protecting him with lies, getting myself in more trouble for someone who doesn't even care if I'm alive or dead. These bitches. Next they'll scrub my taste buds off with Comet, or pop my eardrums with a safety pin, and I'll be entirely without senses.

"Take it, I don't care. It's just something I stole." And I'm pushing myself up off the bottom of the slide, running toward where I think the school is, where I hope Dad is working late. I can't see. Hot tears are freezing in two lines down my face as I stumble along across the snow. I smack into a wall. I ease myself along with both hands until I find the door, push it open, and fall in a heap on the hallway floor, sobbing. I don't care who hears me. The tears are cleaning away the burning, and by the time Mr. Levy comes out of the office I can see a little bit, enough to tell him I'm fine, I just fell down, that's all. I sneak into the Kindergarten classroom, where I lie on the nap mats in the back, hidden by the water table from anyone walking by. The smell of crayons and Plasticine is comforting. I feel like sucking my thumb. There is a raw, sore line around my neck where they yanked the yarn off.

The next day, in school, Carla wears the snowflake over her Metallica t-shirt, and makes sure to say hello to me. So do the other girls. I know that girls do these things everywhere in the world, these initiations, these tests, and I know that once you've passed you're okay. I'm not so sad today. I even pretend that it didn't hurt at all, the stuff in my eyes. I pretend I don't know what they're talking about when they ask if I'm all right. Instead I tell them they should meet me at the playground after school. I've got something to show them.

Mina shows up first. She says I didn't cry as much as Lucy did when she had it done to her. She says now I can be part of the group and I'll be much happier. She says now I'm like a real Inuit girl who knows how to be tough and laugh at pain. Also that when I'm done my homework today, I should go to her shed. I don't know what to say to this. Mina says she's not stupid.

"Don't worry, he's my brother. I not gonna tell anybody you talking to him."

The other girls are coming. I show them my own little torture. In pairs, under my instruction, they crouch and face one another. They put their hands on each other's necks. They breathe really hard and fast for two or three minutes, then blow all the air out, hold the nothingness in their lungs, and squeeze. The girls squeeze their friends' necks and no one breathes. They all pass out. I have eight small Inuit bodies piled around my feet like I'm some sort of conquering empress or a saint everyone bows down to adore.

The one that is unconscious the longest wins. That used to be my specialty, in St. John's, when the other groups initiated me. Where my Cream of Wheat coloration, my hippy-child tangle of uncut hair, my handmade corduroy overalls made me different from everybody else. Even there, I was the butt of many jokes and the subject of many pain-games, although these appear to differ according to geographical location. Kids in St. John's play the fainting game and kids in the Northwest Territories play with Inhalers. Also, in St. John's you yell "Ow!" when someone's really hurting you. "Ow" is the Newfoundland word for pain. I used to think it wasn't really a word, it was a sound, an instinctual kind of a sound that all humans make in reaction to pain. But the kids here don't say "Ow," they say "Aiii." These are major cultural differences. In the St. John's fainting game, I always stayed passed out the longest, sometimes so long people thought I might be dead. I was a little bit famous for it. Even the smokers circled in to watch.

Mina and Lucy come to in time to see me holding my hands to my own neck, panting, eyes rolling back into the glorious black space of the faint. Inside, there is nothing, and then coldness, and a tugging. The sick trip back up.

Mina is holding my hand. "Teresa, you gotta wake up."

The rest of the girls are going home. They look shaken by what they've seen in the black falling place within themselves. I'm pretty sure they won't bother me quite so much anymore. I go home without going to Willassie's shed. I won't let him ruin this moment of victory. These kids play hard, but I can out-tough anybody when it comes to pain.

There are many hard games to play here. Crotch tag is like real tag, but you have to hit the person in the crotch as hard as possible, and squeeze too, if you can. I have a splendid display of purple and brown to show how much I play. There's the game to see who'll be burned by the older kid's cigarettes, at recess. They pick out a person to burn on the arm, and if you cry they hold it there for longer, till you can smell your own skin frying. To win this game you have to laugh in their faces and beg them to do it again.

There's a game which involves holding your naked palm to the flagpole, to see who can hold it there the longest, without freezing to the metal. I'm not so good at this, and can report from experience that Band-Aids do not stick to palms. There's one game that's the same in St. John's and Sanikiluaq, the one where two kids hang from the monkey bars and try to pull each other off by latching on to the other's waist and yanking with

204

their legs. This game wrenches your arms from their sockets and gives you wicked blisters on your hands, and causes one child in five to hit their head on the gravel with a dull, slightly liquid, thud. In St. John's we called this Challenge, but here it's called Killer. The rules, however, are the same. There's a game where you put a piece of broken glass into your hand and squeeze. Who can squeeze the hardest, the longest? Who can survive anything, better than anyone else? Who is tough enough to live here? Who is tough enough to love the North?

The next day, news of my fainting game has reached the older kids. They want to learn. I say maybe. Annie from Grade Nine makes me put out my arm. She pushes up my sleeve and burns me in the crook of my elbow, the most tender spot besides your neck, and they never burn anyone there. I look her in the eyes and I don't even cry. This is easy compared to the Inhaler. It's just skin. She's impressed. She says I should go sniffing with her. To see if I'm good enough to take it without getting sick.

I say maybe. I tell her it can't be any harder than the fainting game. She says "try glue first and see if you like it." These older girls have different pastimes. They pierce each other's ears with sewing needles. They call each other sluts. They smoke cigarettes and shove each other and spit in each other's hair, like the tough girls back home hanging out in the park across from our house. Annie says she can give me a tattoo. Ink from a ballpoint pen on the tip of a sharpened, heated paper clip. She's got one that says "Skid Ro" on her inner arm. She says it hurts like a bitch, so she's been doing it one letter at a time, and hasn't gotten around to the w yet.

Willassie pushes the books off my desk in science. I have to bend down to get them. He steps on my hand. When I look up he's smiling the chocolate-bar smile I've been avoiding since forever already.

"Get off my hand."

"Meet me at the shed. I mean this."

I pretend I'm deaf. I'm Helen frigging Keller, Willassie. I leave school as quickly as possible and walk across the river. The cigarette burn is chafing against the sleeve of my jacket, but I don't mind. I'm becoming addicted to these little hurts. They help keep my mind away from the more complicated things which are hurting me. It's easy to deal with the pain of a burn, or the skin coming off of your palm. It's easy to endure. There is even some pleasure in mastering these sensations. Mom knows. Being alone is much harder to cope with. I stop on the rock where Willassie gave me the hickey. I feel fairly invincible, and decide to go to the shed, after all. To see what he has to say, and maybe to tell him that I hate him, that he'd better not do anything dumb like make me a present ever again unless he wants everyone to know about the day on the river. I'll threaten him with publication. The headline, Sanikiluaq's Toughest Boy Exposed as Real Sucker for Qallunaat. My new status among the girls has given me gumption. I'm not afraid of a stupid boy. I'm going to tell Willassie exactly what I think of him. I open the door. He's sitting in his carving place, drinking tea.

"Come here," he says.

"Why?"

"Because I ask you to."

I go over to where he's sitting, calm like we haven't been ignoring each other for practically a month now. He holds out his hand. My snowflake.

"How'd you get it?"

He smiles. "I give Carla five hickeys, she give me anything."

I grab it from him, and when he reaches for my hand I throw the snowflake onto the dirt. "You're a jerk."

"I just get it back for you. The hickeys mean nothing."

I'm crying now, despite all the gumption I thought I'd mustered. The last thing I wanted to do was cry. "Yeah, nothing."

He picks up the necklace. "Quanniq, don't cry. I will do anything for you not to do that."

"Then why do you hate me? Why do you let them say all those things to me? If you're my friend, how come in school you won't even look at me? Did I do something wrong? Whatever it is, I'm sorry. I'm sorry, I'm sorry, okay? I'm sorry." I'm sobbing now. The predictable waterworks. Sooky baby.

"I gotta be careful. You know."

"No, I don't. Careful of what? Afraid I'll bite you?"

He hugs me. I lean into his shirt. He puts his chin on top of my head for a second. We both shift our weight and Willassie pulls back.

"Carla means nothing. I hickey her to get your thing back only," he says.

"Carla can go to hell."

He smiles but not the whole way, not the face-splitting smile, not the pencil-in-the-cheek smile. I'm drawn to this small little smile like a diabetic to a bag of Tootsie Rolls. I know it's bad for me. I'm so close that I can see each tiny soft line in Willassie's lips, the most elegant cross-hatching. I can smell cigarettes on his breath, and tea. I can smell the sugar in it.

Our lips touch. The breathing stops. Our lips stop touching. The breathing starts again. This cycle continues as I open my eyes to find Willassie so close to my face that he only has one eye. We touch and retouch our lips together, while looking into each other's single eye. Blink: goodbye. Wink: hello again.

He presses the snowflake into my palm. I put my hand up to his face, and feel the skin below his eye and beside it. The smooth skin of his forehead with the smooth bone underneath. His rounded jawline, the soft curving complexity of his ear. My other hand holds my recovered necklace. I let the sharp points of the snowflake dig deeper into my palm. If I don't hurt myself, I might start crying, and never, ever be able to stop. I might drench myself in my own tears and freeze standing here, an ice sculpture of myself, a statue of a girl in the middle of her first kiss. One-eyed wonder. Wink, blink.

Hello. Goodbye again. Hello. Goodbye.

33

Mark has brought the Art-Van over to my house and parked it. Next week, he's taking off with his new piece of ass, Solange, for two months. In the meantime he doesn't want to spend his cash on gas, so I'm taking the van early. Solange is hitting the fringe circuit with her solo show, *Je me suis le ciel*. On the poster, she has her hands lifted heavenward. Bare feet. A white laundry basket full of red clothes on a stool beside her. She stares at us, imploringly, with eyes full of sadness: come to my show. She wears the core of a Granny Smith on a piece of lace around her throat. In tiny print after her name, and the director's name, and the ticket information, it says Mark's name: sound design/technical assistance.

Me:
You've got to be fucking kidding. Are you having your mid-life crisis? Mark, you tame old pussy. You sold your soul for a round trip to Winnipeg?

Mark:

Shut your hole, Teresa. It's my first performance collaboration.

Me:

Oh, sweet Jesus.

Mark:

But we've got to take her car. The Art-Van will never make it to Vancouver and back.

Me:

I doubt it'd even make it to the ferry, dude.

The Art-Van is glorious. Mark's had it as long as I've known him—an old-school green Westfalia with scabrous rust creeping up its belly, and a white top that used to open up but doesn't anymore. The inside is fitted with a mattress and a wooden chest of drawers with candy-pink handles and bolts across the drawers to keep them from swinging open. There's Christmas lights and curtains with roosters on them. A lot of pieces of the van have been replaced with reasonable facsimiles made of orange electrical tape. It shows Mark to be a lot less cynical then he likes to let on. He's lived in it from time to time, when he couldn't make rent. There are charms made of twigs and leaves, tied up in hemp, hanging from the rear-view. They've been there since I can remember. The leaves are beautifully translucent. They're from British Columbia, like Solange.

Near the beginning of our friendship, Mark and I went outdoors a lot. We drove around, looking for something to happen. We busted a gut laughing. Everything was funny or profound.

I remember one time, in particular, right near the start. It was a gorgeous Sunday morning in the summer. Mark came by, and we decided to go messing around outdoors. We drove to Signal Hill to kick the whole thing off. We sat on the rock wall and looked out at the ocean and the Narrows. Cape Spear a distant gleam. The wind so adamant about blowing us into the sea that we had to cling to the wall with our thighs. Mark said, "Did you know you have the most beautiful skin in the world, like tracing paper?" and "Do you want to eat chocolates filled with mushrooms?"

I said "No, I didn't know that," and "Yes, I would like to."

We went back to the van and ate these chocolates he'd made himself. You couldn't tell there was anything in them. The mushrooms powdered in a coffee grinder then mixed into the melted chocolate, poured into an ice-cube tray lined with tinfoil and left to harden in the glove compartment. We drove through The Goulds to Bay Bulls, the rank manure smell coming in the opened windows. I got Mark to pull over at the beginning of a trail that went through the charmingly-monikered Bread and Cheese Cove. Mom used to take me there for picnics. Havarti on rye. Baguette and brick. I wished I'd thought of bringing something to eat. Mark produced his pipe and we smoked some hash to make our ascent less steep when it hit. Mark opened his arms and hugged the sky. He made up a song about clouds. For once, he was in love with everything.

We started hiking. Once we'd crossed the river and were wandering between the foundations of the old abandoned houses, I could feel the changes. Parts of me were tingling or heavy. My joints seemed oiled more lavishly then ever before, and I could move them smoothly, with total grace, instead of thrashing around in the confines of my own stiff skeleton, as it seemed I usually did. Everything looked crisp and rich, the harlot-red dogberries, with their strange matte finish that absorbs the sunlight, the concrete of the old foundations with the pebbled surface that left marks on my palm. I took close-ups. One was of my palm itself, a complex thing: the tiny lines, the whorls, the pinkness of the pebbled denting. I put my hand to my forehead and let the full weight of it press into my skull, onto the pulse of thought underneath. I tried to press all thought right out of me. I just wanted to feel the sensation of this heavy thing, my hand, pressing onto this soft stuff, my skin, over this pleasant hard stuff, the fused bones of my skull. I just wanted to experience that sensation indefinitely. To the full extent of feeling. I looked over to where Mark was crouched on a rock, picking up blades of grass and kissing them. We were coasting. Eventually we walked on. I was unable to stop grinning even though my cheeks ached. Nature overwhelmed us. The light alone was orgiastic. Occasionally one of us would stop and kneel to put our face in the moss, or touch sap bubbles in the bark of birch trees, letting ourselves get sticky. On the beach by the lighthouse, I looked for shells and found a seal vertebra, bleached white by the tide.

"This is a seal's vertebra," I said. I remembered you carving them, carving faces into the soft, porous centre where I guess the marrow was. Larger faces in the whale vertebrae.

"You can carve a face into this middle part." I gave the vertebra to Mark. Impossible to hold such a thing in your hand and deny the existence of death. We walked back along the cliffs and the sun was setting. Mark said that mushrooms were unrelenting, you had to be ready to face the intimacy of the world for at least eight hours straight. I didn't tell him this was my first time. Despite the eyeliner, I'd been a pretty good kid. My mouth was numb. I didn't say anything.

I'd thought I would hallucinate something, that I might see you floating just underneath the surface of the water where the breakers were crashing, staring up at me. I half-hoped to hallucinate you, in any form. I wanted a shamanistic experience, to see you like Atanarjuat, running naked across the ice, sun flashing in the puddles behind you. But it was summer. There was no ice. I wanted the mushroom chocolates to open up a doorway between real and imagined worlds, and let you step through, just for a minute, so I could remember later how you came to me in a vision, grown up. How you gave me a particular leaf in Bread and Cheese Cove, how I pressed it in my dictionary. How you told me to go on, to go forward, to stop getting stuck in you, like a fox in a snare, and how that somehow healed me, although it was a drug-induced hallucination and not reality. This didn't happen. Instead the world was just lovelier than before, the colours brighter, the sounds clearer. My body moved more slowly. Even my eyelids were taking their time opening and closing. I said, "Let's be blood brothers. Should we get tested first?" "I'm clean, baby," Mark said, and cut into my thumb with his pocket knife. I did the same to him. We pressed our hands together. "I feel like a Hardy Boy," I said, and laughed, although I half felt like fainting.

Now Mark and Solange are going to fringe their faces off for two months, and I have the Art-Van. Which means I'm free. I can go anywhere the van will take me, which might not be far, given its duct-tape interior. But it's further than I've been able to go since the death of my dear old Pontiac. Out of city limits.

Into the wild.

Now that I have wheels, I have possibility. I might even take a few gigs out of town, who knows. Gay Stevie is going out to Trinity to do the festival soon, and they probably need some shots done for their brochures. This used to be a yearly gig for me before I started full-time at the gallery, and I bet if I called them up they'd hire me for a few days. I could do some kind of photo essay on the place while I'm at it. Visit Evan and Nan like I promised my mother. Get my eye back in shape. It's a very pretty town.

Mark might have gone over to the Dark Side, but he's still been a saviour to me. I'm weak with the thought of getting out of St. John's, city of claustrophobia. I need the water and the dirt and the sky. I need to be away from the people, their open mouths, their eyes.

34

The day rushes past me and I'm oblivious. I care about nothing but the feel of Willassie's hand on my back, my neck, my head where the soft spot used to be. Willassie's lips, the smell of Willassie. He's intoxicated me.

in-tox-i-cate\[L *in-* + *toxicum* poison – more at TOXIC] **1:** POISON **2 a:** to excite or stupefy by alcohol or a drug or a touch by a boy named Willassie, just the smallest little touch esp. to the point where physical and mental control is markedly diminished **b:** to excite or elate to the point of enthusiasm or frenzy so nothing else matters, not even the tauntings of my classmates or the collection of burns I am growing on my smooth arm skin <*intoxicated* with joy> <I am *intoxicated* by him. My heart is a helium balloon, ready to float up through my throat out of my mouth into the air of this classroom, and nothing can pierce the heart-balloon's shiny pretty skin, and no one will be able to catch it because it's going to float above the world forever, like some kind of magic voyeur organ, and report back the beauty of what it sees to me as I sit here, unbothered by everything,

because, Ladies and Gentlemen, Willassie kissed me in his shed and nothing is ever going to be the same again. I know it. I'll transform my enemies with the brilliance of my smile. All is good, isn't it, all is good, because THE BOY KISSED ME>

I'm in the Kindergarten classroom at lunchtime, with Danny. Danny is my new friend, so I tell him. He's eight, but still in Kindergarten because he has some sort of disease that makes his brain not quite the same as a normal kid. I can relate to that. Since Ms Jenkins lost her marbles, there's not enough teachers to take shifts with Danny. He's got to have someone with him all the time, even at lunch. Dad volunteered me for three lunchtimes a week. I don't really mind. I like Danny. He's got a sweet smile and it's easy to make him laugh. He likes drawing with crayons and having tickle fights. Danny wears jogging pants, and special shoes with braces coming out of them, because his body, not just his mind, has been affected by his disease. He's always snotting and drooling. He can't walk very well and prefers to shuffle along on his bum, giggling at the crackle sound of the diaper under his pants rubbing along the floor. He doesn't talk or read or write, but this doesn't seem to bother him. I take his hand and he shuffles on his bum beside me, done up in his coat and mitts and his hat with the chin-strings on it. His mitts have idiot strings, to keep him from losing them. Danny's fast even though he can't walk. He scoots ahead of me on his bum, pulling at my hand.

"Slow down, okay, we're almost there."

We're going to the front part of the school where most kids don't go. There's not much to do out here. The playground and berry hill and smoking area are all on the other side, this is just the driveway. The window to the staff room is in full view, so no one wants to come here. But it's sunny out and I don't want anyone to bother us. I like being out here with no one to talk to. Danny likes to play with the gravel. He puts it in a salt beef bucket, then dumps it out again. I sit on the front step and think about Willassie.

We're still not talking in school. Now it's my turn to want to ignore him. I don't want Carla and the others to cause trouble. And it's so easy to be with him at other times, in his shed or out on the land, walking. Mina and Lucy are my accomplices. I have sworn them to secrecy. Now that I'm tough, like a real Inuit girl, they're eager to help me. They think I'll get them a sniffing invitation from Annie, their hero. Dad thinks I'm at Lucy's house, tutoring them in math every day from three till five. He thinks I'm explaining long division, but really I'm walking out on the land with Willassie.

We walked over the barrens the other day, but not near where everyone goes fishing. Willassie showed me his favourite place: a little hill and a little hollow with the frozen ocean on one side. No one goes out to this place because they say it's haunted by the old-time people. They're angry because they've all died out. I asked Willassie if he believed in ghosts. He laughed and said he didn't believe in things he couldn't see. I said that I believed in ghosts but wasn't afraid of them. They would protect us if danger came. The ghosts would warn us. He told me I was funny and held my hand, out there on the tundra with the frozen ocean spread out in front of us. If I didn't look back, I could pretend we were in Newfoundland. This is what I'm thinking about.

I look up. Danny is crouched down playing with rocks. I can't see what he's doing.

"Danny!"

He's putting fistfuls of gravel in his mouth. Only my hand

on his face, squeezing, and my other hand in front of his mouth, scooping, can get him to spit the rocks out. If he were alone, he'd probably eat the whole driveway. I take him back inside to get a drink of juice from the staff room, to rinse out the dirt left in his mouth. His chin is muddy with drool. I knock on the door. Mr. Levy opens it, a piece of bannock in his hand.

"Teresa."

"Could he have a sip of juice? He started putting dirt in his mouth."

"You've got to hold onto his hands and watch him carefully."

"I know."

"Are you unable to do this for me, Teresa?"

"No."

"Because I need to know if you're up to it." He looks sternly into my eyes.

"I'll be more careful," I say.

Mr. Levy crouches down in front of Danny.

"All right now, would you like some apple juice?"

Mr. Levy takes Danny's hand and brings him into the staff room. Dad's in there with Nancy, eating soup at the table by the window. Dad's doing the crossword. Mr. Ilsat is having a lie-down on the couch.

"T-Bird." Dad wipes his mouth.

"Hello," says Nancy. "You like to have some soup with us?"

"Dad made us peanut butter and jam."

"Are you sure?" She gestures to her bowl of brown, murky liquid. I shake my head. Danny's pulling on my pant leg. He's spilling juice on the carpet.

"If that's it, Teresa?" Mr. Levy opens the door. "The staff room area is private."

He shoos us out and closes the door. I was always allowed in the staff room before. Anywhere Dad's ever taught. I did all the dittos of the school paper yesterday, for God's sake. What's so special that I can't be in there now? What are they doing? Counterfeiting? Making moonshine? Is there a whorehouse hidden behind the wall?

I take Danny back to the classroom. Maybe we can play with the water table or read a book together. There's those wooden tangram puzzles that he likes, too. I wipe a little stray dirt off his cheek with the sleeve of my shirt. He beams up at me. We'll stick to indoor activities for a while.

35

Down at The Ship in my brown lace flapper dress and combats, hair twisted into pale knots like lumps of sugar all over my head. I have a sugary brain tonight. Everything is sweet. Even the music, although Mark would hate me for saying it. It's his band, Crayfish Aftertaste. This is the last gig before he hits the road tomorrow, so the place is even more packed than usual. There's chicks sitting on tables and spilled over into the entrance to the washrooms. Mark's singing about stolen cars and dead dogs. I find the whole thing endearing, especially the way he looks so angry. His fingers coaxing furious riffs out of his guitar strings.

I don't buy Mark's act. I've been angry in my life, and it doesn't have this grace to it, this infectiousness. Real anger is clumsy and hot, a spark of magnesium you can't look at directly. Mark's just pissed off. Real anger wouldn't attract this cloud of nubile girls in heavy eye makeup who've flooded the dance floor and are seriously sweating it up, whether or not they'll admit to it. Everyone has a crush on Mark when he's singing. He looks good with his mouth obscured by the microphone. They can't help moving their hips seductively and staring at him, hoping he'll look them in the eye while singing something significant. Most of these vapid little chicks would settle for a wink during the "yeah yeah yeah" part of one of his punked-up Beatles covers. Something to think about while touching themselves in the bathtub.

He's looking at me now. I'm dancing, enjoying the loudness of the music, its solid presence in the bar. It won't be ignored. I can appreciate that. I jump around, filled with the joy of movement, and a splash of something like motherly pride. I'm going to miss the prick. Solange can stand in the back in her skimpy dress looking all pouty and metropolitan if she wants to, but Mark is still singing to me. Everything is how it should be.

Someone falls into me. A stream of cold booze down my back. I yelp and spin around. It's Delith. Fuck off. Shitfucker. Where'd she even come from? She's spilled her beer down my back and is looking so sorry for doing it. Like why couldn't she have spilled shit all over anyone else. I'm sorry I smoked up ten minutes ago. I smile, and pat her head—why the hell am I patting her head?—and go to get napkins in the bathroom. I think she was drinking Jockey but I can't be sure. I suck on my dress but it just tastes like beer, plain and simple. I order Jockey anyway, and scotch for me, bending over and fishing for my money in my shoe as three loaded university dudes make stunned comments about my ass, one going so far as to give me a quick, timid pat. I stand back up and turn to pay the bartender. I hand the ass-grabber a napkin, saying "This is for the mess you probably made in the front of your pants, touching a girl and all," and go back to the dance floor. Not a very good insult, but, hey, I'm fucked right now. It'll do.

I find Delith's back in the crowd. It's dry, unlike mine. She's wearing a soft blue tank top. I can tell it's soft, even though I haven't touched it, by the way the light catches in the fabric and doesn't reflect. That's what we call an expert eye. A soft blue tank top and a skirt made of old corduroy pants, cut up and sewn back together again. Her hair in a messy ponytail, exposing her neck. Fuck-me boots.

I don't know that I have the guts to give her the beer. It's her hand I'm worried about. If I touch it. I'm just going to drink the beer myself and find some other place to dance. She turns around. She's trying to be cool but she's freaking, and it's leaking out her face in nervous jerky smiles. I go ahead and hand her the bottle. I down the scotch in one go: a forest fire.

The boys end the song with a sweet harmony. Mark's asking me over the microphone to go get drinks. Like I'm his girlfriend or something. Like Je me suis le Solange isn't even here. She's standing by herself near the sound gear in the back, compulsively adjusting her fashion tam, sipping on a kiwi cooler. If I didn't have a bitchy streak, I might take pity on her, but I let her sweat it out. She's got to learn. This is how things are with Mark and me. He doesn't need to tell me what to get everyone. I already know.

When I hand the drinks to him, he's glossy with sweat and has an equally wet and ecstatic cast to his eyes. It's going really well, better than usual. The room is with them. The crowd is clamouring for more music, more, more, more. The clink of pints knocking on the tabletops. He gives me a quick kiss on the cheek for bringing the drinks, and when I turn back towards the dance floor I can't tell if Delith cares, but I know she saw. I deliberately stand in front of her. I don't know what I'm doing, but it looks like I'm doing it anyway. I dance for several songs, aware of every time she brushes up against me, inevitable, in the throbbing mass of bodies. I close my eyes. Mark is singing straight into my medulla oblongata, bypassing all the logical bits of my brain and going right to the basics. The primal shit. Making me itch. I could stay like this all night, in perpetual motion, these occasional grazes along my back, my ass, my calves, which may or may not be Delith, and which may or may not be accidental. I could fucking care less if anything else ever happens between us, because she is dancing and so am I, to the same music, and sometimes she cannot help but touch me. I can feel myself getting sticky. It's a novel sensation and I am interested in prolonging it. Medulla oblongata: these are elegant words, good words for whispering.

Something cold goes down my back. I jump. More beer. Unbelievable. She's saying something I can't make out. I bend my head towards the heat of her.

"Sorry. Jerkface decided he was going to have his own little mosh pit up my butt. Let me help you clean that."

"What?"

"Mosh pit! Up my butt!"

"I can't hear you!"

"I'm sorry!"

"I'll go clean it up! Don't worry!"

"Let me help you!"

We're yelling in each other's ears. I put my hand on her arm to steady myself in the crush, as people push forward to dance. Mark's playing his most popular song, "My Baby Jocasta." We pass Solange. She isn't even nodding her head to the beat. I wink in her direction but she pretends she doesn't see me. Delith heads towards the bathroom. I follow her through the crowd and into the light.

"Oh God, I'm really sorry. Fucking mosh guy kept shoving me. I should've shoved back but he would've taken that as encouragement. Jesus, two whole beers! Hope it doesn't eat through your dress."

"Don't worry about it. Everything I own is from the thrift store anyway." I'm trying to wipe off my back and she's taking the towels from me, patting outwards from the spine.

"I can reach this better." She's getting the back of my neck in gentle wipes. "I'm sorry."

"It's okay."

She's wetting paper towels, putting them on my neck. I flinch. I can feel her wiping inside the neckline of my dress. The backs of my arms.

"Hey Delith, you smoke pot?"

"Sometimes." She dries me off with fresh paper towels, patting my neck down gently.

"You want to go for a walk with me?"

We get our coats and go outside into the alley.

"So much for being stunned by my grace, huh?" She's kicking around in the dirt, not looking at me.

"Well, stunned, definitely."

We smoke a joint, passing it from hand to hand, mouth to mouth. It burns down to a nub and I have to hold onto her fingers to get it from her. I am high and don't let go. She is stoned and doesn't either. I am holding hands with Delith in the alley. Correction, I am holding hands with Delith, who is also the most gorgeous, bird-boned, animal-eyed, big-voiced Burlesque Performer/Waitress/Wonder of the Natural World.

224

Who shimmies and shakes all dressed in scarlet fringes. Whose hand fits into my hand as nicely as wrench into socket, as gun into holster, as penis into condom, as key into keyhole, as Kindertoy dismantled and cleverly manoeuvred to fit inside the tiny orange egg. I touch her hair. She isn't looking at me.

"Teresa, I'm not a lesbian, you know."

"Haven't we been over this? I say, "Hello, there." You say "I'm not a dyke." I say, "Me either, dumbass." Now can we get on with it, please?"

It's true and not true. I don't know what's true. I'm only sure of the feelings in my body, with Mark's music jolting out the back door to meet us, and the cold air all around. We kiss. I don't know who starts this and it doesn't matter. Girls' lips are the softest things. We make involuntary noises in our heterosexual throats.

Other people are coming to smoke or grope in the alley. We leave without discussing it. I take Delith to my house, with my mother's possessions still in their staid, lunatic piles. We don't speak and we don't turn on the lights. You can barely see the psycho paintings, and, besides, she doesn't take much time to look around. We take our coats off in the porch. I ask Delith if she'd like anything, and she shakes her head. I take her by the hand and lead her through the dark house, up the stairs to the bedroom. I close the door behind us and we begin immediately to remove each other's clothing in the glow of streetlight and moonlight through the sheers, my hands trembling with the softness of her shirt and the smoothness of her skin beneath it.

Delith is kind of laughing. "I can't believe we're doing this." She's trying to undo the hasps on the back of my dress.

"It's taking too long," I say, and reach up to undo them myself while she kisses down the length of my side. I get her tank top off, no sweat. The happy pucker of nipple. The ribs, each politely in its place, the perfect curve where neck meets shoulder. The smell of skin so good after the smoke-laden clothes are gone, fresh-shucked. The slight and gorgeous swelling of her belly. I put my hand there. She kisses my sternum. I feel it crack and shift under the weight of her mouth. Delith takes bites at me, big wolfish ones and also kitten bites along my shoulders and into my armpits, making me twitch and gasp, elbowing her in the ribs. We both laugh. I look at her. I really look. I dare to look at Delith the way I always wanted to look at someone. That powerful/powerless way. All openings.

All those boyfriends, strung out in a neat, forgotten row. All those nights I lay and waited for the motion to stop, for the man in question to sigh in his ecstasy and tumble from me, leaving me in peace. My muscles held tight against any tremors of feeling, proving myself a perfect, whorish actress as I murmured and sighed and secretly clenched my teeth, counting the minutes going by. All those years that I lay still with someone touching me, down where all the panic is. Thinking that was all there was to it. That I deserved to feel nothing. As punishment for my sins, my genitalia had been fossilized, turned from flesh to stone. I had long ago resigned myself, like Elizabeth, to an indefinite period of penance. I believed it was my birthright. My inheritance.

My left hand is in Delith's hair, the other with its fingers slowly inching inside of her. I have slug-trails of tears down into my ears. Delith is smiling. I feel the shape of her smile when I put my wrist to her mouth. I offer up for the bite. Her fingers now inside of me. Strange to know exactly how your ministrations feel. Delith with her mouth upon my nipple, my nipple suddenly a beautiful thing to me, an O'Keeffe peony, not the colourless, deformed gumdrop I am used to examining disappointedly. No shame. We are radiant beyond our bodies. My tongue upon her neck, tracing its arteries, like words nearly faded away, only readable by touch. She is twitching with pulse. I can feel it through my tongue on her neck, as well as in the slick hot space my fingers are curled up in, rubbing themselves against the wet velvet on all sides. I look and I let her look at me. We breathe together. This is scary. I can't remember any words in my own language, and can only breathe the word quyanaq onto the curve of her neck. She puts her whole hand up inside me. Her little hand. Both of us wide-eyed to bursting, caught in each other's gaze. Aiii. Good God, I might die from this feeling. I slide my fingers out, and she's sighing. I move downwards, the quilt gathering at our feet in heavy piles. I kiss Delith in all the places Willassie never got to kiss me. The shock of taste makes me salivate. Her thigh with its translucent sheen of tiny hairs against my retina, so hard I see sharp bursts of light. Private fireworks. I press in further, tastes changing, a new taste, delicate. I try to get it everywhere on my tongue. I must get my fingers in it. She's starting her period soon, there's a metallic bite to the saltiness. I rub myself into her knees, the bedclothes. I reach up with one hand and run my fingers along her throat. She can't bear it any longer. She cries into the bitten pillow, into the white sheets of my white bed, Sedna-bed, resting place beneath the frozen sea. Further and further I sink myself in. I take some of her onto my fingers and rub it on her nipples. I put my fingers in her mouth, so she can taste herself. Her hips push my head skywards, towards the surface.

Quyanaq is the only word I can remember. I luxuriate in how deep in the throat it is, the Inuit q behind the tonsils, down there where coughing and growling start. Down in the involuntary muscles of the larynx. Qi. Qa. We howl a little. We laugh and gasp and moan, we shiver and bite things. We sing the praises of our nerve endings. I say, iiiiiii. She says, ohhhhhh. So this is what everyone's been talking about.

Now that I've experienced what it is to be really intimate with another person, to be fully in the tide of life, to have it overflow the senses and make me temporarily feel beautiful, to have the world move through me like that, to—just say it—to have an actual orgasm, now that I know what that feels like, it occurs to me to ask myself, Self, what took you so long? Are you really a Lesbian, after all? What conclusions have we drawn? Was it the privates themselves that were preventing you? But it can't be. Because that would be saying that the love I had for you, Willassie, was some kind of fabrication, some kind of play I was acting, and not the blood-and-bone thing we had between us. No. So, I was too young. I was barely thirteen. I was faulty. I was the wretch who got shoved behind the door in Heaven the day they gave out working cunts. So I thought. Up till now. Or didn't think. More fool me. Is this the dawning of my new decade of the body?

I grin and finger Delith's perfect ear. I tell myself to shut up. It's better when I think less. Delith curls herself into me and we stick in places, thigh to thigh, nose to neck, hand to breast. We stick that way until morning comes. I dream of nothing, the whole night. There is no need to take my midnight photograph; I don't wake myself in fright.

Delith is beautiful, and she wards away nightmares.

36

There are some things I know I shouldn't see, but I can't help looking anyway. It's my journalistic curiosity. Dad says there are things about the Inuit that I won't understand. He says they're different from us, and sometimes these differences might scare me. He says I shouldn't ask too many questions, because Nosy Parkers get their noses lopped off to spite their faces.

But I have to peek. I need to know all the secrets that Willassie won't tell me.

Tonight I'm going to look into the windows of his house. I've never done this before, having officially given up the spying thing. Tonight, however, it's necessary. I tell my father I'm very tired, and go to bed at nine o'clock. I always shut my door and he never checks on me, because I'm almost a teenager now and that kind of stuff is for babies. If I'm quiet, it should be easy for me to get out through my window. I dragged one of the crates from the playhouse over underneath it this afternoon. The trickiest part of my preparation for escape was getting all my outdoor clothes without him noticing, but I waited till he was in the bathroom and then quickly brought my coat and boots from the porch into my room and put them in my fort, where he wouldn't see. It was all very easy for someone as experienced in sneakery as me.

At ten o'clock, after faking snores and sleep-mumblings, I get dressed and ease my window open. I climb out and pull the window almost shut, wedging my copy of *Little Women* into the sill so I can get back in, later. I feel a little guilty doing this, but every important Top Secret Mission requires some sort of sacrifice, and Louisa May Alcott is going to have to take one for the team tonight.

I hop down from the crate and sneak my way to the other side of town, where Willassie and Mina and their mother live. All day I've been picturing their house, trying to imagine what horrors I'll see. I know they don't have any curtains, which should make things easy. Carla and her big mouth and her stupid stories.

She grabbed my arm yesterday when we were leaving school. "You get your thing back?" she asked.

I knew what she was talking about—my snowflake necklace—but I told her it was none of her business. I nearly added Dad's saying about Nosy Parkers, but I was pretty sure she wouldn't get that part.

She wouldn't let go of my arm. She said I should go out back with her so she could tell me something about Willassie.

"I know you like him and you needs to hear it."

I protested that I didn't like him, that we weren't even friends, which is true and untrue. Mostly untrue. True in public. Untrue when we're alone.

She touched my snowflake where it lay under my shirt with the tips of her fingers. She looked into my face, her hand on my jaw. Her neck had that splotchy look from where he'd sucked on it, and my eyes kept running over the patterns of it.

"You gonna come talk to me."

So we went outside, to the back. Carla got out her smokes and gave me one. I told her I didn't smoke and she said "tough titties," so I accepted her offer to light it for me. She had to stand close, with my coat opened and wrapped around her, sheltering the little flame from the wind. I could feel waves of heat off her body. She smelled like fat from frying bannock, and also cigarettes. I held my smoke carefully between my fingers, like her. The taste was so strong and dry it made me cough.

She took a drag and blew the smoke towards me. "You don't know nothing," she said. "You're so dumb about everything in Sanikiluaq. You think it is easy to kiss a boy, to like him, and that's the end. You think this is for just you two and no one else got nothing to do about it."

"So?"

"You know Marguerite?"

"Mr. Levy's daughter? What about her?"

"She had a necklace too."

"Good for her."

"Willassie give Marguerite a thing like he do for you."

"So."

"So."

"Willassie can give things to anyone he wants to. I don't care." The first day of school: banging on the desks. Her weird French name. I put my hand in my pocket and close it around the stone bird.

"You shut up now and listen, Teresa. I am telling you this so you have a warning, all right?"

I started to speak and she put her hand over my mouth. It

tasted like cigarettes. Everything tasted like cigarettes. I licked her palm and she let go, wiping her hand on her pants.

"Okay. I tell you the whole thing. No one else gonna talk about this. It's not for talking about, don't ask no questions to nobody because they's not gonna tell you nothing. Got it?"

"All right, all right. Just tell me."

"Willassie will get in trouble with his mother if she knows that he sees you. She don't like Qallunaat."

I have to lean against the door because I'm dizzy from the smoke. "Carla, nobody likes us."

"No. His mother hate you more than anybody. She's so mad with the Qallunaat. Her husband died because of them and she never forgot about it. So she never talk to the whites and she wants to see them go away."

"A white person killed her husband?"

"Qallunaat Jesus."

"Jesus killed Mr. Ippaq? I'm not dumb, Carla."

"You shut it. I can tell you. Before I was born, when the church came here at first, it scared the people. And then, over the years some of them still hate it, but some of the people love it so much they think they's special. There's two men in the town who started to think they are God, and Jesus too, and they tell the others to follow them or else they go to Hell. And most of the people think they are crazy, but some believes them and follows them out on the ice with no clothes on and they all get lost out there and freeze up and the people found all these dead Inuit and also the two crazies who thought they were Jesus and God. Willassie's mother had to go to the bodies and pick out her husband and she is only a young mother then, Mina is a baby still. She will never forget what the Qallunaat God do to her husband.

So now she hates them and she will very hate you."

"Is this true, Carla?"

She looked at me for a minute, taking a drag off her smoke. "I know you don't trust me. I want to tell you because I want you to stay away from Willassie. He knows about it but he never talks about it so don't ask. But he make you that necklace to protect you and it's okay by me you have it back. I want it, but when he told me why he gave it to you I said you can have it back, okay. I don't want you to get hurt. I'm not such a bitch as you think."

"What do you mean?"

"Willassie's mom is arnagtoq. You know what that is—someone who knows how to do the magic things. She knows how to do the scary things. She makes people hurt if she's mad with them. She makes them go away."

"No way."

"She made Marguerite go away."

"Carla, Marguerite is in university. I don't think Willassie's mom made her go there."

"Mr. Levy tell you that?"

"Yeah. Everyone knows."

"Everyone knows their own thing. I knows that Marguerite had a fight with Willassie and she took off her necklace and she don't go to school. She go away and she don't come back. I don't know where. But she go and she was chased by the tupilak that his mother made and that is true because I seen it."

"Tupilak."

"Thing a magic person can make out of bits of skins and bones and it get up and walk around and chase the people you don't like away. Her one look like a fox and a walrus mix together. It is small but very evil."

"So, Willassie's dad thought that if he went out naked on the ice with some guy who said he was God then he'd be saved. Because of this Willassie's mom wants to hurt me, becauase Jesus was white, like me, and so she's going to make a weird creature out of hoofs or whatever and send it after me, and the only thing that can stop her is my necklace."

Sarcasm is lost on Carla. "No joking. She don't know you like Willassie. If she knew about it then that is what will happen, yes. She never wants for him to be mix up with any Qallunaat. She'd rather kill him or make him crazy herself."

I put out my cigarette on the step. "Well, thanks. If I see any weird-looking creatures around town, now I'll know where they came from."

She wasn't smiling, though. "I mean it, Teresa. No one's going tell you, so I do. You listen and you take it true. Her tupilak is powerful and it's out there now. It didn't come back. It made Danny have no brain. His mother Eva once fucked Willassie's dad right before he died. Even though it was a long time after that when she is pregnant, Willassie's mom think her husband must be the father of Eva's baby, that it is his spirit in there. So she send tupilak to the stomach and curse Danny before he's born. Now he can't talk and he's stupid forever. These things I know you don't think can happen but this is not your world, Teresa. There are things you don't know and if you are smart not stupid you listen to all I say and you take it true. Magic is real here, and powerful, too."

I don't take it true, of course not. I mean it's all as silly as Mom's talk about Fairies, for God's sake. But I was really freaked out for two reasons last night. Firstly, when I went to bed I touched the back of the bear that Willassie made, on the coffee table. I do this every night. Then for some reason I looked over at the carving of the woman and the baby. Was the baby Willassie? I leaned forward into the lamplight, and for a second I could have sworn that they were really smoking those ivory cigarettes. I looked over, and the first thing I thought was that there were real eyes watching me, and real smoke going up. Then Evan ambushed me from behind, and when I looked back, the stone was just stone. Still, it gave me the willies.

And when I went to sleep, I had those nine fully-grown men and women, in their birthday suits, lying on the ice around me. They were touching my feet and calling me Saint Liz.

"What do you think you're doing?" I asked them. "Only lunatics would come out here! Put some clothes on!"

And they told me that I'd promised them a miracle, and they were going to lie there on the ice and wait till it happened. Willassie's dad was there, but he looked like Willassie to me. He lay on his back with his dickie bird, as Evan calls it, all swelled up and pointing to the sky. My father hovered above me in the air, perfectly normal except he was wearing a tuxedo with a frilly blue shirt, and was surrounded in light. Mr. Ippaq started crying, rubbing at my ankles, kissing my toes and licking between them, saying "ii, yes." This lady who looked like Nancy with no clothes on came and kissed my father on his glowing mouth. She didn't have a belly button and neither did anyone else. She bent down and put her breast to my mouth. I licked and sucked. I sucked her like I was gluttonous for her taste. Mr. Ippaq tongued into all the crannies between my toes and Dad stood about eleven feet tall looking down at us. Everyone shouted thanks for the miracle of being shown the face of God. They died in ecstasy, writhing blue on the ice. Pointing their swelled-up dickie birds and their rigid nipples at the sky.

I woke up aching. Was some kind of dark magic taking hold of me, infecting me from the inside out? This could get ugly. I decided that the only thing to do was dust off the old Harriet the Spy equipment and go see for myself whether Mrs. Ippaq was using magic to look through the eyes of her sculpture into our house. Maybe she's overheard me and the girls talking, and found out about me and Willassie. Maybe she's doing Arctic Voodoo, making me think about all those dirty things, in order to break me. Spying is the only way I can be sure I'm not just going loopy. I hope I'm not turning into the "moon-eyed, slathering, slack-jawed animal, also known as a human adolescent" that Dad always said I would become, sooner or later.

I can see a flickering of light even though I'm a few feet from the window. I take a breath and edge up to the glass. Shit. The room is flickering because no regular lights are on. The only light comes from a kuudliq lamp on the floor. It's shaped out of soapstone in the half-moon way, filled with what I assume is seal fat. There's moss on fire along its edge, a neat line of miniature flame, giving off a surprising amount of dark smoke. There's no chimney, and the smoke stays in the room, making it harder for me to see clearly.

But I can see enough. I see her. His mother. She wears an amautiq in the old style, with bands of colour at the cuffs. Her hair is loose and knotty. She is kneeling, rocking back and forth in front of the kuudliq lamp with her back to me.

She throws something into the lamp. It flares up. In the flash of brightness there are two more figures in the room, their faces closed in, their bodies just as shut. Willassie and Mina are sitting in opposite corners, on the linoleum. They watch and do not speak as their mother sings words I cannot understand, and does things I know nothing about.

I never should have come here. There are bones on the floor in front of Mrs. Ippaq. She picks them up. I am goosebumps everywhere. I'm so afraid, I feel like I might shit. She is singing louder and rocking more, and the light is so bright it's electricity.

I have no right to be here. Even if Carla made everything up, even if Danny wasn't cursed and no one thought they were God or Jesus, even if all Mrs. Ippaq is doing in her living room is cleaning out the kuudliq, even if all that stuff I dreamt is just my dirty mind, I still shouldn't pry. I want to be inside Willassie's world. I don't just want to live in his heart. I want to understand the things he understands, to see things the way he sees them. I'm just a white kid hiding in a snow bank. I'll never be on the inside of that window. I'll never be on the other side of that pane of glass.

When I reach the houses on the other side of the road, I look back once. There's no light in the window now. All I can hear are the husky dogs whining, the dull thud of my heart through my parka, and the unrelenting wind.

37

As soon as the rat-faced, rat-tailed boy takes our tickets, I know that I don't want to visit The Wildlife Museum. I know this place is going to upset me deeply, I can tell from the sign. Hundreds of Animals in their 'Natural Habitat.' A 'Photographer's Paradise.'

Delith says, "I've always wanted to see a photographer in Paradise. Will you grow a pair of wings, or speak in tongues, or what? Shout "Hallelujah, Daguerre!" and writhe on the floor in ecstasy?" She has a nice laugh at herself.

Her extensive working vocabulary makes me horny. That is the proper name for it. There's nothing sexier than a sexy girl with brains. I grab her around the waist and lick the back of her neck while the boy gets out his key. I blow on it. She shivers. I press my ticket into her hand. "My camera's out in the van. Sorry."

She grabs me by the shoulders. "Come on."

"No, really, I don't feel like it."

"There could be anything in there."

"That's what I'm saying."

"Teresa, please. When are you going to get a chance to see this sort of thing again? It's going to be one of those moments that you remember when you're dying, know what I mean?" She takes my hand, wraps it back around her waist, under her shirt this time, and holds it there with hers. I'm captive, captivated.

The boy has to walkie-talkie someone to turn on the generator. The lights are dim, and flicker.

"Enjoy yourselves." He smiles slowly, showing pointed teeth. Why hasn't Evan warned me about this place?

Next to the doorway is the stuffed shape of a collapsed moose, obviously salvaged from a car collision, its bones not set back into their right piles. A deer's head has fallen from its place on the wall above and lies on the moose's broken back, staring at us with badly set eyes. The sound of running water. Walls painted with trees by someone who doesn't know how to paint. Maybe schoolchildren. Giant caribou head on the wall, its body completed with flat brown latex in the roughest approximation. In amongst fake plants and gravel lie a few broken squirrels, twisted about like overeager high-school thespians, in a dramatic interpretation of Flanders Fields, directed by some theatre school intern. In Flanders Fields the squirrels blow/between the crosses, row on row. There is an Arctic section. Jesus, Mary and Joseph.

Delith grabs my hand and forces me further inside. She says, "We have to. We don't get the chance to visit alternate realities very often, right?" She sounds like Mom. It's a sin to pass up a visceral experience.

"All right," I say, but I want to throw up, I want to scream, I've got my sweater pressed tight into my mouth. The stuffed seals lounge on dingy Styrofoam floes next to plastic penguins and a disproportionately tiny replica of The Matthew. There is a grizzly

239

bear and cub leaned in the corner, less terrifying somehow than the small broken rodents so obscenely strewn about. We are the Dead. Short days ago/We lived. Everywhere birds with partial wingspan are hanging from the ceiling at a dangerous height, their mangy tail feathers threatening to brush against my ears. In the corner is a plastic wading pool with two eyeless, crushed beavers leaned up against it, and a couple of pallid fish swimming balefully, around and around. Left in here with the door locked and the power off until stupid girls from the big city ask to see the wildlife. The whole room stinking of dust and damp fur, a serial killer's bedroom.

"How do the fish survive in here?"

Delith shrugs. "Maybe Rat-Boy feeds them?"

"Rat-Boy didn't know where the light switch was. He probably doesn't even know they exist."

"This is the secret at the heart of the Trinity Loop. Today we saw fish impossibly surviving in the Room of Ultimate Death. Let this be a lesson to us."

Down by the beavers, there's a doorway with a few planks nailed across. Behind it, I can make out old chesterfields and car parts in sloppy piles. Disintegrating crates of Passion Flakies and the choking, clotted smell of mould. I can't help thinking about Mom.

"I want to go now," I say. This was a bad idea, this whole trip. A shitty, hungover idea. I shouldn't be here. With Delith. A crazy idea. Practically fictional. We just drove out to Trinity in the Art-Van, it was as simple as that. I hadn't planned to come out here till next week, for the brochure gig at Gay Stevie's theatre company, but Delith called in for two days off work and I got extra volunteers to gallery-sit, and we just got in the van and went. Hard to believe that last night she was spilling Jockey on my dress and declaring her staunch heterosexuality. On the drive out, she sat sideways in her seat, with her feet on my lap. Looking at me. I mostly kept my eyes on the road, but there was the smell of her, and the feel of her calves, warm and heavy, across my thighs. She read out the crossword, and, of course, there was the scenery, which made us sigh. Those verdant cliffside meadows, overrun with lupins, drunk in the wind, their tender tops trembling against a perfect blue backdrop of water and sky. Trucks, boats, corner stores. Kids on dirt bikes. As we went around sharp corners I had to grab onto her legs while she held onto the dashboard. The Art-Van seat belts don't quite work, Mark's just got them rigged up for show. Delith laughing with her head back and her hair streaming out of the window. Delith, here in the Room of Ultimate Death. I'm squeezing her hand and trying not to bolt. My breathing feels funny. She's totally fearless, laughing at the taxidermy.

We couldn't find her underwear this morning, not even after ripping all the sheets off the bed, tossing them out in the hallway, and shaking out our clothes. Finally we gave up and I lent Delith a pair of mine, my favourite ones, with Wonder Woman on the ass. Although we swung by her place on the way out of town, and she changed into jeans and sneakers and a sweater, she didn't change her underwear. I tried not to think about it. I turned up the oldies station and handed her the cigarette papers. Mark's leaves brushed against the windshield on the downbeat, and the two of us sang along: "Michelle, ma belle." "Sweet as cherry pie." "Billie Jean is not my lover."

We found the turnoff to Port Rexton and I didn't follow it. I didn't want to face Nan and Evan, not yet. Instead, I kept driving toward Trinity proper, until Delith pointed at a sign with a train.

"The Trinity Loop—Newfoundland's Most Comprehensive Amusement Park. Oh, Teresa, come on, we have to go!"

There was a Ferris wheel with low-backed seats that threatened to dump you out if you rocked too much, and one of those big plywood scenes, with conductors and vagrants, the yin and yang of humanity, on a train, with holes cut out to stick your head into and pose. The park was nearly empty, a ghost town. We rode the paddleboats in Loop Pond and nearly got sick from laughter, once we spotted the cartoonish wooden cut-out of the topless Beothuk man standing on shore. There was a sickly giraffe not far from him, leaned up against a snotty var. A tiny train with an open, canopied caboose passed by slowly. "By the power of Greyskull!" The lone child sticking off the back thrust a light-up plastic sword in the air. It made battle sounds.

The water in Loop Pond was dark and still. The rickety Ferris wheel spun a handful of sticky children till they screamed. We headed back into the dock and decided to wander. The Boat Man looked part ferret, or weasel. He wiped the seats of the paddleboat carefully with Wet-Naps when we climbed out.

"Our asses must be diseased," I said.

"Perhaps he'll catch a case of The Gay."

"If he's lucky."

"It is highly contagious."

"Highly."

Choo-Choo Charlie lumbered up to us in his rotting fat-suit and told us to play safe. His head was too large. Creatures with terrifically outsized heads scare me.

Delith shook Choo-Choo Charlie's enormous fuzzy hand.

"Want to get a picture with him?"

I took off up the gravel hill and across the railway tracks before she could catch me. She chased me and pelted into my back, bowling me over on the tracks. We lay there laughing, in plain view. The dinky little train crawled toward us, fifty feet away. I acted out the girl part in some silent movie melodrama. I had betrayed my overtly insane millionaire fiancé by bonking the gardener, and for revenge he was going to run me over with his miniature locomotive. There was no escape. Eyes wide, lashes fluttering, I expressed the universal definition of terror perfectly. Delith was Choo-Choo Charlie, solemn-faced, the Keatonesque Hero-at-Large. She removed the fictional shackles from my ankles. "I told you to Play Safe!" she cried. She gathered my limp body into her arms and wiped my brow as I sighed, "Oh, Choo-Choo!" and swooned with my hair in the dirt. We jumped up and bowed to the Americans, with their John Cabot fanny packs, staring from the train car, as it moved off toward the wooden cut-outs of Batman, Captain Canada, Shanadithit and Bart Simpson. We weren't in the real world anymore. "We're somnambulists," I said.

We wandered hand in hand up the road and decided to penetrate the inner sanctuary of the Animal Kingdom, where you could ride a donkey or an endangered, stumpy Newfoundland Pony, and even meet Willy, the Billy Goat. The pony was out with a pack of Girl Guides. I couldn't bear to ride the donkey. I didn't want it to exert itself on my account.

The girl at the ticket booth was about eight years old. She wore a large black t-shirt proclaiming her love for Creedence Clearwater Revival. Delith asked her what she would recommend, and she sold us the tickets to the Wildlife Museum. We

243

paid our two dollars and slogged up the muddy path, while the girl went back to setting out stacks of souvenir lighters in neat neon pyramid formation in front of her giant cash register, gun-grey and covered in stickers: Cannabis Forever/I Brake for Canadians/Heck is For People Who Don't Believe in Gosh.

I knew right away that I shouldn't have stepped inside the Museum. The dead things piled in here make the air thick and sour. I dread the necessity of inhaling. The birds are swinging slightly on their wires, and the shadows pass back and forth across Delith's back as she keeps exploring, seeing if there's a way in past the beavers, into the other room, so she can poke through all those piles of old junk that we can see through the holes in the boarded-up doorway.

"I have to go outside for a minute," I say. I'm afraid that I might seizure after all, but not in ecstasy, as predicted.

Delith grabs my hand and makes me look at her first. I can feel the dead animal eyes on every part of my body. Even the ones with no eyes are staring. The air doesn't feel like air in here. I make sounds like a humidifier. She drags me over to the pool of water and I look sideways at the pale fish swimming around.

"I dare you to put your hand in with me."

"Ha."

"It's easy, they won't bite."

"No."

"Come on, I'll give you a prize and everything."

The water is stagnant and unpleasant and the fish are so colourless they're nearly transparent. They don't remember rules from the outside world concerning the proximity of humans. It's like sinking your hand into a bowl of peeled grapes for eyeballs on Hallowe'en. We hold hands underwater. Delith kisses me.

Those staring glass eyes want things from me that I'm not yet willing to surrender. I can't bear the thought of accidentally brushing against the stiff, damp fur around me, those scrotty old feathers, dust coming off on my skin. I pull away, wipe my hand on my pants. I can't breathe. She takes my arm.

"All right, we can go now." Delith leads me out. We blink like moles in the sunlight.

"Wow," she says, "that was so worth two dollars."

"You're some kind of sadist, aren't you?"

"Oh Teresa, you poor little thing, I thought you were going to faint!"

"Shut up."

"Should I carry you back to the van? Need some sniffing salt?"

"A smoke." I put my hand out for her pack.

"Funny."

"A smoke, please."

She looks at me.

"Really," I say.

Next to the Museum, in the fenced-in field, there is a day-old foal covered in shit and straw, walking on noodles instead of legs. His bones have not yet solidified into straight lines. We watch him for a second, then Delith fishes out a smoke and lights it for me. I take a few drags, until the sick nicotine rush kicks in, then I hand the cigarette back to her. I lean back against the sign, dizzy.

She laughs. "Feel better now?"

I don't answer. The foal leans against his mother's nonchalant jaw as she pulls up the patches of grass. The parts of his mane not covered in shit look soft and fluffy. I'm suddenly overcome with the feeling of being here, where fish meets foal, the undead and the just-born shimmied up against each other in this fucked-up, perfect little place.

When she sees I'm crying, Delith laughs again, and shakes her head. "Oh my dear. What are we going to do with you?" She puts out her smoke. "Too tender-hearted to live." She uses the hem of her shirt to wipe my tears away.

38

We're at Lucy's house, rehearsing for the Christmas concert tomorrow night. Our act is going to be terrific. We're doing a lip-sync with costumes and fake instruments. We rehearsed every day this week. The first two days were really fun. We watched Video Hits and tried to decide on what song to do. Samantha Fox is cool. She has neat hair. In Reading and Writing class we wrote letters to Samantha Fox. I asked if she had any post-secondary education. She didn't send us back any letters, but we each got a little Video Hits pin in the shape of their logo. Everyone wears them on their jackets now. My favourite video of all time is "Like a Prayer." It's beautiful and scary too. That black Jesus guy is so handsome and Madonna is so pretty. When his face is not a real face and it's melting, and also when there's those burning crosses and Madonna is so in love she's trembling, those parts make me kind of excited because I know exactly how Madonna feels. I know about someone calling your name and it sounding like home. When Willassie says my Inuit name it feels like that. I know about closing your eyes and thinking you're falling. I know about things seeming like they're dreams. She totally understands me.

We're not doing "Like a Prayer" for our act, though. When we asked Mr. Levy if we could do a lip-sync instead of being in the *Santa in Florida* skit with the rest of the class, he said yes, but we weren't allowed to do Madonna or any heavy metal, due to "inappropriate content," which I think is stupid but we said okay.

Finally we decided to do the song "I Think We're Alone Now" by Tiffany. She twirls around in shopping malls, with her long red hair cutting dazzling swaths through the air as the public look on, jealously. The girls decided that I had to be Tiffany because I look the most like her. I didn't want to do it and Carla really did. She pulled my hair a lot when she was braiding it yesterday, and I know it was partly because she was mad that I was Tiffany and she wasn't. I wanted to be the drummer or something, I wanted to have sunglasses and a big hat so no one would see me. Normally I would never do something like this, stand up on a platform for the purpose of having people stare at me. They stare at me anyway, and it gives me the creeps. But I have friends now and my friends really wanted me to be in their act, so I said I would do it, even though I want to pee or puke instead.

We made instruments out of cardboard and painted them. We even have one of those keyboards you hold like a guitar and play. Carla called dibs on it because she didn't get to be Tiffany and everyone agreed. Which left Mina for bass, Lucy for guitar and Sarassie for the drums. I made a microphone out of a toilet paper roll. We practiced moving along to the song, which we taped off the TV. I had to practice tossing my hair around a lot and swinging my hips. Making those retarded kiss-me faces.

Carla kept yelling "Shake that ass!" over the music. I have to wear these high-heeled shoes that Nancy lent me. We have the same size feet. She's helping us with our costumes, because we want to look like real rock stars. That's the whole point. So Nance is making us costumes out of some of the clothes I don't wear all that much: belly tops out of regular shirts, miniskirts out of old jogging pants. She even cut the fingers off some old gloves and put studs on their knuckles. I swore her to secrecy about the whole thing. I said I wanted it to be a surprise for Dad. She told me she was sure he'd be very proud. Nance is cool.

Tonight, though, what we're doing is a secret even from Nancy. Carla stole a bottle of hair dye from the Bay. Ravishing Red. Semi-Permanent. Washes Out in 2-3 Weeks. Do Not Get In Eyes. Will Stain Clothing. I say, "Won't they know it was us who stole it when I show up with red hair?" and Carla says, "Shut up, Smart Pants." Sarassie tells me to take my shirt off so they don't get it full of dye. I agree. It's a new shirt Nanny Norman sent up and Dad would really lose it on me if I ruined it. Or he'd force me to wear it every day after that, as a punishment, Lest I Forget. I strip down to my training bra and stick my head in Lucy's sink. She gathers up my hair and they wet it for me. Someone makes sure all the bits at the base of my skull get wetted down with water on their fingers. It's cold. I can feel the goosebumps starting to rise. Carla combs the dye through my hair. She doesn't try to work the knots out gently, she just rips right through. The jerking and tearing heats up my skull. I don't make a sound. Mina's in charge of wiping up drips of dye so I don't get weird red patches of skin around my ears. That would be a lip-sync catastrophe. We wait for my hair to set. Everyone paints their fingernails one after another with the bottle of Positively Princess candy-pink nail polish that Aunt Cack sent me. We listen to Tears for Fears and jump on Lucy's bed. Only two of us at a time, it's small. Carla dunks my head back into the sink, pouring the hot water out by itself for at least five seconds before mixing any cold in. I refuse to flinch.

We blow-dry my hair and it is shockingly red. It is beyond red. It verges on neon. Nowhere on the box did it say, if you are nearly albino, this dye is going to work at three hundred times its intended strength, but I guess I should've known better. This is probably the exact shade referred to as "fire engine" because it really would stop traffic. It really would cause people to pull over immediately and let you get past.

The girls like it, though. I think maybe they worship it. They look like they're having a religious experience as they gently pick up strands of it in their fingers, rubbing it, testing to see if it really is my hair after all. Holding it up to their eyes for closer examination. Lucy puts an end in her mouth, to see if it tastes red, I guess, and then Carla smacks her, and we all have a smack fight. We end up in a big stupid pile. We lie there and pant for a minute and I turn and bite into Carla's side. She squeals and elbows Lucy in the head who kicks Mina who smacks Sarassie on the bum. The smack fight starts all over again.

We tie my hair up in a scarf so no one will know about it till we're up there on the stage tomorrow night. The other girls are going to wear scarves too, so I won't arouse suspicion. It's our fashion statement. Like if we had our own gang. Dad is really going to have a canary over this one.

The next day I'm so nervous I can barely breathe, and I can't even think about eating. Dad calls me Aunt Jemima because of my headscarf, but he lets me wear it. It's the first time I've ever done something to fit in with a group, and no way is Dad going to stop me from fitting in. It's his secret impossible wish. Mine too, I guess. For Teresa to Belong. Somewhere. To Something. Even if, as Dad said, it's the Pancake Posse.

Evan's class does a Christmas Pageant about the birth of Jesus, who's an Inuit kid born to a couple in an igloo. There are kids dressed up as polar bears who bring him offerings of seals made out of cardboard. They crawl on their hands and knees, dressed in white with paper ears, carrying the seals in their mouths. There are walruses and caribou and narwhals too, but I watch the polar bears the most because Evan is one of them. They don't put Danny in the skit. That's too bad. I bet he'd love to dress up as a ptarmigan or something and drop a mouthful of rocks at the feet of the Virgin Mary, the baby Jesus on high in the hood of her immaculate amautiq.

The kids in One and Two do a play with shadow puppets, and then the teachers do a skit where they dress up like teenagers and smoke. The music from *Grease* is playing. Dad is wearing his Cure t-shirt and has his hair gelled back. A smoke dangles from his lip like James Dean. He and Mr. Levy yell insults at each other. "Challenge! Challenge!" the others scream. Dad and Mr. Levy hook their fingers inside each others' mouths, as the other teacher/hoodlums circle round to watch. They snap their fingers to the music, and the fight starts. The object is to see who can make the other surrender by yanking on the inside of their lip. The prize is a dance with Ms Ikusik, who's leaning shyly up against the wall. Dad and Mr. Levy grunt and paw at the ground like angry ponies while they haul on each other's mouths, twisting their heads in impossible directions and pulling so hard their lips turn white and stretch out into nightmare worms. I don't want to see a finger pop through a cheek. Dad brings Mr. Levy to his knees. Everyone in the gym is cheering. He spits on the gym floor. Mr. Levy crawls away in shame, clutching his face. Dad takes Nancy by the hand and they begin to dance, Dad wiggling his bum at the little kids to make them laugh. He kisses Nancy's hand, pulls her close to him in one swift motion, and dips her so her hair touches the floor. She pretends to faint. He shakes her awake and stands her upright, takes her hand and slowly leads her offstage. She winks at the grade nine girls in the back and takes a drag off her fake cigarette. The other teachers catcall and eventually dance backwards into the washrooms, which they've been using as entranceways. John Travolta wails: "Sandy!"

The Grade Threes and Fours are next, but we have to leave the gym and go to our classroom to get ready. We're going to miss our class's Florida thing, too. Mina and Sarassie help me with my makeup. Nancy lent us her lipstick and eyeshadow and blush, and Carla already has eyeliner, and mascara too. The girls start talking about the big Country Feast tonight. When they say "Country Food" they really mean mussels and char and seal meat and duck and caribou and sea urchins and whatever else, everyone pitching in together and making a feast. Of course there's bannock and cookies and homemade jam and everything too. It's funny, I'm all excited about this. A couple of months ago I probably would've been so grossed out I'd puke, but this is the food that belongs here. It tastes like Sanikiluaq. I am looking forward to the Country Feast as much as Mina, now that I've begun to let myself adjust. There's going to be a big dance, with the whole town joining in, making patterns and circles and swinging each other around. There'll be a Santa Claus who gives each kid a present. Drumming with the old-time Inuit drum. And a midnight service in the church that I'm allowed to go to with Nancy, where everyone gets a candle stuck into an apple to hold on to. They all get lit up one by one till the whole church glows with light and smells like apples too. I can't wait: the cold pew and a shiny Macintosh, oozing juice onto my thumb, everyone's faces lit with candlelight, except the people who don't go to church, the Ippaqs and others who won't forgive those naked people, how they died. Lucy said "You pick the candle out and eat the apple." I said, "We'll plant apple trees out of the seeds," even though no trees grow here. "No," she said. "We eat it all. We eat those too."

Nance comes to help us with our costumes. She doesn't even bother to take her silly teenage clothing off. We look great. We don't look anything like ourselves. I've taken my glasses off. The dental tool doesn't compliment my ensemble. With all the goop on my eyes, I look way older. I'm dressed older, too. I even have a ripped-up mesh shirt with a belly top underneath. I wear my snowflake necklace, I want to show it off. No heeby-jeeby magic talk is going to stop me. I'm sure Willassie's mom doesn't come to Christmas concerts, anyway.

I take off my headscarf. Nance gasps and clutches her string of pearls. She puts her hand up to her mouth. The glare off my head is probably blinding.

"Oh, Teresa," she says, "you look just like her." She kisses me on the forehead. I blush and punch her lightly on the hip. That's all the affection I've got in me. The rest is pure nerves. The girls pick up their paper instruments and I grab my ghetto blaster with the song in it. We wait by the door to the gym to hear our act being announced. Mina is giving her hair a final tease.

Mr. Levy announces us and Carla busts open the door with her boot. I press play and do my best runway-model, hair-tossing, shoulder-shaking, butt-wiggling walk down the middle of the gym in Nance's wobbly heels, with the whole town sitting on either side. My skirt is very short. I hope my panties aren't showing; they have teddy bears. I shake and pout. I toss my hair all the way forward, then all the way back. The singing part comes on, so I start doing what I practiced, mouthing along into my toilet paper microphone, winking and pointing at some lucky members of the audience, or so I hope. I can't see anyone clearly. Everyone is staring at my hair, and probably my panties too. They're laughing at the way we're dressed. They can see my belly behind the thin pink mesh. Someone says, "Qallunaat caught her head on fire." I look back and squint. Mina and Lucy and the others haven't even started up toward the stage yet. Tiffany keeps singing about running just as fast as she can, and I wish I could do that right now. I am going to turn off this stupid music and run. I squint into the audience and realize that the people sitting nearest to me are actually my class. Benny is grinning and wiggling his eyebrows up and down, done up like Santa Claus. Willassie is looking at me like he never knew I had such guts. So I keep on singing, or pretending to, even though I'm mortified beyond description and am praying for the tundra to swallow me up.

About halfway through, Carla comes up and joins me, pretending to play her weird purple keyboard/guitar thing. She can't stand being out of the centre of attention too long. Benny and Willassie and the other boys in our class put their hands in the air and make the rock symbol that is also the sign language symbol for I love you. Mina and Lucy and Sarassie finally make it up the aisle in time for the end of the song. After the applause we run back out the door, flushed and shaking with excitement. We jump up and down and hug.

"I'm never doing that again. Ever," I say. No one listens to me.

We head back to the classroom to get changed before the feast. Dad comes up behind me in the hallway and I think he's going to yell at me in front of my friends for dyeing my hair and parading around in skimpy clothing. I can't see his face. I wish I had my dumb glasses back.

"Look, Dad," I say. "I'm sorry, but I had to. For the act. Nancy said it was okay. Well, not the hair. It'll go back to normal in two to three weeks, it said on the package."

"Teresa, I came to give you a hug. It's good to see you stand up like that. You looked very confident. We should see more of this from you, T-bird. You have a lot to be confident about, although next time please alert me before you decide to radically alter your appearance. Save your old Dad the heart attack."

He grabs me by the shoulders and gives me a hug. I stand stiffly and let him do it. It's the first one in a while. I'm almost too old for it now.

39

Delith and I peel out of the Trinity Loop and head down the hill to Trinity Proper. We park the Art-Van in a field and go for dinner in a historic bed and breakfast overlooking the lighthouse on the isthmus in the bay. Trinity is this tiny, almost too-scenic, too-perfect town, where people in period costume buy smokes on their lunch breaks at the one and only convenience store. They work at the museum or with the theatre company, and pass their handfuls of change in hand-stitched gloves to the sweaty cashier who barely tolerates them. The whole town is geared for tourists. Gay Stevie likes to say, half joking, that there are more craft shops than residents. The first wave of retired Americans, with their camcorders and Polaroids, have already set up camp in the graveyards, on the wharves. The buses hurtle down the narrow hill like army tanks, and disgorge masses of elderly bodies like locusts, or like those grubs that completely destroy the maple trees in town each summer, ugly green things that drop like hailstones and in August turn into a blizzard of albino moths that fuck for a week, lay their eggs and die away again.

Our waiter for the evening is a middle-aged gentleman named Fern. He can understand what whales are saying. He knows when they tell each other, "If you're looking for Trinity East, you've got to turn around and go to your right and swim for about ten minutes." He somehow knows that whales use our systems of measurement and also our place names. He is co-writing a play with Gordon Pinsent, Newfoundland's Favourite Fairly-Famous Progeny. It's about the ascension of humans into whales, in the afterlife, and will be staged in this very dining room. Gordon will stand on a table and give a moving speech, in whale costume. He'll play the piano. Fern tells us all this while we eat our grilled cheese and garden salad with Catalina dressing. We drink a bottle of cheap red wine as quickly as possible. He gives us a photocopied booklet detailing his scientific collaborations in whale communication with four anonymous "Nobel-Prizewinning" scientists. He sits at our table and sips a glass of tomato juice while we eat, and promises to send me research and information once a week for the rest of my life, if I'll just give him my mailing address. I twist and twist my napkin. Mom's one hundred percent stable compared to this whack job. Delith's getting red from keeping a straight face. She's busting a gut. But Gay Stevie has warned me about this guy. The women in town forbid their sons to hang around the expensive playground across the street from this particular B and B. The boys leave the shiny new monkey bars to the girls, and play on the shitty wooden swings up the road. There've been charges, but no court date thus far. I don't tell Delith. It seems ungenerous, somehow. We take the pamphlets Fern presents along with our bill, and I write a fake address in his book: Kitty Fleming, Manuels.

After dinner, it's dark, and the town is tiny, its streets full of ankle-twisting holes. I get my flashlight and take Delith to the nearby beach. We walk within the thin circle of light on the rocks and gather up broken shards of china with patterns in blue and white and brown, the edges rubbed smooth by the ocean. Delith puts them in her satchel-thing. It bangs against her hip and makes a soft, clinking sound. She starts singing Dolly Parton. No one else I know sings old-school Dolly. We get a little pretty harmony on the go.

We hear faint sounds of raucousness and follow them to the one bar in town, Rocky's Place Lounge. Both a Place and a Lounge. Really just a big dim room with a few pool tables, a row of video lotto machines and a big deck out back where someone lights a joint and everyone smokes it. Kevin Spacey came here to shoot pool while they filmed *The Shipping News*, that execrable joke. At Rocky's they have Kev's autograph, framed, above the VLTs.

We go in. The door to the deck is open. I can hear Gay Stevie and the others laughing out there, singing Meat Loaf or something, blissed-out beyond conversation. The whole theatre contingent is hiding out on the deck, because tonight is Dance-Up. This woman with a riding crop, which she smacks against her hand for emphasis, teaches people traditional Newfoundland set dances, the kind with swinging partners and group activity, the kind my generation is allergic to. She has a fiddle player and an accordion player and a headset microphone. The Dance Dominatrix. She is fierce and beautiful and we are terrified of her. We young artsy types never participate in Dance-Up. It's for old people and tourists. Instead, we sit at tables and laugh at the drunk women with fanny packs and wrinkled cotton dresses spinning into the wrong men, tripping up the other couples. Or we go out for tokes on the deck and don't come back.

But tonight Delith is with me, and I don't recognize anyone when I take a gander around the room, and I'm drunk on cheap red wine and using phrases like "take a gander around the room." I'm feeling reckless. I buy us scotch and tell her to down it, fast. Which does not count as a shooter. She makes a face at my choice of drink. "So macho, Teresa."

"It'll put hair on your chest," I reply.

I want her so badly I wish we were still on the beach right now, down on the rocks, groping each other, getting driftwood in the spine. Or out in the van, which I left by the B and B and which is therefore probably being used to stage some kind of whale version of *King Lear*, by this point. So close, a two-minute walk down the road, less if we really beat it. It would be so easy. But, I am determined not to give in to my own urges, playing a new kind of pain-game with myself. I am sticking to my plan and I press on, despite Delith's collarbone, its smoothness and nearness and its shape, perfect for sucking on.

"Delith, damnit, let's Dance Up!" I say. "It's time we took part in our Living Heritage."

We join the circle of couples and the Dance Dominatrix smacks us lightly on the ass with her riding crop. We blush furiously and introduce ourselves to the other dancers, most in jeans and sweatshirts, male and female alike, wearing practical shoes, unlike our girly ones, primed for accident. We don't tell them we're from St. John's, for fear of summoning the disdain, often dormant in the hearts of older Newfoundlanders around the bay, for those young things from Sin City who don't have a clue how to dance right. We tell them we're from Toronto. They love us and our adorable insistence on dancing with each other, even though set dances are in man-woman pairs. This is a strictly hetero activity, but the old folks are willing to smile upon us cute little dykey Mainlanders with our cute little dykey Mainland ways, so different from theirs. Delith is the man, even though she's shorter than me and wearing a frillier dress. We Strip The Willow, Dance To Our Partners, Thread The Needle and Spin Till We Drop. Our faces are slick and dripping. Our wet bodies stick together as we spin around so fast the floor comes with us. The accordion is loud, almost punk-rock. Mark would be digging it, although he'd never admit it. Trad music is for losers, he says. Case closed.

The Dominatrix picks Delith and I as the anchor couple to Crack The Whip. We all join hands in a circle, then Delith and I split, and the line of people starts winding itself around her, tightly, until we're all coiled up together, heaving, Delith in the middle and me on the periphery, our eyes wide and searching for each other past the perms and ball caps. The punk-rock accordion starts up again, the fiddle getting pretty hardcore too, and the Dominatrix lady shouts "Crack it! Crack the Whip, my love!" Delith turns and we all spin outwards with the aftershock of her movement, in one organic, quick spiral that spins us around and back in. We Crack The Whip and I'm flying, I really feel like I might be flying, Delith and I and so many happy, sweating, shouting strangers, dancing together.

Our forebears knew how to have a good time. Who would've thunk it? Afterwards, we're all so tired we collapse around our elbows on the sticky tabletops. I'm shiny with sweat. I'm wet on every surface of my body. Where Delith touches my arm, she slides. We glide our skins together and look with concentrated affection into the dark pupils of each other's eyes. I kiss Delith in Rocky's Place Lounge before she's caught her breath from the Whip-Cracking. The locals stare openly and guffaw or tut or look quickly away, silently blessing themselves. There is weak applause. Rocky himself offers to buy us a round. Delith tells him we'll have two scotch, please, no water no rocks, and that's when I know it's official. I'm smitten. Capital S. This girl has sorcery.

We finally wander out onto the deck, where Gay Stevie sweeps us each into the air with many kisses. "My loves! I could just squat you! Swear to God! You're just so cute, the two of you!" We let ourselves into the circle and talk to people we don't know. The actors are all sleeping with each other, or at least putting their hands up each other's shirts. Travis is here, my brother's friend Travis. He passes me the joint, shoving my shoulder, shouting, "Hey, missus, I remember you!"

I shove him back. "I remember you too!"

"How about that?" we both say, and there is general laughter. Last time I saw Travis he had more acne and his voice was cracking, playing Super Mario or some shit with Evan, who must have been about fourteen and was in his I'm Going To Ignore That You Even Exist phase of dealing with me. Travis. Weird. Back then he hadn't grown into his body like he has now. Now he looks fucking indestructible. The draw smokes in my fingers, flaring up its pretty orange head as I put my lips where everyone else has already sucked. I inhale the smoke—hash oil in there too, I'll be damned—and blow a stream straight up to where Ursa Major is teaching Ursa Minor a thing or two. I pass the joint to my left, to a girl in a neon-green dress with a cartoon frog on the front. She peels my fingers back carefully to avoid getting burnt. Instant connection: the eros of the communal spliff.

I ask Travis how Evan is, as casually as I can manage, with

what feels like Mount Rushmore lodged in my throat. He says he hasn't seen him in a while, he doesn't know, they don't really talk a whole lot any more. I wonder what that means. I wonder about the weight and the history behind it. It seems weird to ask, so I don't. Travis says he thinks Evan is working at the FoodLand in Port Union, but he isn't sure. "Don't tell him I'm here," I say, "I want to surprise him." Travis says, "Well, he shoulda seen you making out with your girlfriend in there. That woulda surprised him all right."

The Dominatrix has started the most evil dance of all, the Kissing Dance. One person has a scarf, and they place it over their victim's face and kiss them through it, then grab them by the waist from behind, forcing the kissee into motion. That person then has to kiss someone else through the scarf, and on and on, forming a giant conga line of the embarrassed. No one in the bar is safe. We barricade the door to the deck with a patio umbrella wedged under the doorknob. No one wants to dance the Kissing Dance. Several people try to escape from inside, but it's too late to help them. We have to save ourselves. They rattle impotently at the doorknob. The umbrella stays put. I high-five Travis, who crammed it there. He's my hero now. Eventually we want to leave but are afraid to go back in, so we climb over the side of the patio and drop into the grass. Gay Stevie leads Delith and I into a small river, by mistake, before we find the road. We stumble in the dark toward where I parked. Delith and Gay Stevie do a number from *My Fair Lady* as I walk behind them, looking up at the stars, which shine like cups and saucers in the perfect black sky.

We drive Gay Stevie to his place, a dirty little basement apartment with a toilet that leaks all over the linoleum. Beside the bathtub, mushrooms are growing out of the wall. They look like little ears. He sleeps on a mattress on the floor. From what I understand, actors are used to this. His fridge is broken, as are half the elements on the stove, and the heat in the living room refuses to turn off. There are two hard-backed chairs and a coffee table. No other furniture. No kitchen table, no couch. He gets put up for free, so he can't complain. He lives as though he might leave at any minute. Not even his scarves thrown over every available light fixture can redeem this place. He offers his mattress to us but we wave him off and crawl into the back of the van. We get under the sleeping bag and Delith falls asleep quickly, leaving me to lie awake and enjoy the sensation of her warm, solid leg across my body, her head tucked into my armpit, my other hand stroking her hair. No nightmares.

We awake to the noise of dogs going cracked next door. Radiohead playing through Gay Stevie's open window. After breakfast, we decide to go on a boat trip. It's Monday, the theatre company's day off, so there'll be no use for me till tomorrow, when Delith will get the Town Taxi back to St. John's. I will live in Gay Stevie's driveway till Thursday, when I told Nan I'd be out to stay with her and Evan for a couple of days. I'll finish the shots for the company, maybe even drive up to the Northern Peninsula, if the Art-Van seems like she's got that much go in her. Who knows.

We sign up with a group of tourists for a day trip to Ireland's Eye, a small island with a graveyard in the woods and abandoned communities. The tourists are loud and overexcited and start videotaping as soon as the boat trip starts. They are most likely from landlocked, urban centres. A school of porpoises appears. The tourists have their camcorders out and they're hooting.

A lady in a fuchsia sweatshirt and cowboy hat is screaming "Holy Doodle!" and jabbing her finger apoplectically at the school of porpoises, as if no one else can see them flipping lazily about. I wonder if anyone will keel over with a heart attack if a minke decides to show itself.

Delith and I go below deck and smoke a secret draw. Then we go up into the vacated stern and lean back on the bench, looking up at the beauty of storm clouds rolling over. We picture the skies opening up and raining blood down on us. Although this image is disgusting and terrifying, we also think it is beautiful. How beautiful it would be if the ocean turned to blood. The tourists would collapse from shock, shouting "Holy Doodle!" to the end. We would stand up and lift our arms and open our mouths to the sky, for if the sky rained blood, we would have to see what it tasted like.

"I started my period this morning," she says.

"So did I," I say. "How about that."

Ireland's Eye. So green and perfect. A Narnian field. The kelp is the bright yellow of kelp in dreams. The wind is whispering in the dry, thin grasses. All the buildings are in piles. They're lichen-coloured, like the rocks. Delith picks blueberries and feeds them to me from fingers stained with juice. I lick them thoroughly, but they stay purple. Every murmur echoes like a shot across this perfect valley and into the cliffs where the tourists are lumbering about, flirting with broken ankles.

We're sitting on the back wall of a church, keeled over and almost entirely stripped of its rust-coloured paint by the seasons. Three gothic windows lie near my feet, their stained glass patterns now replaced by the intricate green of grass and fern. Something scampers through the foundation. I can hear its thump. The others all walk past, looking for the cemetery in the woods. Delith and I walk the treacherous piles of fallen lumber and find a Bible, half-disintegrated, held together in an organic lump by its own startling mint-green mould. It opens in three places. The words legible are the famous ones about loving thy neighbour and also a lesser-known bit about it being impossible for a man with a good heart to do anything but good. No mention of women with good hearts.

"Women's hearts are never wholly good, thanks to Eve," I say. "Damn her and her predilection for fruit."

"Yeah," Delith says, putting her hand on my neck. My scalp comes alive, and of course we stop and kiss each other.

I take pictures of the Bible which I know won't turn out properly. We place it under a pile of lumber to protect it for a few months more. Our hearts are full of that strange painful feeling. Houses and churches fall down quickly after people leave them. They collapse into themselves, purposeless. There are patterns of decay and sadness in the swollen lines of timber, wet and wasted, barely resisting complete disintegration and a sighing return to the arms of the earth.

The church steeple has fallen down, but appears intact except for the very top. The cross is gone, perhaps shattered in the collapse or stolen for a heathen souvenir. Delith walks the length of the fallen church wall. I shoot and shoot. The light through the drizzle is gorgeous. She crouches and stares into the steeple where the cross used to be. The hole is big enough to climb through. She does. When I look inside, she's crying, and although we barely know each other yet, I know her well enough to know she rarely cries about anything. I climb through the hole. There is no gravity. We're frozen with the feel of it. We can't sit and can't stand, for the laws of motion don't obey us. We lean into the beams, clinging to them. No words. No poking or prodding. Delith's eyes turn upwards to the thin light filtering in from the neat grey portals. The trap door floats above us in slivers of sky. I don't deserve this. Each straight strong plank spirals inconceivably into a beautiful swirl. The words "straight" and "curved" have no meaning. Words are pitiful and cannot describe this. How did I get here? I do not deserve this.

Delith props me up while I point my camera in every direction. I know these pictures aren't going to turn out—it's too dim in here—but a girl's got to try. We peer through the windows of the steeple as the rain comes on. The others scream and run for the boat. We take our time, trying to sink this feeling down deep, into the roots of our bones. Eventually, we head down in the rain. I carry my camera underneath my jacket to protect it. Delith clings to my back for support.

We have just been touched by God. We have read His words from a chunk of living decay. We crawled inside the ruined hub of His worship and found it beautiful and disorienting. If only every church would fall and crumble, there might be more sacred places where you can regain your sense of amazement. Awe. Where the smell of things crumbling is like incense.

The look on our faces and our extreme lateness might make people think we'd just had sex in the ruins, but these people are Mainlanders, lost in whale-wonder, incapable right now of contemplating anything else beyond minke and sperm, baleen and fluke. Not God in ruins, not ghosts and rot. Nothing but whale. Not even two girls fucking, or loving each other.

40

We're in gym class and Dad's making everyone do push-ups, with elbows making perfect right angles, or else it doesn't count. I can only do two or three, with my spindle arms. Willassie does the most—he can do sixty-seven—but even he can't beat me at long-distance running. I could run all day and still keep going. The trick is to think about running toward something really important that you really need or want. You can run right through your own exhaustion this way. I'm attempting Push-Up Number Four when the fire alarm goes off. This has only happened once so far this year, the day Benny got suspended. We all pile out through the gym door, shivering in our jogging pants and t-shirts in the cold April wind. The snow going over our shoe tops.

Dad jokes about making us keep going out here. We all laugh at the thought of having to get down and measure right-angle elbows, our faces getting pressed into the snowbank. He goes to find out what's happening and we're left with the Threes and Fours. I can see Tom-Tomas and Evan on the other side of the playground with the Kindergarten class. They're ninjas, of course, kicking at nothing, making ridiculous sounds supposed to scare the girls.

We start having a snowball fight, the whole class, and pretty soon it's getting out of control. We're chucking snowballs at the Grade Threes and Fours, who are running after us, falling down and getting their knees satched. It's boys against girls, because every game ends up that way. The girls have their backs to the school, where the dirty snow is, and the boys have taken over the igloo as their home base. We all built the igloo as part of our cultural education curriculum, along with the fish-skin parka that I helped to sew up with sinews, and the tent made of sealskin in the library. When the snow melts, we're going to make a real Tuuniq house too, with stone walls chinked in with moss and a sod roof and everything. Everyone gets to sleep for one night in the igloo, in groups of four, and we get to light a kuudliq and snuggle in together under caribou hides, just like in the olden days. Mina and Lucy and Carla picked me over Sarassie as the fourth person for their night. I don't think Dad ever felt more proud.

We make a running attack towards the igloo, sending the boys scattering with pitiful yelps. Everyone's wrestling in the snow, shoving snow into faces and down shirts. So cold that it burns, and makes you scream at the touch of it. I'm being attacked by Benny and Willassie. I clutch my sides in an attempt to stop the stomach ache I've got from laughing while they shove snow in my face.

"Mercy!" I scream. "Please, mercy!"

"No no no, Missy Polar Bear. You likes the snow!" Benny is fierce. He's taking a handful of snow and putting it inside my shirt. His hand brushes past my nipple. Willassie hurls Benny to the ground and starts punching him, hard, on the head and in the stomach. I don't think Benny even meant to touch me there. Everyone comes running to see the two boys fighting, mashing each other's heads into the snow and punching each other's stomachs. I stand to the side, wringing my hands, doing my best Scarlett O'Hara imitation, ready to swoon as soon as I see blood.

The crowd pushes me back until I can't see what's going on. This is no longer about me. I heave out a last, sighing sob, and wait for everything to end itself, preferably before either of them lose any teeth. I start to walk away. Maybe I'll go sit on the monkey bars till the alarm goes off. I see someone over by the door to the school, slouched in the gravel. It's Danny. I run over and pull a fistful of rocks out of his hands. He's swallowing furiously. There's pieces of glass in the pile of gravel around him. There's blood coming down one side of his mouth. He's rocking back and forth, his legs splayed out uselessly. I don't know what to do and try screaming. Everyone is so engrossed in the fight they don't look my way at all.

"It's okay, Danny. Don't worry. I'm going to help you, okay? We're going to go to the nursing station and get one of the nurses to help you feel better. Okay?"

I drag him by the hand towards the nursing station, him choking and not able to breathe properly, me trying to think what my Nan or Mom would do. I sing "O Danny Boy," although I only know half the lyrics. The rest I just make up. I'm worried he can't breathe properly, and I never learned CPR. Not far to the Nursing Station. Not far. "But come on back, when summer's in the meadow/Or when the valley's humped with too much snow." I can see the door. Danny is slowing down. I'm half-carrying, half-pulling him the rest of the way. I get the metal door open, it's stinging my palm. I'm yelling for help.

Other Body nurse comes out. If she's surprised to see me and Danny, she doesn't let it show. She pleasantly asks me what happened while heaving Danny into her arms and carrying him towards the examination room. I tell her and she tells me thank you, it's what she thought, they might have to make a cut to get all the rocks out, depending on how big they were. I tell her about the shards of glass. She hands me off to Birthmark to get some dry clothes, and calmly calls Braces to come and help her. They lead Danny away, and I yell after her to sing "O Danny Boy" if he's getting scared. She doesn't answer. They're gone. And me so preoccupied I didn't even notice what new slogan was on her t-shirt.

Birthmark says her name is Wanda and she's glad I brought Danny straight here. She says this isn't the first time he's been brought in for consuming inappropriate items. Nicely put. I ask her if he'll be okay. She says there's no need for me to be concerned. But I've seen her poker face, on the plane ride here. Danny was gobbling up those rocks like a bulimic. He was eating them like it was something his body needed, but also like he wanted so bad to stop. I wonder if it was the fighting that made him do it. Or maybe it's like Carla said, and he's cursed. Someone wants to hurt him, and they're inside his mind, controlling it, whispering bad things that paralyze his free will till he's nothing more than a puppet to the mean little voice that's whispering, "Eat the rocks. And the glass. Go on. You deserve it. You deserve how bad that's going to feel." Danny does what the voice says, because it's hard to ignore some magic tupilak thing from a powerful shaman sitting right in your ear, telling you what to do. And also he's retarded or delayed or disabled, or whatever the right word is, and so it's probably harder for him to resist the nasty tauntings of the tupilak. Who made him that way in the first place.

I'm wearing a pair of Wanda's jeans and her pink shirt, both huge on me, and sitting reading a science magazine, when Mr. Levy brings Willassie and Benny into the nursing station. Benny's missing a tooth. The fight went too long. Willassie's bleeding above the eye. The sight of it makes me want to spew. Mr. Levy is telling Wanda they need to be seen to right away. You can practically see his blood pressure rising. He demands to know why I'm there. When Wanda tells him about Danny, he sighs. Sits. Benny won't look at me, neither will Willassie.

Mr. Levy smiles tiredly and thanks me for bringing Danny in. Calls it mature. Says "You look nice in pink. It was Marguerite's favourite colour." Benny smiles and repeats her name. He looks at Willassie, who looks at the floor, and for a few seconds no one moves. There's a pause that follows every time her name is spoken. I wish I'd never heard it.

Willassie appears not to have heard either of them. I wonder if he knows about his dad and Danny's mom. How Danny is his half-brother. How his own mother can lay such a powerful curse. He must know. This town is very small, and Carla has a big mouth. However, most of the kids wouldn't admit to believing in that old stuff. It's superstition, like believing in Fairies. Even if Willassie has heard the stories, he probably thinks they're shit and blocks them out.

He's only looked at me once, since coming in here, and that was an angry look. Like he hated me. But I know he doesn't hate me, he doesn't, oh no. He kisses my neck. He kisses it soft, so

I don't bruise. I know he doesn't hate me, but he has to try very hard not to let it show. That could be dangerous. It could get his head kicked in. I am the dreaded Qallunaat. They spit at me and tell me to go home. It could make him turn retarded, if the stories are true. You never know. Willassie looks at his sneakers and Benny fidgets in his chair, occasionally making his eyes cross to try to get me to laugh. I pretend to read a tattered copy of *Time* magazine. Mr. Levy breathes loudly through his nose and makes notes in his day planner.

Danny is crying somewhere down the cold, white hallway, where they're hauling rocks out of his gut. None of us go to him. Nothing was on fire.

41

Gay Stevie is a wonderful man, but I worry. I worry about him like a mother would. I drove him back into town on his day off, and we spent a delightful evening getting stoned and making carrot cake. We also set up the sewing machine and made swanky matching pants out of my orange bridesmaid dress. Finally we fell asleep on the couch, using each other's feet as pillows. I woke up with a serious crick in my back, so Gay Stevie insisted on plunking me face down on the floor and sitting on top of me. He is giving me a massage, a Gay Stevie Special, and telling me about his various escapades. Lifting up my shoulder blade like a piece of heirloom china and then viciously shaking it out.

"Yeah, so anyway, April Fool's Day this year, I was at Bianca's, right, there was some cabaret on and I was done up as Dorothy from the Wizard of Oz. I found these killer ruby platforms at this shoe store in Corner Brook, of all places. Anyway, I got pissed and I mean really pissed…"

"Drunk or mad?"

"Both, Bella." He calls me the pet name he normally reserves for Jam Jam, his cat. Starts knocking the knots out of the base of my spine. It kills. "I was pissed on Manhattans, right, pissed in all directions, up, down and sideways, and this guy says "Let's go to the washroom." I say all right, we go, and he fucks me in the washroom without even going in the stall, just drops his pants and lets me have it under my pinafore, out in the open. All these dudes are coming in to take a shit and they see this guy giving it in the ass to Dorothy over by the soap dispenser."

"They weren't in Kansas anymore."

"I think I should give up drinking."

"So, who brought the condoms? You or Ass-Man?"

Gay Stevie moves back up to my neck. He starts talking about the Matt Damon Hot Factor, so I know that no one brought the condoms. Again. This man, my friend, this advocate of gay rights and volunteer with the Tommy Sexton Foundation, this man who is touching me more intimately right now than any other man has in years, this man is a fucking idiot.

"Stevie."

"Darling."

"Don't darling me. Are you a crackhead? Do you hate me or something, you want to leave me and go rot in a hospital bed? For what, for some loser guy to fuck you in a washroom and never see you again?"

"I don't know."

"You of all people should know better, Stevie."

"I do. Forget it." He works back up to my neck. "I want to do things. Extremes. I don't want to talk about it. It's getting me through."

I think about my cigarette burn days. The gas sniffing game. Challenge. Killer. Mercy On Me. Sticking my hand on the cold flagpole and deliberately pulling it off a second too late. Losing crotch tag on purpose to feel my bruises deepen. I made this. I own it, I own the blackening of broken veins above my pubis. This hurt makes joy more joyful. It highlights it. .

"You've got to stop and you've got to get tested, because one of these days you're not going to be lucky, and you're going to get in over your head, and then there'll be nothing you can do about it, and being sorry won't do any good. This is your mother talking."

Gay Stevie's fingers carve out my occipital bone. "I got tested."

"And?"

"And what?"

"Well, what did the doctor say?"

"I didn't go back to find out. I get one day off a week. One 24-hour period in which to return to civilization and live as a free man. Fuck me if I'm gonna freak out in a waiting room when I should be taking it easy for once." ·

I shoot him a look. I have the evil eye.

"Okay, I'm being flippant. Big surprise. But, seriously, if I find out I've got it, what good will it do me? I'll just be depressed. I can't afford the medication. Actors can't afford to get AIDS. Not around here anyway. I can't even afford to go to the dentist, for shit's sake. Unless I get some sort of Canada Council grant that funds the treatment of a terminal illness as performance art, I'll never, ever be able to do it. And I'll just give up. Whereas, if I don't know, I can just keep on living as usual, until my body gives out."

"But you won't ever be able to have sex again. You won't, not in good conscience. And also, what if you don't have it? Wouldn't you want to know?"

"Sure. But the fear is the biggest thing right now. Bigger than anything else."

"But."

"It's eating me."

I picture a big black shadow coming to eat Gay Stevie, spitting out his nipple rings as I would fish bones.

He says, "I want to play myself in the Made for TV Movie. It could be my big break. No one else would really be right for the part."

"You'd better stop being so fucking calm about this, or I'll really be mad at you."

"I had my panic attack already, T. It's okay. It happens to people all the time. They get sick, they die. It'll be fine. I'm still just me."

He has to go. They're due back in Trinity for a show tonight. "I love you," I say. "Watch out for moose on the highway."

"Be a good girl. I love you too." We kiss each other on both cheeks and on the lips and he hugs me. My ribs actually feel like they're cracking. I'd do anything for him.

I still haven't gotten around to telling him about Delith, not really. Not that he hasn't figured it out for himself from our little trip to Trinity. Sleeping in his driveway in my van-bed, not really big enough for two. The glow. The smiles that threatened to crack our faces.

I want to talk, I want to tell someone about how giddy I'm feeling. And about the fear. I'm scared of the hugeness, the hunger of my body. I don't want to listen to its clamouring. I'm used to silence. I'm used to genitalia made of stone. I also wish to remain oblivious to the truth of whatever's going on inside me. Because it's so huge it's dangerous. Even if it's good.

That night, I dream that Gay Stevie is being gang beaten in an alleyway, somewhere off George Street. I have to get to him before the men beat him to death. There is piano music, like in a Charlie Chaplin film, slightly too fast for the action. There is a man chasing me. He's bald, with metal teeth and syringes for fingers. His breath comes out of him in fish-blood and chicken-shit coloured clouds. I know that I have to reach Gay Stevie before the man touches me with the needle-fingers, or we'll both die. I make my way through Buckmaster Circle, down St. Clare Avenue and into a maze of row housing. Every so often I'm shown Gay Stevie bleeding in the alley, from an omniscient third-person perspective so removed from myself that I can't influence it. He can't hear me crying out in terror as I see the men kick at his face with their steel-toed boots, and carve cruel hieroglyphics into his chest with their razor blades. Die Faggot. On Your Knees.

I'm lost and about to give up hope and then that girl is there, that poor girl who was murdered last year or the year before, her face on TV for a month or two. That Inuit girl adopted by white people and raised in St. John's. I used to see her downtown, she actually wore a chain from her nose to her ear. They never said why she was murdered, though some people said it was Sex and some said Drugs, and a few radical thinkers said Both. No one said she's an Inuit girl all by herself in a sea of white skin. No one said it's because she was brown, but maybe it was, who knows.

She had a shaved head and purple lipgloss. Eyebrow spikes and knee-high cracked Doc Martens that I was jealous of. I would sometimes see her walking, the only Inuit girl I'd ever seen in St. John's. She'd go by with her eyes on the sidewalk, like she didn't know she was stunning, like she wanted to disappear. But she was stunning. I saw her high-school picture on the television and she was dead. And I thought, is it a coincidence that in a city of few murders and fewer Inuit, is it a coincidence that the two things merged? I cried when I saw that picture, I felt at a loss, because every time I'd see that girl on the road, I'd want to talk to her, to ask her out for coffee or something, and to use the few Inuktitut words left to me before I forgot them too. I was too shy to step in front of her and put my hand out. I was a self-deprecating sidewalk-starer too. And I had to ask myself, if I had fucked fear and talked to her, could I have helped? Would she somehow not be dead now?

At any rate, this dead gorgeous punk girl is in my dream. Suddenly we're close enough that I could kiss her if I wanted, and I think that I want to, and I might even do it, except now she's putting a tab of acid on her tongue. It's got a little arrow on it, pointing to the left, so I veer that way, because in dreams those are the rules. I run around a corner and into the tundra. The tundra is waiting in the middle of St. John's to consume me whole. It lies somewhere between Victoria Street and Bates Hill, somewhere in there where I didn't notice it before. The dead girl won't come with me. I can't breathe, the wind is suffocating. I have no clothes on, I'm turning blue and stiff with cold. Where did my clothes go? Nan made me that sweater, and she'd be vexed if I lost it. I don't need the aggravation of another argument right now. Gay Stevie is almost dead. He's bleeding through the letters on his body. The man with needles for fingers is grinning. Hey, Dead Girl, come and help me! The needle-fingers come toward me. They sink into my neck.

"Jesus Christ! Jesus Christ!" I jolt awake so violently that

I pull a muscle in my back. A wave of pain if I try to move anything. I lie there for hours, helpless, unable to move, the pain searing my sides every time I start laughing at how retarded it is to hurt yourself while you're asleep. Pathetic. It kills when I start to cry. My nightmares have worked themselves into my waking life. I'd shudder if it didn't hurt. I'd scream. Will I next wake up to find myself martyred, my fingers lying like stunted sausages on the bedsheets in a sauce of my congealing blood? Are my outsides and insides switching on me? I roll over slowly and sit up. I stagger to standing, lurch to the dresser where I left my stash, and lower myself back into bed. That's all the go I've got in me. No one's home: Mark, Nessa, Delith, not even Dad. The smoke takes on the room. I get ashes on the pillowcase.

I think that girl's name was Jenny, but maybe it wasn't.

42

Mr. Levy is going to teach me how to use his big, super-powerful microscope. He said sometime he'll also teach me how to use his camera and how to develop pictures in the darkroom. Me and Evan are going to his house tonight, after supper. I help Dad make the rice and corn, he does the rest. I mix up the powdered milk that Evan and I hate so much. It's yellow, with lumps that turn gritty in your teeth, nothing like real milk at all. We have to drink three glasses of it a day, as some sort of punishment for being born. Here, real milk costs six dollars a litre, yet we still have to be careful about developing brittle bones. Especially me. Mom says people with "the fair blood" are prone to brittle bones. I drink my milk through clenched teeth, straining the gritty clumps out and smearing them into my napkin.

It always takes Evan three times as long as everyone else to finish his supper, because he talks constantly. Even when Dad and I are done and gone off to do something else, Evan keeps talking, while everything gets cold and lumpy on his plate. He's definitely going to have a life in the entertainment industry. I set down the glasses of cruddy powdered milk and he gets into his chair, already talking.

"If you could do anything right now, what would it be? I would go to ninja school in China and learn all the best moves and then come back, and Tom-Tomas would be so mad! Wouldn't that be funny? This milk tastes so gross I'd rather drink anything else. Would you eat snails rather than drink this? I would. I'd also eat boogers, or live tarantulas, or dead people's fingernails."

"How about Honey from the Honey Bucket?"

Evan scowls at me. "Don't be so gross all the time, Teresa."

"All the time? I said one thing about Honey."

But he's off on another subject. "Judy Arnaq's older sister just had twins and Judy knit them sweaters, even though she's only eight. Can you knit, Teresa?"

"No."

"You're almost thirteen. How come you don't know how? If you ever have twins, they won't be very warm, because you don't know how to knit them sweaters. Unless you got Judy Arnaq to do it. She would because she's nice. But I wouldn't marry her. She wants to marry me, but I told her I'm never getting married, no matter what. Because no ninjas are married. Did you know that all insects have six legs? Did you know the world is like an orange with lava inside the peel? Did you know that Inuit words don't have the same letters as English, they have different ones made of triangles called syllables? I mean, syllabics? Did you know everyone calls Dad "Tusks" because of his moustache? Did you know that seven plus three is ten and so is two plus eight?"

Sometimes I can't stand the way Evan is constantly talking, especially when he's at the table and half-chewed pieces of shepherd's pie are falling out of his mouth. On the other hand, he's never boring.

"My tooth is loose."

"You'd better not tell Dad or he'll get the pliers out."

"No he won't. You know how to make a paper airplane out of a dollar bill? Tom-Tomas showed me, and it really works. His belt got ripped so I gave him one of my belts. 'Cause we're ninjas and ninjas need belts. Do cowboys need belts? Yes, for their guns to hang on. Right, Teresa?"

"Yeah. That's all completely true."

He grins across the table at me. Red lips and tiny white baby teeth, skin now almost as brown as Tom-Tomas.

"Pass the salt, Seven." Mom used to call Evan "Seven" as a joke. I thought it was hilarious when I was little. We're laughing about it when Dad comes in from the kitchen with the fish.

"What's so funny?" he asks.

"Nothing," I say, and give Evan the Be Quiet look. Any mention of Seven or any of the other old jokes my mother had with us makes Dad sad for the entire night. And he can't afford to get depressed right now, because Nancy's coming over.

I'm not supposed to know that, but I do. Teresa the Spy. What can I say, I'm a natural. Even though I've officially retired and am no longer actively seeking out clues, I'm so good the information just makes its way to me, all by itself. Also Dad talks pretty loud, even if he's in the bedroom with the door closed, pacing along the lines in the linoleum, absent-mindedly chopping at the air with a pair of scissors as he talks. I don't need a glass pressed up to the door to hear what he's saying. The words come through my wall, clear as anything. Nancy is coming over and Dad had better be in a good mood.

That's why Mr. Levy invited me and Evan over, tonight

specifically. Dad wanted Nancy to come over and he didn't want us around while it happened. Because they want to have sex. Mr. Levy said I can sleep in Marguerite's room and read her books, and that means he thinks I'm pretty excellent, because no other girl has ever gotten to sleep in Marguerite's bed before, besides Marguerite herself.

Mr. Levy's a real pal. That's what Dad calls him. He's doing Dad a favour. Dad thinks I won't understand about his love for Ms Elbow. He thinks I'm still mad. And I must confess, I'm enjoying the ability to make him uncomfortable, to make him sneak around. And I want to sleep in the pink bed in the special room full of old secret things, and maybe do some investigating on the former most popular girl in Sanikiluaq. Miss Marguerite of the Mysteries. Let Dad sweat it out for the moment. I'll tell him he's got my blessing when I break the news about Willassie and me. How, on my thirteenth birthday, eleven days from today, he's going to make love to me.

I've made green Jell-o for dessert, Evan's absolute favourite. He says it looks like what aliens would be made of on the inside, instead of blood and lungs and stomachs. They'd just be green and wobbly the whole way through. Soon Dad will be telling him that he doesn't know where he gets his imagination. But that's obvious. He gets it from me, and I get it from *Star Wars*. I pack up Evan's pirate book before I go. He won't go without it. It's his favourite book of all time. I put it in with his jammies and toothbrush and help him get dressed up for the cold. I tuck his mittens into his cuffs all the way around, so his wrists won't get chapped in the wind. Dad makes farting noises with his mouth on Evan's cheeks and does the dumb thing where he raps my skull with his knuckles and says "Still not ripe." He tells me to

283

have fun.

"Goodnight, Teresa. Goodnight, baby. See you in the morning, okay?"

"Can we have pancakes?" Evan says.

"If you're good."

Dad hangs out of the doorway, shivering, watching us walk. He calls out, "Make sure to thank Mr. Levy for letting you stay over."

I'm only bringing the essentials, my best nightgown, clean underwear and socks, my flashlight, and *The Once and Future King*, in case Marguerite had terrible taste in books. I knock on the door.

"Welcome, Monsieur et Madame, to my humble lodgings." Mr. Levy bows. He's wearing his purple sweater and there's a thread sticking up out of the collar, like a vein going up his stubbly neck.

I curtsy. "Thank you, kind sir." Evan copies me. He can curtsy pretty good.

The three of us play Snakes and Ladders and Mr. Levy wins, which embarrasses him. I help Evan get ready for bed. I sit with him and read the pirate book before he goes to sleep. He knows nearly all the words off by heart, so we take turns being the different characters. For fun he pretends to be me and I am him. He gets the way I squint just right. I pull the blankets up and tuck them underneath him all the way around. Evan agrees with me that lying tightly wrapped in the sheets like a mummy is the best way to go to sleep. You feel safe and warm and like someone is holding on to you. Mom used to do the blankets like that for me. I guess I'm too old now anyway, but it really did make a difference. My dreams used to be so sweet.

When Evan falls asleep, it's just us grown-ups. I go back into the living room where Mr. Levy has set up the microscope. He makes me hot chocolate. It's so sugary I can barely drink it, but I do anyway, because I don't want to hurt his feelings. He shows me how to work the microscope. It's basically the same as my little one, but a lot stronger, with five different magnifying lenses. Mr. Levy puts on classical music that sounds like a thunderstorm and I put in the fruit fly slide we made together awhile back. There's so much more detail. The dark lines in the slide turn themselves into linked cells, each with a distinct, crisp patterning.

"Mr. Levy, do you have a pencil and some paper I could use?"

"Sure thing. More hot chocolate?"

I say yes. The kind of person I am, if I like somebody, and I want to be nice to them, I'll drink their hot chocolate, even if it's sickitating. We spend a long time in the living room. Mr. Levy drinks alcohol, but thinks I don't notice. He's not allowed to drink it or even have it in his house. Alcohol is banned here, because too many bad things happen to people who drink it. Which is why, I guess, he's putting it in a mug and calling it tea, when we both know better. I'll never say anything.

I draw the cells of the fruit fly. Mr. Levy says that lots of artists have used science as a basis for their work, like Leonardo da Vinci, who also used to write backwards and invented weird flying machines, way before the first airplane. He reads aloud to me about Leonardo da Vinci from his encyclopedias while I replace the slides, over and over, and draw what I see. I draw the close-up insides of many things: a bit of dust, a drop of hot chocolate, a wood shaving, a shred of ham. Mr. Levy gets a toothpick and tells me to open my mouth. He puts his hand on my chin and scrapes the toothpick along the inside of my cheek, then wipes it on a slide. I look at the slide of my own cells and draw them. They don't look how I thought they would. They're not as complicated as some of the fruit fly cells.

"Who would've thought you're made of simpler stuff than a bug, eh, Teresa?"

"Not me." The line where he scraped the toothpick stings inside my mouth.

At ten o'clock, I tell Mr. Levy I'm getting tired and he shows me to the bedroom. I thank him for a lovely evening, and he bows again.

"My pleasure, fair lady. I shall excuse myself and let you go to sleep."

"Goodnight."

"Goodnight, Teresa. Sleep tight."

He closes the door and walks back to the living room. I can hear him sink into the couch. The inner sanctum of Marguerite is mine alone. I get the flashlight out. Might as well do this professionally.

She had decent taste in books. There's no *Sweet Valley High* or *Fear Street* like the girls in my class in St. John's used to read. I took my copy of *The Odyssey* to school when everyone else was face and eyes into Christopher Pike horror books, the titles spelled out in raised red slashes dripping blood. Marguerite has no books like that. She's got the usual L.M. Montgomery and C.S. Lewis stuff, nothing I haven't already read. Probably she took the best books with her when she left.

Marguerite liked flowers. The bedspread and curtains are made of pink material with purple flowers all over it. There's also a picture on the wall made of real flowers squished flat and framed. I recognize pansies and forget-me-nots among the different blossoms.

Other than that, the pictures on the walls are all of boys, from magazines. The kind I think I'm supposed to put up when I turn thirteen. I nudge open the closet but then stop, because it's really creaky and I don't want Mr. Levy to hear me snooping around. Instead I go to the dresser, and peek at what's inside. The drawers are full of papers, school work mostly. Boring stuff, unless I want to read about Marguerite's brilliant math scores and pretty terrible spelling. That's one thing I can do better than her. I can spell nearly any word correctly, even long, difficult ones like schizophrenia, juggernaut and unconstitutional. In the last drawer, I finally hit treasure, solid gold. Marguerite's photo album. This should be good.

Lots of baby pictures of chubby-cheeked Marguerite in a house that isn't this house. Grinning in a meadow, evergreens in the background. Being held by Mr. Levy, skinnier and without the purple sweater, on a boat. Her hair the colour mine was when I dyed it and it had faded a little. For a while there I looked like an actual redhead. One with a woman holding the baby. A blonde woman with narrow, nervous shoulders and a surprised look to her mouth. Mrs. Levy. I wonder what happened to her. Marguerite gets older, page by page. She graduates from Kindergarten in a lavender robe that pools around her feet, holding a bunch of tissue-paper flowers. She sits underneath a massive tree, holding up Barbies at Christmas. Marguerite skates. Marguerite slides. Marguerite does ballet. Marguerite turns twelve. There's her cake, an angel food cake made into a beautiful ball gown, with a doll stuck into the middle, its body decorated in icing, like the bodice and sleeves of the dress.

Something Nancy would've made for Evan, if he'd been a girl. Marguerite arrives in Sanikiluaq. There she is with her Dad, no Mrs. Levy. There they are on the airstrip, grinning beside their pile of stuff just thrown off the plane. Arms around each other. Marguerite in her girly gypsy costume, for Hallowe'en. Bobbing for apples. Dad said they don't do that anymore, because Inuit kids never blow their noses, and after ten or twelve bobbers the surface of the water gets all covered in snot. But that can't be true, because Marguerite wouldn't be caught dead with boogers on her face. I'd bet a hundred dollars on it.

Marguerite, at a dance. Her head thrown back, laughing. All the faces around her laughing too. The picture freezes everyone mid-clap as Marguerite and Mr. Levy dance. He dips her so low her hair touches the floor. They're both wearing patent leather shoes, Mr. Levy's face a shiny beet. I look closer at this picture. The older kids I don't really know. I think that might be Jolene in the corner. And that boy.

Willassie is in the picture, grinning that woodshed, candy-bar grin. I know it's him. He's about thirteen. Willassie is in this ghost-girl's album, looking at her like she's Isadora Duncan and not some kid being stupid with her father. Like she takes his breath away.

I look through the rest of the book. In several of the pictures, Marguerite is wearing a whale-tail necklace made of ivory.

A loose photograph falls onto the bedspread. It's one of those stupid pictures everyone likes to take of themselves and their friends with their faces squished together, looking down their arms at the lens. Huge foreheads, out of focus, in the middle of some great time you're having that you want to remember forever. But you can't get very much background in when you can only get an arm's length away from yourself, so the pictures leave everything else out, and aren't really a good record of the event you want to remember. It's just you and your friends' giant faces, all smudgy and squished like a couple of overripe peaches.

This picture is Willassie and Marguerite. When I see it I want to vomit, but I don't. Everything tastes like cigarettes. All I can think about is Carla talking and me trying not to listen. And Willassie looking at me when I'm Tiffany and making the rock symbol which is also sign language for I love you. And my red dumb Tiffany/Marguerite hair and my gooped-up face.

I hate this picture where Willassie is looking at Marguerite, and Marguerite is looking at the camera with big glassy wet blue eyes, huge enough to go swimming in. Willassie's lips are on Marguerite's cheek. He's scrunching his face up. She's smiling.

I put the album back in its drawer. I don't want to snoop anymore. I put on my best nightgown, with the lace at the cuffs, made of the thickest flannel. I crawl into Marguerite's perfect princess bed. Even though I'm full of some kind of new, unsettled feeling, I finally go to sleep.

I dream that I'm St. Liz, doing time up on the cross. The jeering crowd throws their bread crusts at me and the pigeons peck me dead. Marguerite stays, afterward, and so does Nancy. They're the ones who really know how much this dying thing is killing me. My cross is made of walrus tusks and there's dust in the air from a fresh sanding. They cry into their blue Virgin Mary costumes. They blow their noses in Kleenex and turn the Kleenex into a nightgown, to cover up my skin from the heat of the sun.

"We fair-skinned people have to be careful about getting

sunburns, don't we, Marguerite," I say.

"Oh, yes. Once I got burned so bad my face came off. Even though you're dead, you don't want to peel."

"Can't expect you to understand, Ms Elbow," I said. "All you Inuit do is tan, tan, tan."

Marguerite shakes her head. "She won't talk to you. She's taken a vow of silence. Nancy's becoming a nun."

Nun-Nancy is crying a single, beautiful tear, which I magnify under a microscope and draw. It is made of hundreds of snow-flakes, all strung together in intricate chains. It takes me so long to draw that I die all over again. I can feel someone touching my cheek. They don't want me to go away and leave them. And I'm St. Elizabeth, so even though I'm tired of being crucified and I don't want a sunburn and I don't want to be stuck up there with the nails through my palms, I come back to life anyway, to help the person with the soft, sad touch. I open my saintly eyes. Mr. Levy is standing over the bed. He starts backwards, the rum or whatever in his cup slopping a bit. He shakes out the hand that was touching my face and clenches the fingers into a fist, white-tight.

"I'm sorry. For a minute, there... I thought you were my daughter for a minute there."

"Oh."

"I just thought you were Marguerite for a minute. It's been a while since there was someone in this bed."

I sit up.

"I used to come in like this when she was sleeping. It's perfectly normal. There's no crime. "

"It's okay."

"I used to come in and touch her face and say I loved her,

290

when she was sleeping."

"It's okay."

"Your father must do the same."

He turns around and stands there for a long time. It's dark so I can't really be sure, but I think Mr. Levy is crying. His shoulders are hunched and jerking a little, and that's usually a telltale sign. Also he gropes for the doorknob like he can't quite see where it is. He leaves the room without saying anything else. I settle my head back into Marguerite's soft pillow, way softer than mine at home. I say to myself: Self, Buck Up. Self, Get a Grip. Marguerite is not you. You are not Marguerite. You are Quanniq. No two Quanniq are alike. I am not Marguerite and Marguerite is not me. I am Teresa Norman, daughter of James and Elizabeth, sister of Evan. I have thoughts, and all my thoughts are my own. My hand is my hand, and so is my face. No one else has that pencil scar on their cheek. No one else is as pale and see-through as me. I maybe even have Fairy blood. Anything is possible. Willassie loves me. Quanniq. Me. TLAF: True Love Always and Forever. TTEOT: Till The Ends Of Time. Mr. Levy is drunk and Carla is a bitch and I didn't see that photograph. I made it up. It's me he loves. It's me he loves. It's me. It's me. It's me.

43

It's been two weeks since Delith came home with me, nearly two whole weeks since we sat in the steeple of the church on Ireland's Eye, ten days since I drove back to St. John's without even stopping in for tea at Nan's, though I'd promised. Nine days since I put my back out dreaming about Gay Stevie and the violence of death, as represented by a man with needles for fingers. Nine heinous, boring days, but who's counting. Gay Stevie calls me long-distance from Trinity. He says, "Hang in there, princess," and makes kissy noises into the phone. Curtis lugs around the furniture and Vanessa makes casseroles that shrivel in the fridge throughout the week: lasagna, scalloped potatoes. Curtis does the dishes when they're used up. We drink Black Bush out of travel mugs.

And as for Delith, I left three messages on her machine, first to say I fucked up my back and was home being a lame-o and would love it if she came by to alleviate the unrelenting boredom which has engulfed me. The next week, "Don't worry, I'm walking and even sitting now, doing the slo-mo version of tai chi, if you can comprehend something that slow. The melting of the polar ice caps is faster than me. I'm on glacial time. Oh God, stopping now. Call me."

I know she checks her messages obsessively. I won't worry. She said she'd call.

Actually, she said "Thank you. Trinity changed my life. Safe to say that. I need to get my head together. I'll call."

Okay. Fine. If I were to attempt to get my head together, it'd take more than three weeks. It would take years to fit back together the soft, woollen unravellings of memory, logic, REM, instinct. Each going their separate ways, further and further from the cortex.

So, fine. I said that, if for some reason she didn't want to see me anymore, didn't want to talk to me, if perchance she found herself retching with the memory of touching my body, if all those tiny noises were just put on for my sake, if I was maybe as embarrassing as a cartoonish tattoo the morning after, bumpy, crusty and too garishly bright, if I proved distasteful in the light of post-intimacy, if she could please just call to tell me that, then I wouldn't bother her anymore. Because I need to know. I did say that. If she wants to tell me to fuck off, I told her, if you want to tell me to fuck off and leave you alone, then fine. I do at least deserve the fuck you. But no anti-conclusions. No tearing out the last chapter. After enthusiastically declaiming our anti-sexism, we both agreed that men had done this to us on several occasions and it was the lowest form of cowardice, worse than a litany of your faults, worse than a door slamming in your face, or your belongings packed into a cardboard box labelled Property of The Whore of Maxse Street and left on the curb for the neighbours to see. At least these crude gestures of anger really let you know where you stand. Hence my current upset at the lack of communication, my disappointment in Delith. I should have done the gutsy thing and told her I loved her as soon as I knew that I did, even though it's arcane and dangerous to say that shit. I should have said Fuck Fear. I should have said something else than all that meaningless shiss I did say: goodbye, take care, be safe, call me. Shiss: shit that has the consistency of piss, usually symptomatic of a hard night on the rum. I touched her clitoris with my tongue. I let her put her fingers up inside of me.

Today I stood in the bank lineup and experienced what felt like appendicitis when I thought I saw her coming through the door in the reflections of the mirrored wall. I mean, I got this stabbing pain. The woman who entered looked nothing like her, but she was wearing a canary yellow headband, the plastic kind. Not that Delith ever wore those headbands, but I'll take any excuse to get worked up. Curtis says, "Chillax already."

I'll finally be able to go back to the gallery tomorrow. It's actually a relief after the week of lying around the house, doped up on Atasol 30s, furiously incapacitated, fed up with the clutter but unable to do anything about it. I haven't been able to do much at all. Nothing that involves moving. I watched television for a few days. CBC in grainy black and white. Night after night. The polar ice caps melting. Entrepreneur-types putting a positive spin on things. Earnest men in natty suits saying that the melting is going to be a boon, economically speaking. Lucrative trade routes will open up between Russia and North America, imagine the possibilities.

I picture Sanikiluaq in the year 2030, which is when the men in the suits tell us all this melting will really start kicking in. The tundra, shrinking, turning to mud, leaving behind the sickened remains of newly endangered species. Morphing gradually into lush jungle, with monkeys and magnolias. Trees heavy with papaya and starfruit. Snakes instead of foxes. Gone the flora and fauna of yore, gone the monsters of yesteryear. Now it's *The Jungle Book*. The calfskin loincloth clings to your thighs, Willassie. You're practically type-cast as Mowgli. The happy Russian sailors are all tanned dark as Eskimos from their trip round our tropical northern waters. They've done good trade, beef for borscht, and are giving sentimental toasts to one another with futuristic Tetra-Paks of Canadian lager.

I wished momentarily that I had cable. I wished that television had never been invented. I wished humanity was a more elevated club to belong to. I turned off the TV and huffed around the kitchen, grimacing, picking at various casseroles, cold, right out of the fridge. Finally, I heaved my way back up the stairs, threw the remote down over them, and flopped back into bed. Curtis had the foresight to bring a box of books up from the basement. The dull-coloured spines are coated with dust. I ease apart the brittle, splotchy pages. *Kidnapped. The Wizard of Oz. War and Peace. Owls in the Family.*

If you love words, they'll never desert you. They will always be there, waiting patiently in their ordered pages. I can reread the same books over and over and be surprised, every time, by some detail or nuance that didn't appear before. I've reread *Wuthering Heights* and suddenly sympathized with Catherine, after years of thinking her spoiled beyond reason and, at root, common. Unworthy of Heathcliff's burning, wild love. The sudden affinity for the simpering, scratching Catherine shocked me. Like rediscovering olives after a childhood spent making puckered faces at the mere mention of the word, now to find myself lusting after the saltiness, the shape and texture of an olive in my mouth. Always, it seems, the story or the food has changed and I've remained constant, when, really, the object is an object, a thing unchanging, and it is I who continue to metamorphose. My heart, my tongue.

I've been without the time or volition to read for a while now. I've laid this old love by the wayside, replacing it with other preoccupations: dancing, drinking, smoking pot. Mystic journeys with Art-Man in the Art-Van. Sex with girls. And taking photographs, of course. Images instead of words.

Flat on my back with my new-found treasure, I am falling in love with words again, after such a lengthy period of abstinence. Sentences so beautiful they make me itchy. I rub my face across the pages. I press the cool covers to my cheek. Lay before me, Words. Lie there naked on the bedspread. Put your head upon my shoulder, or, better yet, nestle into the hollow of my lap and let me comb out the pretty tangles in your hair. I am yours, forever. I swear this on everything I've ever read, cross my heart and hope to die, stick ten thousand needles in my eye. I stand atop my paper fortress, defending Literature's honour, a devoted knight in her Court of Love. Commanding imagined armies into the fantastic breach, bookmark raised like a shining sword, dust jacket shielding me. The book? *A Sin City Townie in King Arthur's Court. Donna Quixote. The Sword in the Stone Walrus. Love in the Time of the New Plague.*

Oh, and *One Hundred Years of Solitude*. That one I can leave intact. The title needs no clever twist to describe my life perfectly.

44

I sit with my back against a rock, looking out at the ocean, with Willassie's head on my stomach, my book resting on his forehead. He blows the pages around with an upwards stream of breath, still visible although he says soon it will be spring. "Wait till there are flowers out here," he says, "the little purple ones. Wait till it's berry time and the owls are hatching and the tundra is blooming."

Out in the haunted valley, where no one else comes, I read to Willassie from all sorts of books. Out there in front of us on the ice is where the crazy fake Jesus and crazy fake God led the people that time. His dad was one. I try not to think about it. Willassie hasn't said anything. We don't talk about that kind of stuff, our families. Instead, he teaches me Inuktitut and how to read the land for signs of different kinds of animals. He tells me about the kinds of berries, the stars and what their stories are. I read my books to him. He likes stories with made-up creatures in them, so I'm reading *Beowulf and Grendel* and acting out all the parts. I'm so brilliant I think I may have to become an actress instead of an archaeologist or a journalist or a prizewinning cosmetician or any of my former chosen careers. I'll play Catherine (New and Improved! 65% Less Whining!) in *Wuthering Heights* opposite Willassie. He's much more handsome than Laurence Olivier.

Heathcliff is supposed to be swarthy, brooding, not quite white. Heathcliff is dangerous, physically imposing. Willassie is the toughest boy in school. He loves me like Heathcliff loved Catherine. He'd do anything for me. If he knew that anyone ever hurt me, Willassie would kill.

He interrupts the story. "How many days more?"

"Four, counting today."

"You are happy?"

"Are you happy?"

"You don't answer my question, Quanniq."

"I'm so happy I could bust." I kiss the dent the book made in his forehead. I try not to think about those stupid pictures in Marguerite's drawer. I try not to even think her name to myself. It rankles in my brain, like a festering sore. Willassie pulls himself around sideways into a little ball, his breath warm in my crotch, making me clench all the muscles down there. I want him with my heart and my mind and my soul, if it exists, but not with my body. I know that's wrong. I know I'm supposed to feel different. All panting and hot. But my body wants no one. My body wants a suit of armour, and a sword or machine gun to keep intruders out. It wants a Rottweiler to guard the perimeter of my underwear. It's terrified, it doesn't know what's going on. I feel very small. I feel like I'm a baby. I'm afraid of all the swelling, twinging feelings I get down there when Willassie lies like this in my lap, his breath getting me warm. I'm scared of those sick dreams, the dickie birds like flagpoles. Although Juliet was only thirteen.

Willassie hands me a piece of bannock. The end of the coil, my favorite. More crispy outside and less dough in the middle. I've brought tea in my dad's thermos, sweet as drinking a liquid cupcake. We eat outside, where our appetites are sharper. Willassie is planning things for my birthday. He's planning a way that we can be together for the whole night.

"You don't need to do anything special. I don't deserve it," I say.

"You deserve everything. Not just one night."

I can't help thinking about the whale-tail necklace.

Willassie talks to me about Inuit philosophy, although he'd never call it that. He talks about using everything, wasting nothing, reinventing old things. I think my mother has the same ideas, even though they're more about composting and recycling and second-hand clothes, and not about using seal sinews for string and seal bones for children's games. In the old days of Sanikiluaq, there was no such thing as garbage. Nothing got thrown out, not a scrap. It was the white men who brought the idea of garbage to the land. Things that you used once and then didn't need. We both tell each other that people and our feelings for them come first, everything else second. That simple is better, less stuff is better. We want to live in a time before convenience and disposability.

Although I'm only twelve-nearly-thirteen, and a dreaded Qallunaat to boot, I think I would like to try this new-old way of life with Willassie. Living in an igloo or a Tuuniq house, depending on the season. We could hunt and pick. Even though we both know my father would never let us, and neither would his mother, that it's all a big wish we're investing too much time in. Chances are just as good that I'll move in with my infamous ex-boyfriend, Romeo Montague. Dad found his name pencilled into the wall of the playhouse and makes fun of me on a weekly basis because of it. He thinks this is the extent of my knowledge of boys. He thinks Shakespeare is my teacher when it comes to love, and not this boy with the strongest hands and smoothest skin and softest earlobes, especially between my lips, and finest eyelashes and, yes, most perfect nipples. Like chocolate chips. Willassie deserves everything, not just a skinny kid with scabbed-up knees and no breasts at all and these weird coarse hairs starting to grow through her crotch-tag bruises. I have nine of them already, and no tweezers. I cut them down with my scissors but they grow right back. Another thing I have to keep hidden so as not to embarrass myself.

We'll build our house in the haunted valley when the spring comes. I make him promise. We'll drag rocks from all over, we'll decide how to best match the edges up. We'll get moss to fill the cracks, and mud and grasses. Caribou hides to line our bed, a small bed in the middle of the house, barely big enough for both of us. And when we're sleeping close together, we'll dream that we've become one person, and then, waking up in the tundra, we'll discover that it's true. I'll have come into my Fairy inheritance, granted a miraculous transformation at last. Sleeping, the Good Folk will visit us. Upon awakening we'll have merged into one hybrid person, half-tall/half-small, half-Inuit/half-white, half-boy/half-girl, half and half of everything about ourselves, and all the way beautiful. Teresassie. Willesa. I laugh out loud, thinking about it.

Willassie takes this as his cue to fling me to the ground for a vicious tickling, and I narrowly miss knocking my teeth out. But it's better when it's dangerous, our foreheads nearly hitting the sharp edges of the rocks as Willassie fumbles for my armpits and I fend him off the only way I can, being on bottom and much smaller. I kiss him so soft that he's got to stop tickling me. I tell him in our private language of tongue-touch that no one has ever touched me before. That he's the explorer of brand new territory. The privileged navigator of virgin waters. Fuck. Shit. He is. I am.

45

Bringing Mark to Dad's house was either the best or worst idea I've ever had.

It certainly unleashed an avalanche of embarrassing Teresa Stories, from both of them. Boy, was I excited. On the other hand, I haven't seen Dad look so animated in a long time. Finally, someone to argue philosophy, and, worse, politics, with. Someone whose personality is not inseparable from events of the past, with whom one can exchange pleasant banter, minus deeper reverberations. I can't begrudge him that.

As for Mark, he loves playing my nearest and dearest. He gets off on the idea that he's the only one of my friends to meet my father. This gives him an elevated place in the universe. He thinks he knows everything about me, but, if he did, he'd break apart with the density of it. It'd be like trying to carry an anvil around between your ears. Mark is terribly naive when it comes to these things. He thinks that just because he says "I know you, Teresa" and I agree with him, the statement is true. When nobody knows anyone else at all. I don't really know either of the men sitting next to me, Dad on the left, Mark on the right, me in the middle, squished into the couch cushion normally reserved for buffer space. The men talk over my head about genetic warfare and how Mark found Calgary as opposed to Edmonton, and I become smaller, trying to sink myself away from the contact of their bodies, the moist heat.

I don't want to feel Mark's thigh touching mine. I don't want him to talk like we're lovers, in that staid and comfortable tone. That intimate tone. I don't want Dad to reminisce about my childhood antics as though they haven't been soured and turned bitter in his brain. Not one of us is honest, here, in this room. We're pleasant, honesty's antithesis. We say nothing that we think someone else will object to. Even Mark reins in his tongue out of deference to Dad, and talks about driving through the Rockies. Even Mark is more or less pleasant. I tune them out. Think about that night that Delith came back to my house. For once I let my heart do the moving. I let myself be vulnerable as I haven't been in ages. And it sucks now, but. I really felt something. I felt something huge. I felt that l-word feeling. I found myself mouthing it: l—. L—. And even if it sucks right now, even if the thought of Delith incapacitates me, even if Delith is a two-Kleenex thought at the best of times, I don't regret it. For a few days I actually felt the way I used to feel with you. I was alive again.

Dad flicks on the TV. He compulsively watches the CBC news to catch the weather. Carl is live from Rennie's Mill trail tonight. "Back to you, Debbie." I hate Debbie because she looks like Mom. Minus the nasty edema, swelling her up like a blowfish. Healthy Debbie is telling us about the newest shame in Sheshashit. Dad and I both hold our breath and pretend we aren't listening. I pick at the coffee table, fingering a rough spot in the wood, as we hear about the gasoline and rags and the Native Youths with their eyes rolled back into their heads.

It's a lot like the fainting game. There's a quick fall into unconsciousness, usually. The headache afterwards, the stink. Mark starts up a discussion on the subject which immediately crashes and burns. He'll get no opinion on Sheshashit from any member of the Norman family. The TV cuts to commercial: shit about disposable super-facecloths that you chuck away twice a day. They keep you looking younger for longer and pile up in the landfills with our disposable maxi-pads and diapers and our fast food trash. Even in the relatively pristine environs of Newfoundland, garbage lines the chain-link fences around schoolyards. In St. John's harbour the bubble of raw sewage continues to swell. Recycling is a running joke. I can't wait till we put the movie on. Zeferrelli's *Romeo and Juliet*. No more talking, and none of the sad stuff about the world we live in, buffered between ads for pastes to make your teeth whiter, other pastes to keep you regular, some to wax your car, pastes that turn into instant gourmet diet supplements, and vaginal pastes, even, for birth control.

Give me period costumes, lush scenery and poetry full of swoons. Give me delicate British accents: even ugly words sound as if they're wrapped in linen napkins. Give me Olivia Hussey's eyes with the stars and planets inside. The morning he leaves, she'll expose her breast to us in a milky flash. He'll stand with his buttocks chiselled by sunlight. She'll drink the potion. She'll lie in the tomb. He'll find her body, leave no drop to help her after. She'll put the dagger to her perfect breastbone. She'll push it in, her neck arched back, determined. Killing yourself is a difficult thing to do. The story will go on around them. The plot must tie itself up. Her molasses hair will drip and drip, and she'll lie on her love's cold body till she turns cold too.

46

Nance made me a cake. Vanilla, in the shape of a snowflake. She cut out all these holes, so it's lacy and delicate, and for emphasis there's white icing and shredded coconut and those silver balls like on wedding cakes, in all the nooks and crannies. I can tell that today is going to be the best birthday I've ever had, better even than the bowling/pizza party I had in Grade Three. Dad split the ass out of his worn brown cords when he bent over to throw the ball, and spent the rest of the party with his pants come apart and his tighty whities showing. Circling around like a dog after its own tail, asking my classmates if they felt a breeze.

We're having a small supper party. I just want a few people here: Dad and Evan and Nancy, of course, and Mina and Lucy, and Carla, who really isn't all that bad. Now that we're all bosom friends, I like Carla. When it was our turn to sleep in the igloo, she told us all her secret. Now I know it's okay to trust her. I know she's really my friend. Mina asked her who the father was and Carla said she didn't know, exactly, and she listed all the people it could've been. None of them was Willassie. Lucy made a point of asking, and Carla patted my hand.

"He's the only one who would refuse me," she said. "That's why he makes me crazy in the head."

Who knows if it's true, but at this point I'm willing to accept anything. Carla's no threat. Her mom is letting her keep the baby, and even said that, once she starts to show, she doesn't have to go to school anymore. I offered to help her keep up with her schoolwork at home, so she could come back once the baby's born, and she laughed and said, "That's it, now. That's the finish of school for me. I'm gonna be a mother only." She looked happy, even though she doesn't know whose baby it is and she'll never learn anything beyond Grade 6. She wants someone on whom it's okay to lavish all her hidden wellsprings of love. Carla's not so tough. She's off the cigarettes.

Willassie can't come to my birthday dinner, of course. But Lucy told Dad she's having me over for a sleepover after dinner tonight, and instead Willassie and I are going to the igloo. He and the girls are in cahoots. Mina's a good friend to me. She gave me my present already, a bottle of perfume that she must have been saving up to buy at the Co-op for months. She would've had to sell nine or ten pairs of mitts to get enough. The bottle is shaped like a horse and the perfume inside is pink. *Free Spirit.* To spray it on, you take off the horse's head. It smells like my Aunt Cack and the basilica, the makeup counter at Sears. When I smelled it I got so homesick I thought I was going to cry, but I didn't. Not even when Mom didn't call, like she said she would.

She probably forgot about my birthday. Probably she forgets a lot of other important things, now that I'm not there to help remind her, even easy stuff like when to pay her phone bill and how to make spaghetti. She throws it at the wall uncooked.

Probably she forgot to pay the phone bill and they cut off her line and then she forgot that the line was cut off, so all day she's been picking up the dead receiver and dialling my number, desperate to talk to me on the day that I become a teenager. Because she can't reach me she's decided to paint me a birthday picture, and mail it here, and if I'm patient and hold my perfumed horses and wait a few weeks, there it'll be, the biggest, most fragile package on the plane, wrapped in brown paper with my name in capital letters, carefully stencilled in red. Inside will be the most beautiful painting. It'll make the brightness of the snow seem dull as Barbie hair, in comparison. I don't know what the painting will look like exactly, but there'll be flowers and angels in it, for sure.

Evan's been doing the It's Teresa's Birthday dance all day. It involves a lot of bum-shaking and jumping in circles and has been banned from the kitchen. He knocked into Dad while Dad was taking the caribou out of the oven and nearly got hot meat juice all over himself. This scared everyone except Evan. He thinks he's invincible to danger, due to his imaginary ninja status. Besides caribou stew, we're having corn on the cob—from a can, but good anyway—and rice with mushroom soup mixed into it, and bannock. Fresh milk, one whole litre, as a treat. I can already taste it: creamy, smooth. Slightly sweet. And the most beautiful cake in the world for dessert.

I'm setting the table with Evan's help, which means he's dive-bombing my knees while I try to put out the wine glasses. Dad said we can use them for our milk. He said maybe God will come down and turn the milk into wine and save us all from the horror of living on a dry island. Then he and Nancy shared a secret adult look because they think I don't know that Dad has a bottle of

Bailey's and a bottle of Grand Marnier in his bottom dresser drawer. Dad thinks I don't know he's breaking the law. But I'm a super-spy, so of course I know, and I'm prepared for the day the RCMP come to the door and take him away to serve his time in the single cell of the police station. I've got *Miss Manner's Guide to Child Rearing*, the First Aid kit, multivitamins, and extra socks and underwear for me and Evan all in a suitcase under my bed, ready to go. If Dad gets arrested for liquor possession, I'm not going to stick around to suffer the consequences of being left alone. We'll run away and live as orphans. We'll build a Tuuniq house and Willassie'll live with us. I'll bring my books in a big waterproof bucket. Maybe two buckets. There's a lot of books. Evan will grow up bilingual and will also learn the language of animals, so he can be safe playing out in the nothingness with the polar bears and wolves.

Supper is delicious and we eat noisily with greasy chins full of caribou juice. Nancy and Dad touch knees under the table. They think they're being secretive, but when Evan drops his corn on the floor, I pick it up and see their thighs pressing up to one another. It reminds me of that time on the plane here, long ago and far away, when the dentist and She Who Is Now Named Wanda But Was Once Only Known As Birthmark did the same thing under the pullout tray. Are all people in love so obvious?

When the kids look at me and Willassie sitting next to each other in class, not talking or touching or looking at one another, do they see how obvious it is that we were meant to be? All the fake-o nonchalance is just a disguise for that fragile, bursting feeling that is devouring us both in our seats. Monday to Friday, nine till three, I look hard at my textbooks and try not to get suckered into the bright, glowing thing in my periphery that is Willassie Ippaq. Of course, the halo of light that I imagine I can see around his arm and head and throat and other parts isn't really imagined. It's just invisible, it's just his energy that I can feel radiating out towards me. I know it's there, even if no doctor or scientist or other learned person says it's possible. In between our desks, and above the staticky carpet, the invisible parts of ourselves are kissing and caressing and conversing with one another. You don't have to do anything stupid, like hold hands in public, for this to happen. Our secret selves are joining together, between the spaces of our bodies and our desks, without us looking at one another, or acknowledging it in any way. Our spirits are doing it themselves, always.

If only Dad could learn this trick he'd be much less nervous, in the staff room or at the dinner table, with his furtive thigh longing for release. You'd think he'd have figured it out by now. He's more than three times as old as me. He gets up to bring in the most beautiful birthday cake of all time, and there's a knock at the door.

Dad lets Mr. Levy in. He puts down a big box wrapped in Santa paper left over from Christmas. He reaches his huge red-haired hand across the dinner table and gets his sleeve in my beautiful icing.

"Teresa, happy birthday. Thirteen, eh? You're officially embarking on your journey to adulthood. I wish you smooth sailing, my dear." He hands me the box. It's heavy. I pick apart the tape, thinking Book, Dictionary, Almanac. But it's his camera, all wrapped in pink tissue paper inside an old oatmeal box. I can't believe he's giving me this.

"What do you say, Teresa?" Dad says. "That's very generous of Mr. Levy."

"Thank you."

"I think it's time we had a photographer on staff at the paper, Teresa. You up for the job?"

"Yes, sir." I salute. He likes it when kids do this.

Mr. Levy shakes my hand. "Good man," he says, and Nancy gets him a plate.

I let Evan get on my lap and look through the smooth metal eyepiece. I let him fiddle with the focus. Mr. Levy tells me how to clean it and what the numbers all mean. I think about Willassie, who isn't here, and Mom, who isn't here either. I wish they could be here too. I wish I could have all the people I love together at once. That'll never happen again. I know it's true. Dad and Mom will never be together again. I can't deny that anymore, not now that I want to be an adult and not a kid. Not with Nance and Dad right in front of me with those sparkly love eyes. And Dad would never in a million years let me be with Willassie, not out in public. No one would. They'd say I was too young. And if they didn't say that, they'd say I was Qallunaat. Go home, they'd say. White girl, we don't need you. We hate you. Get out.

Even Dad would be angry about it. Rubbing thighs with Nancy, under the table. The same rules don't apply to him and me. When it comes down to it, Dad can be a hypocrite. Because he loves Nancy he thinks she's Different. She stands out more to him as who she is. To Dad, Willassie is no one. He's a stunt double. He's one face in a crowd: the Troubled/Troublesome Native Youth. He's big, and nearly a grown-up. Sometimes he looks kind of tough, sometimes he spits. He's the boy who threw the pencil and carved those things about me in his desk and fought with Benny. I know Dad would just see all that and nothing else. Willassie's right. This can't ever stop being a secret.

The whole town would practically kill us. It's never going to be allowed for us to walk down the street in daylight together. Or go to the dance together, or anything. And forget him ever coming to my birthday parties.

I take the knife and cut the cake, and carefully wipe the blade, and cut again. I don't slit my wrists. I don't even cry. I put my fork into the soft side of my slice and lift it to my mouth. Like a cake made of snow in a fairy tale. I scrape every last smear of icing off my plate before I calmly get up and thank everyone for coming and calmly and graciously and maturely exit the room and go to the bathroom and calmly lift up the cover of the Honey Bucket and serenely pull my hair back and kneel and calmly stare at all our collective shit. I breathe the smell of it in and, beginning with the beautiful birthday cake, I vomit everything out of me, straight from my gut and out of my wet red face. The Beatles are singing too loud for anyone to hear me. They all think I'm having the time of my life. The music gets turned off. I hear the telephone ringing. Dad answers it. No one's calling my name, but it has to be for me. It's my birthday. I go back out to the living room after swishing some water in my mouth and wiping my face. Dad's on the phone trying not to be heard. I ask him who it is. He won't answer me.

"Let me talk to her," I say.

He hands me the phone. It's warm from his ear. I hate that.

"Hi, Mom."

"Teresa, my darling, I love you and I wish you all the best today and every day, you know that." She's talking fast.

"I love you too."

"Did I ever tell you about St. Elizabeth of Hungary?"

"Yes, Mom."

"She's my namesake, if you didn't know."

"I knew."

"She was the most amazing woman, and I think we could all learn a lesson or two from her. When I'm angry with the world, I think of St. Elizabeth and her trials and accomplishments, and I take them as my own because they are for me to learn from, and for you to learn from too, if you wish. Do you want to learn about her?"

"Yes, Mom," I say, although I already know everything there is to know about St. Elizabeth of Hungary. I impersonate her in my fucking sleep. But when my mother gets upset, something takes over and replaces all the things I know she wants to say with the facts of St. Elizabeth's life. I'm not supposed to notice this or comment on it to anyone. There is nothing to do but ride it out. I turn my back to the room full of guests and stare at the shiny patch of wall above the stove.

"Well, Teresa, you may not know this, but although I am a devout Catholic and do my best to do well by God, marrying your father was certainly not a step towards Christ. I let myself get distracted, honey, and before I knew it I had agreed to toss a coin when you were born. To see if you could get baptized or not, but that's another story. Get your father to tell that one. Shocking. The point being, I'd lost my way. But when I came upon St. Elizabeth of Hungary, I was truly saved. She loved Jesus so much that it led me to the true faith as well, as one day she'll lead you, I'm sure. If only I'd named you Elizabeth instead of Teresa, although I didn't want anyone to think I'd named you after myself. The sin of pride is a heavy burden, and it leaves a stain."

Then the usual stuff about St. Elizabeth's childhood engagement at the age of four, getting brought up with her groom-to-be, riding horses together. He won her little heart with ponies. Very smart. Then he dies and the second eldest brother, Ludwig, takes over the engagement. Elizabeth gets weirder by the day, and more religious. Walking around with rocks in her shoes, pulling her hair out.

"She was fourteen when they married, and he was twenty-one. She had never known any other children. He held her hands as she prayed by the bedside at night, but he didn't understand how special she was. He couldn't see it. All those miracles. Once Ludwig surprised her, trying to sneak bread from the castle out to the poor in the fields. When he caught her, the bread turned to roses, and so she had stolen nothing. How beautiful and unnecessary, this miracle. Wouldn't he have loved her when he saw her helping others? Why roses? And more importantly, did they have thorns?"

Mom pauses for a second to consider the thorns pricking slightly into St. Elizabeth's sides under her horsehair petticoat. I can hear her on the other end, sighing at the beauty of her own mental picture, before going on with her lecture. I would think that a more useful miracle would be to turn roses into bread. That way, St. Elizabeth could go out in the garden and pick a bouquet and have enough bread for an entire family. What's more, I bet her husband wouldn't give a rat's ass about the flower beds, so he'd never know what she'd done and would never be angry with her. But leave it to God to make up this frivolous little bread-to-roses scheme instead.

Mom goes on, about Ludwig dying in the crusades, and Elizabeth renouncing her family and her children and everything she ever owned.

"She had a love of poverty. She lived in a pigsty for quite some time, and was desperately happy. The love of Christ is also the love of His Cross. This she teaches us."

This monk in charge of her "spiritual education," Brother Conrad, beat her with a rod and made her do things Mom won't even tell me about, but after her death he was the one who got her named as a saint. "Which is how the world often works," Mom says. "Those who seem harshest really want the best for you."

I look back out into the living room. Dad is cutting Evan another slice of cake. Everybody's faces are lit up like a Norman Rockwell painting. My mother doesn't have a sweet clue what she's saying. She's just talking.

"St. Elizabeth of Hungary died at twenty-four. She barely lived at all. And yet her miracles continued after death. Healing was said to occur at her tomb: the paralyzed could feel again, cripples could walk again, mutes could talk again, boils and sores vanished and were replaced by shiny pink new skin. That's why they ripped every piece of her apart. People took her lips, her ears, her fingers, hair, toes, anything they could get as relics to heal their pain. The only thing that remains is her skull, which is protected as a religious artifact. She can be yours, too, you know. She'll wait for you. We'll wait for you, for as long as it takes, Teresa, my little dove. I know you'll be coming home eventually."

I thank my mother for her uplifting conversation. She tells me she's been working on a personal modification of the traditional prayer to St. Elizabeth, and that she will recite it to me as a birthday present. Oh joy.

"Holy Elizabeth, mother of the poor, St. Elizabeth, who didst fear God from thy heart, St. Elizabeth, whose nights were spent in prayer and contemplation, St. Elizabeth, who was consoled with heavenly visions, St. Elizabeth, holocaust of penance and humility, St. Elizabeth, admirable preacher of meekness, St. Elizabeth, lover of the Cross of Christ, St. Elizabeth, light of all pious women, St. Elizabeth, cheered by angelic choirs in thy last agony, hear my prayer for my daughter above myself. Make me a gnat, a snail to be crushed underfoot, a cripple, an outcast, a leper, an exile, so that she might lead a charmed and charming life, safe from adversity and the perils of weakness. Help us, St. Elizabeth, to despise the pleasures and indulgences of the world and to delight in the consolations of Heaven. Help us, St. Elizabeth, to delight in our pain, for it is sacred, akin to the pain of His Cross. Pray for us, Holy Elizabeth, that we may be made worthy of the promises of Christ. Amen. Hosanna in the highest."

She hangs up without saying goodbye. I hold the phone to my ear until the echo fades away completely. I swing my body around the pivot of my heavy heart, and face the cozy scene in the living room again.

There's nothing I can say. I don't get to say anything.

47

I open the mailbox. There's the usual Columbia House envelope flogging sanitized, sugary punk-pop, the power bill, and, hilariously, a subscription to *Chatelaine* magazine, addressed to Norman, Elizabeet. Finally, one precious and rare object, an actual piece of mail, for me, my name handwritten in purple Sharpie in big letters on the front of a large manila envelope, folded in two to fit into the box. No return address. I open it on the front step, thinking no one but Gay Stevie would send me something so mysterious. There's about ten pages of thick, expensive drawing paper, filled with ragged handwriting in coloured marker, salmon-pink, olive and teal.

Dear Teresa,

I'm a shithead. In case you haven't come to that conclusion yourself in the past few weeks, I thought I'd point it out. I know that explanatory letters for abrupt disappearances are passé, and that it's awfully old-fashioned for me to be doing this, but I'm too chicken to phone you and don't have your e-mail address, so here goes. I don't really have any excuses for not calling you in the past three weeks, but that's not going to stop me from saying I'm sorry anyway and attempting to explain the situation.

I turn the sheaf of paper over to find out for sure who it's from, and there's her name, signed in pink Sharpie, underlined, with a couple of xs and a heart. My eyes go out of focus. I sit down quickly in the doorway. Above her name is something about newborn kittens. Do I want a newborn kitten. I wipe my eyes and shuffle back through the letter. The first four whole pages are dedicated to what seems to be a blow-by-blow account of fracturing her tailbone, developing a yeast infection and midwifing her cat's birth, all at once. Then the Sharpie changes to brown and it's something about fucking up. Excuses. Fucking up. Guilt about fucking me over. Feeling fucked and being depressed about it. I'm the only person she'd ever want to go inside the Wildlife Museum with. Did I know what she meant by that? I'm the one she dreams about. Do I get it? In grey on page six: I want that beautiful memory kept intact. On the next page it turns to orange. How she got back with her ex-boyfriend. Three days after Trinity. How it was because of me. How I'd showed her what she had inside. Her generosity. Scarlet: I deserve happiness and should hold out for it. There's someone out there who is waiting to find me and kiss me on my pretty mouth, she promises.

I fold the pieces of paper up and put them back inside the envelope. She's put some other shit in there too. My Wonder Woman underwear, washed and neatly rolled up. They smell like detergent. Springtime Fresh. I'm holding a pair of panties to my face, clinging to them, while sitting on my front step. Pretty sick.

The fucking bums in the park are giving me pitying looks from across the street. They're my panties, people, don't judge! I shove them back in the envelope and haul out the last little thing. A ripped and crumbling fragment of something. A leaf of the Bible, from Ireland's Eye.

I start crying in my open doorway, my bare legs sprawled out on the curb. The image of her there inside the steeple. The rain. Her eyes, looking upwards. What I've been trying not to think about. Her dazzled expression. How tenderly I felt. My heart inside my chest, filling it. How alive I was. How it felt to be there with her, there together at the beginning of something.

I stand up and go inside, put the envelope in the recycling bin. I wash my face, burn some incense, make a pot of coffee. Put on my sweatpants and decide to clean out the basement.

I won't think about her anymore. I shall strike her name from my memory. I will clean my house and thus cleanse my spirit. I'll harden up my guts. I'll seal myself shut, turn those little throbbing bits back into stone. I had my shot, it was stupid. I can't feel any kind of L-thing. I'd rather die. I should have known.

48

My family doesn't know how handy their birthday gifts are. I have the warm new nightie that Dad gave me on underneath my snowpants, I have the sealskin kamiks that Nancy made for me on my feet. She sewed caribou-fur tulips around the top edge. They fit like a glove. The picture that Evan drew for me is tucked between my skin and the thick elastic on the bottom of my training bra. It's of Evan and me and Dad and Nance, with Mom in the corner, in a black-crayoned box separate and above everyone else. He's forgotten one of the E's in my name. The guy that is Dad has a big gut, and the little girl that is me stands next to an inukshuk, my arm around its rocky neck. Evan's smart.

I've also packed my new camera, freshly loaded with its first roll of film, my copy of *Romeo and Juliet,* a flashlight, my toothbrush, and a slice of leftover cake, for Willassie. The essentials. We all leave for our "sleepover" and head quickly to Mina's house. She hugs me and I can feel my ribs shifting beneath the squeeze. They all hug me.

"Have fun, Quanniq," Carla says.

"Thank you."

"Listen, you make sure he takes it out before he's gonna come."

"Come where?" I say.

"Just try not to get it inside yourself."

I realize that she's referring to his sperm. That tonight Willassie will insert his reproductive organs into my own and wriggle them around inside of me.

"Now go wait in the shed," Mina says.

They go inside, Mina's kamiks slipping noiselessly on the linoleum, the other two in squeaky Qallunaat-style boots. I go into the shed and sit on my tire in the corner, and wait. I sing myself a song Mom taught me.

She's like the swallow that flies so high
She's like the river that never runs dry
She's like the sunshine upon the lee shore
She's lost her love and she'll love no more

I don't know what a lee shore is. It sounds tiny and remote, maybe undiscovered. An undiscovered shore. I wonder how many of those are left in the world, shores no person has ever stood on, dragged their boat up on, split fish on, cut up walrus carcasses on, watched capelin beach themselves on, suntanned on, skipped stones on, had bonfires on. Where no one's ever sat and listened to the roaring of the water. Down in our haunted valley, facing out towards the ocean, I could swear I was at home on Middle Cove beach. The exact same sound. When I turn, though, and there are no trees and there's no road sloping down, I have to admit that I'm still in Sanikiluaq. I can't remember the second verse to my song, but it doesn't matter. I hum and fiddle with the camera, focusing on different things in the shed. I take a picture of the weird walrus-man that Willassie's working on. It weighs so much that he has to get someone else to help him move it. The walrus-man is wrestling something that doesn't quite have shape yet. Maybe a dog. I bring the chisel marks into focus. This camera makes me see things I wouldn't notice before. The whiteness of dust particles on a piece of dark green stone.

Willassie stops in the doorway with a serious face and his arm extended. I take his picture. This makes him smile. He walks right to me and puts both his hands on the top of my head. They cover the whole thing. He gives me the longest, slowest, warmest kiss. I feel like I might die from any sudden movement.

"Happy birthday, Quanniq." In the innermost part of my ear the cilia jump around.

He leads me out into the night. We hold each other tight and run like we're in a three-legged race. He takes enormous leaps that I need three steps to keep up with. I'm glad I'm wearing my new kamiks which allow me to move faster on the snow than Qallunaat boots. Made out of sealskin, they're used to it. When we're nearly at the igloo, Willassie makes me stop and turn to face the school. He tells me to stay there while he goes ahead. He says for me to wait for him.

Looking at the back of the school is pretty boring. I look up instead. Billions of tiny pinholes in a thick curtain. So much light that it isn't really dark outside, once you let your eyes adjust. Mom and I would sometimes drive out to Flatrock in the middle of the night to go stargazing, away from the glare of the city's lights. She taught me how to look sideways at stars. When you stare at them directly, they get shy and dim their shine. It's only when you nonchalantly appear to be looking somewhere else that the stars truly let themselves go, swelling with light in your periphery. I look at the northern stars this way, letting my eyes haze over. When we went to Flatrock, Mom would tell me the old Greek stories about the stars. We had a book. We'd lie out there on the cliff, with the waves crashing away below us, wrapped in our coats. Mom would tell me most often of Artemis, who was the virgin goddess of the hunt, and her consort, Orion, who was a giant. Artemis's brother, Apollo, didn't think goddesses should be knocking around with lowly giants, so he came up with a plan. He challenged her to a bow and arrow competition to hit an object far out at sea. Apollo knew she was a perfect shot. She won without breaking a sweat and was very proud of herself till she found out that the target was her lover's head. Her arrow right through the skin and bone of it. Now they chase each other around the sky in star form, and will for all eternity, but anyone can see that it's a lost cause. There's all the vastness of space between them.

Sometimes Mom would cry a little when we lay out on the cliffs. I'd hold her hand and rummage around for Kleenex, pretending I didn't know what was wrong. She'd say it was just in sympathy for the giant with the arrow through his brain, but I could tell that her poor tender heart was breaking, and maybe other parts of her as well. It was obvious.

I hate the thought that Dad left her alone while she was like that. That their love went away, poof! Evaporated. That love can do that, just leave you alone some day. By the time Willassie gets back to me, I'm sad. I can't help it. For sure he won't understand, so I don't tell him about my mother sobbing on the cliffs till the sun came up while I huddled in a ball beside her. I certainly don't tell him about her crazy saints and lonely paintings and scrubbing my face so hard that time she caught me trying her lipstick on. The stain of Jezebel I was bringing down upon myself. I said I wanted to be like her. She said no one should ever want that. Removing doorknobs so no one can get into the house. Painting on everything: the fridge, the stove.

Dad with his voice too loud. "You're painting us out of this fucking house. You're doing it. You're doing this, Elizabeth, this isn't me." Evan's crashing dinkies in his room. I'm in my bed with a book to read and ears made of stone.

"You're doing this. I can't fix it. I can't fix everything, I can't do anything about this, I'm not a superhuman, you seem to think you're married to a superhero, I'm not the Green Lantern, Elizabeth, I am not Clark Kent. These kids are getting messed up, don't you see how she shies away from people, don't you see how I'm not doing that, don't you think when your kid goes to get a glass of milk there shouldn't be a painting of the crucifixion on the damn fridge door, staring her in the face. I don't care if He's smiling. Don't you get how you're not just hurting yourself now, she can't even make any friends, Neville's been talking to me and it's getting worse, she's reading too many books. Yes, books are good, but they can't replace people. She never talks to the other kids. I can't trust you to be alone with them. I'm sorry, but you're not the same person I married. I know that's a cliché, but clichés exist because they're true. I'm sorry if I'm being unsympathetic. I can't anymore. I can't deal with you. I can't live like this. I don't want her to. He's small enough to get through this, but look at her and tell me you're not messing something up. Look at her. She's got the eyes of an old lady already. She looks older than my fucking mother. And I don't need to start in about myself. There's twice as much money. We'll talk to you on the phone. You'll feel better. It'll be less stress. More room. Rest.

Quiet. No more kids yelling. You can paint, that's what you said you needed, isn't it? You could make some paintings that aren't attached to our furniture and maybe even sell them. Remember doing that? Remember making a living, Elizabeth? Remember working? Do you? Because the market is waiting for you to make some more work. You're very talented. You know that. You just have to get down to it. Just start to work. On something that isn't our washer and dryer. Try a piece of canvas. Try something other than the bloody Last Temptation, for Christ's sake. You've got to shake yourself out of this. Take care of yourself. The kids won't forget you. I won't forget you, but. I love you, yes, I love you. Don't, please don't start. Yes. Yes, I love you. But. It's too hard. This doesn't work, and it hasn't for a while now."

And even though I've asked the fairies to turn my ears to stone, I can hear every stupid syllable of every fucking word.

When Willassie asks me if I'm okay, I don't say anything. I don't want him to worry. I pretend that I'm not afraid of turning into my mother when I grow up. I pretend that I have no reason to lose my mind, although I do. It runs in the family. I pretend there's nothing wrong, that I'm completely happy and can think of nothing but my own Willassie, inside this perfect cold night with no one else around and the entire sky shining down clear and bright upon us, lighting us up. Pretending to be happy is what people in love do. Willassie takes my hand and turns me around to face the igloo, now glowing warm and orange through all the chinks and seams. He's lit it up from the inside.

"It's a good thing your birthday is now. A few days more and this whole igloo will just be water. It's soon spring."

"Carry me inside like a proper gentleman," I command.

He kisses my mitten and kneels down. "Okay, Miss Teresa,

but it's gonna be on my back like this. The door is very low."

I sling my leg over him. He carries me horse-style on his hands and knees through the entrance tunnel. I have to flatten myself to his back, the ceiling's so low. Not exactly textbook romance, but pretty perfect. To reward my steed, I kiss his horsey neck. He whinnies softly, stands up, and takes me to our bed.

We sit awhile and look at each other in the light of the seal-oil lamps. I remember about the cake. I watch Willassie eat it and I take a picture of him there, with a little bit of icing on his chin, all glowing and beautiful. I want to remember the way this feels forever. I want to remember how it feels to be here, sitting with my one true love in the thick, jittery anticipation before we come together like adults do. I've got butterflies in my stomach, like they say happens. Also some of those prehistoric moths that are as big as dinner plates.

Before he gets undressed I make him blow the kuudliqs out. The only way I can do this is in total, conspiratorial darkness.

49

Crayfish Aftertaste are back! The Aftertaste Forever! It's Mark's first gig since getting back from the fringe circuit, and the whole damn town seems to have showed up to drink their faces off. Rock on. I'm so drunk I could lie down on the bar and float away to the ends of the earth on the ocean of beer I've consumed tonight. I've drowned every part of myself, except for my ears. My eardrums are alert, ready for action, getting action, getting itchy inside with sound. Mark is the best singer in the entire universe and no one in this bar can deny it. I'm gonna stop thinking forever and I'm also gonna stop feeling anything. I'm just gonna hear stuff and taste stuff. Just use my senses. Like an animal. No explanations, no feelings. Just the action, the thing that needs doing. The impulse, the reflex. The fuck and the kill.

I'm leaning on the pole in the middle of The Ship, the one that's painted like a mermaid. Someone's put a picture of Rex Murphy's gorgeous pout over the mermaid's face. Her arms cross behind my head, holding me up. I want my best friend Mark to sing so hard in my direction that he cuts a wake straight to me, through the sea of sixteen-year-old snots shaking their shiny little asses. The slight but wobbly flesh on their upper arms so scarily hairless. Then they'll all know that I'm the one at the centre of the song, and everyone knows that if you can't be a Famous Artist (FA) yourself, the next best thing is to be the Muse of a Famous Artist (MFA). I want to glow, visibly.

I jump higher than all those other girls. Even though it aches, I can't stop grinning. I close my eyes and jump in circles, tight high circles at the back of the dance floor. I'm dancing on other people's feet but they don't care because I'm so full of music that it's oozing out of me like light. The music and I have clear ownership of one another. The songs are too short and there aren't enough of them. I want to dance till my legs fall off and my brain gets jiggled to shit and I can do nothing but lie stunned and trusting and legless on the floor. I want someone Mark or non-Mark to come and touch me, lightly touch me on the shoulder or maybe the base of my skull, the occipital bone, just one finger, just briefly, girl finger boy finger I don't care finger, just for one second, to remind me that I'm here and these are my people. Not the lycra mass of jailbait, but the music people, the meaning in abstraction people, the archaic notions people, the impulsive people, the self-abusive people, the self-mythologizing people, the people obsessed with people, with specific types or shapes of people, the gourmand people and the ascetic people, the really shy people and the feral, slouching idols. The ragged, hand-sewn people. The hand-drum people, the shroom eaters, the pot smokers, the ones slouched in the corner making notes for novels on their napkins, the dream makers, the poets, the clowns and puppeteers, the modern dancers, the yoga masters, the macrobiotic health nazis, the actors—yes, the actors!—the activists, the radicals, the shit-talkers, the experimentalists and the plain old-fashioned drunks. The man who helped invent Spellcheck, God bless his heart.

These are my people. Why should I feel ashamed if I can't stand up when I'm amongst my people? They'll pick me up if I fall over with drinking, they'll let me sleep on their couch. They won't ask about my obvious depression, but maybe in the morning after tea and toast they'll walk me to the corner and see me on my way with fraternal concern. I'll walk home slowly, full of the weight of the morning with the crusts of mascara falling scale-like from my eyes. I won't be sad about fucking Delith and her fucking yeast infection and her shitty boyfriend, or anything else. I will thank my people for preserving my dignity to the full extent of their capabilities while my dumb old heart comes around.

I slowly edge down the mermaid pole till my butt touches the moist carpet. Even with my ass petrifying itself in a pool of Jamieson's, this is heaven. I'm never moving. Or if I do it'll only be to jump up and down on as many of my people as possible, forcing them to touch me, to hug me or push me, I don't really care which. I just want to be the subject of physical energy, of intent to touch. Some friction of skin.

Now that I'm on the floor, there's nothing but feet. Sally Ann army boots, expensive sneakers and strappy platforms below neatly nicked ankles, hastily shaved in scummy tubs. A pair of steel-toed boots with paint flecks, gallery-white. Mark's shoes. He's huge. He's going to fall on me. I put my arms up to protect my giant soft baby head and he grabs me. Human contact. His thumb is pressing into the hollow of my wrist. He wants me to get up, he doesn't want to crouch. People will kick his back and he'll resent them for it. He doesn't want to resent anybody. I can see him trying. He doesn't want to resent me for being so upset that I'm fucking piss-loaded like an amateur, except I think he's loaded too. He hates me for being so sad, except he's sad too. I'm crying now. Mark's hugging me. "Whoever's making you so sad is going to get his ass kicked."

"Thanks, man."

"Who is it?"

"Never mind."

"Come on."

"I'm embarrassed."

"Come on, girly. Tell me."

"You don't want to know."

"Want to bet?"

"I'm betting."

"Do I know him?"

"It's Delith."

Mark says "oh," but maybe it's actually "no," and I just misheard because of the beer in my ears. He's disappointed that he didn't know everything about me. He doesn't like it when I change. He doesn't say anything else. It's the end of the conversation before I even find out what he thinks about this. I know Mark, and from now on he'll pretend he doesn't know what I'm talking about. He's the expert of emotional delay, of deflecting anything tricky. I must admit, I'm jealous of this ability. Sometimes I cry so much that my face chaps and bleeds under the eyes. The day I got that fucking letter, I barely cried at all. I held it in, and then that night when I got in bed I sobbed so hard that the salt water ran into my ears and chapped them too. No one is worth chapped ears, not even Delith. My skin almost as sore as that time Mr. Fuckhead swung me around in science class and I skidded on my face on the carpet. Nowadays a teacher caught doing shit like that would be blacklisted. I think Dad said that eventually he was promoted to some school board job in Manitoba somewhere.

I put my cheek against the carpet to see if it's rough or soft. Mark picks me up and chucks me over his shoulder like I'm something he shot out in the woods and is dragging home to gut. My people recede away from me, inverted and jiggling. I wave to them and blow kisses to the sound man on his gummy plastic chair. Mark is removing me from the people. Bastard. I run my ice-cold hands up under his shirt to make him stop, to make him reunite me with the people, who need me. "Specifically me, don't you see. Without me, this evening will be missing one detail, one essential detail. Without me, it's David without the slingshot. David without the slingshot is just a naked dude. How can you deprive the people of their slingshot, you A-hole?" And so on, as the street jiggles backwards and upside down, away from me.

There are stairs and there's a couch. "Couch is a funny word. Turn the u upside down, you've got a seashell."

"Pretty clever, T."

"Turn me upside down, you've got a mermaid. I need to dance some more."

"You need to sleep."

"I need a fucking lover. For fuck's sake. Lover, oh anonymous lover of the future, yoohoo! Where are you? Hello? Someone! Anyone! Please!"

"Shhh. There, there." He pats my head. His voice is more beautiful in the quiet with his neighbour peeing loudly through the thin wall and the Void, the Slip, the Fall waiting to gobble me up the moment that I dare to close my eyes. "You're my guard dog, my angel. The goddamned wind beneath my wings."

"Sing that and it's over between us. I'm serious. No more crazy foreplay or equally crazy sex."

"Speaking of sex, where was Solange tonight?"

He says nothing.

"You broke up with her? Say you didn't break up with her. What'd you do, leave her in Regina?"

Nothing. Nada.

"So long, Solange, hey buddy? It was the two-month limit? Freaked you out?"

"You know me."

"Jesus Christ, Mark." The room is spinning, worse now that I'm lying down. I am going to quit drinking. I am going to quit drinking. "Jesus, you're a fucknut. That chick loved you, dude. She loved you. I mean, I fucking hated her, but she loved you. And I didn't hate her. I didn't know her. I knew her enough to know she loved you. Anyone could see it. Do you know how long it could be before something like that happens again?"

"Yeah."

"Like, maybe never."

"Yeah."

"So?"

"So what, for fuck's sake?" He plows around and kicks the furniture.

"Why? Just because of your stupid two-month rule, which is like the lamest rule ever made, and I can't believe you even bring it up in conversation with people. So, because of your stupid rule, you have to break up with every girl before things get going, even if they love you? That's retarded. That's retarded to the max.

Dude, you're so fucked up."

"Fuck you, Teresa."

"She loved you."

"Fuck off, honey."

"I'm just saying."

"Teresa, please."

"Just saying, all right. You do this every time. You need to figure out how to deal instead of freaking out, dude."

"Stop saying dude."

"Sorry. You need to deal."

"I didn't love her."

"You didn't let yourself love her."

"No."

"You didn't let yourself love her. You could've loved her. I bet if you'd given her a chance you could've loved her. Did you even try?"

He shakes his head.

"You didn't try. You didn't wait. She didn't have enough time."

"No. I wanted to feel like shit over someone. And I couldn't. I couldn't. I don't know what the fuck is wrong with me. Of course I wanted to."

I'm crying now, wiping my nose in the tail of Mark's shirt as he stands in front of the couch. I pull him down by the hand. He huddles into my belly. We're both very sad. We're both drunk and weepy.

"Why can't I love someone?" he says into my stomach.

"You will."

"When? I'm old."

"You're not that old."

"Why can't you be my girlfriend?"

"Mark," I say. "Do you have to be like this right now?"

"I'm kidding, T. Fuck."

"Good."

"But we almost love each other enough."

"Mark."

"We almost love each other enough to love each other forever."

"We love each other, honey. But."

"Yeah. But."

He wipes his snot on my knee and I smack him softly on the arm. His eyes are rimmed in soft pink, from crying. Bunny eyes. "I feel like I'm you, I'm so sad," he says. "Am I a headcase? Someone, please, tell me if I'm crazy!"

"Stabs at my mental health are not cool."

"Sorry."

"Mom's crazy."

"Your mom's a genius."

"She's fucking bipolar."

"She's also a genius."

"That kind of shit is hereditary, you know."

"Lucky you."

"You're funny."

"What?"

"Can we just go to sleep?"

"Sorry," he says.

"I'm really drunk."

Mark sighs. "I am too. Don't tell anyone I said that shit, all right. It can't leave this room. I don't know what's wrong with me."

"No one'll know the tin man has a heart. Don't worry."

"Sweet dreams."

"Don't let the bedbugs bite."

I close my eyes and start to drift a little, through the tilting feeling, into sleep. Mark stays crunched into my belly. He's nice and warm and smells like The Ship. Cigarettes and weed and local beer. It's comforting. He's talking. I try to stay awake, but I'm falling.

"Isn't 'but' the worst word in the English language?" he says. "You're brilliant, but. You're perfect, but."

"Yeah. It sucks."

"I love you, but."

"Mark. Count the little sheepies."

He covers his face with the blanket. I can't make out what he's saying. He's never acted like this before. I'm totally loaded. Is he crying under there? I rub his back. I can feel the hard spots where he holds shit in. He keeps the blanket over his face. I wait. I wait to make sense of what he's saying or just to wait, to be in contact, to communicate something with the warmth of my hand through the ratty blanket through his shirt onto his skin and through it, into the muscle and nerve and hard shitty bits and bone and guts and heart, all of it. He keeps talking into his own little vacuum, talking to himself I guess. I wait for him to come back into the room with me.

"But what?" That's what he's saying. "But what?"

I rub his back. I rub up and down the column of his spine. He's so fucking sad. I smooth the bumps out of his shirt.

"But what? But what?"

50

With the lamps blown out, it's better. This hot skin on mine is the skin of my one true love. It burns me in the places where my flannel nightie has been pushed aside, unbuttoned, twisted and fondled as though it were also a part of my body. The heavy feeling of his mouth. I can't let myself go completely. If I try to relax into the feeling of the kissing, the hot skin, the gentle tracing of his fingers, then I'll start thinking about what sex is for, which is to procreate. To make babies. I'll think about babies, about Carla's beginning of a baby, and how technically my body is ready to make babies too. All it takes is your period. Period. I don't want to think about how we all used to be babies, about how I used to be a baby and how that means my parents had sex. How, when I was conceived, they were in love so deep they could barely breathe. They vowed never to leave each other. Under that willow tree. He did up her shoe. Now Dad's rubbing Nance's thigh under the dinner table and Mom is ripping her hair out and painting the Sacred Heart on her chest of drawers. And there's nothing she can do and there's really nothing he can do, either.

Love just went away. I can't think about that right now, because I might cry. Not only that, I might throw up into my true love's beautiful mouth.

I need all my strength to make it through tonight without vomiting or crying. Mental discipline. It's all got to do with ignoring the bad thoughts and only letting the good ones in. It's about shutting out all the paranoid, tupilak voices that are whispering to me about Marguerite. How Willassie liked me better with my Tiffany hair because I looked more like her. How I'm sure she had bigger breasts than me, and no sickitating hairs growing out down there, and probably no bruises from crotch tag either. How, this whole time, Willassie's going to think about how much better it was to have sex with her than with me. How I don't know what I'm doing. The dictionary and Shakespeare's *Collected Works* didn't tell me everything.

He wants to keep a lamp lit, to look at me, but I won't let him. I won't let him touch me down there. When the time comes, it's me who reaches down and guides his penis in. It's smoother than the rest of him, with wormy ridges of vein under the skin. It's warm. His wiener. Dickie bird. He moves gently. Even so, I'm not very big—in fact I'm very small—and with each soft push I leak tears out of the corners of my eyes and into my ears, feeling my skin straining, trying to stretch. Sighing, saying "Yes." Saying "I love you. You make me feel so nice. Please, yes." I say all the things I think I'm supposed to say, based on the soap operas, and the tears start falling in their slow streams on either side of my face, leaking down onto the caribou hides. Willassie is sighing, his hands wandering sometimes to lightly brush my nipples, maybe making sure they're still there, I don't know. Every so often he attempts to feel his way further down, further into intimate territory, until I distract him by kissing his face, his smooth arms and his smooth hot chest. I grab his bum, so strong and perfectly round. Willassie moves deeper inside me. I feel something give way. I cry out and he thinks it's because I'm happy. His hot sperm comes spilling out over and inside me, stinging in where the new rips of flesh are. Carla's going to be upset with me. I grip the hide so tight the ends of fur cut into my palms. Willassie covers my face with kisses and I struggle to keep breathing.

"I love you," I say. He kisses me again.

He scooches down to lay his head on my chest. I cuddle him like he's a little baby. I softly stroke his forehead. My precious relic. I worship this skin, these ears. We lie together and he drifts off to sleep. My heart sounds like a Salvation Army drum. I can feel him twitch with the effort of some dream state arm-wrestling match or komatik race. He grunts softly and his shoulder jerks into my rib cage. I imagine his komatik hitting a rock, Willassie holding on for dear life off the side, jolted out of equilibrium. Calm, even though he could've died. When I cry, I do it silently, so he won't wake up.

When I finally sleep, I dream I'm Saint Elizabeth, handing Jesus the relay baton. In my dream, He's delighted when I take his place. He especially enjoys divesting me of my clothing. Jesus looks good in my new nightdress. He smoothes the lace out with his womanish fingers and saunters away across the tundra. On my cross of ice there's no need for nails. I stick there with my own freezing rivers of snot, blood and sweat. Like a tongue to the flagpole. My tears form thick bands of ice which divide my face in three.

I am my own triptych, to use the correct artistic terminology.

51

There's nothing so awkward as dinner on your birthday with friends and relatives who are sick and tired of your shoddy behaviour, especially when you agree. I'm turning twenty-five today, and I feel like lying down and giving up. I'm not worth the effort it takes to drag myself from place to place. I've dug myself into a pit of despair and there is no hope of climbing out of it, not when my father sits across from me with his eyes unfocused and shallow as puddles. Bereft. It's my birthday, and that day is one we'd both much rather forget.

Instead, we dress in our most respectable clothes and pick up Mark and go to India Gate. We eat luscious, rich platefuls of baigan masala and navrattan curry. We suck the cool lassi down our parched throats. We drown everything in tamarind sauce, and we pretend that this eating is the celebrational kind, when really we're eating to fill a gap, to fill up quickly the gaping maw of sadness that surrounds this accursed day. Blackest of black.

My mother was asleep when I called her. I left a message with a nurse named Cheryl, but no one called back. What odds, probably would've been agony anyway. Nanny Norman called and asked if I had a boyfriend yet. I refused to answer and she said she was just tormenting me, no need to get upset. Which I wasn't. She put Evan on the phone. I said hello and he forced out a Happy Birthday. I asked him how school was going. He said he had to go. I could hear him sit down again at the table as Nan picked up the phone.

"Evan had to go out," she said. "He's got hockey practice."

In the background I could hear him telling Misty to roll over. "Good Misty."

This isn't my brother. "Good girl," he was saying, "good girl, Misty." This isn't my fucking brother, not the one from before, from when he was small. Before all that court and before he had to go live with Nan during the first year, what with all the lawyer crap going on and my unstable condition and Mom's too. Those temperamental Norman Ladies and their Unpredictable Behaviour. Before. When he went to live out in Port Rexton while the trial was on and after it was over too, when he didn't want to come back. He was seven (that was his nickname too, Seven) and he decided he didn't want to come home, ever. He said, "I hate you, Teresa. I only love Nanny and I really hate you."

"What about Mom and Dad?" I said.

"Who're they?" he said. "Who's that?"

After that, any smile from Evan was only the possibility of a smile, a manipulation of the most superficial facial muscles. He built anti-Teresa deflector shields, and really I couldn't blame him for it, so I never tried too hard to knock them down. And the longer we go without communicating, the harder it is to start.

340

Any other day but my fucking birthday and I would've just hung up. Good girl, roll over. But today I said to Nan, "Put my brother back on."

"He's gone out the door by now."

"Nanny, I can hear him. Put him on the phone, will you?"

She covered the receiver and after a second or two of listening to the smother of it in her moist old palm I heard her cough and put the phone back up to her ear.

"No, I checked the house, he's out, my love. Call back around 8:30 and he might be home."

"Hearing things, am I?"

Nan paused long enough to let me know just how possible she thought that was.

"Now, lovey."

"I can't believe you're covering for him."

She sighed. "Oh my. He's gone out, you understand?"

"Oh, fuck then," I say.

"Teresa Eleanor Norman, the tongue!"

"No, fuck it. Fuck it, okay? This is mean. It's mean, it's my birthday."

"Teresa…"

"All I want is to fucking talk to my brother for longer than ten seconds. Is that a crime? Is it? Is that a crime?"

"I can't talk to you when you get like this," she said.

"Like what?"

"You're the emotional kind, Teresa. You know who you take after." A low blow. I attempt restraint.

"I just want to talk to Evan. I can hear him talking to the dog."

"Since when have you been so desperate to get ahold of him?"

"Since now. Since now, all right? So put him on the phone, please, or I'm going to be really upset. "

"If you're having a mood, there's no need to take it out on the rest of us. The rest of us are getting along fine."

"Are you? Great. Glad to hear it."

"Goodbye. I'm hanging up."

"Nan…" The bitch.

"Bye-bye."

"You hate me, you hate me," I said.

"Yes, the whole world hates you. That's how much you thinks of yourself."

As a last resort I said, "I'm having sex with women. Tell that to all your Bingo friends." But she'd already put the phone down, and was most likely re-enacting the most salient parts of what I'd said, for Evan's amusement. Mocking my uppity, Townified accent.

I help myself to more okra. Mark's asking about my most memorable birthday. My bile begins to churn the spices around. I lie and tell the story about Dad splitting the ass out of his pants at my bowling party. Mom wasn't there. She was home with Evan, who was still so tiny he couldn't walk yet. It was just me and Dad and my friends, like today. Without the resentment hanging thick in the air like the smell of pea soup on the stove.

Dad walks us to The Ship. He gives me sixty dollars and tells me not to drink it all, at least not all at once. I ask him for a hug and he thinks I'm joking. After the blowout with Nan I decide not to force anything.

"You know me," I say. "Jokey McJokenstein."

"Mark," Dad says, "you make sure she behaves herself."

Mark salutes and we head down the steps. God love Dad, even if he doesn't want Him to.

The Make-Work Project are playing. I hug everyone I know. I drink modestly expensive scotch, no water, no ice. Curtis and Vanessa come by to give me a spice rack they made. It's in the shape of the province and has my name burned into the Stephenville area. The guys in the band get me to bring it up to the front to show everyone. Jason, the drummer, holds it over his head. The bass player kisses me. He smells like tinned tomato sauce. There's scotch on the house, and bacchanalian revelry. A birthday mosh pit. I jump up and down with Curtis and we shout at each other about how gorgeous Vanessa looks standing over in the corner, chewing on her thumbnail and kicking at the wainscoting. Her long legs in thick black tights, her black hat. Attempting invisibility. Afterwards, Curtis kisses my hand. His moustache digs its little edges in. He tells me I'm a beautiful dancer and buys me a bag of Hawkin's Cheesies.

"Go on," I say, "you'll have me spoiled." He gives me a kiss on the cheek. I catch Vanessa's eye across the bar, and wink. She looks upset, and I wonder if Mark has talked to her since she came in. I tug on Curtis's elbow. We make our way over.

Vanessa reports that when she tried to talk to him, Mark dicked off out back. He's toking it up with the band, who are taking a break between sets. Vanessa wants to go home and work on her quilt.

"I'm sick of this city. It's like a wading pool. Pop asked Curtis and I to come out and stay for a while. He's getting lonely. I think moving out around the bay might be the answer to retaining my sanity. No one wants us around here, anyway."

Curtis is fingering the button on her cuff. "Come on, darling."

343

I realize she's about to cry. She laughs to herself and says, "I've committed the sin of being happy." I take her hand and lead her to the bathroom, tell Curtis to watch the drinks. We sit on the bench and I roll a joint.

"Dear Vanessa. It'll be all right."

"He hates me. He hates me."

"He loves you. That's the point."

"How can you just cut yourself off from your family? It's not normal."

"People do it all the time. My brother hasn't really spoken to me since we were kids. Mark's angry. That's not to say he won't come around."

"It's been so long now. I've been married nearly two years and Mark still hasn't acknowledged my presence yet."

"Dear Vanessa, don't cry." I wipe her face with my fingers. Her poor sad face is breaking my heart.

"Why is he punishing me?"

I kiss her forehead. "He can't understand what's going on. He doesn't trust it because he's never had anything so good happen to him."

"Poor bastard." She smiles a little.

"Yeah. He's old and sad."

"I'll say." She laughs, and blows her nose. "You have a brother? Why didn't I know that?"

We get Curtis and go out into the alley for a draw. Mark's still out there. He spits on the pavement and goes back inside when he sees us. Despite her bravado, Vanessa can't stay after that. Curtis leads her up the alleyway onto Duckworth Street, whispering "darling" into her hair as she sobs openly. I share my draw with Jason and the bassist. His name is Neil and he's also a poet. He brushes my ass with his palm on his way back inside and during the next set makes eyes at me. I make eyes back. Around three AM Gay Stevie shows up. He's got a flask of rum in his panties. We take a few swigs each and I go to find Mark and slap him around a bit.

"How's she going, buddy?" I say.

"Not bad. Quite the night. Are you loaded yet?"

"Nearly."

He turns around and orders me a scotch.

"You're going to have to forgive each other sometime," I say.

He's leaning on the bar. "Forgive who now?"

"This town's pretty small. You're going to disappear every time she shows up?"

"Maybe."

"She's your sister."

"So."

"It's Vanessa. You love her."

"Love's a construct."

"Oh please."

"Prove me wrong, then."

"God. I can't believe you. Stop being so stubborn about everything."

"Mind your own business."

"Fuck you," I say.

"Jesus," he says. "I don't need this shit."

"I'm not going to stop being friends with her. Or Curtis. He's really great."

"Just drop it."

"No."

"T, for real."

"What?"

"I said stay the fuck out of it." He looks at me. His eyes are miniatures. There's no affection left. Our friendship lies murdered on the dirty Ship carpet. They start to turn the lights on.

Gay Stevie and I head down to The Zone, which'll be open for a good while yet. In Sin City, the fags drink till the sun comes up. Till the suits are out on the pavement in the morning, sipping their coffee from Styrofoam cups, tripping on the drunken gaylords tipped out onto the sidewalk, stars still shining in their eyes, swooning with booze. Today I'm twenty-five and I'm going to drink myself to the other side: unconsciousness, death, the nuthouse door. I don't care which. It doesn't matter anymore.

52

It's the dead of night. Willassie is snoring and I'm just lying here. I'm not used to sharing a bed with someone. I get out my flashlight and read *Romeo and Juliet*. I pace the igloo in my kamiks. I take out my brother's drawing and look at it. I lift my nightdress up and examine the little crusts of blood. That's not so bad.

The air is old in here already. It smells like we've been living here all our lives, not just one night. As though this one night equalled whole lifetimes.

I put on my snowpants and parka and go outside. Down by the shore, I watch the sun come up. There's still ice for a ways out, and then slob all jammed up against itself, and then the open sea. I walk out on the ice as far as I dare. The air is so cold it cuts into my lungs and the sky is getting orange and pink like it's supposed to. If I was ever going to see a narwhal, now would be the time. I search the surface of the water for a glimpse of ivory horn. Every time a wave breaks there's a possibility that in the foamy white there's another white and it's the white of a narwhal's horn. Sea unicorn. Barely even real. In the sunrise there, in the glowing, sparring for territory, the clink of their horns drowned out in the noise of the waves and breakers. If I saw a narwhal, I'd be eternally blessed. It's considered extremely lucky. But most likely they're like regular unicorns and only show themselves to virgins.

I stay outside until the sun is up. I should sleep at least a tiny bit. I can't afford to be late getting home. If Dad ever found out about this, he'd see red and charge. Steam would come out of his earholes. I go back inside and lie down next to Willassie, who is so warm and limp with sleep that he doesn't flinch from the chill off my body. I snuggle my head into his side. I breathe with him, slow. And soon I know I'm sleeping.

In dreams I grow kelpy hair which swirls like peppermint through the clear, icy water. Small fish swim by. Marbles rolling across linoleum. My fingers float around me, trailing thin strings of blood. My pinky finger floats close to my eye. I can see the core of bone framed daintily by the layer of flesh all around it. It transforms itself into an arctic char, into a million arctic char who circle my head, swerving through the blood-threads. My thumb swells itself into a polar bear. I know that everything else is inevitable. In time the wounds will heal over into smooth nubs. A seal swims by and tickles my breasts. I let it nuzzle me. I feed it raisin bread with butter on it. My seal has deep black eyes and the softest fur. It brushes slowly down my torso and touches fire.

Willassie's head, hastily pulled back from my stomach, where he was tickling it with the thick prickle of his hair. He's looking where I didn't want him to look. I think maybe he might spit on it. God, let me faint and delay this moment. I'm hideous.

He brushes my bruises with his fingers. "I did this?"

"No, that's from crotch tag."

"You play the baby games still?"

"Shut up. Everyone does it."

"You're not a baby now, Quanniq." He kisses me. "You're my only girl."

I don't say anything.

"Quanniq." He's got my arms pinned on the hides. "Why are you sad for?"

I look at the melt-marks on the snow ceiling. He squeezes my wrists.

"Why are you sad?"

"I'm not sad," I say.

"Yes you are."

"No."

"Why are you sad?"

"I'm not your only girl."

"I told you Carla means nothing."

"Not Carla, Willassie. Not Carla."

"Who?"

"Not saying."

"Who?"

"I don't want to say."

"Say it." He squeezes my arms tighter.

"Nope."

"Yes. Say it."

"Marguerite."

It's like I've just shot off a gun. The air has that extra-quiet quality to it. Willassie stops breathing for a second, and for a second his eyes get full of stuff. Like a film.

"I am sorry you think that," he says.

"No, I'm sorry. Forget it."

"That was a long time before now."

"I know. I'm sorry."

"I was a kid then. I only want you now."

Willassie puts his thumbs on my cheekbones. His hands are heavy on my face. "You are the one who makes me crazy in the head. No one else can do this." He knocks my forehead with his own. "Yesterday you said you love me."

I try and look at something else, but there is nothing else. His one big eye above me.

"I want to hear you say that again." He puts his hand down there, and I flinch. I can't help it, there is no moaning feeling coming over me. I'm defective. He puts his hand there. I try to do nothing. Willassie kisses my eyelids. They cool with his spit in the morning air. He rubs my nose with his nose, an Eskimo Kiss. Now that's funny. Willassie kisses my neck in that river spot. It makes me feel like someone else. I feel different with his mouth there. I can picture the curving of my throat, white against the black of his hair, the hides and snow underneath us, the sunlight coming in through the chinks like exclamation points. The picture is beautiful and, because I'm in it, I must be beautiful too.

"Willassie."

"Mmm."

"What time is it?"

"Near nine." He keeps on kissing my neck. I try to concentrate.

"We should go soon. We don't want to get caught."

"It's Sunday. No one wants to come to school."

"I have to go home for lunch."

"Okay."

"We don't want to get caught."

He stops kissing me. He keeps his hand down there. He says, "Get up then."

I want to feel that thing I've heard about. "Don't stop. Please," I say. I want to make it right this time. I want to lose my body to the unbearable waves of feeling.

"I am going to make you say that thing again." He puts his finger up in there. It's so surprising that I gasp. There's a wriggle to it. His finger is sliding against me. It's soft, but it's insistent, it won't stop, I can't ignore it, there it goes, rubbing and rubbing away. I want desperately to love my love. I want my body to want him. I want that swooning sensation. I want the fantastic screaming feeling. Gigantafantasmatastic, that's my new word for how I want to feel. His penis is inside me. The cuts are cutting themselves brand new. I'm making those animal noises. Willassie makes them too. We make the noises together, they fill our ears. I howl from hurting and he thinks it's love. I think that it's love too. We hear nothing else. We don't hear the footsteps. We notice nothing until the door flap is lifted and the light comes in. There's a man standing there, with no face at all, because he's lit up from the back.

"Christ Almighty," he says, and the silhouettes of his fists swing around in the air.

53

Gay Stevie and I are at The Zone, which is not half as much fun as it promised to be. He's disappeared somewhere, and I swear to Jesus if it's to have the bum sex with some shitty old math teacher in the Little Boy's Room then there really will be hell to pay. But probably he's at the bar. I won't worry.

It's me versus the sea of fags in tight pants, touching each other. They're playing old-school Madonna and I'm still feeling sad. I have, however, perfected the technique of appearing outwardly serene, even if inwardly I'm racking my guts with sobs, so to the innocent bystander I appear to be having a nice time. Or as nice a time as one can have while indecently sloshed at a skanky gay bar with no dance partner at four-thirty AM on your fucking twenty-fifth birthday just after your best friend has cut you out of his life and your Nan and brother have also practically disowned you. I'm having just the nicest time. Seriously.

I paid the creepy cover man with the oil-slick eyes. I climbed the stairs in the harsh night lighting that's supposed to make you feel sexy and dangerous and subversive, but actually makes everyone look pallid and unwell. I checked my coat alongside the fun-fur jackets and pleather bombers. It camouflaged itself immediately. And then I did shooters, blue stuff, red stuff, peachy pink stuff, something that tasted like coconut and lime. I never do shooters. I'm opposed. Not the 1-800-FUK-MEUP, the 666, the 747 or the 911. No After Dark, After Eight or Afterbirth, no Ball and Chain, no Barney on Acid, no Beam Me Up Scotty. I would rather choke back a glass of powdered milk than drink a Bitter Pill. I don't do Blue Balls, I don't occasionally lean up against the bar and ask for a Buttery Nipple with a Cherry Kiss. No Cocaine Lady, Cowboy Cocksucker, Cunnilingus. No Dead Hitler, Dead Dog Vomit, Dirty Bong Water, Disco Ball, Double Pucker, Duck Fart, Duck's Ass, Duck Fuck and certainly no Duck Shit Inn, for shit's sake. No Easy Does It, no Eat Hot Death, no El Bastardo, and, for the well-being of mankind in general, do not try to get me to toss back an Eskimo Joe. Never that one.

Shooters are for engineering students and Stagette parties. Left to my own devices, no evil shooter would cross my lips. I am surprisingly vituperative about this. But tonight I promised to do whatever Gay Stevie wanted me to, because on a person's birthday, that's the rules. No free will, lots of sucked-back booze. My head is full of ghosts. I don't want to keep dancing, but stopping seems a more dangerous option at this point. Who knows what interrupting the momentum might do.

Some shitty slow song is playing. Some Mariah Carey crap. Gay men have no taste in music. No one can slow dance alone without looking like an asshole. I'll make as many sweeping generalizations as I want to. I look for something to lean against. The mirrored wall across from me is a psychological torture device. In it, all the girls have found other girls to put their arms around. They remind me of Delith. The buttery skin below her armpit. Inside her elbow. The underside of the arch of her foot, and her toes and ankles. Men are dancing close to one another, hands in back pockets, one prolonged kiss. There I am, too, the freakish white hair and paper-white skin. The shapeless pink dress, hopelessly inconsistent with the dark, throbbing mass of bodies all around me. I'll never hide myself here. In the mirror, I'm a pale afterimage superimposed on an already complete scene. A cheesy double-exposure, two and a half times per second, in the flashing of the strobe. I see myself in stills. Every third of a second there's a new, static image flashed up on the back of my eyeball, the light so bright I think I can see the inside, all the muscles in there. Blood in tiny vessels, pulsing everywhere I look, transparent, underneath the flashing images of what's really in the room. In the mirror I compose the picture. Self Portrait Inside Own Eyeball. Depressed at the Gay Bar, Study #1. That stripe across my throat is a blood vessel, my own, an enlarged and impossible projection of a blood vessel from inside my eye, full of blood, pulsing. Like a cherry-red garter snake or Angela Carter-style necklace, for Bluebeard's wife. I reach up to brush it off, like a creepy crawly mystery something that I hit at, quick, before I really know what it is. Like when a dead moth falls onto your face at night, from nowhere, and you fling it off, screaming, coming fully awake in the split second that the dry thing touched your skin. You bolt upright and think, irrationally, Death! The strobe flashes, you move from asleep to awake, two unrelated states of being, nothing but darkness in between. Like that.

I'm going to pull an Elizabeth Norman soon. I'm gonna go berserk. See Her Blind Herself With Science! See the Albino's Eyes Roll Back! No more, please, no blood vessel roping at my throat. No inside shit. I walk up to the mirrored wall. I press my face to my own face, hard, trying to crack the mirror between my eyes. To break it with frowning. To make the insides of me get lost already. Shove off, Self, you're smothering me. If this mirror girl would come to life, I'd have someone to dance with. She'd come home with me later, share my bed, never leave. That's sick. That's—what's that story? I peel my face off the mirror. A print of my nose and forehead is left behind, a greasy, fatheaded T. Narcissus. Happy Birthday to me.

All of a sudden I think I might puke. I hurry to the bathroom. I wait with my head hung over the toilet bowl, seeing if I have the urge to purge. I think about Mark and almost get something to come up. I don't want to leave this toilet stall. Or I want to leave it right now and start walking towards Signal Hill. Maybe I'll go hiking in my pink dress and combats at four in the morning like a whack job—might as well embrace your Living Heritage, Teresa—or maybe I'll just go to bed. I'll climb through the bathroom window. I'll drop the three storeys. I don't care. I can't go back into that bar, not even for my coat. I can't be anywhere there are other people. There are too many similarities. You and other people. Her and other people. People and other fucking people, always looking alike. I won't leave my house again. I won't sleep. I can't risk the accidental ambush. There's no way to drag myself forward in time, and fucking get over it, when every attempt I make just ends in new ghosts. Delith in my head like the memory of a dead lover, even though she's not dead, she just doesn't love me. Not that she made any promises. Not that she said she would.

You're not dead either. I don't think you are. But you live in my past and that's as good as dead, really. That shit can't survive the other shit. The bad shit. There's a reason that all the world's most celebrated love stories are made up. Mark is sloughing me off, like dead skin. Evan would rather communicate with fucking Misty than with me. Someone's knocking on my stall. I try to sound chipper. "There's someone in here already."

"Teresa. What's happening?"

"This is the girl's washroom, Stevie."

"Oh, formalities. Open up."

"Why?"

"Because I know you're not taking a leak in there. You're having some kind of existential crisis, and those happen to be my specialty. I have anti-existential powers."

"Like what?"

"Besides the buckets and buckets o' love?"

"Yeah."

"I have a birthday surprise for you."

"Yeah?"

"Uh-huh."

"Is it drugs?"

"Teresa! My stars!" Gay Stevie's being his mother now. What a card.

"It's drugs, isn't it."

"Once we go outside and smoke the drugs, I think the surprise will present itself."

I have no idea what that means. I don't really want to come out of the washroom, but I know that I should. Otherwise I'm just acting immature. Heaven forbid.

"Come out, come out, wherever you are!"

I sniffle. "Why don't you come in."

"Not usually my style, honey, but hell, anything for you."

Gay Stevie hoists himself over the top of the toilet stall somehow, the crazy bastard. He hurls himself in on top of me. I shield my face and narrowly miss getting plowed into the napkin disposal unit.

"Now everyone's going to think we're doing it," he crows. He pulls up his shirt seductively to reveal two gorgeous fat joints stuck into the waistband of his pants.

"That's a hell of a lot of drugs for two people," I say.

"Happy birthday, Bella."

"Who are we meeting, Stevie?"

"Just come on." He takes my hand and opens the stall door. He pulls me out of the bathroom into the thick air of the bar. The strobe is off now, thank you Merciful Jesus. He gets our coats. Gay Stevie gestures with flamenco hands towards the back door, out to the alleyway. I follow him into the crisp night, our breath in faint clouds around our heads. He baptizes Joint #1 and lights her up. I do a little soft-shoe in the dirt around him.

"My stars!" he says.

"My stars!"

We gad about in the alley like both of us are Gay Stevie's mom. According to legend, that's what she said when he told her, age eleven, that he was a homosexual. She didn't cry or laugh or disown him or anything. Just fanned her face and said, "my stars."

"So where's the surprise, anyway?" I say.

"What?"

"You said there was a birthday surprise that would appear."

"Right. My stars!"

"Your stars!"

"You have to close your eyes, first of all."

"Okay."

"Then I'm going to go away for a minute. I'll be back post-haste."

"With wonders untold."

"That's right."

"Okay then."

I do what he says. I can't think of any reason why not. These kinds of surprise-type things always freak me out. Secretly, I'm hoping it's Delith, that she's here somewhere. Okay, not even all that secretly. I really hope he's hidden Delith in some seedy little corner of The Zone and now she's going to appear. She'll brush away my tears with her pinky finger and fix the collar of my dress. She'll bring me a birthday cupcake with one candle sunk into the icing. "These past few months have been a mistake. I've finally realized that you're worth the hassle of changing my definition of myself. My patterns. Not everyone's worth that much energy." There'll be icing on her thumb, which she'll hold up for me to taste.

Gay Stevie grabs my shoulder and I jump about a foot. He takes my hand and leads me around the corner to the fire escape. There, under the stairs, he's lit up about thirty or forty tea lights. They illuminate the brick wall, sheltered from the elements. The green lettering is fresh and fastidiously neat:

MY HEART BEATS

T WITH BLOOD AS

RED AS THE ENVY

OF EVERY OTHER

(HU)MAN

"I can't believe you did this!" I exclaim.

"Say you'll never leave me."

"Oh, Stevie. This is the most romantic moment of my life."

The letters seem to undulate in the candlelight. Gay Stevie lights the second joint. We sit on the dank ground under the fire escape, admiring his brushwork. I tell Gay Stevie how much I love him. He says the same to me. Then he wants to go back inside. They're playing The Strokes, who he thinks are deadly. We decide not to squander it. Could be George Michael from here on in. We head back inside, past the irksome doorman, putting our stamped hands up to the light.

We do a kind of frenetic pseudo-Charleston that quickly clears a space on the dance floor. No one wants to lose an eye to us. We shake our limbs like we're having acid-induced seizures. We grin and whoop and spin each other around. Gay Stevie kisses me on the mouth, a little indecently. I give him some tongue just to see what he'll do. I accomplish the impossible and actually make him blush.

"I rule!" I shout. All the dykes are staring at me. Gay Stevie hangs his head and I wave my fist in victory. I do a war dance. I give myself high-fives. The dense thud of the bass line kicks in. Cher or bust. I roll my eyes. Gay Stevie takes my hand. Even if the music blows, we have no choice. We're dancing.

54

Mr. Levy's waiting outside. He's yelling at us to get dressed. He's sputtering with swears. Willassie and I are clutching each other, what's he going to do, how'd he even know we were here, is this a random act of fate or did someone tell him, did he see my naked self, I know he did, what a creep, is he going to tell Dad, of course he's going to tell Dad, of course he is. Mr. Levy is yelling. Leave the sock just put the kamik on quick. Leave the bag leave everything. We don't have time to even kiss and I'm a little glad. The lack of meaningful gesture lets me believe this isn't the end. I picture Willassie doing something drastic. Kicking a hole through the back wall of the igloo and whisking me away to the other side of the island. But it's a small island. We'd never get far enough away. Even if we took off by kayak across James Bay, they'd send out boats or they'd get the planes to fly low, until they found us.

We walk to the front of the school. I manage to squeeze Willassie's thigh as Mr. Levy unlocks the door. He keeps the keys in his fist, he holds them out way in front of him, like they're dirty. We go straight to the staff room and he locks me in. As if I'd run. Although I guess it'd be better than doing nothing, even if it's dumb.

I can't just sit here. I'll go crazy. I don't know what I'll do but it won't be pretty. There'll be blood and St. Elizabeth of Hungary. I have to distract myself, but the staff room has nothing good in it. There's the jar of pickled seal eyeballs. Anywhere you go, at least one pair of eyes is staring at you. There's the dartboard with the picture of the Prime Minister over it. The ancient book of crosswords. The ditto machine with its wet, streaky pages. I could make copies of crossword puzzles. I could get some eyeballs to eat.

I sit and pick at my kamiks. I rub the fur against the grain and draw pictures in it. If Dad brings Nance with him I'll be okay. She'll take my side. Inuit girls do all this stuff early. I'm probably the last girl in my class to start. Carla's having a baby and her mother isn't having a conniption. She's knitting booties. It's no big deal.

When they unlock the door I've fallen asleep. I jolt up, my face trailing drool. Dad comes in. No Nancy. He's got the oldest eyes in the world, like he saw it end already. I did that.

"Dad…" I can't say I'm sorry because I'm not sorry. I can't say it didn't happen. I can't lie. So I say what I know is true.

"Dad, please, I love him."

He laughs one of those sad laughs.

"He loves me too."

"You're a baby, Teresa. You're a kid. Love isn't part of this issue."

"What issue?"

"He's five years older than you. He's nearly grown up. He's

361

Inuit. I don't think he wants you to be his soulmate. I'm going to talk to him, don't you worry. I'll make sure this situation is ended properly."

"Dad."

"You don't have to talk about it now. Mr. Levy told me."

"But Dad."

"Sometimes people pretend to be nice so they can take advantage of you. Do you know what I'm talking about? This boy made you do things. I know it's not your fault. You don't have to get upset. I didn't properly warn you. Maurice said I should have, but I didn't think…"

"I wanted him to."

"No, Teresa. It's rape."

"No!"

"Rape. Statutory."

That ugly word is in the room with us now. It's sticking its fat ass where it doesn't belong.

"He didn't do that."

"Don't lie."

"He didn't rape me."

"Teresa, don't lie. I won't allow it. Mr. Levy saw you. Are you telling me that he didn't?"

I say nothing.

"That he didn't see anything?"

"No."

"Did that boy touch you?"

"What do you mean?"

He rubs those old eyes. He laughs another horrible, resigned laugh with sedimentary layers of pain shot through it. "Did he put his penis in you?"

"Yes."

"What?"

"Yes." I can't lie. I can't.

He's looking at the wall and talking very quietly. "If he put his penis inside of you then that's definitely what it is."

"But I wanted him to."

"You're twelve. It doesn't matter what you think you wanted."

"I'm thirteen," I say. "It was my birthday."

"Right. Your birthday." He won't look at me.

"The other girls do it."

"They're different."

"I know they are."

"You don't know what you want when you're this young."

"That's not true."

"You don't know, Teresa. You're vulnerable."

"Dad."

"He tricked you."

"He didn't."

"You're a baby."

"I'm not."

He grabs my arm. He's never grabbed my arm before. "Listen to me. You're a child. Having sex with a child is wrong. It's a crime. It's a damaging action that has to be accounted for."

Those dumb seal eyes won't stop staring. "Dad," I say again.

"I love you, Teresa. I'm supposed to take good care of you. I'm sorry I didn't do a better job so far."

"He loves me too."

"He took advantage."

I shake my head.

"Whose idea was it?" he asks.

Shit. He's got me there.

"Well?"

"His," I say. "But I wanted to."

"His."

"But I wanted to."

"You don't have to talk about it now." He puts his arm around me. He smoothes down my hair like he used to when I was a kid.

"It's all right, T-bird. It's fine. This isn't your problem anymore." I lean on his shoulder. I don't say anything, because my Dad who loves me is going to cry. It's broken hearts all around, today. I'm just letting him take care of me how he thinks he needs to. What's the real harm in that? It'll make him feel better, and then at least one person can have some peace of mind today. I don't protest anymore. I don't plead or beg or get down on my knees. I slump my weight into his side and let him hug me. And of course I'm fucking crying. Dad hugs my face into his shirt. I can hear the uneven thumping of his heart underneath. "And was this the first time?" he says.

I nod. I feel him sigh.

"Well, that's something, at least."

I keep nodding into his chest. It feels nice to squish my nose into it. I suck in a few deep breaths. "What's going to happen?" I ask.

"Nothing, for the moment."

"Please don't punish him."

"He'll be dealt with by the police, not me."

"But."

"Don't worry about it. Go home and wait. Evan is at Nancy's house. I'll call her and tell her to bring him over. I'm going to go to the RCMP with Mr. Levy. We'll probably have to come to talk to you."

"No."

"Yes, Teresa. I'm sorry, but that's how these situations end. We've got to keep our chins up."

"I hate everything."

"Teresa."

"What."

He collapses into the couch. "Don't tell your mother, all right?"

He doesn't have to worry about that. I'm done with words. No more fat-assed r-words and no more shiny l-ones either.

"Go home now," he says.

And I do. There's nowhere else to run to. I picture Mr. Levy and Dad locking Willassie up in the skin room. They slap him silly. They call him a rapist. They say, "That's statutory rape, son, we're putting you up on charges." He beats his fists against the floor. He screams my name. He quotes Shakespeare, something about crossed stars. Or maybe he doesn't. Maybe he gives up too. I'm so sorry, Willassie. I could've fought more, I could've made Dad listen to me. But he needed me to be a kid. His heart was beating irregularly. I could hear the skip. I know I'm the biggest fuck-up in the entire world. I'll get everything I deserve. It's coming to me.

I kick at the melting snowbanks and cry. It's warmer out so my tears don't freeze. Somehow this makes me cry harder. I want to go back in time. I want to go back to yesterday, when it was still winter, and just run away. Just run away from Willassie. I'd hide out for a while. Refuse to see anyone. I'd publish a nasty story about him in the paper. I'd throw his necklace at him and tell him it's over. I'd give an Oscar-winning performance. I'd say, "Sorry, Willassie, I have feelings for Benny that just won't go away. He looks so hot with that missing tooth." Or some other lie. I'd find some way to make him never want to see me again. I'd rewind all the way to the pencil stuck in my face, and I'd keep it like that, permanently.

They think he attacked me. They need to think that. Otherwise they don't understand. But sometimes you just can't understand, and that's the end of it. I guess that's hard to accept, especially if you're a grown-up like Dad or Mr. Levy and you think you're smart enough to understand anything. And I can't go back in time. Even if I could, I probably wouldn't have the strength of character to say all those things. There's no way it would turn out differently. We'd eventually always end up here, on this stupid morning where it's spring out and I'm thirteen.

I'm weeping and kicking the snowbanks. I come toward the house. The snow is melting ferociously now, in great white puddles on top of itself. There's a skim of water over everything. My kamiks are getting soaked. I dry my face with my mittens. The snow will be gone soon and those stupid purple flowers will be out.

I put my hand on the doorknob, aware that this is the defining moment. This is the moment where I step through the door into the new reality that is waiting, post-rape, whether there was rape or not. This is the moment where I swallow down the truth. This is where I go, just go with the flow, wherever the grown-ups are steering it.

I can't do it. I can't sit at home and wait for the police so they can make me talk. God. I don't ever want to talk again. I hate words. God. Fuck. Shit. I hate the capacity for language. I wish

I was like Danny, with no language at all. Then the word 'rape' wouldn't exist and Dad wouldn't be able to look me in the face and say it to me. Goddamn fuck. Fucking shit.

I've started sobbing full force, the kind with yelling in it. That compulsive, shuddering kind of sobbing has kicked in, and now I really can't help it. I've slid down in the puddle by our back door. My snow pants are soaked, but who gives a flying fuck how wet it is.

I've taken my stone bird out of my pocket at some point and started squeezing it and I think I must've hit myself in the face with it, because my vision is all messy, too. I can't see anything but colours. Blurred. I broke my glasses hitting myself in the face with the dirty sharp beak of the damn bird and didn't even notice I was doing it. The glass has cracked in pieces. I squeeze some in my hands.

I will rail against the flesh. I want the blood to come out. I want to see it. I stuff some gravel in my mouth and swallow like Danny. It's the only sensible thing I can think of doing. It hurts and I eat more.

I take off all my clothes. I don't care if everyone is peeking out their windows. I will expose my pitiful body. Those dumb crotch-tag bruises and the scabs down there. I blame it on my body, feeling those stupid feelings it didn't know anything about. I blame it on my body and also I will punish it.

I'm a little kid still. I'm a fucking slut. Those dickie birds pointing in the sky. I sucked upon the tit and worshipped it. Stupid body. Stupid body. I can't say those words they're going to make me say about how it was his fault and how he made me. I rip the necklace off and put it on the pile. Let Carla have it. I have no magic thing that can protect me.

I'm shaking with no clothes on. It's fucking freezing, even though it's spring. I keep the picture my baby brother drew and the bird I've been using to knock some sense into myself. I'll carve the scar out of my cheek so they can't use it as evidence. I hold the bird so tightly that the points of its wings cut into my palm. I take some pieces of my glasses, but leave the dental tool. Its blunt handle won't be much good.

I start heading away from Sanikiluaq, everything a blur, leaving the abandoned pile of clothes in a pile by the back door. The snow cramps my feet before I'm out of sight. It's so flat here that you have to run and run before you lose sight of anything. No hills to hide behind. The wind's in my mouth, pushing my breathing down. I stand facing this wind which wants so badly to flatten me. I ask it to do it, to kill me, have done with it, please. Have mercy.

I sit in the snow. My body is shaking with cold and refuses to go any further. The houses look like tiny spots of mildew on white bathtub tile. Stupid body. The sun is bright but I feel nothing. My bare arse in a puddle. I hate all puddles. Also I want to drown in one.

I'll be camouflaged until the last of this snow melts away, and that won't be for another day or so. Without my glasses I can't tell the difference between my leg and the snow. I'm nearly invisible. Even my hair shines clear-white. I'm cold. I take the stone bird. I don't know how to keep the drawing safe. There's no place to put it except inside me. And I do, because it's the last thing I have that's worth saving. I would die for this picture that Evan made. I fold it as neatly as possible, my freezing fingers working numbly an inch or so from my face, eyes squinted into focus. I take the lump of paper and put it up inside of me. This hurts, but I want it to. I only hope no blood spoils the paper. I take the bird. It's not going to work, too dull. Good for bruising, but not sharp enough to do real cutting. Good thing I brought the glass as well. Dad says think ahead. Mom: just trust your gut, darling.

I suppose it should be one wrist, then the other. If Mom were here she could tell me. She knows about these things. If Mom were here she'd listen to my side of the story and she'd stop this from going too far. She would've adored Willassie. Although the glass is jagged and sharp, it's also slippery and hard to use with my hand close up to my face and my fingers trembling. I make long scratches which begin to show red. I will break through to bone. This is the last thing I can do that means anything. I take one last look around. There is nothing to see but white, above, below, in between. Those shitty houses wrapped in shine. I drag the glass harder. There are pearls of blood. I examine them closely. I squeeze the bird in my fist and the drops stream out. The other wrist now, the harder one, with my awkward hand. I am patient. I have all day. This is the only thing I have to do today. No homework. The blood is coming out faster now as I press the glass into the other wrist. When I squeeze my hand, I get giddy watching all that rich colour spilling out into the white. I can't hold onto the glass anymore. I know what'll happen next. I'm going to faint out here, and that will be the end of it.

Ashes to ashes, amen. Surely I can't last long, with this river of blood and the other wrist starting too, a rivulet, this river and rivulet of blood and this cold and grief. Soon I'll die of exposure, my body defining itself in blue against the fucking puddles.

My vision is going and even the sound of the wind disappears. I think I feel a little licking at my wrist. I struggle my eyelids open. I can't be sure, but there's a thing. Tusks and fur like a wolf or a walrus. Like something weird. It's licking me. I'm seeing things, and the thing I'm seeing is snuggling into me. I can feel its body heat. It knows I need something warm pressed up against me. Its fur is soft. I can hold it if I want. I can feel its soggy made-up breath. Evil little tupilak, my only companion. It doesn't care that I'm worthless. I feel it cuddle into my neck. The tupilak nips at my breastbone, trying to keep me conscious. Too late. I'm headed into the dark expanse. I've made my bed and now I'll lie in it. Not even the old magic things can keep me here. I'm going to my fucking rest.

55

I don't know why I'm here. The fireworks are happening but we can't see them. The neighbours are in the way. We can only see the faint aftershocks of colour around their rooftops, soft shimmerings of pink and green. Canada Day is a heinous little holiday anyway. Especially in Newfoundland, where July First means the decimation of the Newfoundland Regiment at Beaumont Hamel as much as it means patriotism to the large landmass we're invisibly attached to. There tend to be bar fights on Canada Day. Dorks with maple leafs painted on their faces pretty much ask for it when they go down to The Republic singing their anthems with the Newfoundland flag hanging green, white and pink above the booze. I usually do nothing on Canada Day. I avoid celebration and instead hole up with, I don't know, a Liz Taylor movie or something. *Taming of the Shrew*.

Tonight started off well, though, me and Vanessa and Curtis smoking hash and painting my house. I took three bazillion photographs first. The paintings are, after all, very good. My mother's last body of work. Full of that rankling, unsettled feeling. Messy smears of paint, scraps of cloth or garbage worked in. While in her prime Mom was known for vivid landscapes and floral imagery. Angels did creep in there near the end, but they were pretty angels, peaceful angels, suitable for gardens. The murals in this house are different. The saints feature prominently, in their glory and their agony. Other creatures as well. Winged, horned men with bees for teeth painted inside the kitchen cabinets. Bird people and fish people dancing wildly round the shower walls with great hunks of meat in their hands, dripping gravy. There are angels, but they're awful ones, ones that look sick as cancer patients. I think I might show the prints somewhere. A mother/daughter collaboration. *The House of Mad Women.* I'll get famous off my name, like Sean Lennon or one of those odd Zappa kids: Moonsuit, or whatever he/she is called. Mark was right about one thing: Mom's a genius. There's no doubt.

It felt blasphemous to paint over everything, but I had to do it. There's only so much a girl can take before she spontaneously combusts. We're painting it white, the whole thing. Every room, hallway, light switch, radiator, closet, baseboard, stair. Beautiful white. Clean. All possibility. Except for Mom's old studio, which I've made over into my darkroom in traditional black, and my old rainbow-papered bedroom, which I couldn't bear to destroy. Curtis brought drop cloths and a stepladder. While we rested between coats we watched Cirque du Soleil on TV. Girls turned themselves into orchids and men stood on top of each other in mathematically dazzling configurations. I marvelled at the suppleness of the human body. I can't even touch my toes. Already fossilized.

At eleven-thirty or so, I went into the kitchen for top-ups on everyone's drinks. I saw the Kodak envelope on the counter, and stuffed it into my overalls pocket. Those pictures. Even feeling them through the envelope was freaking me out, and I knew I wouldn't open them, I'd just burn them or something, unless I did it with Mark. I knew it was a bad idea, but he was the only one I'd let look at them, if they are what I think they are.

We hadn't talked in over a month. I was high on hash and given over to the whims of fancy, but still fully cognizant of the potential destructiveness of my actions as I picked up the telephone and dialled his number, my eyes tracing the paths of flame-coloured trapeze artists swinging each other by the neck. I was hoping he wouldn't be home and I could leave a message, something nice to let him know I was thinking of him when he got in at three AM, drunk and tripping over the boots in the hallway. I knew he wouldn't be out, though. Mark doesn't believe in going out when everyone else is.

"Hello?" His voice cracked a little, but I didn't laugh. Normally I'd milk it for all it was worth, but tonight I couldn't. My tongue seemed to weigh a thousand pounds.

"Hey," I said. "Happy Canada Day and what are you up to?"

"Smoking a joint in the tub."

"I told you not to do that."

He doesn't say anything.

"Gay Stevie's nanny died when she fell asleep in the tub." I was suddenly getting concerned. I wanted him to be intact, at least, even if he hated me.

"First of all, I'm not going to fall asleep. Secondly, after many years of practice I've become an expert at lucid dreaming, so, if I did happen to slip under the water, I'd know what had happened, asleep or not, and it'd all be okay. A little water in the lungs. Thirdly, I'm a grown adult. I'm almost forty. I can decide what to do with my body, thanks very much. "

"You're thirty-three, nimrod."

I wanted to tell him about the endorphins. How when you're drowning, on the first inhalation of water you choke, but, on the second, your body releases all these endorphins. You feel fantastic. It's like heroin. I know this because of Gay Stevie, whose grandmother died in the tub. The endorphins make drowning one of the best ways to die.

"Can I come over?" I said.

"Sorry?"

"Can I come over?"

I could hear him taking a drag off his joint, holding the smoke in.

"I guess. You want to come over?"

"No, just wanted to see if I was allowed."

"Still a comedian."

"You'd better put some clothes on."

My mouth was moving. Sentences were coming out. On the TV a man with hair like seaweed was placing metal balls along his spine. If only they didn't use that cheesy synthesizer.

"I'm putting my shoes on," I said.

"I'm getting out of the tub," Mark said.

"Tonight I save you from drowning," I said. "Tonight I save your life."

I told Vanessa that she and Curtis should stay and hang out at my house but that I had to go out. I didn't say that I was going to see Mark, but I didn't have to. Vanessa's like that.

Now I'm in Mark's stairway with the window overlooking the neighbour's window, through which we can see straight through to the other side of their narrow house, out the other window, and on to a distant view of the harbour. The wine in my glass splashes onto my wrist when Mark leans forward to look at the soft glow of blue explosions, the fuzzy suggestion of the actual fireworks. We've been standing awkwardly in the stairwell like that since I arrived ten minutes ago. Mark handed me a glass of wine when I knocked on the door, and then came and stood at the window. Neither of us wants to bring up the night of my birthday, me getting the fuck out of his fucking shit. Instead, we talk about how expensive fireworks are, and how they disappoint everyone.

"Let's toast the soldiers born as ghosts today," Mark says. "To the boys of the Newfoundland Regiment."

I lean my head back. He's on the step above me. From this angle he looks like a stranger. He looks down and says nothing. I bend further backwards, imagining myself in a see-through sequined suit, glorious pink streaks covering my face, a circus queen. I bend as far back as I can go. Mark leans forward a little to steady me. He clears his throat. I can see the vibrations of it. His eyes are wet with the thought of those dead men.

"Turn the right way up," he says.

"I'm an acrobat. I can backflip over anything."

"You're crazy."

I smile. "You are, for not just ravishing me. What have you got to lose, really?"

"Don't say that."

"What?"

"Don't say shit like that unless you mean it."

"Okay. God."

"Don't 'God' me, you little heathen."

"Mark."

"Fuck right off."

"Mark."

"Fuck off."

"Mark."

"Teresa, please." He's pleading. He's going to push me down the stairs. He's got a face like a plastic mask. He's scared of me.

"Mark."

How is it possible that we've never stood this way before, close enough for him to tear into my throat, to slit it beautifully with an ordinary kitchen knife, leaned up in the narrow stairwell, just the two of us?

"Mark, I'm sorry I've been a loser. I wish I could've been a better friend."

"Oh, fuck off. What is this, your death speech?"

"Seriously. I shouldn't have tried to make you talk to your sister."

"Let's not talk about it."

"But, Mark. It's none of my business, like you said."

"Look, I was upset. I'm sorry I was an asshole. You weren't doing anything I wouldn't have done to you, under the circumstances. And I'm going to call her soon. I miss the shithead. I just..."

"I know," I say.

"I just wish I could look out for her."

I look him in the eye. "Vanessa's fine. Or she will be once you speak to her."

He nods his head. "Good."

We both go at our wine.

"I feel like there's shit I should've seen," I say.

376

"We're all like that."

"I always figure things out way too late."

"We're all like that."

"I'm sorry I'm not in love with you."

Mark turns away. "I said forget about it. I was fucking drunk."

"I'm baring my throat to you. I'm letting you slit it if you want."

"Don't say shit like that. You're so melodramatic. Jesus."

"I wouldn't mind. I was supposed to die a long time ago, but something got fucked up. There was this animal thing that saved my life. It was punishing me."

"Don't say anything," Mark says. "You're giving me the creeps. Stop talking. Turn around."

"Did you know I had a brother?"

"Yeah. I guess. "

"I had a brother."

"Yes?"

"His name was Evan. He was five, then six. He had his birthday."

"Where is he now?"

"Port Rexton. He lives with Nan. Mark?"

"Yeah?"

"Someday do you want to hear the story of my brother and why he could never forgive me?"

"Yes."

"Are you sure? It's scary and sad. There's blood and guts and everything."

"You can tell me whatever you want. Now turn around. I need a hug."

"Mark."

"Come on, a big old Canadian hug. Gender-neutral. I promise I won't feel you up."

"Mark. Mark. Mark." I can't stop. If I don't keep saying his name he might disappear. He might fall asleep and drown. He might have a dream so beautiful he won't want to wake up. "Mark."

"Come on."

"I tried to kill myself. I tried my absolute hardest to make everything stop."

He doesn't know what to say. I can't look at him.

"There was this Inuit boy. They said he raped me. He never did. They said it because I was too young. Very ironic. It was my birthday. Well, the day after, but close enough. I turned him in. The shit I've got stored up in me, the shit that squeezes at my throat. I was thirteen. It was my birthday and I couldn't even slit my wrists, for shit's sake. I couldn't even die of fucking exposure and anyone could have, if they'd done what I did. You shouldn't get a heart before you're twenty. Your body doesn't know what to do with it." I wipe my nose. "He used to call me this word that meant snowflake. I can't remember the actual word. My heart was always up in my mouth. He got three years in a group home. No permanent record. But, Jesus. I'm a blight. Like locusts."

I haven't told him the whole story but I've started to speak, and that's something. There's so much I've never said, to anyone.

56

I'd been out there for hours by the time Nancy and Evan found me. The pile of clothes. She couldn't keep him from looking at his sister lying naked and bleeding with her face beaten in. Those bruises. Blue with cold. Skin coming off, thin pieces like the pages of the dictionary. I remember opening my eyes and seeing these blurry figures. One was a little boy, hitting into my side. The other was a beautiful brown lady. Saint Elizabeth for sure. She was saying that she loved me. Rocking back and forth a little. "I'll take care of your pain, my Teresa."

They took me out that night on an emergency plane. We took nothing but the clothes on our backs, or, in my case, the clothes hurriedly piled around me. Everything else got left behind, or so I thought. That was the end of it. There was no neat epilogue where everyone gets their heartfelt goodbye, their last kiss, and the truth of what happened. I didn't see Willassie again, not till the trial, and never when we could actually talk. He signed a paper that said he wouldn't try to contact me. There was only that last shitty thigh-grip outside the school that could've meant anything.

We left the Northwest Territories behind without saying goodbye to anyone. It was impossible. I was sick. My skin in tatters, like an old map. I wouldn't let go of Nancy's hand. She kissed my crusted-up knuckles when she pried herself free so that Wanda could dress my wounds properly. Nancy kissed my dirty knuckles with her perfect mouth. She stood in the snowbank by the runway, looking up at us, getting tiny.

I didn't speak for months, I didn't go to school. We called it Home Schooling, but mostly I just lay in bed, long after I had to. When Dad ordered me new glasses, the world jumped into focus again. I could concentrate on lines of shadow and light for hours, their precision. I made a frame out of paper. I would make photographic compositions in the air and frame them. I made a million still lifes.

I lay in my bed in our new house in Cowan Heights. An empty bedroom where Evan should've been. At first we thought he'd only be gone a couple of weeks, till the skin grew back and the swelling went down and my wrists healed over and I was basically less of a terrifying sight. Then Mom tried to off herself, too, so there was no way he could come home, Nan said. Not with two psychos around. Then it was wait until the trial's over. Then wait until the school year's out. Pretty soon he didn't want to come home at all. He thought of Port Rexton as home. Dad said to give him time, we'll wait it out, and other passive shit. He was tired and unsure of his parenting abilities. Fuck it, it was hard enough for us to exist as we were without a little kid around, asking about everything. Neither of us had any strength left to put into keeping up appearances.

Total economy. I just lay in bed, sleeping or reading or taking imaginary air pictures, undisturbed by my father, who didn't wish to fall to pieces and therefore didn't want to speak to me, even though the clicking sound I'd make with my tongue while pressing my eyelids together reminded him of Mom, and made him uneasy.

I atrophied. I didn't dream. Grown-ups came to talk to me, in ones and twos. Some were lawyers or social workers and some were psychiatrists. I answered all their questions. I said yes a lot. It was the easiest way to get them to stop talking. They never did figure me out, one way or the other, although I went on the meds for a while, before I gave it up. They made my hair fall out. I wanted to grow backwards, to lose my adult self. I only read children's books, where animals were more important than people. When Aslan died I cried myself to sleep.

I stopped menstruating for nearly a year. I assumed it was due to Evan's drawing which I had let disintegrate inside me. I assumed I was a born-again virgin, what with all the grief, and no better explanation ever presenting itself. No stillborn, mixed-race baby. Just the paper pieces falling out one by one, sodden along the folds, unravelling themselves amid my feces.

Months went by and I did nothing. The one time I saw my mother, we had matching wrist bandages that no one mentioned. She said, "what are you doing?" and I said, "taking pictures in the air" and she said, "do you want to be a photographer?" and I said, "yes" and Dad said, "I saved your camera." He gave it back to me, even though it came from there, I guess maybe because I got more excited about it than anything else in recent memory. It was heavy, and real, unlike everything else.

The Northwest Territories weren't real. They were made up. My fairy story. Evan wasn't real. There was no boy named

Willassie and no smack-fighting girls and no pretty Inuit lady. In this new clean house on Frecker Drive there was no history. Dad turned Evan's room into an office with a couch-bed. We kept nothing. It had to be that way, in order for us not to keep on shattering further until we ceased to exist.

The camera was magic, having survived. I wiped it all over with a pair of underwear, the softest cloth I had. It had spirits inside of it, ones that maybe could help me. See things. Focus clearly. Even though it was as impossible to prove as seeing the inside of my eyeball, I could tell the camera had changed. It seemed sentient. I took it to bed at night. It came to school, eventually. It helped me wait it out. Ride the motherfucking wave. Just wait and see.

I took it back with me for that awful two-day trip we had to make, me and Dad, back up there to testify. My headphones on any time I could get away with it, looking through the camera lens at my feet. No one would make eye contact with me, not Mina and her mother, or Benny, or even Carla in the back with her baby. Nancy didn't turn up. I didn't blame her. I could understand how hard it would be.

I sat before the judge. He was unimpressive and ordinary, sitting in the gym behind a fold-up table with a cup of instant coffee. They showed pictures that they took when they found me. It didn't really matter what I said. Those pictures looked bad. Dad cried and so did Mr. Levy. They had all the evidence they needed without my testimony. Willassie was an Inuit boy, much older than me, and I was white. They asked if it hurt when he penetrated me. I said that it did. They asked if I tried to kill myself and I said yes, I didn't want to be any more trouble to anybody. I never had to say the r-word. I never once got to look in Willassie's face. It was like he had a blind spot. I had ceased to exist. I knew that was as good as I deserved, so I didn't cry, not even when Benny spat on me as we left the building, and screamed that I was a lying cunt. The RCMP set up camp outside the hotel that night, and decided it was best if we didn't have any visitors, not even Mr. Levy. You never know in these cases. Emotions run high. Best to be on the safe side. I took my camera up with me, not to take any pictures, just to hang onto. I just had to hang on and remain conscious. It was the only real thing left.

57

"Mark, do you forgive my transgressions?"

"Teresa. I had no idea."

"Mark, do you forgive me my sins?"

"Yes. I'm sorry. Yes."

I take the Kodak envelope out of my pocket. The film was in that box I didn't know about, the TERESA MISC. box in my parents' old bedroom, with the plaster over the door decorated with tumourous angels, that Curtis and I decided to hack right through. He said it was bad feng shui to have a walled-up room, and started in with the sledgehammer, a snowstorm of plaster dust whirling to the floor around his feet. Dad must've brought shit over to Mom's house, to store out of sight. I had no idea he'd kept all of it. My coat. The beautiful kamiks. My little snowflake, smaller now. It's been twelve years, and now is when I'm ready for the TERESA MISC. box. These things only appear when you're able to deal with them. When you won't just burn them up, or drown.

"I hate going to a commercial developer, but."

"What are those?"

"I really didn't want to fuck this up."

There's only a couple of prints. It was a new roll of film, put in fresh on my birthday after we ate our dessert. Mr. Levy showed me how.

"Mark. Shit. I don't know if I can do this."

I brace myself against him. I move my thumb; it was covering you up. There you are, looking surprised, caught in the act of saying something. There's your nose and your eye and your other eye, back together again. You're standing inside the door to your shed. You've got your arm extended and your hand is more in focus than the rest of you. The scar on your thumb.

Picture two is in the igloo. There's a warm glow off the kuudliqs. You're eating cake. Shiny eyes. Icing on your fingers and your chin.

You wanted to take one with the camera in your hand, with our heads squished together, out of focus. Even though I thought of that Marguerite picture, or because of it, I agreed. Look how worried I am. Look how meek and pale. There's that necklace. Look how hard you're kissing me. In the picture I've taken my glasses off. My gaze is totally unfocused. Do I still look like that?

I tilt my head back and look at Mark, who isn't you. I lean back against him. I say, "Thank you for seeing these with me."

I say his name. I bless him with his own name: Mark. I turn around and say it with my lips lightly touching his collarbone. I say his name into the sharp line where his beard starts. I say it on the place where he swallows. I say it into his mouth. I say "Mark" into the mouth of Mark. He says nothing. I put my fingers in his hair, testing to see if it'd hold me, should I fall. His hair contains biblical strength. I put you outside of the window. In my mind, I'm piling you into the fireworks, dissolving you in the pale blue bursts of blurry light. Mark's lips are almost as soft as girl's lips, but not quite. He's making a small sound like a child sleeping. I could die from it. We're taking this moment by the balls. I don't care if there's regret. We don't know what we need. We don't know much of anything. The answers aren't immediate and they are not easy. Or there are no answers. Anything could happen. Things will go on happening. It's okay to muck around and get things wrong and feel like shit. We all do that.

It's good to know, finally, that being without a lover does not mean being without love. I'm a slow learner. There are so many things I should have figured out by now. I ooze love for everyone, like sweat. I say, "I'm dead inside, dead," but it isn't true. I want to fling love down, on Delith, Gay Stevie. Curtis and Vanessa. My brother and my mother. Even poor old Solange.

Tomorrow I'll call my father. I want to tell him about seeing Nancy that time, how I thought she was a saint. How it was her who saved me, if anyone did. I can give him that. And I need to tell myself that I'm okay. I am not a bad person, a coward, a plague. I'm all right.

I turn from Mark and look out towards the city. You're outside the windowpane. In my mind, I'm wearing the most beautiful costume of translucent fabric. Organza. It's patterned with lines where my veins are, rimmed in clever red at the cuffs. Forgotten for a decade, the word Quanniq returns. Snowflake. I touch the necklace on its new bit of yarn around my throat.

I've been kissed into purity, into absolution. I'm removing layers of myself. A kiss can have great power, given the right person and the right moment in time. Given the circumstance, a kiss can change a life. The writers don't lie.

Goodbye, old guilt, old shame! I'm shedding the unnecessary. Only my body remains, this foreign fleshy thing which I've just begun to investigate. Which just now is unfolding itself from the inside, from chrysalis to butterfly, growing taut with blood at the thought of how alone I am, how rife with possibility.

I myself am the tundra or a pure white room. This thought is more erotic than any other thought I've ever had. One sexy thought begets another. Soon enough I'm swollen with them, full and buzzing hot. It's easy to go forward. Now that there's momentum, I'm a genius of the trapeze. I can let you free of all our transient burdens. Or try to, at least.

One eye closes, the other opens, transferring the wink. The shift in perspective is a fucking relief.

Quyanaq. Seriously. Thank you, and goodnight.

Acknowledgements

I would like to thank my editor, Stan Dragland, and my publisher, Beth Follett, for their belief in my work and their wise coaching through to its final form. Thank you to Zab, Sarni Pootoogook and Michael Crummey. Thanks as well to Lisa Moore, who mentored the first drafts through the Banff Centre Wired Writing Program in 2003, and to Fred Stenson for his warm encouragement. To Lynn Moore for the legal information, and to first readers Robert Chafe, Jason Sellars, Ryan Davis and Craig Francis Power for their feedback on various drafts. To John Jamieson for sending me the time capsule materials that I buried as a child in Sanikiluaq. To Isabell Takatak for the vocabulary. This book won the Percy Janes First Novel Award in 2004, and I would like to acknowledge adjudicator David Freeman for his belief in the manuscript and his kind words. In 2006 the book won the Fresh Fish Award for Emerging Writers, and thanks are due to Fresh Fish Award judges Susan Rendell, Joan Sullivan and Leslie Vryenhoek for their support, especially Susan, who has become the book's Fairy Godmother. Thanks to Libby Creelman and Claire Wilkshire, also Godmothers. Thanks to Conor Green, Stephanie Saunders and Rae Ellen Bodie, all of whom, eight years ago, propelled me into writing this book in the first place, though I'm not sure any of them know that. And to my family, for remaining patient while I refused to divulge any details or let them read a single page. Giant thanks are due to many members of the arts community of St. John's, whose names are too numerous to mention, for continuing to be a source of friendship, inspiration, collaboration and mutual support. You know who you are.

This book was written with the assistance of the Newfoundland and Labrador Arts Council..

SARA TILLEY's *Skin Room* won both the 2004 Newfoundland and Labrador Percy Janes First Novel Award and, in 2006, the inaugural Fresh Fish Award for Emerging Writers. Sara has received several Newfoundland Arts and Letters Awards for playwriting, prose and poetry, and her work has been published in *TickleAce* and *Zeugma* Magazines, and featured on CBC Radio. Sara's activities span the theatre, writing and Pochinko Clown Through Mask. She has written, co-written and co-created ten plays, and in 2006 was the recipient of the Rhonda Payne Award, which celebrates a woman contributing to the development of theatre in Newfoundland and Labrador.

Sara was born in St. John's, but spent most of her childhood in rural and isolated communities. Her work is inspired by sense memories of life in Brigus South, Newfoundland, Nain, Labrador and Sanikiluaq, in what is now Nunavut. She currently lives in St. John's with her partner, Craig, and their cat.